CHASING THE LANTERN

BOOK ONE OF THE DAWNHAWK TRILOGY

BY

JONATHON BURGESS

Cover Painting © 2015 Ksenia Mamaeva

Book & Cover Design by Vladimir Verano, Third Place Press

Edited by Susan Defreitas, Indigo Editing & Publications

ISBN: 978-0-9909604-0-9

SECOND EDITION

BRASS HORSE BOOKS

JBURGESS@BRASSHORSEBOOKS.COM
WWW.BRASSHORSEBOOKS.COM

For Shawna

PROLOGUE

Captain Fengel pushed open the door. But only an inch or so. Beyond, the alley was dark and foreboding. He ignored the unhappy rumblings of the other pirates and listened to the faint, late-night city sounds that echoed back to him: a horse and carriage upon the cobbles of a nearby street, an argument in some upstairs tenement.

It was a hell of a thing, to be hunted.

That people wanted him dead he took for granted. Such dangers were endemic to the life of a pirate. It was the setting that disturbed him so. Being trapped in a foreign city, where the only friends and allies were those in his crew, that was alarming.

Nothing for it then. At least at the moment things seemed safe.

He stepped back from the door, adjusting his monocle. Fengel turned in the small foyer to address the mob at his back. His remaining band, maybe twenty in all, stared back at him, tense and worried. They were a motley bunch of rogues, cutthroats, and scallywags. But they were his, and he was responsible for them. Not that he'd been much good for it, of late.

"All right, you lot," he said quietly. "We've lost our ship, our employer wants us dead, and so do most of the locals. Our host has graciously offered to take us to another hidey-hole until we make our run for that weather balloon down at Paine's Yards." His gaze flicked to the red-headed woman standing off to one side. She watched them, darkly amused. "Follow her in ones and twos, and for the Goddess' sake, try not to look too much like wanted men. All right? Off you go."

He pushed open the door for Sharper Mary, the mistress of the bordello where they'd gone to ground. Mary pushed past him to the alleyway outside.

She didn't bother speaking. She didn't need to. Fengel knew what she was thinking; she just wanted them gone.

None of his crew moved. Henry Smalls, his short, faithful steward, stepped forward. "Captain?" he said, voice reedy. "Is this wise? I mean, you think he'll show? You can't trust an aetherite." Henry blinked and looked over his shoulder towards Maxim, their own magician. "No offense."

Maxim only glared at Henry.

Their ship gone, the artifact lost, and their employer cutting his losses, Fengel and his men had barely managed to find a halfway decent hiding place. With much apology they'd invaded Sharper Mary's brothel, boarded it up and prepared to make a last stand against their pursuers. It had taken outside intervention by an aetherite, Mary's friend and the very same slippery bastard who had killed Fengel's beautiful airship, to find a solution.

Fengel adjusted his monocle. "Trust him? Not entirely. But he's wanted by the same individuals who are hunting us. I think this is our best bet. Now quit gabbing and get moving. One and two at a time now, off you go."

The crew moved up to the door. Sharper Mary rolled her eyes and walked up the alley out of sight. A few at a time they followed, trying to look discreet and only succeeding in looking furtive. Finally, the last of them were gone and Fengel made to move outside as well.

Someone grabbed his elbow.

Fengel looked back to see a slip of a girl, one of the prostitutes who lived and worked in the brothel. She was small, waif-like, the long golden tresses cascading down her shoulders her most noteworthy attribute. Unlike the sheer dresses of the other prostitutes, she wore trousers and a man's shirt, with heavy leather boots one size too large. A pair of long daggers poked up from her waistband.

"Captain?" she said, in a voice that all but squeaked. "Mr. Fengel, sir?"

Fengel frowned. This was going to be awkward. His crew hadn't hurt the girls, he'd trusted them to behave, and made sure of it to boot. But their stay had certainly been a tense, frightening time. What grievance did she have?

"Yes, madam?"

"Take me with you."

Fengel blinked. "Absolutely not."

"Why?"

He fought for a moment to martial all the reasons. Then he fought with himself on the proper way to say them without giving insult. The young woman cut in before he could start.

"You misunderstand. I don't want to come along as your ship's doxy, or any such thing as that. I want to join you. Be one of your crew."

Fengel blinked. "This isn't a game, young miss—"

"I can fight if I have to, and I've no qualms about stealing. I'm quick and clever, and I'm sure I can haul a rope if I have to. I've got no problems with hard labor, and if you want me to duel you or some such stupid ritual for the chance, I'll do it and I don't care how much blood gets spilled, mine or yours."

Fengel opened his mouth, shut it, opened it again. "Miss," he said finally. "We've got the whole city after us. We're pirates. Why on this good earth would you want to do such a thing?"

She gave him a flat look. "I'm a whore, Mr. Fengel. And I'm tired of it. Have you ever been a whore?"

He had to admit that he hadn't.

"I sleep with men in exchange for money. Sometimes the nice ones send me flowers or little gifts. More often I get sore privates and a fat lip to go with them. I'm tired of this life, and tired of being the one who gets things taken from her. Take me with you. I don't care if your road's a dead end. The one I'm on certainly is."

The little whore stared at him, unwavering. There was an intensity to her that Fengel found unsettling. She reminded him of someone he knew, someone he hated, yet respected. That she was small, well, that was troubling. But being a woman wasn't a problem; some of the most vicious and successful pirates in the world were women.

He made his decision and stepped aside to hold the door like a gentleman. "Very well," he said. "You can join my crew. Until you've had enough."

She let out a breath he hadn't known she'd been holding. Then she nodded, and left the brothel. Captain Fengel did the same.

CHAPTER ONE

Lina stared at her hand of battered cards and realized that they couldn't save her.

"I'll raise ya the bench bottom," muttered a pirate.

The day was warm. Mid-afternoon sunlight reflected off the waters around them, shimmering on the chop of the ocean. Its brilliance pained Lina, the way it prickled at her sunburned skin. She hid from it as best she could by sitting low against the gunwales. But the sun still found her periodically, as the makeshift longboat crested each shallow swell with its rolling up-and-down sway. Clouds floated by up above, all puffy and rumpled with rain. Lina frowned at them. She wasn't the only one watching the sky. The others were bound to raise the stakes even higher.

"Oarlock," said Oscar Pleasant. He rubbed the week-old stubble on his chin, glancing furtively at the others playing the game.

"Gunwales," croaked Henry Smalls. Lina spared him a glance; the older pirate was tired, his features sunken and sallow. He showed worst the effects of dehydration and exposure that was slowly killing them all.

"Floorboards," said Sarah Lome, the huge piratess.

The castaways raised the stakes, bidding with the small part of the longboat that they could each lay claim to. Only half of the pirate crew played, gambling with the battered packet of cards Oscar had produced. Everyone else sat quietly, too tired to grouse, focused on their own misery. The oars lay athwart the gunwales, useless without anywhere to row to. Captain Fengel sat in the bow of the little vessel, quiet, confidently watching for any sign of their lost home port.

The pirates were watching her. Lina realized it was her turn. *All right. Time to decide.* Her sunburned fingers held a pair of deuces and nothing else worthwhile. Lina gazed at the cards a long moment, then shook her head. First chance at next morning's dew would be good, maybe keep her going long enough to spot land or a passing ship, but it wasn't worth risking the little fresh water she could suck up from the baseboards of her own tiny spot. Growing up poor had taught Lina to look after herself. You didn't do that by frittering away your only chances of survival on a losing hand.

"Nothing worth betting," she croaked aloud. "I'm out."

Oscar moved to stop her, his confident smile undercut by shaking hands. "Hold on. Maybe there's something else you can throw into the pot."

Lina glared at him. *This again?* She didn't know the pirates very well at all, but they all knew who she was, what she'd been. So far Oscar had brought it up every chance he could, even during their harried, ramshackle flight from the city of Triskelion. That part of her life was done with. Why didn't men ever seem to get it?

She glared at him. "And what would that be?"

The pirate smiled. "Those lovely golden locks of yours."

Lina blinked in confusion. The others did as well. "My hair? What? You want my hair?"

"Aye," grinned Oscar wickedly. "It's so long and soft. I've watched you each morning. It gets wonderfully damp. Throw in first lick off those, lass." He leered at her.

Lina flushed in embarrassment. This was the most disgusting thing anyone had ever asked of her, and she had heard a lot of disgusting things over the years. Her long tresses were a source of pride. They had taken years to grow and had always served her well. The gangers and sailors always paid more for a pretty head of hair.

The other pirates watched to see how she would react. Lina had done her best to keep pace with them, even chased by constables and assassins. She'd held it together and pulled her weight as they fled through the streets, then out and away from Triskelion in an old longboat attached to a weather balloon. Lina had even kept quiet after that mad, terrifying flight had ended and their makeshift airship crashed into the ocean hundreds of miles from shore. Still, through all that, the crew had yet to warm to her. They couldn't seem to understand why a prostitute wanted to be a pirate.

A hot coal of anger settled in Lina's gut. *I'll prove myself, one way or the other.* They wouldn't catch her backing down from a challenge. And if she happened to lose? Well, she'd put up with worse. "Fine," she said. "Winning hand can suck on my hair tomorrow morning, all they want."

Oscar chortled happily. "That's that then. Anyone else? No? I call." He threw his cards onto the bench before them. "Three knaves and a pair of knights."

Raspy groans and sighs of disgust echoed from the assembled pirates. Maxim, the crew's aetherite magician, threw down his cards and cursed in his thick, native tongue. He wasn't the only one. Not one of them had a hand to beat Oscar.

"That's all for me then," the ferrety pirate said with a smile. Oscar collected his deck and winked at Lina. "And I'll be seeing you girlie, first thing in the morning." He puckered wind-chapped lips and kissed at the air.

Lina glared at him. The coal of anger burned brighter. *No.* That part of her life was done, and long hair was a liability now, anyway. "No need," she said. Lina drew a long dagger from her belt, one of two knives taken from her old madam in severance. With her other hand she grabbed the back of her head and wadded her tresses into a thick mass. Growling, she cut, sawing through until the whole mess came free. Her head felt suddenly light. The ocean breeze tickled the now-bare skin at her neck. She swung the fistful of hair onto Oscar's lap. Strands like threads of gold fell down into the bilge of the boat, or flew away with the wind. "There," she said. "Have at it."

Everyone stared at her. Then the pirates broke out into laughter.

"She got you there, Oscar!"

"Good one, lass."

"Hey, Oscar, you lucked out. Now you can pretty up that ugly mug!"

The game over, the pirates all moved back to their places, chuckling to themselves. Oscar was the only one not amused. He glared at Lina, face dark. She ignored him and scuttled slowly back to her usual spot. Glancing back up towards the bow, Lina froze.

Striking green eyes held her. Fengel, captain of the pirate crew, was watching her. Even dehydrated and half dead from exposure, he sat with a stiff spine and a proud countenance, as if such fleshly concerns were beneath him. The pirate captain affected a short brown beard and mustache that his steward Henry Smalls trimmed every morning at dawn. He wore a broad tricorn hat and a golden monocle. Lina thought the latter ridiculous, yet still it somehow fit. Middle-aged and well-tanned in his tattered blue jacket, he was the very image of an officer in His Majesty's Royal Navy, which made his status as a notorious sky-pirate all the more incongruous.

Fengel's skin looked clammy and his eyes almost sunken. He gave a short, slow nod of approval, then turned back to face to the bow. As seemed to happen every time he looked her way, Lina felt butterflies in her stomach. She quashed it down and hunkered against the gunwales.

This whole idea was a mistake. He is not *the reason I came.* Prostitution in the machine-city of Triskelion had been an ugly life, and she'd been looking for a way out for a long time now. When Fengel's men passed through her bordello, airship destroyed and desperate to flee the city, she'd finally found one. *That doesn't change the fact that I should have stuck to whoring. Even that beats dying of exposure, adrift on the open ocean.* The crew all seemed confident that the captain knew where their home port was and could get them there, but Lina had never heard of anyone crossing the Atalian Sea in a weather balloon. And so far at least, they hadn't.

With a sigh, Lina crossed her arms on the gunwale and rested her chin atop them. She regarded the ocean waves for what seemed the thousandth time. The bay back home was a dark green, and rather cold. Here the water was a deep cerulean, clear for a dozen fathoms below. Lina idly wondered if it would grow so clear she would be able to spy the very ocean floor, hundreds of feet beneath them. That seemed unlikely.

Something moved in the water just below her. It swam out from underneath their longboat only a few feet below the surface, wide and very long. *Some huge fish? A shark?* Lina had never seen any of the weird creatures that sailors sometimes talked about. This thing was as wide across as her armspan and covered in silver scales that shimmered in the daylight.

Her belly grumbled. Lina shook herself, realizing the opportunity. Fish or shark, it was still food. She half-turned to look back down the boat. "Hey," she hissed. "Hey. Anyone have a spear? Or a fishing line?"

Sarah Lome blinked at her sleepily from the opposite side of the boat. The woman was huge, seven feet tall and stocky. Her biceps were thicker than Lina's thighs. Lina didn't think she'd ever be called pretty, especially with the sunburns she now wore, but no one would ever dare call her homely. "What? A spear?"

"Quick," said Lina. "There's a shark or something. A big fish. Just over the side."

The woman blinked at her again then leaned forward, with far more quickness than Lina thought someone her size should have. Her thick strawberry braid fell over her shoulder as she moved. "Where?"

Lina pointed over the side. "Just here," she said quietly, turning to peer back into the water. Then her mouth fell open and she stared.

The creature was still swimming out from under their boat, but now it curled *down*. What she'd thought a shark or fish was a massive serpent, thicker than her arms could stretch and at least thirty feet in length, growing longer with every passing second. Dimly, just at the edge of what she could see, Lina thought she spied the reptilian head of the thing.

Coming back up at them.

Lina turned back to the boat. "Serpent!" she yelled.

The ocean erupted at her back. Saltwater drenched Lina while the pirate crew let out shouts of alarm. She threw herself to the opposite side of the longboat and turned to face the monster.

The serpent rose up some fifteen feet above the waves. It glared down at them, two black and belligerent eyes peering down from above a coffin-long maw. A rough frill descended from the top of its skull down its length. A wide pair of vicious horns crowned it. Sailors of all kinds agreed that of the many dangers of the sea, none was so terrible as the serpent. Like their land-born cousins, the dragons, sea serpents were large, powerful, and very dangerous. Lina had heard that the biggest could even threaten armored steamships.

This one opened its mouth and hissed. Lina spied rows of razor fangs and a bright red tongue. The smell of rotted fish wafted over them and she thought she was going to gag. It almost seemed to grin. Then the beast rose even higher, bending its length over their heads, and dove back into the water on the side opposite. The whole boat shook with the impact and the gunwales beneath its body cracked. The crew shouted and scrabbled about for cover, reaching for their weapons.

"On your feet, you laggards!"

Sarah Lome grabbed up an oar out of the bilge and held it like a club just as the serpent rose again, enclosing their vessel in a single coil. She stepped forward and swung the oar in a huge two-handed blow. It connected with the maw of the beast before it had risen more than a few feet. The monster jerked back, shaking the whole boat, yowling and rearing in surprise. Lina stumbled and clutched the opposite gunwale. Out in the water she spied the writhing humps of its body in the surf; the monster had to be eighty feet long.

"Drive it off!" yelled Henry Smalls. "Don't let it crush the boat!" The little steward had a dagger in hand and was hacking and jabbing at the coil in the middle of their ship. His blade scraped and scored and finally hit home. The serpent gave a grunt.

Other crewmen set about the monster. A man with filed-down teeth and patchy red hair struck a solid blow with his hatchet. The serpent yowled again, its voice like bending iron. It darted in, lightning quick, knocking Sara Lome down and biting at the other pirate who'd struck. He shouted and swung at its nose, just ducking aside.

Lina stared in horror as the maw of the thing passed just inches away from her. Then the serpent shifted back. Something in the wooden hull of the boat cracked as it moved. *Yet another challenge. All right. I won't back down.* Lina drew a dagger and threw herself at the coil of the serpent. She scrabbled over Sarah Lome to hack and stab at the monster. Its scales were too thick though, too tough. The beast was going to break their ship and then devour them from the water, one by one.

Sarah Lome caught Lina's eye. "Keep at it," she said. Then she stood, took her oar up again in both hands, and yelled. "Hey! Hey, beast!" She turned and swung at the coil of the monster. The oar cracked in half with a sound like a gunshot.

The serpent roared. It reared back and glared at Sarah Lome. The piratess grinned a feral grin and took up a stance with her broken oar. The monster darted down at her.

Glowing arcane liquid sprayed across the face of the serpent. It roared again and jerked backwards. The whole vessel shook with its throes, flinging the pirates about. Lina lost her footing and fell down against the gunwales, her dagger landing next to her in the bilge. More liquid fire shot out to score the thing, turning its scales black and pitted.

Maxim stood upright near the stern, half-cloak and long black hair flapping in the breeze, eyes stern above his prominent nose. The aetherite had both hands clasped together over some arcane Working that seethed and seeped liquid light. Drops of it dribbled down to the waves, crackling and spattering where they touched the water.

"Back!" he cried, accent thick. He flung the conjured liquid in another scalding spray at the serpent. The creature darted away, but coiled as it was around the boat, it couldn't dodge far enough. A few caustic drops still caught it across the side.

The serpent roared and sank back down beneath the waves. Its coiled length loosened and shifted, pulling free from the longboat. The little vessel rocked and shook, until the finned tail slipped over their heads, then down into the waves.

Pirates stood frozen, waiting for another attack. Henry Smalls crouched with his knife like a bulldog ready to pounce, Sarah Lome clutched her broken oar. Oscar Pleasant stood in the middle of the boat, looking frantically around at the roiling sea. He had a dagger clutched in one hand and Lina's severed hair in the other. Maxim scowled and released the rest of his conjured hell-spittle. It scattered overboard with a sizzling pop, like hot bacon grease poured into cold water.

"Is...is that it?" asked Oscar. "Is it gone?"

The ocean exploded beside him. The serpent reared up, skin blackened and smoldering. Oscar flung himself aside with a scream as it struck out, jaws wide. Lina drew her other dagger, pointing in futility at it. But the serpent pulled back and sank below the waves before anyone else could react.

One minute passed, then another. The pirates spread out to watch the water, weapons held at the ready. It did not rise again though. The serpent was gone.

The crew relaxed. Sarah Lome lay down her oar. Then she spied Oscar and belted out a laugh. Lina glanced over to where the pirate lay in the middle of the boat, shaking, pale and white. He clutched his knife still in the one hand. In the other he held only a small tuft of what was left of Lina's long hair.

Oscar looked down at the bits of hair, then up at the huge woman. "S'not funny!" he yelled. "That could have been my arm!" He scrambled to his feet as others joined in. "It's not funny, damn yer eyes! I almost died, and we're worse off now than before! That damned snake cracked the hull. Look, we're taking on water!"

Lina grabbed up her dagger as she glanced down at the bilge. He was right. Water was dribbling in through several cracks in the wood. And the waves were just level with the gunwales where the sea serpent had crushed them.

"Mr. Pleasant," said their captain.

Lina glanced up at the bow. Captain Fengel had half-turned to face the crew. He had a hand upon the pommel of his sword, though the blade was only drawn an inch, as if he had only just now decided to involve himself in the serpent attack.

"If you are quite done with histrionics," continued Fengel, "I suggest you begin to bail, and the rest of you, row." He swayed slightly, certainly just the swell of the waves beneath the boat. Fengel pointed out at the horizon. Distantly, Lina could just make out a dark speck. "The Copper Isles. We're finally home."

Silence reigned as the crew peered out over the ocean. Then they became ebullient.

"We made it!" cried Oscar Pleasant. "We made it!"

"*Wir werden leben!*" yelled Maxim, reverting to his native tongue in excitement.

"The Captain did it," said Sarah Lome, voice soft with wonder. She threw herself back down onto a bench and reached for an oar as the pirates all praised the Goddess, their leaky longboat, and the Captain himself. "Quiet," she bellowed at them. "Oscar's right for once. Captain's got us this far, now it's time for us to do the rest, before we all sink. Henry, get to the tiller. Oscar, Geoffrey, Maxim, start bailing. The rest of you, row!"

What followed was some of the most backbreaking labor that Lina had ever been subjected to. Stroke by stroke they approached the horizon, Sarah Lome doing the lion's share of the work, rowing as much as any three other men combined. Henry Smalls guided from the tiller. The rest used their hands to help paddle or bail leaking water from the bilge.

The distant speck resolved into a small island chain as the sun crawled down from the sky. Lina spied no beaches, only sheer sea-cliffs riddled with shining veins of copper and topped with thick and impenetrable jungle. Jagged rocks and outcrops protected the approach from every direction. These were the Copper Isles, a notorious pirate haven and the bane of shipping between the Western Continent of Edrus and the newly discovered continent of Yulan.

Evening found them paddling out of a small canyon waterway into a lagoon deep within the interior of the isles. The cove was ringed by the same sheer, hundred-foot-high cliffs that Lina had seen everywhere else in this place. Green vines and vegetation crept down from the heights to drape across the other waterways that led here, most only big enough for a longboat. The far end of the cove was gentler, and the cliff there slanted down to the water in a series of natural terraces. A town had been built upon these, an echo in wood and stone of the creepers and growth hanging elsewhere above the cove. Lina spotted houses, shops, and workmen's huts, all hanging precariously, linked by rickety bridges and suspended boardwalks. A series of piers stretched out from the bottom of the township, a pair of sail ships now at dock. Mirror to its twin below, the top of the town supported another harbor, though for a very different kind of vessel.

Like great bulbous fish, the skyship gasbags stretched golden and gleaming in the fading sunlight, shining sails spread wide along their lengths. Beneath each hung the long shape of the vessel itself, a hull like any other ship attached by thick cables to the oblong balloon frame. There were half a dozen of the wondrous vessels, and Lina's breath caught in her chest at the sight of them.

This was Haventown. Home port of Fengel's Men and the only sky-pirate den in all the seas that were known.

"Just a little farther," croaked Henry Smalls.

The steward's voice brought her back to the present. Lina bent back to bailing, cupping her hands and tossing water overboard. The crewmen around her were ready to collapse in exhaustion, and she was as well. The only one who did not row or bail was the captain, sitting serenely up at the bow, confident that his crew would not fail him. By now the water in their bilge filled a quarter of the boat, and was halfway up Lina's calves where she sat on a bench.

"Put your backs into it!" roared Sarah. The piratess heaved at the oars, seemingly indomitable. The dying vessel surged with each powerful stroke, leaping forward in fits and starts.

Lina felt like she would die. Slowly they crossed the lagoon, sinking lower with every passing moment. Two-thirds of the way across, the water came up to her waist, the bench seat she sat on only just above the waterline. When they finally made it to the town and pulled in along an empty pier, only the tips of the gunwales were above the water.

The longboat scraped to a stop against the stony shore. Up above the tideline the pier turned into a weathered boardwalk bordering the docks from the rest of the town. Captain Fengel stood and nimbly climbed the ladder up to the pier, conveniently having stopped just next to it. His crew half-walked, half-swam after him, or made for the bow and the shore.

Lina floated in the drowned longboat, resting. Then, in floundering fits and starts, she pushed away from the boat and dog-paddled her way up to the shore where the boardwalk stretched out to the pier. She collapsed, panting, and barely noticed the shadow that fell across her. Lina glanced up to see Captain Fengel peering down at her through his monocle, a vaguely surprised expression on his face.

"You can't tie that wreck up here!" shouted a voice.

A figure appeared out of the gloom. Tall, sandy-haired and ruggedly handsome, he was a pirate straight out of the penny-shows that Lina had loved as a child. He looked to be several years older than her, in his early twenties, his smile easy and cocksure. He held a mug in one hand, brimming with foamy ale. "Other ships need the space," he said with a smile.

Fengel and Lina both glanced back down the dock at the empty piers. Henry Smalls crept over to join them, standing deferentially behind his captain and looking like a scruffy, half-drowned bulldog.

The stranger stepped over Lina as if she weren't even there and came to a stop before Fengel. He grabbed at the captain's hand and pumped it, slapping his shoulder as well. "Goddess' teats. I was waiting for you up at Skydock near our usual watering hole. Then I saw the little longboat floundering around down here in the lagoon. Where's our bleeding ship at?"

Fengel considered the man calmly. It must only have been a trick of the light that he seemed to sway. Henry stepped beside his captain. "It's gone, Lucian," said the little steward. "The *Flittergrasp* is gone."

Their captain reached out, took Lucian's drink, and downed it in one smooth gulp. "First mate Thorn," he said to Lucian, his voice a harsh croak.

"We've had a rather rough time of it. I would appreciate if you could take up the command for now."

Lucian stared at Henry in dismay, his drink forgotten in the face of their news. "But how? What happened to the ship?"

"Aetherite blew it up in Triskelion," said Henry. "We've barely made it back."

"In a *longboat?* Across the Atalian Sea?"

"It was a kind of balloon at first. Someone's idea of an airship. Happened to be attached to the longboat, thankfully."

Lucian covered his eyes. "Our ship. Our beautiful ship." He straightened with a sigh. "Captain…there's no loot either, is there?"

Captain Fengel only frowned.

The first mate groaned. "Captain, you need to pay off Mr. Grey. Very, very badly. And now, without a ship…" He looked back to Fengel. "Captain, we need to talk about this. But you'll have to go pay obeisance to Blackheart first."

Fengel staggered as if he had been shot. An ugly scowl curled its way onto his face. "Ah. Yes. Obeisance."

"She's up at the Bleeding Teeth. But—hello. Who is this?" The first mate stared down at Lina, one eyebrow raised.

Lina tried to stand and talk at the same time, and failed. Lucian reached down to help her up. "Lina," she tried again, attempting a smile at the dashing first mate. He winced, and she knew she had been less than successful. *Oh, that's right. I've no hair anymore.*

"Doxy from Triskelion who wanted to be a pirate," said Henry. He turned to Fengel. "Sir, you can't put off your obeisance to Blackheart, but we can't be going up to Natasha in this state."

Fengel shook, as if surprised to find himself where he was. "What? Poppycock." His voice wavered. He looked around, as if taking in the dock and the town for the first time. His eyes darted down to the groaning pirates laying about the pier and he frowned as if surprised to see them there. "Mr. Mate, I would be obliged if you could take care of the crew."

Lucian nodded. "Of course, sir. Of course." Then he blinked. "How should I take care of them, sir?"

Fengel swayed. "We've just come back to port. Do what we usually do."

Henry Smalls spoke up. "It's exposure, Lucian. Lots of small beer, clean water, and food."

Lucian nodded, then turned back to the captain. "But with what money, sir?"

"Lucian, I leave that…in your capable hands."

Lucian peered at him. So did Henry. Fengel didn't seem to notice. Lucian sighed and ran his fingers through his hair. "I'll just take them to Garvey's Hole. Put it all on the tab." He frowned back at Henry Smalls. "That tab's still good, yes?"

Henry rolled his eyes. "Until tomorrow, apparently."

Fengel clapped Lucian on the shoulder. "Good. You have your orders, Lucian. Henry, you're with me. And…you too, Miss Stone."

Saying nothing more, he staggered past them onto the boardwalk and up the hill.

Lina stared after him, then turned to the other two men. She worked her mouth to get enough spit to talk. "Obeisance?" she asked. "To who? Who's this Natasha? Not even the serpent made him flinch."

Henry and Lucian both narrowed their eyes. "His wife," they said as one. The loathing in their voices sent a shiver up Lina's spine.

CHAPTER TWO

THE HEAT-FATIGUE WAS MAKING THINGS RATHER DIFFICULT.

Fengel concentrated on putting one foot in front of the other. The wooden stair he climbed was steep and built haphazardly into the earthen slope between terraces. His breath came in short gasps, stolen in the moments between mounting one step and pushing down upon the last.

A platform landing appeared halfway up this terrace. Grateful, Fengel stopped a moment. It was not large. Several small shacks clustered on it like a clutch of frightened pups backed into a corner. Their brightly painted signs advertised a tailor, a tattooist, and a black apothecary. A drunk sailor knelt at the edge of the platform, retching his rum over its lip. Two rogues stuck to the shadows, peering at Fengel and fingering daggers. To his right rose more of cliff-hugging Haventown. At his left the slope continued down to the docks and the lagoon. The air stank of brine, beer, and subtle jungle smells. Nostalgia washed over him and Fengel sighed. *Home. I'm home at last. Hurrah.*

The failed job in Triskelion, the loss of his *Flittergrasp*, and then the mad flight from that city. It made him want to shake his head, except that the muscles in his neck ached and his mouth was dry as a bone. Dimly Fengel realized that he should get food and water, though he didn't feel desperate. Just confused.

Fengel tried to focus. Where were they going again? Was this it? The upward stair looked rather imposing. Surely he hadn't meant to climb it now? Visible weakness in a captain was anathema upon a ship, and he was a little off at the moment. He certainly wouldn't have put himself in a position to show it to any of his crew. Or would he? Fengel pulled at his beard. *This will take careful deliberation.*

"Something wrong, Captain?" The voice came from the stair directly behind him.

He turned to peer at the duo below. Henry Smalls, his faithful steward, looking grizzled and drawn. Beside him stood a young...boy? No, not with that figure. A woman then, petite and with knife-hacked hair. Probably. If only she wouldn't stop shifting in and out of focus, he would be able to tell. *Miss Stone. That's right, I brought her along.*

The silence stretched. Not good. *I need to say something.* Fengel grinned. "Absolutely capital, Mr. Smalls. Here we are, after all."

His steward blinked up at him. "Sir? It's still a goodly distance to the Bleeding Teeth."

Blast. This landing wasn't their goal then. "Of course, of course," replied Fengel, making a dismissive gesture with his hands. *Think fast.* "I meant here, the view of the lagoon. Positively charming. Should the Servants flitter down from the Goddess on high, this is the place where they would choose to do it."

Smalls and the young woman looked out over the placid but scummy lagoon. "If you say so sir," he replied dutifully.

Fengel sighed and rubbed his forehead. He really didn't want to climb anymore. "You are a man of simple tastes, Mister Smalls. Still, I persevere."

He continued in their climb, taking care not to groan at the ache in his calves. Prim, proper, and impervious. Never let them think that you did anything against your will, and never show them your limits. Never let them see you stumble. That was the key to success, though by itself it only took one so far. What was the Bleeding Teeth? He had known a few minutes ago, and felt a peculiar undercurrent of dread at the thought. *Ah!* He had it now. The place was a tavern atop the highest terrace. Which explained the dread; more climbing was needed. Still, Fengel brightened. A tavern meant food and drink, both of which were sorely needed.

Night fell as they climbed the switchback stairs and terrace boardwalks, and Haventown blossomed to life around them. The air filled with catcalls, raucous laughter, and the sound of breaking glass. Lanterns and candle flames were lit, illuminating foggy windows and setting dirty glass aglow. Pirates, smugglers, and sailors appeared as they ascended, all swaggering and strutting through the rebel town. Barkers stood before the brothels and better taverns to hawk the goods inside. Three footpads waited in a narrow alley while a young woman lured in victims. Past her two rival captains shouted at each other while their crews placed bets or called out barbs of their own. An aetherite conjured up dancing, living flames for his own amusement. Fengel spied Blackheart's Bandits, keeping things peaceable if not exactly keeping the peace. High above them floated the airships in Skydock, the fabric of the gasbag frames and their skysails reflecting the light back below like great, soft lanterns.

Fengel focused on the buildings, ignoring the crowd. Where was the Bleeding Teeth? Farther up? Had they passed it already?

Henry's voice floated up to him. "The Sheikdom of Salomca started it all."

Fengel started to prepare a response. But the steward was talking to Miss Stone, not to him. *Hmm. This could help a bit. I must remain canny.* Fengel slowed, eavesdropping as they made their way up Haventown.

"This was, oh, twenty years back or so, lass. The Sheikdom started preying on Royal Navy ships, the ones making the new trip to the Yulan Colony, what everyone now calls Breachtown. They founded Haventown here to launch their raids. When the fighting heated up back home they left, and the towns here had to fend for themselves. Between that, and the merchants sucking treasure out of the Yulan, well, you get pirates."

"But why doesn't the Kingdom just clean us out if we're such a bother?" asked Miss Stone. *Lizzy?* No. *Molly?* Fengel tried to remember her first name. *Lina, that's it.*

"They try, on occasion. But we're two weeks away by ship and they still wage war with the Sheik. Also, the Copper Isles are bigger than you think, lass. A whole chain, not just what we saw outside."

They ascended the last stair and found themselves on the topmost terrace. Here the town spread out to either side, its boardwalk stretching out across the clifftop like a crescent moon. Taverns, sailmakers, warehouses, and brothels all clustered together in the middle, dwarfed in turn by the wide platforms and cleared-jungle enclosure of the Brotherhood Yards where they spilled out over the cliff. Opposite the Yards at the far end hung the Skydocks, piers stair-stepping up a slope in the cliff. Several airships floated at mooring there; the closest caught Fengel's eye.

The *Copper Queen* was crafted from dark oak, an old sailship in truth, rope and cabling hanging it from a gasbag balloon. Thick hawsers and chains lashed it to the overhanging pier of the Skydock. There was something about that ship, some important fact that pricked at his memory, demanding recall. But the information was hidden, and he turned away. It was obvious that the ship hadn't flown in years, and wouldn't again anytime soon.

Fengel turned back to the nearest buildings, peering through the crowds for the Bleeding Teeth. He seemed to recall that there was a signboard above it, with a scarlet smile carved into the wood. *There.* It lay a hundred feet up the boardwalk, sandwiched in between two other buildings and half-built onto the slope of the jungle cliff top. *Food and drink!*

Henry and Lina conversed behind him as he approached the tavern. "That's good to know," said Lina. "But what's this about obeisance?"

"Well, we're not really like a proper town now, are we?" replied Henry. "Haventown works because even pirates need a place to sell the booty, repair the ship, and have a few drinks. But it's anarchy lass, everyone's only real allegiance is to their ship. Sometimes things get ugly. Twenty years ago it was pretty bad; ships firing on each other, vendetta murders in the brothels. Then one of the first sky-pirates had his drink shot out by a stray pistol-ball. Euron Blackheart put his foot down, knocking heads and sinking ships until everyone agreed that he was in charge, the king. So now whenever a captain comes back into port they have to swing by and acknowledge him before anything else. Usually he holds court in the Bleeding Teeth."

Fengel reached the front of the tavern, climbing several steps up to the porch. Henry's story was familiar, was right, but he had forgotten something, something important.

"So who is Natasha?"

"Well...Euron's getting a little long in the tooth. Copper Queen back there is his ship, and it hasn't flown in a decade. Day to day things are run by his daughter now, Natasha Blackheart."

Lina's voice dropped low, conspiratorial, with a strange edge to it. "You mean Captain Fengel's wife?"

"The same."

Oh. The fog clouding his brain dissolved. Not food and drink. Natasha and obeisance. That was why they were here. Fengel grimaced, fighting down the swell of mixed, mostly negative emotions that welled up inside him. Through the door came music, braying laughter, and the sound of something breaking.

Smalls had fallen silent. Fengel could feel their gazes upon his back, both his steward and the girl. *Never let them see you stumble.* Still. Natasha. He wanted to spit. Instead he squared his shoulders, adjusted his monocle, and pushed through the wooden door.

The interior of the Bleeding Teeth spread out before him. A hundred different lanterns lit the room brightly, all affixed to the walls or hanging from the ceiling. There were hand-lamps, ship's lamps, garden lamps, oil lamps, and even streetlamps. At the far end of the room a great stone hearth blazed merrily, combining with the lanterns to fill the room with an oppressive heat. A narrow bar dominated the left wall, a fat barkeep glowering behind it. Despite its warmth, the room was almost full. Pirates of every description lounged at tables spread out throughout the space. Fengel recognized a few of them, captains of skyships and sailships sitting apart, clustered together with their crews.

The middle of the room was empty, set before a heavy chair placed with its back to the hearth. It was a throne, really, carved of a single piece of heavy wood and pillaged from who knew where. A woman reclined lazily in its lap, leaning against one armrest with her leg stretched out over the other. She was tall and thin, wearing captain's boots, tight leggings, and a puffy blouse cut low to reveal ample cleavage. Her skin was dusky, and long tresses of curly black hair spilled down over her shoulders to frame an elegant face. Striking golden eyes gazed out hungrily at the world, balanced by a crooked smile. At her sides, on each arm of the throne rested a simple wooden mug. One was cracked and broken, as if it had been used to stop a pistol-ball. The other was still in use, a thick head of foam crowning its lip. In spite of his other feelings, Fengel's heart lept into his throat at the sight of his wife.

Mordecai Wright, Natasha's first mate, stood beside and a little behind her chair. The man was a thin, sinister shadow. He wore black, well-suited to his dark hair and beard, and glowered at the world as if it constantly did him some disservice. In the space before the throne stood a young, handsome pirate.

Leaning down, Mordecai whispered into Natasha's ear and made a gesture at the man standing in the empty space before her. "So," she said, voice sultry and slow. "You think you're good enough to join my Reavers?"

"That I am," said the pirate. "I've served three years with Ruckshaw on a sailship, I know the Isles like the back of my hand, and I can out-fight and out-drink damn near any man alive." He grinned, cocksure.

Natasha returned his smile. "That's quite the boast." She glanced lazily back at Mordecai. "And I think you're wrong on at least one part. But tell me. *Why* do you want to join my crew?"

He grinned lasciviously. "Because of all the captains in Haventown, there's only one that men dream of, and that's Natasha Blackheart."

Natasha smiled coyly at him. "Flatterer."

"That I am!" he laughed. "But it's not just that. Your ship, she's a work of art. The *Dawnhawk,* she's the finest in Haventown. A skyship, and a masterpiece of the craft. The Brotherhood has come a long way since that old garbage scow, the *Copper Queen.*" He chuckled dryly.

The room went silent. The barkeep ducked down behind his bar.

"Mordecai?" Natasha held out a hand. The first mate drew a flintlock pistol and passed it to her.

The would-be sky-pirate stared, eyes wide. "No," he cried. "Wait!"

Natasha took aim and fired. Thunder erupted in the room, the blast setting Fengel's ears to ringing. The dashing pirate slumped to the floor, sending the sawdust flying. Face pensive, eyes dangerous, Natasha blew smoke from the barrel and passed the pistol back to her first mate.

"No one insults my father's ship," said Natasha quietly. Then she smiled, sat back, and took up her mug. "He was right, though. The *Dawnhawk* is a very fine ship."

The tension in the room evaporated, the crowd jeering laughter before turning back to drinking and jesting and games of chance. Mordecai made a gesture and two men jumped up from a table. They grabbed up the corpse to haul him away. Then one paused and turned back to their captain. "He's still alive, ma'am."

Natasha quaffed from her mug, the drink sloshing a bit over her delicate cheeks and spilling down her throat. She wiped her lips with her sleeve and raised an eyebrow at the crewman. "Really?" She looked up at her first mate. "You need to clean your gun."

"Mayhap," said Mordecai, "you need to work on your aim."

She sighed. "Nonsense. Fellow might be as tough as he said. Fancy that." She raised her voice. "Take him to the ship. If he survives maybe he can have his wish. After all, a little stamina in a man is a rare thing." Natasha raised her mug for another pull, then paused to belch.

Fengel squared his shoulders. *Time to get this over with.* Sidestepping the two crewman and their bleeding, groaning cargo, he moved to the middle of the taproom floor. Mordecai noticed him first, and smiled thinly. Natasha didn't see him. She was taking another drink, mug upended.

"The crew of the *Flittergrasp* has returned to port," he said loudly, clearly. "And thus, I have come to give my obeisance to the rule of Blackhand."

Natasha's eyes widened. She choked, leaned up, and spit her mouthful of ale in a geyser that soaked a nearby pirate. "Fengel?" she gasped, staring at him.

Up close he saw the familiar signs. *She's drunk. Again.* He pursed his lips disapprovingly. "Indeed," he said.

She laughed, wiped her chin with the sleeve of her shirt, then laughed again. "Oh, now this is a day. What kept you? Triskelion isn't that far away."

Mordecai smiled like a serpent. "Alas, ma'am, I believe that good Captain Fengel had to take the long way home. I spied him coming into the Waterdocks in a broken longboat."

Natasha blinked up at her mate, then at him. "What? Where's the *Flittergrasp*? Why weren't you on your ship?"

Cold anger and hot embarrassment writhed in his stomach. "The *Flittergrasp* is...no more. There was an incident over Triskelion. It was destroyed."

The room quieted abruptly. Natasha stared at him, her face slacking into surprised sympathy.

Then she laughed. Great big choking belly-laughs that set her form to shaking uncontrollably. She threw her empty mug at the floor and it bounced. "You...utter...*tit,*" she howled. The rest of the room joined in, mocking laughter echoing from wall to wall.

Fengel grimaced. "Your sympathy is appreciated," he said. "However, after a bit of rest, I plan to make my way to the Yards to resolve this inconvenience."

"And what," asked Natasha, gasping for air, tears in her eyes, "do you plan to do there? The head Mechanist is gone missing. The Brotherhood of the Cog aren't taking any more ship orders."

Fengel started. *What?* What did she mean?

"I tell you what," said his wife, slurring slightly. She took a deep breath and then cleared her throat. "A pirate's no pirate without a ship. I've always had a soft spot for you, I'll admit. And it seems you're in a bit of a bind. Here, drop that group of press-ganged losers you call a crew, and join mine. You can even be a mate. First or second I don't care, should be fun seeing you try to best Mordecai. It's been a bit since I've seen that swordplay of yours." She smiled back woozily at her first mate. "My husband here is probably the only one on the Atalian Sea who can give you a run for your money, isn't that right?"

Mordecai Wright stared her down. Then he turned to Fengel, eyes narrow. "Hardly," he drawled.

"Hmm," said Natasha, turning back to Fengel. "What do you say?"

"Never," he replied instantly. "My crew is my crew. They stand behind me, and I behind them. I will simply have to acquire a ship by some other means."

Anger rippled across Natasha's features, turning her fair face into something ugly. "How *dare* you. Fine then. That'll teach me for trying to throw you a bone. It's just as well. I would have loved to watch you crawl, making do with second best when everyone knew that you'd had your own ship. I would have loved to watch you choke on that swollen pride of yours. Go then! Get out! Starve to death instead, you incompetent fool. When I find your beggared arse down on the Waterdocks, I'll laugh! Now go!" She stood and pointed with a wavering finger, chest heaving.

Fengel felt himself flush. He bent in a short, terse bow. Then he wheeled about, looking past Henry and Lina and making his way to the door. He pushed through it back to the town outside. The cool night air hit him like a hammer. Descending the stair, he closed his eyes and let out a sigh, willing away the turmoil within. *Ridiculous harpy. Besotted slattern. Raging—*

Two hands grabbed him roughly. They swung him around to smack into a wall with a thump that jarred his thoughts and his sense. Distantly, he felt his monocle fly free.

"Mr. Grey would like to speak with you," said a voice like heavy gravel.

Fengel looked up into a face made wholly out of scar tissue. The man holding him was huge, though not quite the size of his gunnery mistress, Sarah Lome. Still, he himself was slight in comparison. Another massive fellow, partner to the first, glowered down at him. Past these two Fengel spied Henry Smalls on the stair, watching in surprise and concern, Miss Stone standing behind him.

"Ah," said Fengel. "Yes. Mr. Grey. Of course I will pay him a visit. Just as soon as—"

"Just now," rumbled the other thug. "Mr. Grey would very much like to speak with you, an' he won't be taking 'no' for an answer."

Fengel felt his heart sink into his stomach. *I do* not *need this right now.* But he smiled up at the thugs. "Well, then. Lead the way."

The man released his grip and stepped back, indicating their desired direction. Fengel paused to straighten his jacket and replace his monocle, then he strode ahead. The men moved to frame him, and he heard his two crewmen jog up to behind him.

"Captain, should I go and fetch—"

"No, Henry," replied Fengel. "Let's just go and see what Mr. Grey wants. Attend, Miss Stone. I am sure that this shall be an extended education on the life of adventure you so desired."

They walked on in silence along the uppermost boardwalk. The thugs led them along the northern edge of the cliff, past shops and craftsmen towards the Skydocks and the airships there. Some of the locals observed the procession, scurrying out of the way after a glare from the two massive escorts.

"Who is Mr. Grey?" Lina asked quietly.

"Local factor," whispered Henry. "Financier and fence for all the big criminal cartels back on the Western Continent. The Sindacato. Funds a lot of people here."

"Oh." She fell silent. Fengel wasn't surprised. *Everyone* had heard of the Sindicato.

The troupe reached the border between the Skydock and the town proper. Grey's thugs led them to the last building before the Skydock, an older manor-house of a style at odds with the rest of the shanties and shacks of Haventown. A low ramp led up to a front door elegantly carved out of fine wood. Fengel paused halfway up to catch his breath and stare longingly at the great dirigibles moored only a hundred feet away.

Lina spoke up again, her voice a whisper meant not to carry. "That was his *wife?* What a bitch."

"That she is, lass," replied Henry. "And pretty much in charge here, more or less."

Fengel gazed out at the airships, a sense loss almost overwhelming him at their sight. They floated gently in the breeze, the watch crewman bantering with each other from the underslung decks. Sailing on the open ocean was a fine thing, but nothing compared to the wind-born sway of flying through the air.

"But why?" asked Lina. "Why did he marry her?"

"A moment of raging insanity," said Fengel. The two thugs turned back to him, fists ready to chivvy him along. Fengel smiled at them and continued up the ramp to the building.

The front door opened onto a richly appointed parlor. Fine carpets covered the floors and oiled teak paneled the walls. A small couch sat against one wall, facing a portrait of a distinguished Perinese gentleman next to a door hanging slightly ajar. Past these a stair led upwards to the floor above.

"Thomas? cried a voice through the door. "Is that you?"

The second thug who'd manhandled him strode over and pushed open the door. "Yes sir," he said quietly. "And I've brought the debtor you asked me to go find."

"Fengel?" said the voice. "Ah, excellent. Show him in please."

Thomas glared over at him. Fengel was already moving. He sauntered over to the door, Lina and Henry falling in behind him.

The room was a small, well-decorated office. Bookshelves lined the walls and expensive rugs lay upon the floor. A massive mahogany desk dominated the small space, a single chair facing it.

Mr. Grey sat behind it, as bland as his name suggested. Middling height, average weight, and light brown hair, his skin tanned but not so dark as an islander. His eyes were an unremarkable shade of brown. As if in compensation, his clothing was wealthy and refined. He wore a suit, expensive and slightly unreasonable considering the climate, and his hair was slicked back with pomade.

"Ah," he said in a soft voice. "Captain Fengel, have a seat. So good of you to drop by." His eyes flicked to the pair of crewman behind him. "Would you and your crew care for some refresh—"

"Yes," said Fengel, Henry, and Lina all at once.

Mr. Grey blinked, taken aback. "Some tea, Thomas," he said. "And biscuits." Thomas grunted and backed out of the room. Grey turned to face Fengel again. "Have a seat. Now, let's get straight to business. It's come to my attention that you and your crew returned to Haventown in a leaky dinghy tied up down at the docks."

"Longboat, actually," replied Fengel. He took the lone chair before the desk. The floor creaked as Henry and Lina moved up behind him.

A moue of annoyance fluttered across Grey's face. "Yes, a longboat. As I take it, your most recent venture has failed?"

Fengel nodded, despondent. His ship. His beautiful ship, blown to smithereens by arcane flames. He forced the thought from his mind.

"Then, most importantly, I take it to mean that you cannot pay off your loan?

Despite himself, Fengel winced. He could feel Henry's eyes on his back. Fengel smiled a brittle smile. *I need to say something. Something quick, witty.* He opened his mouth but Grey bulled on.

"And the distinct manner in which you arrived suggests that the collateral is...unavailable?"

Fengel sighed, like a balloon letting free its air. "Gone," he admitted. "Dead by an aetherite's infernal magics."

"I see." Grey steepled his fingers. "Mister Fengel. You are aware that you owe me in excess of two hundred and forty-five thousand gold sovereigns?"

Henry sucked in his breath. Miss Stone whistled. "How?" asked his steward. "For what?"

The financier consulted a ledger on his desk. "The details are extensive, but in short; your captain owes me, and by extension the western cartels, for five separate loans over the last year and a half. Ostensibly to repair, refit and supply his ship."

Henry quieted in shock. Fengel was glad for that. "I am aware," he replied to Grey.

"And you cannot pay."

"No."

Grey tapped his ledger. "Well then, it is quite fortunate for you that I have a task all lined up."

Fengel blinked, his confusion returned. "I'm sorry?"

The financier rolled his eyes. "I had the suspicion that your latest venture west would be fruitless, if not quite so catastrophic. Simply put, there is something that you can do for me to square your debt to the Sindacato, saving your skin and perhaps making a profit for once in your life."

He turned in his chair and retrieved a sheaf of papers from a bookshelf, which he then rolled out upon the table. Grey hunted for a moment, then tapped a space at one side. "Here," he said.

Fengel peered down over the map. Though dizzy, he made out a sketch of the Copper Isles and the Yulan continent. As he examined it, Thomas returned with a large platter which he set upon the edge of the desk before backing away discreetly.

Fengel lost all interest in the map. The platter held a fine silver tea service with a steaming teapot, cups, a large pitcher of water, and several small plates stacked high with sweet biscuits. His mouth watered painfully at the sight of it.

"Feel free to help yourselves," said Grey. "Now—"

The financier fell silent as the trio descended upon the platter. Lina moved quickest, grabbing handfuls of biscuits and shoving them in her mouth. Fengel cursed her speed and found himself fighting with Henry over the pitcher of water. They tugged it back and forth until Henry seemed to remember himself and abashedly, yet regretfully, gave in to his captain.

Fengel raised the pitcher to his lips then stopped, spying Mr. Grey out of the corner of his eye. *Never let them see you stumble.* He smiled, and with an effort took a teacup and filled it, which he immediately drank. Then he poured another. And then another.

"At any rate," said Grey, eyebrow raised, "I have had a recent dispatch from Breachtown. The *H.M.S. Albatross* has gone missing with all hands en route to Triskelion. The vessel was carrying a large number of very valuable items, but most of all a gemstone, big as two fists, carved of a luminous and unknown material."

Fengel paused in pouring himself another cup of water, and Henry wrenched the pitcher from him. "Gemstone?"

"Yes. A recent find, known as the Governor's Lantern. I want you to attain it for me. Now. I have paid a pretty sum for an aetherite divination, and that augury seemed to indicate that the ship had run aground here, in the southwestern coastline, along the mouth of the little-known Silverpenny River. Take whatever treasures you can find from the wreck, but the gemstone is mine. Return it to me and I will clear your debt to the Sindacato. Oh, one other thing. The Lantern may be cursed."

"Cursed?" asked Fengel, one eyebrow raised.

"Possibly. At any rate, that isn't my problem. We have an accord, and I'm not taking no for an answer. You've much to do, and I as well. Take the map. A description of the gemstone is attached."

Fengel felt flustered. "But I haven't got a ship anymore."

Grey looked bored. "Also not my problem. Thomas! Please see Captain Fengel out." The financier rolled up the map and handed it across the table to him, along with another sheaf of paper. "Oh, and Captain Fengel? One more thing."

Fengel blinked. "What?"

Grey suddenly looked anything but mild. He met Fengel's eyes and held them. "This is your final chance. No more loans, no more time. Return with the gemstone. There is no other option. You can not hide from the Sindicato. And you cannot fight them. Bring me the Lantern. If you don't, we will be taking your head instead." He held his gaze another moment, then looked down at his ledger.

The three of them were escorted outside, Lina gulping down a cup of hot tea and Henry shoving sweet biscuits into his pockets. Fengel tried to regain his composure. The Sindicato were dangerous, but he'd always believed that he could deal with them. Now, with Grey's threat hanging in his ears, he didn't seem so certain. He tapped the rolled up map to his chin and strolled down the ramp to the boardwalk. Halfway down he stopped, frowning. *What am I going to do?*

"Oh sir," said Henry, through a mouthful of sweet biscuit. "How could you get in with the Sindacato? And for so much? What are we going to do?"

The airships of the Skydock caught Fengel's eye. Maybe he was looking at this the wrong way. *Grey's honest, if cutthroat. His information would be good. And if I can get that gem, everything's fixed.* The airships bobbed gently in the evening breeze. Closest, the *Copper Queen* was a dark blotch against the night, the finer vessels easily visible past it. The *Dawnhawk* was the largest and most magnificent, a beautiful airship, brand new and unscarred. The complex network of skysails hung against its hull like glimmering fins, shining in the light of the rising moon.

An idea began to form within the murk of his receding confusion. So what if his old ship was gone? He still had his crew, he now had a job that could take care of everything, and he'd drunk about a gallon of water flavored by little lemon slices.

"Mister Smalls," he asked tentatively. "Are you still owed a favor by Wayern the crate-maker?" Fengel turned back to his befuddled, grizzled steward. Then he grinned.

CHAPTER THREE

MORDECAI COUNTED THE KNOTS IN THE WOOD OF THE FAR WALL.

"That inconceivable shit," ranted Natasha. "That pompous, blowhard windbag!"

He didn't bother saying anything. There was little point when she was like this, angry and in her cups. He continued his count. *Forty eight. Forty nine. No, that's a hole from a pistol-ball. Isn't it? Maybe just dried blood?*

Natasha Blackheart was a competent captain and a ruthless pirate. She truly was her father's daughter, and old Euron cared only for booze, booty, and his ship. But unlike her father, Natasha was also quite emotional on a few other, more personal subjects, especially when she was drunk.

The first was Euron's own legacy. The old man was the most famous pirate of them all, and she constantly stood in his shadow. Everyone in Haventown knew the tales of his exploits; she'd grown up hearing them constantly, and both loved and hated the old man for it.

The second was her husband. Fengel was well known amongst the current generation of buccaneers. His crew were fiercely loyal for some reason, and the man was a master with a blade. Beyond that, he was a strangely honorable fellow for a pirate, though priggish. Goddess alone knew what Natasha saw in him; the origin of their engagement was a mystery.

Between these two fixations, Natasha was driven to reach farther and plunder harder than any other brigand in Haventown. When inebriated she would obsess over the two of them, becoming ridiculously petty. Mordecai learned long ago that it was best to simply let her rant until her emotion burned itself out, or she found someone else to burn it out on.

"Fop," Natasha continued. "He's as base-born as I am. Worse! He's the son of a back alley horse-doctor!"

Mordecai kept his peace, still rankled at her meaningless, drunken suggestion that Fengel might replace him as first mate. It was the kind of thing he should have come to expect, but it still annoyed. A great grandfather clock sat along one wall opposite the bar, a relic of Euron's many, many raids. It chimed eight times, presenting an opportunity for escape.

"Maybe I should have him killed," Natasha muttered. She grabbed at Mordecai's coat and glared at him with bleary eyes. "What do you think?"

"An excellent suggestion," he murmured. Faintly, he felt a glimmer of hope— maybe she would finally see sense. Mordecai was wiser than to try to encourage the subject, though; she would only get defensive. "It is eight. I must make the rounds."

Natasha released him, face slack as she considered her words. Nothing would come of it, he knew. She upended her mug, swaying slightly in her father's throne. Finding it empty, she hollered for the barkeep, gesturing for Mordecai to take his leave.

He took his chance and left the bar. Outside, the cool evening breeze of the Isles was a panacea after the stifling heat of the tavern. Most assumed that the heat in the Bleeding Teeth was calculated, that Euron liked to see the pirate captains beneath them squirm and pant while he remained icy calm. For his part, Mordecai always suspected that the warmth was meant to comfort to Euron in his age.

Leisurely, he strolled down the boardwalk, heading in the direction of the Yards. He stuck to the middle of the walk, one hand comfortably on the hilt of his cutlass as he made his way through the drunks, sailors, and whores. All fell back at the sight of him. Mordecai never smiled, but inwardly he let himself feel pleased. Being first mate of Natasha's Reavers, the most feared band of cutthroats in the Atalian Sea, lent him recognition enough. But Mordecai had a reputation all his own, carefully cultivated over many years. No one risked his offense.

It would have been nice to show himself around a little further. *But duty calls.* They'd already overstayed in port. Much longer and the crew would become lazy or rebellious, and that meant he would have to reinforce discipline, which meant in turn that he'd have to find new bodies to replace those that were inevitably lost.

He swung by the Brotherhood Yards and spoke with the foreman, a dour Mechanist in a leather greatcoat and goggles. For all the mystery of his profession, the man looked harried. Mordecai ratified the bill for repairs made and checked to ensure that spares had been delivered to the *Dawnhawk's*

Mechanist in case of an emergency. He took care not to intimidate the man *too* much. It behooved him to have a cordial relationship with the people who made sure his ship flew.

He climbed out to the stair-step pier of the Skydocks where the *Dawnhawk* was moored. Reaching it, he stopped a moment to regard her. A ball of warm pride grew in his belly as he took in her shining skysails and clean, dark hull. She sat anchored on the highest pier of the dock, latest and best of the air-borne marvels of the Brotherhood.

The ship was Natasha's, but he was the one that ran it. In a ritual he performed whenever he approached, he compared the *Dawnhawk* to the other airships, just so he could find them lacking. They certainly flew well enough, and would be worth a fortune to any nation on the Western Continent. Yet beside the *Dawnhawk* they were pitiful and outdated. Mordecai did not consider himself a petty man, but the ship was his passion, and his position on it a singular point of pride.

His eyes alighted on the last and lowest of the moored skyships, old Euron's boat, the *Copper Queen*. *That brash idiot was right. What a garbage scow.* Dismissing it, Mordecai walked down the pier to an assortment of crates and barrels stacked below the *Dawnhawk*, which the crewman he'd left to keep watch were hauling up onto the deck. Konrad Faust, ship's navigator, spied Mordecai and strode to the gangplank above him. Like all airship navigators the man was an aetherite, capable of conjuring forth strange magics from the invisible daemon he carried with him.

"Almost loaded," Konrad called down, voice clouded by the thick accent of his native Greisheim. The aetherite was stocky, and as he spoke the shaggy blond beard he wore danced like a scruffy bush in a windstorm. Mordecai didn't like Konrad. But he acknowledged the man's utility, even if he was dangerous and a little unstable. It was a pity that the rarity of such individuals didn't leave much room to be choosey.

"Good," Mordecai replied. "You've got until first light to get things shipshape. Captain will want to rise with the dawn."

"We be ready," affirmed Konrad, blue eyes crinkling. The man sounded affable. He must have sated his daemon recently. "We plan on being gone awhile? Why so much food this time? It's packed oddly too. Captain thinking of a little smuggling?"

Mordecai raised an eyebrow. Salt-beef, hardtack, black powder, and fresh water? The goods order hadn't been exceptionally larger than usual. He turned and called a pair of deckhands, waving them over with the crate they'd just hoisted. "Set it down," he said. "I want to get a look inside." They nodded and dropped the load before him. Mordecai retrieved a nearby pry bar and levered the top up. Rows of packed biscuits lay tightly within. Hardtack.

He frowned slightly. Another man might feel foolish. He did not. It was always better to be safe, and perhaps a little paranoid, than to be sorry. The pirates of Haventown were a cutthroat bunch; it was never a good idea to think oneself immune to some sort of sabotage, regardless of one's reputation. "Get it aboard," he said to the crewmen. They scurried to obey. He turned back to Konrad. "The cargo's fine. Now quit dawdling."

"I didn't say it wasn't!" The navigator turned away in a huff to yell at another crewman.

Mordecai set his mouth in a line. None of the other crew would ever dare to respond to him that way. But the navigator was erratic, half-mad. There was no point in following it further, for now. One last task needed tending to, and he turned away from the ship, making his way back down to Haventown from the Skydocks.

As first mate he had many responsibilities. Foremost was to be the captain's strong right hand, doling out punishment and keeping ship's discipline so that she could get on with the job of captaining. Second was to care for the ship itself, and Mordecai always made sure the vessel was as well-stocked and in good repair as any in the Perinese Royal Navy. Thirdly, he did what he could to improve the prospects of the ship and crew.

This last he attended discreetly. Haventown was a pirate town and den of smugglers. All the things that pirates brought in from their raids filtered back out through the factors and fences to the black markets of the Western Continent. In return, gold and other goods filled the coffers of Haventown, along with things of more intangible value. Rumors and classified information were traded throughout the town, just as valuable as any other commodity.

Mordecai had built up a fine network of informants over the years, carefully weeding away the untrustworthy and unreliable sources until only the best were left. Tonight they told him of a fat merchant convoy about to sail from the free city of Capricanto. He also heard that the Sheik and the Kingdom were preparing for another naval engagement, and it would be good to avoid the northeastern region around Triskelion. Lastly, he made his way to a smaller, quieter tavern near the Waterdocks and settled in to hear local gossip, brought to him by those who curried favor with Natasha. There was rarely anything useful, but a dutiful mate kept abreast of things.

"You Mordecai Wright?" said a deep voice.

Mordecai took the speaker in at a glance. But for the maze of scars across his face, the man was unexceptional, common as any other dockside brawler and only good for the muscle in his arms. "I am," he replied, calmly sipping from a glass of wine. "And you must have a *very* good reason for bothering me."

The stranger didn't meet his eyes. It was obvious he wasn't used to dealing with his betters, and didn't know quite how he should go about it. He settled on obsequiousness. "I'm Jack. Gorvey up at the Skydocks said you pay good for information. Well, got somethin' might interest you."

"Tell me what you know," replied Mordecai, voice level. "I'll decide what it's worth." Most of the evening's gossip had proven useless. He was bored and wanted to leave.

Jack looked like he might object, but quieted. He sat still for a moment, then appeared to come to a decision. "I work sometimes fer Mister Grey," he said. "Whenever 'e needs a bit of rough work done. Thomas, he comes down to grab me earlier this evenin', says 'e needs help tracking down a posh feller Mr. Grey wants found. The Fengel guy that's married ter yer Captain Blackheart." Jack glanced up at Mordecai from the corner of his eyes, hunting for a reaction.

Mordecai kept his face impassive. It wasn't hard. "Go on."

The thug frowned. "Anyway, we found him, up on the top terrace near the Bleeding Teeth with a few crew. They were all messed up. We hauled him off to Mr. Grey and I kept quiet outside while they chatted. Seems Grey wants Fengel to find something valuable. A lantern or summat."

Mordecai gestured at the barkeep, ordering a mug of grog for Jack. "Tell me everything you heard."

Encouraged, Jack told his tale. Mordecai learned that Captain Fengel was heavily in debt to the Sindicato, and about the wreck of the *H.M.S. Albatross*. He grilled Jack on the details repeatedly. Once he finished, he tossed the thug a gold sovereign and left the tavern. Grey wasn't one to be fooled with, and Jack would likely be dead before the end of the week for letting this slip. Still, that was no concern of his.

It seems this night has been profitable after all. Truly, he could care less about Captain Fengel, though the man's first mate, Lucian Thorne, had been a personal irritation before. Hearing about Fengel's financial straits was amusing, but the only real value to be gained from the news was the fact that would please Natasha. And even that could be taken too far, as evidenced by her current besotted ranting. The location of a wrecked Perinese frigate, heavy with priceless treasure—now *that* was news worth hearing.

He climbed the terraces of Haventown. The hour was late. Overhead the moon shone brightly, nearly full. It cast strange, ghostly illumination over the lagoon, deepening shadows while brightening the boardwalks. The evening's mad revelry had quieted, as it did every night at this time. Life was carefree and unrestrained in Haventown; exertions burned themselves out quickly.

The topmost terrace was empty when he reached it on his way back to the Bleeding Teeth, the few drunks and pirates pointing out the skysails of the airships at Skydock. By the light of the moon the vessels glowed, their strange material seeming to burn with a cold fire.

A wrecked frigate would be quite a bit more worthwhile than a well-armed merchant convoy or walking into a war. Normally Mordecai didn't enjoy salvage operations, but this was ripe for the picking. He did sums as he walked, calculating the duration of already-purchased supplies against distance to the nearby Yulan continent. Shrill laughter distracted him. Another couple, a pirate and his ugly whore, were pointing at the Skydocks and laughing. "I ain't never seen the like!" the woman chuckled as Mordecai passed.

"Oh, it happens, lovie. But on the *Dawnhawk*? Someone's got balls o' brass, that's for sure."

Mordecai stopped. He turned back to look at the couple, then followed the man's finger, pointing up at his ship. A single figure moved about the deck. At this distance he could not tell who it was, but the person's movements were furtive. The figure attached a hook and a satchel to a rope hanging off the deck and slid it down away from the ship to somewhere else, hidden by the rooftops of Haventown and the gas-bags of the other skyships.

Someone was looting the *Dawnhawk*.

Mordecai ran, drawing his saber as he went. Where was Konrad? Or the crewmen set to watch? Were they dead? The idea was preposterous. The navigator was a powerful aetherite, and Mordecai had personally trained the crewmen in swordplay. Who could lay them low? Certainly not a lone thief.

He ascended to the pier where the *Dawnhawk* was moored. It was empty, the cargo missing, stolen or loaded aboard. A chemical stink wafted down from the deck to stain the air. *The damned cargo. There was something wrong with it.* He ran up the gangplank with a growl, heedless of the caustic stink, then stopped abruptly at the scene before him.

The thief was alone. He wore a leather greatcoat and thick leather gloves, a belt at his waist dangling a sword and brace of pistols. A leather-and-brass miner's mask covered his features, allowing him to breathe safely. Several heavy glass bottles lay cracked and broken about the deck at his feet, the source of the thick chemical fog. The missing crew lay all about, either dead or unconscious. Half of the barrels and crates were stacked neatly near the open cargo hatch, the rest presumably below. Two were open, and the lone figure was busily stuffing the contents into satchels to drop onto the guide-rope leading off the edge of the airship.

Mordecai rapped the gunwale with the pommel of his saber. The sound echoed out across the deck, startling the figure. "I don't know who you are," said Mordecai, "but by dawn all of Haventown will know who you were. And they will know that you died screaming."

The thief peered up at Mordecai from across the deck. He held a short pry bar. Turning, he jammed it into the top of the nearest crate and leaned on it. The crate cracked and the lid sprung up, half-opened. Then he turned back to Mordecai, reaching up to pull away his mask. It came away to reveal a smiling, sandy-haired man with bright blue eyes.

"When I go," said Lucian Thorne, "I plan to die laughing."

"Thorne," hissed Mordecai.

"Hello, Mordie. How are you?"

"This is beyond belief," said Mordecai. "You, all alone, are trying to steal from the *Dawnhawk*."

"You leap to conclusions. Always have."

"And yet," continued Mordecai. "You almost succeeded. Killed off my watch crew and the ship's aetherite. I'll have to replace them. That's slightly vexing."

Lucian kicked Konrad, the nearest of Natasha's Reavers at hand. He studied the aetherite with a frown. "Oh, not dead. Just unconscious. Should be waking up any minute now, if my apothecary knows his numbers."

Mordecai took a step forward, raising his blade. "That can't have been cheap. And I happen to know for a fact that your 'captain' is more impoverished than a poxied whore."

Lucian grimaced. "Yes. Had to pay out of my own pocket for this. I'm not exactly pleased about that, I'll admit." He brightened. "Still though, it let me pull one over on the ol' bitch, so I can't complain."

"You act as if you're going to get away." Mordecai smiled wickedly. He took another step, savoring the moment. *I was content to let you be, you little shit. Now I'll have your heart.* "I truly wonder. You've always been foolish. But stupid? Whatever you could have gotten for my ship's supplies wouldn't be nearly worth the risk. Look at you now. Fengel, he might have had a chance. He's good, I'll admit. But you? You're barely a competent swordsman."

Mordecai took up a guard position and approached. Lucian darted back to the far gunwale where the guide rope was tied to a cleat. He drew a pistol at his belt and leveled it at Mordecai's chest, cocking it with a thumb.

"Again, you leap to conclusions." Lucian smiled even wider, as if he were trying not to laugh. "I am not going to be selling off your hardtack and stale cheese. We appear to have need of that."

Mordecai smiled wryly. "Really. How did you plan to go after the *Albatross* without a ship?" Lucian started, surprised for the first time. "Oh yes," continued Mordecai. "I've heard about your little task for Grey."

"That's not your concern," snapped Lucian. He squared his shoulders. "In any case, I've places to be. Time to be off."

"You still have to go through me."

"Mordie, I know full well how deadly you are with a blade. And I've got no intention of fighting you."

"No?"

"No."

Lucian fired. The pistol in his hand roared like thunder. Mordecai was only a dozen paces away. He felt a moment's internal, reflexive panic. Then the earring in his left ear warmed briefly and there was pressure over his chest, right above his heart. The pistol ball whistled past, deflected. Careful not to show, Mordecai breathed out in relief, then smiled up at Lucian.

The other man stared. "So it's true then. You did come by an aetherite's charm somehow. That's like cheating, really. I'll just have to try again harder next time." With that he bowed, turned, and vaulted over the edge of the ship. The guide rope went taut as he caught it in gloved hands, sliding down out of sight. Mordecai charged forward, caught off guard. He lashed out with his saber, adder-quick, but still missed. Lucian could move damned fast when he wanted to.

Mordecai caught his balance on the rail and glanced down the guide-line after Lucian. The other pirate slid down the rope, laughing wildly as he fell to another skyship. It lay moored several dozen feet below and three hundred away, at the far end of the Skydocks.

The *Copper Queen*.

Mordecai hacked at the rope furiously, but Lucian landed on the deck of the old air vessel, disappearing from view just before it parted and fell away. He cursed and pounded at the gunwale with his fist. Then his eyes widened. A flurry of activity was taking place on the *Queen*, pirates moving with purpose along the gunwales, guide-ropes, and the bow.

"You assume..." Mordecai breathed. Startlement and horror rose up in him. *You cheeky little shit. You really weren't going to fence anything. You mean to steal the Queen!*

Konrad stirred at his feet. The navigator groaned and let loose a string of foreign curses. Mordecai turned and kicked the man savagely in the ribs.

"Up! Get up, Goddess damn you!" Others moved and he went among them, kicking and shouting and chivvying them awake. Slowly, far too slowly, the crew climbed to their feet. They groaned and wasted precious seconds tottering about in confusion.

"What going on?" asked Konrad. "What happen?"

Mordecai grabbed the man close. "That bastard Fengel is trying to steal Euron's ship!"

The navigator's eyes widened. "That's madness!"

"I know! Now get your arses down there!"

Lashed on by threats and invective, the crew rushed off the deck and down the Skydock. Mordecai sent one man off to rouse everyone else in the Bleeding Teeth. Hopefully, Natasha was still drunk.

Brash as always, Lucian's plan was still foolish. The *Queen* hadn't moved in a decade. Just to get it aloft would take a complete restoration of its light-air gas cells. And the ropes and chains that tethered it were old and hard.

But.

The ship was a symbol of Euron's rule. And as much as she hated the sight of the thing and the shadow it cast over her own efforts, Natasha cared about it just as much as her father did. If Fengel *did* get away successfully, the Blackheart family would have everyone involved strung up by their toes. And Worked charm or not, Mordecai didn't back his own chances against all of Euron's men, or Natasha pushed past her limits.

Retribution burned in his mind as Mordecai moved with the crew down the slope of the Skydocks to its base. He took the lead and led the brigands of the *Dawnhawk* up the gangplank of the *Copper Queen*. A brawny, shirtless fellow stood at its peak, barring their way. Mordecai cut the man down without a moment's hesitation, pushing past. Bystanders looked on, stunned by the group's charge. He flicked his blade out, slashing and driving them back as the crew followed at his heels.

Something is wrong, he realized. Fengel's thieves fell back, hands up to ward him away. Mordecai paused to breathe and take in the situation around him. Konrad and the others spread out, quieting as they followed his lead, becoming aware of something...off.

The enemy crew were a motley lot, more a gang of dockside scum rather than any real group of pirates. They stared at Natasha's Reavers in surprise and fear. Not a one bore a weapon. Instead they all held mops, brooms, and buckets. Sudsy water made the deck slick and reflective where the light of the moon peeked past the gas-bag frame above.

"Where is he?" shouted Mordecai. He wheeled. "Show yourself, Lucian! Where are you, you tricksy bastard?" A sea of frightened faces stared back at him. Mordecai stalked over and grabbed one of the dock scum by his shirt. "I saw him drop down here. Where's Lucian Thorne?"

The terrified dockworker sputtered. "I don't know! He just ran past, said we should get started. But we waited until the pistol shot! Just like he said!"

Mordecai backhanded the man with the basket hilt of his cutlass. Blood and teeth flew through the air. "Keep talking! I—"

"What, by the Goddess' teats, is going on here?" Natasha stormed onto the deck of the *Copper Queen,* the rest of their crew behind her. She glared about, hair frazzled, and stalked over to Mordecai, stumbling along the way. "Mordecai, what are you doing on my father's ship?"

Blast and damnation. His captain drank heavily. Unfortunately, that also meant that she had quite a capacity for drink. She was still walking, and talking, when anyone else would be unconscious. Or dead. "These scags were trying to steal Euron's ship," he growled.

"No!" howled the bleeding man in Mordecai's grasp. "It was a present!" He fell to his knees before Natasha, sobbing now.

"Captain!" yelled Konrad.

Natasha held up a hand to her navigator, not looking at him. She glared at the man Mordecai held. "One at a time, damn you all! I'm still rather tipsy." She pointed at the pirate before her. "You," she said, finger wavering slightly. "What do you mean?"

"It was supposed to be a present!" he sobbed. "Fengel's man came down to the bar, said he needed some men for a surprise on behalf of Fengel for his wife. Paid us a silver apiece to come up here and clean ol' Euron's ship. We, we just had to wait until we heard the pistol shot. So's he could time it right. That's all I know, I swear! It was just supposed to be a present."

Natasha stared. Then realization struck her. "*Fengel?* she cried. "Fengel's behind this? That doesn't make any sense. The man wouldn't give me anything unless it was poisonous and had teeth like knives!"

"Actually Captain," said Mordecai, "I think he had a plan to steal the *Queen,* but this doesn't—"

"Captain!" yelled Konrad again. "First mate! Look!"

Heat burned in Mordecai's breast. How dare the navigator interrupt him. And in front of Natasha! He dropped the sniveling dockworker at his feet and formed a fist. Looking up toward the navigator, he stared.

Konrad wasn't even looking him, or Natasha. He had crossed to the rail of the ship and peered out up beyond the gasbag. Other crewmen were pointing at something, as well as some of the 'cleaners' involved in Lucian's plot. Mordecai glanced over at Natasha. She met his gaze and the both of them ran to the railing.

The *Dawnhawk* was leaving. People scurried about its deck and gasbag in a flurry of activity. The mooring lines were already cut and the ship floated free on the breeze. It rose above the Skydocks, steam puffing from the exhaust-pipes at the rear of the vessel and taking direction as the propellers began to spin. A single figure stood at the helm near the stern.

"My ship!" cried Natasha.

The figure moved to the railing and waved down at them. From where he stood, Mordecai could see the tricorn hat and heavy officer's coat. Moonlight glimmered for a moment, reflected, as if from a pair of spectacles. Or a monocle.

"My ship!" cried Natasha again. "You whoreson bastard! Give me back my ship!" She erupted into a torrent of emotion, a stunning string of profanity that blanched the faces of the hardened pirates around her and even gave Mordecai pause.

He yelled orders at the crew to run back up to the *Dawnhawk's* pier. Even as they ran off he knew it would be too late. He turned back to his captain. "Lucian Thorne is still somewhere on this ship. Or in town. He can't have gotten far."

Natasha wheeled on him, eyes half-mad, panting from lack of breath. "But that bastard husband of mine has my *ship!*" she screamed in his face.

"And we will get it back," he vowed. "Because I know where they are going."

His captain glared. "Search the deck from bilge to the bags," she yelled to her crew. "Tie these sorry bastards up somewhere I can interrogate them properly. And you," she said, pointing to Mordecai, "tell me everything that you know."

Mordecai took a calming breath, and did so.

CHAPTER FOUR

*I*S THIS SUPPOSED TO BE MY NEW HOME?

Flying on a real airship was nothing like Lina had expected. Her flight from Triskelion on their makeshift conveyance had been a dicey and terrifying experience, as the vessel seemed constantly about to crash into the sea, which it finally had. The *Dawnhawk* was altogether different. It rocked gently but solidly beneath her feet, its deck swaying left and then right at irregular intervals, prodded along by the whim of the wind. The sensation was strange, similar and yet altogether different from travelling a seagoing ship upon the open ocean. These incongruities surprised her, kept her from any easy acclimation. And there were others. It was quiet. No waves crashed against the hull, and no seabirds screamed. While the wind still whistled over the deck and the wood of the vessel creaked, these were hushed, small sounds.

"A bit different, eh?" asked Henry Smalls.

Lina turned. The ship's steward walked up to where she stood in the middle of the deck. His bulldog features were still drawn with fatigue, but she sensed enthusiasm and energy from him.

"Very," she said with a nod. "Quieter, too."

Though different, the airship still had much in common with a normal seagoing vessel. Its deck was long and flat, hanging parallel below the gasbag frame above. There was a bow and a stern, but neither end rose up in a forecastle or stern deck; the whole ship was uniformly flat from end to end. Three hatches led down below: a large one for cargo in the middle, and two smaller openings placed fore and aft for crew use. Low, flat equipment lockers were placed between the hatches, like wardrobes set on their sides.

"

From thick rings bolted along the gunwales, rigging and cable work rose up the way they did on any sail ship. But there the similarities ended.

The gas-bag frame hung two dozen feet above the deck, a fixed axis tethering the vessel to the sky. The ropes and cables anchored to eyebolts extruded from the fabric along the ribs of the frame while ratlines and other rigging crawled up out of sight above. Along the deck lay two thick pipes, one on each side of the ship, parallel along the gunwales. They were anchored up near the bow and ran back out past the stern, blowing exhaust. Mounted along their tops and to the railing were complex chain link mechanisms connected to strange half-sails attached along the outer hull of the ship. The sails were folded now like a lady's fan, their cloth shimmering strangely in the pre-dawn light. Mixed in with them near the stern were more gearwork and the wide propellers that pushed the vessel along. The ship's wheel sat amidst all this near the stern, remarkably normal, save a large gearbox rising up beside it.

Darkness dominated beyond the borders of the airship. Lina hadn't been brave enough to approach the railings yet, to catch a glimpse of the Copper Isles, which she knew would be spread out far below. Instead she stood atop the closed cargo hatch. Until now her only company had been a skeleton shift of the more rested and able hands. Their theft successful, Fengel had reinstated Henry as acting first mate, given orders to the few hands hale enough to maintain the ship, then gone with the others below to rest. Presumably Henry knew where they were going. Though exhausted, Lina was too unsettled by the strangeness of the ship and her place upon it to sleep. She settled for staying out of the way, watching. But as dawn approached she moved up and down the deck, trying to understand the world she found herself in.

"That's the gulls yer missing," said Henry. "Those vermin are everywhere, even followed us in that damned longboat. They'll do the same up here, but it's early still. Once things warm up a bit the pests will be screaming and shitting everywhere. When you get put to work atop the frame you'll have your fill of them; that's where they go to roost when it's quiet. The little freeloaders like to hitch a ride." He sighed. "What are you doing here, lass?"

She frowned at him. "Wasn't sure where I should sleep. Or if I should be or not."

"Not that. Why did you tag along back in Triskelion? This is a hard life, lass. Not like in the penny plays."

Lina sighed. "Ever slept with a man for money, Mister Smalls?"

Henry blinked. "Can't say that I have."

"Well, I have. And there's only three ways you end up. Dead, diseased, or acting the madame yourself. I figured that I'd rather try my hand at piracy."

"We don't end much differently."

"Maybe not," agreed Lina, "but at least I get the chance to fly." Beneath them the deck swayed as a strong crosswind pushed at them. "Though I'm not sure what I think about that, now that I'm here."

Both fell silent, looking out at the gloom beyond the ship. To the east rose a faint glow, herald of the coming sun.

"Well," said Henry after a few minutes. "You stayed up all night, so you'll be on the evening shift under Gunny Lome. You'll sleep and go to mess with her crew. She'll show you the ropes. Aft deck just below has got cots, that's where you'll sleep."

Lina relaxed. She was seriously considering laying down out of the way on the deck somewhere.

"But, I can't let you go just yet," continued Henry. "Got a job needs doing, and you happen to be free."

Lina blinked. "I'm not my best at the moment."

"Shouldn't take long. Come along now."

The acting mate led her back to the rear hatchway. Lina followed him down to the deck below, a tight corridor dotted with doorways to either side. At the far end she spied a wider, open space full of swaying hammocks and snoring pirates. Henry led her back away to where the corridor ended at a heavy metal door, then banged upon it twice.

"Just do whatever he says," said Henry Smalls. "It shouldn't take long. When you're done go grab some shuteye." The acting mate turned away just as the metal door creaked wide.

Through the portal Oscar Pleasant blinked at her, ratlike. "What are *you* doing down here?"

Lina stared in confusion. Henry Smalls wanted her to work under *him*? She frowned. "Whatever you need," she said tiredly, "let's get it done with."

Oscar leered at her and then laughed. "You're an eager one." He waggled his eyebrows. "But it's not me who asked for ya. Mechanist called us down here." A rough voice shouted out from the depths of the space beyond. Oscar frowned, then jerked his head toward the sound. "That's him now. Best not to keep him waiting. Ever."

Resigned, Lina stepped past the pirate through the portal. The room beyond was unlike anything she'd seen. It might have been large, but was so packed with boilers, pipes, and copper tubing that she couldn't tell. Needles vibrated within their pressure gauges and linkage mechanisms whirred. Small puffs of steam escaped through baffles and valve-releases. A bucket-

and-pulley system stood ready to bring loads of coal from compartments down below. A slow, steady thumping sound reverberated throughout, like the echoes of a beating heart.

A furnace dominated the far end of the room. The fire burning behind its grill was the only source of illumination, casting mad shadows among the pipes. Beside it stood a figure in a scorched and stained leather greatcoat, hunched over a long workbench nestled into a space all its own.

Oh, now what have I gotten myself into? Lina glanced back at Oscar. The pirate was smiling, clearly enjoying her confusion. *Ass.* Lina turned away from him and cleared her throat.

The figure whirled. Lina jumped. It was a man, most of his features hidden by the wraparound collar and a pair of thick goggles. Despite that she could tell he was small, roughly her own height and older, his frizzy hair colored salt-and-pepper.

"Who are you?" he demanded, voice muffled by his collar. The figure stalked over and stopped with his face only inches away from her own. "What are you doing in here? This is the domain of the Brotherhood."

Lina took a step back. "I'm Lina. Henry Smalls sent me down with Oscar. To...help you, I suppose?"

"You are no pirate." The Mechanist peered at her through his goggles.

"Yes I am," corrected Lina.

"No. You are not." He gestured Oscar over from the door. "It is no matter. Come."

The Mechanist returned to his bench. Lina followed. Just when she'd reached him the man wheeled, jabbing a finger at her. Startled, she jumped back again, running into Oscar. The pirate smirked and offered a hand to help her. She refused it.

"Here," said the Mechanist. "See." He pointed at a portion of his workbench where a brass pipe was mounted to the wall, its length running up to the shadows of the ceiling while the close end terminated in a horn pointed out at them. "Fengel's piratical shenanigans were most untimely. I had not yet completed my modifications to the vessel. I will do so now, and you *will* assist me."

Lina was surprised at the heat in his voice, at the imperious nature of the command. But she was too tired and bewildered to fight it. "All right," she said. "But what do you want me to *do?*"

The Mechanist pointed at the tube. "I am installing a speaking-tube from here to the captain's wheel," he said calmly. "The two of you stay here and listen until you can hear me, and I can hear you in turn."

"Oh," said Lina. "That's easy enough." But the Mechanist ignored her, already pushing past with a bag of tools in hand. She watched him leave the engine room, and then turned to Oscar. "All right. Who in the Realms Above is that? And what's going on?"

The pirate smirked. "What, you ain't never heard of the Brotherhood of the Cog?"

Lina had, actually. "Aren't they a bunch a bunch of posh types that sit around and drink sherry?"

Oscar shrugged. "Back on Edrus, maybe. A secret society that want to build the perfect world. There are different sects; back there it's rich folks in clubs, but out here it's the Mechanists. They make the skyships. Every vessel's got one of them aboard to keep it running."

"I haven't seen him before."

"Doubt you would have." Oscar stretched, leaning against the workbench, using the movement as an excuse to sidle within arm's reach of where she stood. It was not subtle. Lina wrinkled her nose. He had the oily salami stink of a man who drank too much.

"But isn't he part of the crew?'

"Nope. The Mechanists stay on the ships they service. So long as they get a small cut of the booty, and no one interferes with their work, they don't give a damn who runs the thing. But enough about that." He put one hand up against a pipe, enclosing Lina in a small space against the workbench. "He's right."

Lina narrowed her eyes. She took comfort in the weight of the daggers in her waistband. "About what?"

"You're not one of us. You wanted to get away from Triskelion, I can understand that. But just because you're along for the ride doesn't mean you're a pirate."

She tightened her lips. "Captain Fengel said I could be on the crew. I spent a week dying on that longboat, same as you. I helped row us back into port, steal this ship. I may be green, but I think that counts."

Oscar shrugged. "Captain Fengel's a good sort. Took pity on you back in the city. But being a pirate's not about *asking,* right? It's about *taking.* I can tell, girl, you're a fish out of water. The others can all see it, too. Now, we're not barbarians, Fengel's Men are one of the best crews I've found to ship with. But you've got to prove yourself to join us. That, or have…protection. Now I've got a solution—"

A screech echoed from the speaking tube, startling them both. Lina thought she heard words. Lina took her chance. "Yes!" she yelled into the horn. "Works fine!"

The tube screeched again, discordant and even louder than before. She winced and Oscar started, losing his balance against the workbench. He tripped over a shovel and a bucket of coal and went sprawling to the floor. Lina turned and exited the room.

She paused in the corridor to make sure he didn't follow, then walked to where she'd seen the hammocks, furious. Pirates snored there, hanging like exotic, smelly fruit. Lina found an empty one and, after some trial and error, climbed up into it. Lina lay awake, hand to a dagger, listening for Oscar's footsteps, wondering if he would need further dissuading. She thought that she would be too angry, too worked up to sleep. She was wrong.

No sooner had she closed her eyes than it seemed like she was opening them again. Light filled the room from a number of portholes. The hammocks around her were largely empty, she recognized those still asleep as the skeleton crew from the evening before. Through a door at the far end of the room, opposite the corridor back to the hatchway and engine room, she heard the sound of people eating, the clatter of tableware and muted laughter.

*Food?*Her back ached and her mouth felt parched. But more painful than that was the hole in her belly. The fripperies she'd consumed at Mr. Grey's hadn't been nearly enough, especially after having to fight both the captain and the steward for them.

Lina tried to leave the hammock, failed, tried again, and fell to the wooden deck with a thump. Cursing herself, she climbed to her feet and crossed the room to the door. It opened into another room, longer than the sleeping space. Benches and tables filled it, along with pirates making regular trips from them to a wide sideboard brimming with food and drink. Another doorway at the far end opened into the kitchen.

A few pirates glanced her way as she came through the door. Lina was aware of their overlong stares before they turned back to their food. Unbidden, Oscar's words came back to her. She shoved them aside and made her way to the sideboard.

It was ladled almost to overflowing with stew, fresh fruit, ship's biscuit and other things, a mismatched amalgamation of whatever the cook had found at hand. None of the pirates seemed to care, and made trip after trip, the weird menu pure heaven after a week of starving at sea.

Lina didn't mind either. There seemed to be no order, so she grabbed a plate and filled it, ducking underneath and in between the larger pirates before slipping back to a free space along a bench. Those beside her didn't offer a greeting, only looked at each other. Lina forced herself not to care, tearing into an orange as if it had personally offended her.

She was halfway through her platter when the room went dead silent. *Oh Goddess. I'm eating like a pig.* Face hot, she looked up. Thankfully, no one was staring her way at all.

Captain Fengel stood just inside the door. Lina felt her heart leap a little in her chest. He was as impeccably dressed as always, looking much better for an evening's rest. The clammy pallor to his skin was gone, and he smiled as he took in the room.

Thundering applause erupted. Fengel made a slight bow to the room at large, then a small gesture to the woman at the bench nearest him. She hastily stood and he leapt onto her seat. He held up his hands for silence, and the room quieted.

"Well," he said. "That was quite a little trip, now, wasn't it?" Everyone laughed. Fengel reached down to the table below him and grabbed up someone's mug, which caused the owner to frown slightly. The captain held the mug before him. "I won't lie. Our little trip to the Western Continent was a complete shambles. We lost our ship, any chance of loot, and more than a few good men and women. But! We made our way home, and it was wholly your doing, my good friends. So, here's a toast, from me to you, for your continuing perseverance in the face of incredible odds, and for those who are unable to join us here today."

The captain raised his mug. The mood in the room went somber and the pirates raised their drinks, or hastily acquired one with which to do so. Fengel led them, tipping back a long gulp. He returned the mug to its owner and then suddenly grinned.

"But let's not be maudlin. The *Flittergrasp* was a good ship, but this one's not bad, save the misfortune of being owned by her previous captain." The room broke out into laughter. Fengel grinned and held up a hand. "Now. I've got things to do, and so do the rest of you. We'll be picking up Lucian tonight, and I want things shipshape and the lot of you familiar with your stations. Mister Smalls will have your shifts and assignments settled." He made to turn away when one of the pirates spoke up.

"But Captain, where are we going?"

Fengel turned back, smiling. "Whatever kind of question is that? We're going after the loot, my mates. Buried treasure. Enough to make us all fat as kings." He descended and left the room as the assembled pirates fell to chattering excitedly.

Lina gave a sigh, then blushed as she realized what she'd done. *I've got to fix that.* This was a new life for her. Nursing a flame for the captain would not end well, regardless of what the plays and penny-papers said.

Someone dropped down beside her, and she jumped. It was the thin navigator, Maxim. His unruly hair dangled to his shoulders like a black curtain, and he stared down his beak of a nose at her.

"No one likes to sit near me," he said, a faint accent coloring his voice. "It's the daemon on my shoulder. But you look like an outsider too, so I am joining you."

This again. "I'm not an outsider," she muttered defiantly. Lina couldn't help but notice the small bubble of open space that enclosed them; otherwise, the table was packed.

The navigator raised an eye. "No?

She threw down half an egg. "No! I was on that longboat, same as the rest of you. I fought to the serpent, and helped us get into the harbor."

Maxim peeled a banana. His fingers were long and lithe, like a pianist. "That you did," he replied neutrally. The aetherite frowned, as if he had just been told something that he didn't like. Surreptitiously, he laid down the banana and retrieved both salt and pepper shakers from the table near the others.

"Captain's a good man," he said conversationally. "Most of us here used to work under him. On a Perinese ship. *H.M.S. Reliable*. Know what he was then?"

"No," said Lina. His abrasive manners aside, Maxim's words made Lina curious.

"Petty Officer."

Lina recalled the internal map she'd long ago built of navies and their rankings. In her former line of work, it had paid to know such things. "Not commissioned then?"

"No. Fengel was a better sailor, leader, and swordsman than anyone alive on that ship. But he's lowborn, yes? No patronage." Maxim fiddled with the pepper shaker in his hands, as if he were nervous. "Perinese ships...do you know how most sailors end up on them?"

Lina nodded. "Press ganging."

"Yes. Slavery, really." He returned the pepper shaker to where he'd found it. "Slavery is a rough thing, and the Perinese know they need to be rough in return to make it work. But Fengel...Captain Fengel looked out for us all, took floggings he need not have more than once."

Maxim picked up the salt shaker next and fiddled with it. "What happened next?" she prompted after a moment.

He set the saltshaker down in front of her. "Bad storm. Sick captain. First mate could not handle it. Fengel stepped up and saved us all, took command when no one else was able to." He shrugged. "Made everyone up the chain look bad. They were going to execute him. Now, pirate crews are democracies, yes? So, we took a Crewman's Vote. Then mutinied, made Fengel our captain. Took the *Reliable* and made for Haventown." The navigator touched her hand, drawing in close. "My point is, most of us have been together since the beginning. Others will be cordial, but if you want to be accepted as one of us, you must earn it. Earn their respect, yes?"

Lina felt a sinking sensation. She picked up the salt shaker and her half-eaten egg. "Haven't you ever wanted to make a change? To start fresh?"

Maxim turned his palms upward, leaning back. "It's just how things are. We're mostly good people, though. You've got a chance with us. Any crew really, one must—"

A cry came from down the table. Lina peered past the navigator to a burly male pirate sitting at the end of their bench. He had grabbed the pepper shaker and upended it over his plate. The cap had fallen off, dumping its contents everywhere. Lina and several others laughed at the prank.

"Maxim!" cried the pirate. "You horse's ass!"

The navigator turned around slowly. "The daemon made me do it," he said. "Earned a small Working. Be thankful."

The pirate swore and stood, taking his ruined breakfast elsewhere. He gave Lina a dirty look as he left. Belatedly she realized her mistake. *Great. I really shouldn't have laughed.* The strange navigator was right, she was going to have to earn acceptance.

Lina upended the salt shaker over her egg without stopping to think. The end flew off, dumping a tablespoons' worth of salt to spill over her egg, hand, and the rest of her plate. She cursed and started back, then glared at the aetherite.

"Daemon made me do it," he said with a shrug.

Maxim turned to look out across the room. Lina followed his gaze to a knot of pirates at the far end from them, Oscar Pleasant in their midst. He was telling a story, punctuated by obscene hand gestures and glances in her direction. His assembled mates laughed uproariously.

"He is causing you trouble," said Maxim. "You should do something about that." Then he stood, leaving her alone again.

Lina picked about her plate for anything edible. Eventually she stood and left the mess to find Henry Smalls. As he'd said, she found herself assigned to the night-watch under the huge piratess, gunnery mistress Sarah Lome. Lina was told she would be expected to fight, and help in any emergencies that threatened the ship. Otherwise her time was her own and she was simply expected to stay out of the way. Depressed now, and still feeling exhausted from their ordeal, Lina drank more water, found the head, and then went back to bed. She awoke around seventh bell, late in the afternoon.

Lina ate another meal by herself in the mess, this one not so extravagant as the last, then made her way up to the deck. Pursing her lips, she approached the rails and looked past them down onto the world below.

The setting sun sent shafts of umber light across thick tropical jungle stretching out along the Copper Isles beneath them. The *Dawnhawk* rode a few hundred feet above the canopy, cliffs and rivers separating the land into islets. The Isles spread out in a crescent across the horizon, the blue water of the Atalian Sea surrounding them.

It was glorious. Lina laughed at her earlier trepidation. She rested her arms on the railing and enjoyed the view. *I'm home.* Lina blinked in surprise at the realization. Maybe she'd expected a bit much. Maybe the captain *had* taken pity on her. It didn't matter. She suddenly knew that this was the life for her. *I'm going to make it work. To the Realms Below with everyone else.*

The last of the sun sank beneath the horizon and a shrill whistle rang out across the deck. Lina looked back to see Henry Smalls standing amid the deck with a boson's whistle, Sarah Lome standing behind him, cracking her knuckles. The evening crew was assembling, hurrying from up the hatches or wherever they'd been loitering about the deck. Lina moved to join them.

Henry passed his whistle to the gigantic woman. "Gunnery mistress," he said, "you have the watch."

"I have the watch," she repeated formally. Then both of them relaxed.

"All's straight and clear," said Henry. "This is a good ship."

"When are we picking up Lucian?"

"Around dawn. Captain say's it's going to be the usual spot, along Breakneck Bay."

Lome nodded and he went below. She turned to face the assembled crew. "You all know your normal places," she said loudly. "*Dawnhawk* isn't much different from *Flittergrasp* in that. But, I don't know this ship, and you don't really either. So we're going to go over every inch, and all the work that dayshift has already done."

The next two hours were brutal. By the light of the rising moon Lina found herself holystoning the deck until her back ached. Unused to the work, she fell behind the others, earning a lashing from Sarah Lome's surprisingly vicious tongue. Then they checked the cabling and the rigging along the deck, making sure it was all in good repair and undamaged.

With the moon at its zenith, they greased the linkage mechanisms and exhaust-pipes. Though her fingers were singed by the steam pipes and her back ached from the work, Lina was still fascinated by the devices. They seemed to control the odd half-sails folded along the outer hull, linking them back to the gearbox at the ship's wheel.

The Mechanist made an appearance shortly after this task was completed. He conferred with Sarah Lome, then moved to inspect the mechanism where the crew had worked on it. At each, he found fault. He addressed the pirate responsible for each flaw with withering scorn before moving on. As he moved up the line, Lina's nervousness grew.

Finally, he reached her. But if the Brother of the Cog recognized her, he didn't say so. Instead he bent over the linkage chain she had been scrubbing rust from and then re-greasing. "Satisfactory," he said once, before turning back to Sarah and beginning a withering complaint of the crew and their handling of his machines. Lina let out a sigh of relief.

Afterwards they attended to other, less important tasks. They rubbed oil on the lockers of weapons and equipment, and took inventory. Lina tried to pay dutiful attention to the directions. Unfortunately, the distractions were myriad. She was unused to the hours and the hard work. And if that weren't enough, Oscar Pleasant was in her shift as well. Whether from the incident with her hair or her abrupt attitude in the engine room, it seemed that she had slighted the man. Now he joked and whispered with his mates about her, just enough of which she heard over the groans of their labor and the creaking of the ship.

Sarah let up on them in the small hours of the morning. Seemingly satisfied for the moment, she assigned them off to menial, make-work jobs. She took Lina to a haphazard mound of ropes piled against the starboard railing.

"Get these coiled neatly," she said. "When you're done I'll have someone store them in the lockers."

With only an inward sigh, Lina bent to the task, undoing the knotty tangle and recoiling it a piece at a time. To her surprise the huge piratess didn't leave, but instead rested against the rail.

"You're small and weak," she said. "But quick. You don't complain. Mechanist likes how you respect his machines. Keep this up and there's a place for you here, so long as you don't shy from a fight."

The rope abraded Lina's fingers. Blisters were already forming, and within a weeks time there would be calluses. Once her hands had been smooth and butter-soft. *I don't care.* Her hands could go the way of her hair. "I can fight," she said, hating herself for the squeak in her weary voice.

"I hope you're right. Always comes down to that, eventually." Sarah pulled a pipe from her vest. Filling it, she stood to walk away, then stopped, as if she'd remembered something. "Oscar's making trouble for you," she said conversationally. "You should do something about that. Make sure you don't lose any of those ropes over the side."

Lina bent herself to her task, too tired to respond. As the moon fell beneath the horizon the pile became less tangled, neat coils appearing beside it. She stepped nimbly amongst them; all she needed was to get her feet tangled and trip back over the gunwales.

Without the moon the deck was dark. Lina and the others worked on by the light of two small lanterns, one far to the fore and the other far aft. Over the deck came the muffled steps of someone approaching.

"Here you are, girl," said Oscar Pleasant. He glanced around, ratlike.

"Hello, Oscar," replied Lina, unable to hide the weariness in her voice. The last of the tangle was in her hands and loose. Stooping with a grunt, she tied one end to the gunwales, then began coiling it at her feet.

"We never got to finish our chat last night," said the pirate.

"Nothing to talk about," she replied.

"I think there is." He stepped closer, hemming her in against the railing.

She looked up at him and took in his stance, his cocksure smile. Oscar plainly hadn't intended to give up on her.

"You're playing at this, girl," he said. "Was obvious to me all night. You're too slow, and not nearly strong enough for this work. You're not going to be able to keep up. I daresay it's only going to get worse once a bit o' bloodshed starts."

"I'll get stronger," she replied. "And I've been in a scrap or two." It was true, though she didn't like to think on it much.

Oscar smiled condescendingly. He leaned in, trapping her against the rail with both arms. "You're a whore, girl. On a ship full of pirates. And there's only one way for you to keep riding along." He leered. "I tried to break it to you gently last night, but here I'll say it plain. Now, I'm sure we can come to an agreement."

Lina glared at him. Then she dropped her eyes, pretending intimidation. She looked to her footing, then Oscar's. He was standing in the loose loop of a slipknot. "I...you're right."

The pirate grinned. "I knew you'd see sense."

"Yep."

She stepped on the rope and grabbed the front of his shirt, pulling him towards her as if for a kiss. Then she ducked. Surprised, Oscar pitched over the railing, the rope tangled about his feet. Lina rolled out of the way as he fell.

Lina rose and peered over the edge of the rail, watching Oscar plummet past the lower decks. The rope pulled taut and he jerked with a scream. Lina sighed. It would have been nice if he'd continued his fall. The rest of the crew perked up at the noise and ran over to the starboard railing.

"You hear me down there?" she yelled.

"Oh, Goddess!" cried Oscar. "My leg! Pull me up!"

"Here's the agreement," Lina bellowed down at him. "I'm not whoring for you, your mates, or anyone else on this ship! You're going to keep your paws to yourself, or *I will cut them off.* I make my own way, you prick, and I'll be a better, meaner brigand than you'll ever hope to be! Cross me again and I'll cut off your stones and feed them to you!"

She fell back, panting, ignoring Oscar's cries. She looked up to see the rest of the crew staring at her, like a doormouse that had suddenly turned into a lion.

Sarah Lome pushed her way through the crowd. "Something wrong here, Miss Stone?"" she asked, voice level.

Lina stood up straight. "No, ma'am. Almost lost a rope, but I tied it off. I think we can get it back, if we want it."

The huge piratess nodded. "Well, don't wait *too* long then. Shift is almost over." She looked to two of the pirates. "Ryan, Andrea, take these coils to the front locker." Then she turned and walked calmly back to the stern.

Two pirates bent to pick up the ropes at their feet. The woman, Andrea, winked at Lina as she bent. The rest of the pirates drifted away to their tasks, a few chuckling to themselves. A few, Oscar's mates, glanced her way; Lina caught their gazes and held them, challenging them. All turned away.

Lina bent back to the rail. Resting her elbows on either side of the rope, she looked out at the horizon while Oscar Pleasant sobbed and cursed below.

Yep. I am home.

CHAPTER FIVE

Fengel climbed up out of the hatchway stair. He rose into cool shade, the gasbag frame shrouding the deck of the *Dawnhawk* from the morning sun. The crew on watch moved about their tasks, holystoning the deck and checking the lines. A warm breeze gusted about, bringing with it a bouquet scented by the green growing things on the islands below and the salt brine of the Atalian Sea.

The gust pulled at his hat. Fengel paused to consider the force of the wind. Was it a threat? A real danger? No. Its strength was insufficient. His hat was secure and his hair was safe from being mussed. He returned his attention to the deck. Fengel clasped his hands behind his back and waited to be noticed.

Two minutes passed.

Fengel frowned. He thought about saying something, clearing his throat maybe. But no, that would ruin the effect. Also, the shift watch moved busily. He was loathe to distract them; it was good that they were so focused. The *Dawnhawk* was a new vessel, and not just to them. It had its own kinks and unique that would need to be identified, and compensated for.

Still, this was vexing. *Maybe I can go down and come back up?*

"Captain on deck!" bellowed the acting mate. Fengel breathed a small sigh of relief. His faithful steward had saved him once again.

The crew dropped their tasks at the cry and turned to face him in attention. They didn't salute, that would have been far too much to ask of the men, most of whom had served under a Perinese lash. But acknowledge him they did, and it brought him warmth. It was good to be noticed when one wanted to.

Fengel gave a nod, and the men and women of his crew returned to their tasks. He walked a wide circuit through them, pretending to inspect the work as he made his way back to the helm. His crew knew their duties well. Still though, it was good to show a watchful eye.

Maxim stood with Henry Smalls at the ship's helm, expending just enough effort with the wheel to keep them straight to their course. Fengel took in the navigator's sullen glare and decided not to press it. All aetherites were a little erratic, and their unique skills called for a lighter touch than most crewmen. As well, most crewman couldn't hex a man to misfortune, or light him aflame like a candle wick with just a thought. Fengel had little fear of dark and dour Maxim, though. The man was an experienced hand and could be counted on when necessary.

"Morning, sir," said Henry Smalls. His stout steward was again acting first mate in Lucian's absence, a role Fengel knew he did not enjoy. "Did you rest well?"

"Well enough," Fengel answered. Truthfully, he felt better than that, almost ebullient. Good food, plenty of rest, *and* a ship of his own again beneath his feet. The fact that the latter had been stolen, from under the besotted nose of his erstwhile spouse, why, that was just icing on the cake. And there was more than that. He had a plan, a heading, and a fantastic treasure awaiting them at the other end of what promised to be a quiet shakedown cruise.

What could possibly go wrong?

"Excellent to hear, sir," said Henry, ever dutiful.

"Of course it is, Mister Smalls. Of course it is. But first things first. My shave?"

"Ready and waiting for you, sir." Henry produced a stool and a bucket of soapy water. Fengel sat and removed his hat, presenting his chin so that Henry could go to work. The little steward did so with razor and scissors.

"Anything on the log?" asked Fengel while his steward groomed him. He had rested well, but there were gaps that needed filling. Aside from a small, necessary appearance the morning before, he'd spent all of the previous day and evening holed up in the captain's quarters, recuperating.

"I am happy to say that all's quiet," replied Henry. "We're two nights out of Haventown. Hugged the coastline south. Currently on course for Breakneck Bay to pick up Lucian. No sign of pursuit, so Natasha hasn't been able to convince anyone else to fly out after us."

Fengel permitted himself a small smile, pleased that his expectations had borne out. Natasha didn't have another ship, and would have been forced to begging another captain to help. That wasn't likely to happen. People obeyed old Euron, not his daughter. And for all her beauty, she really wasn't that well loved. Some tried to curry favor with her, but that last encounter at the Bleeding Teeth had produced one nugget of important information: all her real allies were away from port at the moment.

"Yesterday was quiet enough," continued Henry. "Crew are getting a hand on things. The Mechanist here is a surly sort, but seems to have taken a shine to the new girl. Lift your chin, sir."

Fengel thought back. "Miss Stone?"

"That's her. He seems to like how she respects the mechanisms on board."

"A typical Mechanist." Fengel mused to himself as his steward pulled out the little scissors for his beard. "How is Miss Stone doing?" The less he thought about their ill-fated trip to Triskelion, the better. Their flight from the city had been hurried and desperate. When Miss Stone had begged to come along, he hadn't really been thinking about his reply. He'd figured that he would simply deposit her in Haventown. *Not much chance of that happening now.*

"Uncertain, but shaping up. Quite a spine of iron, really. She had a bit of trouble with one of the crewmen, but took care of it last night. Gunny Lome says she'll be fine."

Fengel relaxed. That was a relief. "Keep her on her current shift," he decided after a moment. "But rouse her for anything the Mechanist needs. The Brothers of the Cog are so tight-lipped...maybe she can tease out some of his secrets."

Henry nodded. "Other than that, sir, not much to say. We should be picking up Lucian momentarily."

The steward used a towel to wipe away the excess foam and put away his tools. Their morning ritual complete, Fengel replaced his hat and stood. "Carry on, then."

Fengel left the helm, walking up the deck to the bow and peering out at the world beyond his ship. Below them stretched the coastline, thick, tropical jungle sloping down to meet to a sandy beach and the blue-green waters of the Atalian Sea. This was the southern-most edge of the Isles, where the islets broke down eventually into lone rocks jutting up from the ocean. Fengel picked out familiar landmarks as they flew: a wide seam of copper along a cliff, a particularly large and twisted palm tree. On the *Flittergrasp* they'd made this trip before, many times, and just where he expected it to, the coastline gave way into a small, blue lagoon, hidden in a shallow bowl by the cliffs and jungle surrounding it. The beach was white sand, virgin but for a tiny speck of black; the charred remains of a campfire. A sandy-haired figure sat beside it. Even that far away he could tell that it was Lucian, waiting patiently.

The *Dawnhawk* swooped in over the lagoon. Fengel spied brightly colored fish darting into hiding as the ship's shadow passed across the water. He stood up straight and waved to his first mate. Lucian stood in turn, laughing to see Fengel on the bow of the stolen ship.

Maxim brought the airship to a halt. Fengel called for a rope ladder and watched as one of the crew brought one up, then tossed it overboard. It unrolled itself as it fell, just long enough for Lucian to grab. As his first mate made his ascent, Fengel gestured back to Maxim at the wheel. The navigator called out warning and busied himself with the controls. At his prompting the ship rose, pointing itself out away from the lagoon. Henry Smalls came up from the stern, joining him at the bow just as Lucian crawled over the rail.

"Hah," panted Lucian, winded from the climb. "Beat you again, Captain. Even in an airship. Close shave, though. I only arrived here this morning." Lucian was sweaty and disheveled, his usual debonair appearance dispelled. He spied the steward and gave a nod. "Hullo, Henry."

Fengel smiled. "I will never understand how you can make it from Haventown to Breakneck Bay in less than two days."

"That, my good captain, is because you're not a dashing first mate. We've all got our secrets." He looked up at gasbag frame and then down the deck, taking in the ship. "Well now. Didn't get a good look at her back in port. She's quite the beauty."

Fengel nodded. "Different from our last, but more than adequate. How was the trip out of town?"

Lucian groaned. "Rough. Mordie's getting better. Or I'm getting sloppier. But I can tell you that later. Let's get under way." He faced Henry formally. "Acting first mate, I'll take the watch."

"You have the watch," replied Henry dutifully.

Lucian stood straighter, falling easily into the role of authority. He fired off questions to Henry about the crew, the ship, and the watch log. Fengel left them to it and made his way back down the deck to where Maxim stood at the ship's helm. The aetherite nodded, but stood oddly, slightly tilted, as if leaning subconsciously away from the invisible daemon on his shoulder.

"Bring us up, Maxim. It's time to see how she carries along an aetherline."

The navigator nodded. He gave the wheel a spin and pulled at the levers of the gearbox. The lagoon whirled away as they rose up beyond the cliffs and its treetop canopy. Maxim's gray eyes peered out into the empty morning skies and muttered at his shoulder. After a moment he nodded and turned back to the captain. "Engmann's Run could be flowing stronger," he said in his accented Perinese, pursing his lips as if to keep from adding anything else.

"So long as it flows," replied Fengel. "That just happens to be our bearing."

Lucian and Henry reappeared. The first mate glanced at a gauge on the gearbox and then at the ship around them. "All right," he said, smiling up at Fengel. "Let's see how she holds up."

Fengel nodded calmly, hiding any trace of the uncertainty he felt in his stomach. The *Dawnhawk* was a very good ship to all appearances so far. But each and every one of the Mechanist's sky-vessels was idiosyncratic. While she flew well enough, there was no way to tell how this next step would go.

"We're rising into it now," said Maxim.

"Give the word, first mate," said Fengel.

Lucian cupped his hands and bellowed out at the crew. "Ready the deck!"

The pirates dropped what they were doing and ran to their pre-assigned stations. Some climbed the ratlines to be near the gas-bag. Others ran up to the bow or back to the stern. Hatches were tightened and lines hurriedly coiled.

Fengel felt a slight shudder travel through the ship. It jolted, as if in a strong crosswind, though none was blowing. Slowly, it spun counterclockwise without aid of their rudders, until they pointed southeast, nose out toward the blue sky over the ocean. The skysails along the outer hull rippled, caught by a force that only Maxim could see.

"Dead set," said the navigator.

"Run out the skysails," ordered Lucian.

The navigator reached over to the gearbox and pulled a large lever. A loud, mechanical clank echoed from within, and the gear-link mechanisms running down the length of the pipes stuttered and whirred. The shimmer-cloth of the skysails stretched, opening like the wings of a bat or a dragon stretched wide. The skysails flared brilliantly along the ship and they jolted forward, picking up speed as they went.

The ship settled without any further shuddering, still at speed. All about the deck the crew stood quiet—Fengel and his officers waited for something, anything, to give. He sent a spare crewman below with an order to the Mechanist to cut the engines. After a minute the vibration of the deck changed and the steam-pipe exhaust dwindled. The chain-driven propellers slowed in their spin. Yet the ship kept moving, losing only a little speed. A long minute passed. Then two. Fengel looked to Lucian and the two walked back to the stern. Far below them the waves of the ocean raced by.

"Goddess above," said his first mate. "Smooth as a baby's behind."

The crew cheered, the tension broken. Fengel allowed himself a small smile. They'd stolen the ship, but only now were they *really* flying it. The skysails and the aetherlines they caught were the true secret of flight, the Brotherhood's amazing discovery. No Haventown airship was really worth flying if it couldn't use them; no one could carry enough coal to make flitting all over the Atalian Sea worth it. But it was not easy to make the skysails, and every vessel was virgin until they had been tried. The *Dawnhawk* was well and truly theirs now.

"This," said Henry, "is a good ship."

Fengel bent over to inspect the gauges along the gearbox. He blinked at what he saw and peered up at Maxim. "Have you expended a Working?" he asked. The navigator shook his head. "Hmm," mused Fengel. "Then she's even faster than the *Flittergrasp* was." Despite himself, Fengel was impressed. Not that he'd let it show. "Well and good!" he continued. "Keep to the southeast course then. If Engmann will let us, we'll go all the way to the Yulan. Should only be a day or two until we hit the Stormwall, at this rate." Though the aetherlines didn't run quite straight, they were direct enough, and the coal they saved by not running the propellers would make all the difference. "Lucian, Henry, to the mess. Maxim, send someone down to us if we're needed."

The navigator nodded, resuming his stance before the wheel, focused now on the aetherial current only he could see.

Fengel took his officers down into the ship, over the lower sleeping-deck, and through the aft hatch towards the mess. Passing through the sleeper-rooms he spied the night-watch, slumbering. One of them, the skinny ex-prostitute, caught his eye.

Miss Stone snored uncomfortably in her hammock, arms and legs akimbo, her hands blistered and covered in grease. But she slept soundly. Most green sailors were unsteady and restless aboard their first ship. Indeed, Fengel remembered his own initial voyage all too well. But she was out like a blown lantern. *Then again, a whore's used to a rough life.* Gunny Lome was a demanding woman, though fair.

With her blonde, knife-hacked hair and oversized clothing, Miss Stone looked even more like the waif she truly was. She was stick-thin, and short from what he remembered, barely up to his shoulder. She was attractive, if somewhat boyish at the moment. Could she really adapt to the life of a pirate? *I shall have to keep an eye on her.*

The trio pushed on into the mess. It was empty but for Geoffrey Lords, their silent, terrifying cook, cleaning up the breakfast. As they entered he looked up and grinned, showing off his filed-down teeth, then moved wordlessly back into the kitchen to give the three of them privacy. Lucian piled a plate high with leftovers and sat near a porthole with Henry and Fengel.

"Well," said the first mate, jamming a biscuit into his mouth. "I don't mind telling you, this was a hell of a thing to pull off."

Lucian was capable of being subtle when fishing for compliments. He just rarely bothered. "We could not have done it without you," said Fengel dutifully.

His first mate beamed. "Damned right you couldn't have. Oh, but it was worth it, though. Tweaking both Natasha *and* Mordecai. Right to their faces. That was worth the effort." He laughed. "They were mad as all get-out. Old Mordie chased me down to the Waterdocks, then back up to the top of the terraces and into the jungle. Caught all my blinds, backtracking, and cheap tricks. Almost didn't get away." He paused to take a bite of toast.

"Do you know if she's got any supporters in town?" asked Henry. "Anyone who'll give her a lift after us?"

Lucian shook his head. "When you first cooked this up, I thought Weatherby might throw a wrench in things. But he's delayed, stuck pillaging out west longer than I thought he'd be." The first mate sat back and smiled. "We're free and clear to go wherever we want."

Fengel stole a muffin from Lucian's plate. "Capital. Then we make course east by southeast. Engmann's Run looks strong at the moment, so we'll follow the shortcut of her curve 'til we hit the coast if we can. If Mr. Grey is right, then the *Albatross* should be wrecked along the mouth of the Silverpenny river." He reached into his coat and pulled out a map. Unrolling it, he spread it out on the table, placing the muffin at a recalcitrant corner to keep it flat. "Surprisingly, *Dawnhawk* has an excellent stock of maps. This is a recent survey of the south-western coastline." He placed a finger along a poorly sketched portion. "And here is the river."

"So far south of Breachtown," mused Henry. "What was the *Albatross* doing down there? That's all wilderness and jungle, not even really explored."

Fengel waved this off. "That just means that the ship is ripe for the plucking."

"About that," interrupted Lucian. "This trip isn't going to be as easy as it seems."

Fengel raised an eyebrow. "How so?"

His first mate sighed. "Well, for one, Grey was right. The gemstone's cursed."

Fengel blinked. His steward looked up from the map.

"Really?" asked Henry.

"Really," said Lucian. He paused to take a bite of boiled egg. "Grey's not the first to hear of the thing. It's been causing a stir over in Breachtown since before we left for Triskelion. Grey's been angling for the gem for awhile now. I think he's been watching and waiting for an opportunity just like this one. He's probably been driving his Breachtown contracts all over the place, sniffing about. The *Albatross* has only been missing for a few days."

That explains the timing. "Interesting," said Fengel aloud. "But what did *your* contacts say?"

"That the gem's cursed," continued Lucian. "Looks like it was found only a few weeks ago. Adventurer by the name of Silas Thorn brought it back to Breachtown from the Interior."

"Oh!" said Henry. "I've heard of him. The one in all the penny-papers." The steward paused a moment. "You related?"

"No. My name's got an 'e' on the end. Anyway. Silas brought the gem back and sold it to a local merchant. The merchant was fairly discreet, but one of the porters blabbed and it got all over town; a unique gemstone, big as two fists, pale and milky that glows like a lantern. Apparently Thorn got it from some strange tribe in the jungles of the Interior. Porter wouldn't say much more, and died shortly after. Atop that, more than a few people noticed that Thorn's party was a good deal smaller than it had been going out, just the porter and Thorn himself returning. The adventurer wouldn't talk, just got on the next steamship back to the western lands."

The first mate paused to chew more toast. "Now after all that, everyone was quite a bit curious. All sorts of things are being hauled out of the Yulan jungles, knickknacks of the old Voorn race and suchlike. A completely new type of gemstone had everyone's interest. Thing was, though, the merchant? Became all reclusive. Wouldn't see anyone. But midnight one eve, he was suddenly in the streets, running about like mad and babbling nonsense. Fell over stone dead in front of a constable."

Lucian paused to sip from a mug of freshwater. "That hardly sounds like a curse," muttered Fengel.

Henry raised an eyebrow at him. "That sounds *exactly* like a curse, Captain."

"Hold up," said Lucian. "Our tale isn't finished yet. Listen to this. Our constable, he picks up the gemstone right? Being a sensible and opportunistic sort, he gives it as a gift to his girlfriend. Well, that girl has a lover on the side, and ends up passing the gem to *him*, only that man's the Major of the local Royal Marine contingent. Lover policeman finds out, kills the girl, and then gets promptly done in by our boy in the Service. The Major's accused of murder, but he's got pull— and quite a handsome bribe for the Breachtown Governor." Lucian chuckled. "It didn't do him much good. Apparently his dead girl was riddled with syphilis and the Major was shortly committed to a local sanitarium. That's pretty much the end of him. But the Governor now...he was quite taken with his new prize. Held a week of events, galas, masquerades, etcetera, just to show it off. Incidentally, that's also how our stone got its name. But I digress. It was at about this time that our Governor began to make some very, very poor policy decisions. Such as announcing the sovereignty of Breachtown from the Kingdom of Perinault."

Fengel stared. Henry's jaw dropped open.

"Is he *insane?*" whispered Henry.

"Even with the war in Salomca," said Fengel, "there is no way the King would stand for that. And especially not the Prince. There would be dreadnoughts off the shore of the Colony as soon as they could sail there. Why haven't I heard of this?"

"Fresh news, sir," said Lucian. "And our tale isn't quite over yet. The Marine contingent was leaderless, and easily overcome. The Governor sent them packing back in a merchant ship. However, not everyone sat well with these events. His secretary, a fellow by the name of Joshua Vrey, decided to set things aright. He rallied the militia, deposed the Governor, and restored order. Then, hoping to make amends, he got in touch with the first Naval vessel to make port, our very own *H.M.S. Albatross.* Joshua fills her holds with gold, silver, and rarer things as an apology to the King, with the Lantern thrown in as well. Then sends her homewards, hoping that she'll be able to beat the Marines back to the Kingdom. Two days ago, an aetherite working in Breachtown, who is also in the employ of our very dear Mr. Grey, divines that she's wrecked, in the mouth of the barely-known Silverpenny River. Which is completely the wrong direction from Edrus, I might add."

The first mate quieted, busily feeding himself another egg while the others absorbed his tale. Fengel blinked. Henry was rubbing at his forehead.

"Cursed treasure," groaned the steward. "We're sailing after cursed treasure."

"Poppycock," said Fengel. He sat up straighter on the bench. "While your tale is incredible, Lucian, it is not at all conclusive evidence that the gemstone in question is cursed and that our quest is doomed."

Silence fell over the room at this pronouncement. Fengel felt the faint vibration of the furnace back in the bowels of the ship.

Lucian furrowed his brow. "But...sir. All the deaths? And the madness? And the rather horrible results from anyone who has touched this silly gem?"

"Come now. While the information is alarming, we only have third-hand supposition about a supernatural jinx upon the Lantern. I need not remind you two not to give in to superstitions. There's no such thing a curse."

"Sir?" asked Henry. "Maxim can tell you they're real. I saw him cast one once, when we had that mix-up with the Red Corsairs in Haventown. Other fellow went all diseased and—"

"Magic, Mister Smalls, is another thing altogether." He turned back to his first mate. "Now the far more interesting thing, Lucian, is this tribute. Grey wants the gem, which we haven't any choice in acquiring for him. But how much was loaded into those holds? It stands to reason, that they should be easily much as valuable there as the Lantern, yes?"

Lucian sighed. "Yes, quite a bit more really."

Fengel beamed. "Capital! Well now. We might have to make a trip or two, I don't know how much we can carry aboard yet and still make good time."

"Sir," said Henry. "The aetherite, remember? If Grey knows where the ship is, everyone else is going to as well."

"That's not all," said Lucian. His first mate looked suddenly sheepish. "Dear old Mordie figured out where we're going somehow too."

Fengel started. "What? But how? Grey wouldn't have gone to Natasha."

"I'm not sure. But he knows. And if he does, then she does too."

Fengel considered. "Well. Obnoxious, but we're still fine. She doesn't have a ship, remember? And even if she can convince someone to come after us, we can make off with more than enough—"

The door to the mess flew open. The crewman, Ryan Gae, burst inside.

"Captain," he cried. "Navigator needs you up on deck."

Fengel didn't waste time. He leapt to his feet and ran to the hatch, his steward and mate close on his heels. *A light-air gas leak? Curse it, that's the only thing it could be. Or are we too close to Engmann's Maelstrom? Damnation! This was too easy. I knew it was too good to be true.*

Rising up onto the deck, he took in the scene. The crew were all assembled in the stern. Nothing was on fire, and the ship flew smooth and evenly through the sky. He ran over to the throng, pushing through. "Make way for your captain," he cried, and was gratified to see the crowd part.

Maxim stood at the gunwales, peering out past the steam of the exhaust. He noticed Fengel and pointed into the sky behind them. "There," he said, passing over a spyglass.

Fengel took it, extended it, and looked where indicated. At first he saw nothing at all, only blue sky puffy with high-flying clouds. "I don't—" Then he saw it. Barely visible over the jungle to the northwest, a black speck on the horizon.

It was another skyship.

CHAPTER SIX

"HARD TO STARBOARD!" screamed Mordecai from halfway up the stairs to the aftcastle deck. "Hard to *starboard*, damn your eyes!"

Konrad fought with the ship's wheel. Their navigator threw himself bodily at it, trying to force the ship onto its new course. The man swore in his native tongue, face red behind his bushy beard at the effort. Mordecai ignored him, eyes locked on the aft rudder assemblies. They jutted out from either side of the stern of the ship, connected to the gas-bag frame above by pulleys, wire, and old rope. The linkage controls connecting the ship's wheel squealed and groaned, fighting the foreign navigator. All of it was either moldering or rusted, not yet repaired in the hasty retrofitting they'd undergone.

The navigator turned to the invisible daemon on his shoulder. "Scheiss!" he screamed. "Shut up!" With a growl he threw himself again at the wheel. This time it gave with the sound of metal squealing upon metal, and Konrad went flying past to tumble down the aftcastle deck, landing against the rails, his balance gone. The ship's wheel spun madly, the rudder slamming hard to one side. Mordecai felt butterflies in his stomach as the *Copper Queen* listed. The crew tumbled, yelling and fighting for purchase while shadows cast by the morning sun stretched crazily across the deck.

Mordecai reflexively grabbed the rail along the stair, holding fast as the ship spun. He pulled himself up the steps to the deck, determined to get this scow of an airship back under control. Just as he reached the top a flash flew across his vision; Guye Farrel, the new crewman, leaping up from where he'd fallen to take the wheel. He latched on, yelling in pain as it cracked him across the face, but refused to loosen his grip. Farrel slowly brought the wheel back to even keel against the wind. The ship righted a little, and the crew climbed back to their feet and back to their stations, swearing and groaning.

"Well!" said the Mechanist. "It actually worked. That's a good sign, yes?"

Mordecai turned back to the Brother of the Cog. He stood just below him on the stair, still clutching its rail in a white-knuckled grip. The Brother was young, red haired and freckle-faced. Like all his kind he wore a leather greatcoat, so massive and baggy that it was impossible to tell the shape of his frame underneath. However, unlike the more senior members of his order, his coat was pristine, still smelling of oil rather than the burned leather and engine-grease stink that denoted experience among his kind. The youth beamed up at Mordecai, his silly grin making the peach-fuzz stubble on his upper lip even more apparent.

At Mordecai's withering glare he swallowed. "Of...of course there are still a few kinks to be worked out. Bound to, a ship this old." He rallied. "But I'm positive that I can get that rudder moving smoothly by suppertime."

Mordecai didn't bother with a response. He glanced back at the wheel, where Guye Farrel stood proud and assured as he kept the ship on course, brown hair flying in the wind. The pirate was shirtless but for the bandage wrapped around his chest, holding in place a pad along his ribs where Natasha had shot him two nights ago. He was obviously still in pain, though trying not to show it, still eager to prove himself. Mordecai knew his type; Farrel was convinced he was the star of his own personal penny-play. He would show the man his place as soon as he had the time, after they caught up to their prey.

Farrel caught Mordecai's gaze and smiled, awaiting a sign of approval. Behind him Konrad climbed back to his feet, then roughly shouldered the newcomer aside, still swearing unintelligible foreign invective. He gripped the wheel, then turned his fury to Farrel. The newcomer fell back, startled. Mordecai smiled and turned his attention back to the deck.

The *Copper Queen* stretched out before him, an improbably flying mess of dark wood. His crew scurried everywhere, replacing rope and cable, hauling light-air gas canisters up to the frame above. The ship was loud, creaking constantly. It groaned, sighed, and generally complained like an arthritic old man.

Mordecai glowered. *What a miserable wreck.*

Only one figure wasn't frantically moving about. Natasha stood atop the forecastle on the bow of the ship, staring fixedly ahead. Mordecai sighed and made his way down toward her, straightening his sword and his jacket.

The Mechanist followed his descent, trailing like a lonely puppy. "Those linkages are old; once we get back into port I can swap them for the new pulleys Rontpellier designed. That should increase the speed of the ship's turning by a good ten percent at least."

Mordecai halted, wheeling to face the Mechanist. "Can you keep the ship from wallowing like a drunken sow every time we change course? Can you do that *now*?"

The young Brother quieted, looked at his feet. "I'm...I'm sure I can fix that," he finally said.

"Make sure you do," Mordecai replied quietly, dangerously. "Or I'll tie you to the keel and drag you screaming across the sky. This scow needs to *work*, Mechanist. It needs to *fly* if we're ever going to catch our quarry."

He turned back to the deck, striding down it and snarling at anyone in his way. The Brother followed, but stayed quiet, suitably intimidated.

Mordecai thought black thoughts. Despite his best efforts, Lucian had slipped away *again*, helped along by his network of allies and a damnable knowledge of the Copper Isles. Though he'd scoured Haventown, the rogue had evaded him, and he'd been forced to return to Natasha empty-handed.

She hadn't been any more successful. All her nominal allies were missing from port, anyone who would have helped take up the chase. Conspicuously, every other captain in town was suddenly unavailable, hiding on their ships or otherwise busy. There had been only one recourse left, and it galled the both of them.

But getting the Copper Queen into the air again wasn't easy. Even with Euron's permission, only the hurried, shameful begging of the Brotherhood for a Mechanist had even made it possible, and they'd been forced to make do with the only Brother available, the green pup following him even now. With barely any supplies and a hurried rousting of the crew, Mordecai had gotten the *Queen* cut free from the dock and up into the sky.

They had proceeded to drift north with the wind, powerless, for most of the next day.

Eventually the Mechanist restored the old coal furnace and gave them a modicum of control. Now they were under their own direction once more, pointed southeast towards Fengel's destination along the Yulan and doing their best to make up the time lost. But the old scow wasn't even close to being a decent flying craft. It fought them constantly, forcing them to wrangle it every step of the way.

The forecastle rose up before Mordecai. He climbed the stair up to its deck. It was empty but for the lone figure of the captain, leaning on the bow where the old-style prow stretched forward. He turned to glare at the

Mechanist, warning him to come no closer. The youth jerked to a stop and looked away. Mordecai approached to within a few feet of Natasha, folding his hands behind him.

The captain said nothing. Mordecai waited, knowing better. He was furious—she would be incandescent.

"Report," Natasha finally commanded.

"We're back on course," said Mordecai. "South by southeast heading. We might have over-compensated on our charting. But even under just mechanical power they've got a full two nights gain on us."

Natasha whirled. "Well, if you wouldn't insist on trying to make this broken old wreck dance, we'd have more gained!"

Mordecai flushed. "Or we would still be drifting northwards," he replied calmly. "If the *Queen* collapses under our feet and drowns us all in the Atalian Sea or breaks us on the rocks of the Isles, it won't matter how much of a lead Fengel has."

She snarled, teeth bared. Natasha stopped, and then turned back to the bow in a huff. "Bastard!" she cried, pounding a fist on the gunwales. "He stole my ship. My *ship!* And now he's getting away with her! If I ever get my hands on that poncy, fastidious son-of-a-bitch I'm going to jam that ridiculous monocle so far up his arse that he chokes on it!"

She wheeled back to Mordecai, pointing a finger at his nose. "My father. I had to *ask* my father if I could take this horrible rust-bucket scow back into the air! And he said yes! He *smiled!* Like he was proud of me!" Natasha made a horrible face, like she'd swallowed something rancid. "Get us after them, Mordecai. Fling this piece of shit their way. Damn your safeties to the Realms Below. I don't care how many men you kill to do it, or if you cut your own throat in the process. Get it done."

His captain turned back to the bow. Heat flooded into his face. Mordecai turned back to the deck, lest she see the curl of his own lip.

Unreasonable bitch. He descended back to the deck, marching back toward the helm atop the stern deck. The crew avoided him, taking the ugly look on his face for the warning that it was.

Ascending the aftcastle deck he found Konrad in place at the helm, Guye Farrel standing sullenly nearby. "What are you doing here?" Mordecai snapped at the wounded newcomer.

Guye started. "I was just—"

"Get up on the frame," Mordecai snarled. "Port-side. Check the cloth for tears. Then get over to the bow and make sure the figurehead is polished."

Guye frowned, but ducked his head. "Sir," he said, descending to the deck and making his way to the starboard rigging along the gunwales.

Mordecai stood beside the ship's wheel, fighting for calm. Konrad eyed him, but wisely, for once, said nothing.

The crew were well trained. They kept to their tasks, frantically working to get the rickety vessel shipshape. Other than their shouts and groaning of the makeshift airship, the morning was quiet, the weather calm and pleasant. Though Mordecai worried about sinking, the Copper Isles were visible to their stern, not too far away should he be required to swim it.

If I could survive the fall. The airship worried him. *Damn her obsessions. If this rattletrap contraption sinks into the sea, it'll take us—*

Something caught his eye, to the south along the horizon. Mordecai approached the rail, pulling a spyglass from his jacket. Extending it, he peered through at the black speck floating through the sky. It was too large and far away to be a bird, and flew too fast as well.

An airship resolved through the lenses of his spyglass. The *Dawnhawk.* Her skysails were free and glimmering in the morning sun.

"Ship ahoy!" he cried. "Twelve points to starboard!"

The crew, trained pirates and sailors all, sprang to the starboard-side to see. The *Queen* listed dangerously beneath them.

Natasha ran from the forecastle, leaping down the stairs to the main deck and pushing into the crowd. "Out of my way," she cried. "Damn you. Get out of my way or I'll hang you from the prow by your balls!" She fought her way to the rails and peered out at the speck on the horizon. She cursed, then looked up to Mordecai. "The glass!"

He tossed it to her. She caught it easily, and jammed it desperately to her eye. A wordless cry left her lips. "It's her! It's my ship!"

"She's not so far out as I would have thought," mused Mordecai. "They must have swung back to pick up Lucian Thorne."

"This is it then." Natasha turned to the crew assembled about her. "Men, to arms! Navigator, hard to starboard!"

Mordecai took in the list of the ship, the squeaking of the rudder assemblies behind him, the precarious dangling of Guye Farrel along the gas-bag frame above. "Wait—"

"Hard to starboard, aye," intoned Konrad. The aetherite navigator took a breath and then slammed himself bodily into the wheel. It halted under his weight, groaned, and then abruptly spun as the linkages above were forced into compliance. They swung free, moving over as far as they could go.

The *Copper Queen* whirled out of control again. She spun madly, spiraling clockwise through the air. Pirates yelled in surprise and clutched to railings, the deck plates, the rigging, and each other to avoid pitching over the side. Konrad lost his balance and flew back to slam into the stern railing, its wooden poles cracking audibly.

Mordecai grabbed reflexively at the rail behind him, keeping his balance and footing. He grit his teeth and pushed off from the rail, launching himself at the wheel. The gyre of the makeshift airship pulled at him, but his fingers brushed the wooden spokes of the wheel and he clung to it, pulling himself enough to reach with his second hand, bit by bit until he stood before the helm. He heaved with both arms, teeth clenched. The wheel moved beneath his grasp, but before he could return it true it caught, the rusty linkage overhead groaning again in complaint. The ship slowed in its mad dance, a little.

Mordecai jerked at the wheel. Suddenly Konrad was there, throwing his weight into it as well. Something above them snapped, bits of rusty metal pattering down to the deck about them. They slowed further, still spinning, but not with enough force to dislodge them and send the crew flying over the side. Mordecai turned back to the deck, panting. He spied the Mechanist, gripping the rail by the stair up to the stern deck for dear life. The youth's face was green and terrified. Meeting Mordecai's gaze, he blanched.

"Sorry!" cried the Mechanist. "I—I can fix that!"

Mordecai growled and stalked over to the stair. The Mechanist quivered and covered his head. Mordecai ignored him, glaring about for Natasha. His captain stood still, gripping the rail where she'd been, white knuckled.

"You daft bint!" he cried. He knew it was improper, knew he shouldn't confront her so in front of the crew. Mordecai would pay for it later. But he didn't care. "There's no way this rustbucket and pile of dry rot can catch the *Dawnhawk* in a direct chase. She's got her skysails out! She's running on the southeasterly, Engmann's Run. We'd have to burn everything we've got to even have a chance at catching up. They're not burning a thing!"

Natasha glared up at him, eyes wide and half-crazed. She let loose a wordless cry of anguish, half outrage and half despair, before stalking away again to the bow, watching the spinning horizon hungrily.

Mordecai sighed. He kicked the Mechanist at his feet in the ribs. "Get this scow to stop spinning. I lose my lunch, you lose your head." The Brother of the Cog blanched again, then scrambled to his feet and ran to the deck below for his tools.

Mordecai watched him go, and watched the crew pick themselves up again. The ship still listed dangerously. He called out orders, putting things to rights again as best could be.

The ship gave another lurch as a tailwind caught at it, causing the crew to cry out and grab the rails for safety. With a wild cry, Guye Farrel went flying from the rigging along the frame above. The newcomer flew forward, slamming into the forecastle deck and rolling past a surprised Natasha to fold up just beneath the prow and the figurehead there.

Mordecai paused, feeling an idea take root in his mind. He examined the space where Farrel had fallen from up above, then the bow, then the deck he would have had to cross normally. He turned to the Mechanist, now swaying on a ladder held by Konrad while he worked on the linkage mechanisms suspended from the gasbag frame above them. "Can you get that mess working in short order?"

The youth started and almost fell. He looked down to Mordecai, face uncertain. "Y-Yes. I think. I mean, I should be able to. Only a simple line break. The chain was going to go anyway, so rusted through. I can replace it in fifteen minutes perhaps."

"You've got ten," replied Mordecai, turning to stalk down to the deck. He made his way forward, shouting orders at the crew as he went. *Perhaps we can pull this off.*

Natasha stood waiting for him as he climbed up the forecastle. She'd recovered her composure, but now her temper was up. "You tread thin ice, Mordecai," she hissed. "How dare you counteract me on my own ship?"

"It's my prerogative to do so when you're not thinking straight," he said mildly. "Such as now. This isn't your ship." He pointed to the distant glimmer of the *Dawnhawk*. "That one is."

"You think I need reminding?" she asked, voice low, furious.

"Yes. But more, I think you need to apply yourself again to your post. She's on the Run, skysails out."

"So? We burn all the coal we brought and we can make up the pace."

Mordecai shook his head. "For a little time. But they'd see us, and spin back up to speed. With their furnace to full and the aetherline flowing we'd lose them again, and be stranded to boot. No. We can't beat the *Dawnhawk* directly, she's sleeker than this scow, and has more coal in her holds." He looked up. "But I've got an idea as to how we can catch her."

Natasha's features smoothed, one delicate eyebrow rising. "Oh? Tell me."

"We pounce on them at Engmann's Maelstrom."

His captain blinked. The newcomer Guye Farrel groaned below them. Mordecai outlined his plan. Natasha smiled, and he knew she was convinced.

They were going to get their ship back.

CHAPTER SEVEN

"**A**ETHER'S INVISIBLE." said Andrea. The piratess had dark hair and dark eyes. She took a swig from a hip flask and passed it to Lina. "Here. This is Corsair's Cure-all. Have a shot."

"All right" replied Lina. She sniffed the open end and jerked her head back. The contents had a chemical stench that ate at her sinuses, bringing fresh tears into her eyes.

"Ah, Cure-all," said Ryan Gae through his scruffy black beard. "Found two casks of the stuff down below. Go on, take a swallow. It'll put hair on your chest."

Afternoon sunlight lit the ocean beyond the ship, though the deck itself lay in shadow cast by the gas-bag, as usual. The three of them sat amidships, off-watch, against the port-side exhaust-pipes. Here the tubes were free of skysail linkages and pleasantly warm from the steam within. Through them Lina felt the rumble of the furnace in the Mechanist's room belowdecks.

"That's the second-to-last place that I want hair," Lina said, staring at the flask. She knew she'd have to drink it; her new crewmates were only trying to be friendly. Still though, she worked at getting up the nerve. She'd had many awful drinks before, in similar circumstances. But this stuff promised to be the worst, even more so than the bathtub gin she'd brewed in the slums back home.

"What's the last place?" asked Ryan, curious.

"My back," Lina replied with a smile. She wrapped her lips around the flask and tipped it up. Fire shot down her throat, burned out her sinuses and charred her innards. She gave a strangled cry and fell to the deck, arms and legs curling like a dead spider.

Things felt different aboard the *Dawnhawk* today. Exhausted after throwing Oscar overboard the night before, she had left him to his friends and gone down below to pass out in her hammock. Now there was a subtle change in the crew, they were less wary and more welcoming. Those she passed nodded or gave her a smile.

After rising around noon she'd made her way to the mess, where Andrea and Ryan Gae had made her acquaintance. They were friendly enough, and she liked them. Andrea loved to talk, and Ryan laughed loudly. Now the three of them idled about abovedeck. Apparently there had been some alarm earlier, a sighting of another skyship. It wasn't chasing after them, though, and the *Dawnhawk* had left it quickly behind.

"Good stuff, eh?" Ryan took the flask of Cure-all from her and downed a swig, then pushed it back into her hands.

Oh Goddess. The world swam above Lina. She clutched at the flask, trying for focus. Climbing back up from the deck seemed an impossible task.

"Anyway," continued Andrea as if nothing was wrong, "aether's invisible. Only an aetherite can see it. That's why they call 'em that."

Lina dimly realized that she was still expected to partake in the conversation. She opened her mouth to say something, but only succeeded in gasping.

"That's the *real* secret of flight," said Ryan. "The light-air gas we fly on, I mean, sure, that's important. And coal to push the propellers. But all the kingdoms and city-states back west have got that figured out. The Mechanists have kept anyone from finding out *exactly* what it is, but everyone knows it's a gas."

"By riding the aetherlines for long stretches," said Andrea, "That's how we get anywhere." The piratess slid down next to Lina. "It's about *efficiency*. Coal furnace and propellers blow us along, but we have to fight the wind sometimes. Or burn hard to get out of a storm. Or any other damn thing, just like an ocean-going sail ship or steamship. So long as you've got skysails like ours, it doesn't cost a thing. Captain can order the furnace cold and we just ride along, not losing fuel. Then, when we need to, we can burn coal to leave the lines and chase down prey, though you have to heat the furnace again. It's always better to ride the aetherlines, if you can. Those poor bastards on the older models of airship have to make due, and pillage coal from their victims to boot."

Lina thought about this. "Like that old one I saw in port? The *Copper Queen?*"

Andrea snorted. "*Queen* hasn't flown in years. Probably can't." She rubbed her forehead and pursed her lips, looking thoughtful. "Though if she did, yeah, she'd be burning just coal, relying on propellers. No skysails in Euron's time." She belched. "Heck, could probably put on a bit of speed, that one, assuming it didn't fall apart and the captain also didn't mind losing all their fuel." She shook her head. "But I'm getting sidetracked. Imagine it. Invisible roadways of aether stretching from one end of the ocean to the other, slightly curving. They probably cross the whole of the world. I'd give damned near anything to be able to see them." Andrea gave a sigh and fell silent.

"But you can't?" said Lina.

"Nope," said Ryan. "Gotta be a magician, an aetherite, for that. And most of them can't do it alone, even then. So they bind daemons to help them. Goddess knows how the Mechanists came up with the sails. I wouldn't be surprised if they've aetherites amongst their number. But by and large they're Rationalists. It's probably something to do with Insubstantial Torque and Havelmann's Applied Rationality."

Lina blinked. "I don't know what any of that is."

"High concept mathematics," replied Ryan. "We may be just pirates, but we've got more practical knowledge concerning aether and flight dynamics than any college-bound hack."

"Yarr," agreed Andrea.

Lina slowly recovered from the horrible drink. It didn't smell so bad after all, and the next sip left her feeling warm and relaxed. They chatted easily, Ryan and Andrea relating knowledge about Lina's new career, Lina freely telling some of the more embarrassing stories from her childhood on the streets.

"Can you fight?" asked Ryan after a time. He climbed up to his feet.

Lina giggled a little. "Knife, broken bottle, hairpin."

Andrea gave an approving nod. "Dirty."

"You're going to want something with more reach," said Ryan. "Usually most merchants just heave-to and surrender when we drop out of the sky. But there are some that put up a fight. Between that and the bit of rough play back in Haventown, it always comes down to a scrap. Let me show you..."

The pirate trailed off, staring at something behind Lina's head. Andrea glanced behind them, then scrabbled away from the pipe to her feet with a curse.

Lina blinked up at them, confused. "What?"

Andrea hissed at her: "Get away!"

Curious, Lina twisted around to look directly behind her.

A horror stared her in the face. It sat on the exhaust-pipe, as long as her arm but coiled atop itself like a snake. Thick, ridged scales covered it from one end to the other, so blue they were almost black. The head was smooth and bullet-shaped, serpentine, with a pair of heavy mandibles folded low about the mouth. Behind the head rose a hump that tapered back down the length of the creature. It watched her with two dark, beady eyes.

"What is it?" asked Lina, curious.

"*Chirr*," said the thing. It cocked its head, rising up slightly to meet her gaze. The underbelly was smooth and pale. A glow rose from it, an iridescent red that ran in bioluminescent lines down to form complex patterns.

"It's adorable!" said Lina. Then she hiccupped.

"Uh," said Ryan.

"Lina," said Andrea. She rubbed her forehead. "That's a scryn. A sky-ray. Kind of a runty one, actually. But you really—"

"I've never seen one before," Lina replied. "How does it glow like that?" She held out a hand, tentatively. "Come on, little fella. I won't bite." The scryn reared higher, leaning away to avoid her hand. Lina moved closer. "C'mere little guy." She turned back to her friends. They stared at her, appalled. "Normal pirates have parrots right? Those big, pretty birds I keep seeing all over the place. Is this what we've got instead?"

"Lina," said Andrea. "Come away. They're nothing *like* parrots."

The scryn leapt forward, uncoiling its length. It landed on her arm like a heavy limp rope, but curled in an eyeblink up around her shoulders. The creature was surprisingly light for its size. It smelled of the ocean, and something else, a sharp musk.

"*Chirr*," it repeated.

Lina laughed. "He likes me! I think I'll keep him." Standing, she wobbled a bit. Lina realized she was very tipsy, if not drunk outright from the Cure-all. She pushed the thought aside. "It's so strange up here," she said. "I didn't even stop to think, but you've got probably got all sorts of things living up in the clouds, right? Flying snakes, floating whales..." She grinned at Andrea. "What should I name him?"

"Lina," said Ryan. "Those things aren't pets. They're really, really vicious."

The scryn nuzzled her cheek. Lina laughed. "Look! We're bonding!"

She wobbled as the creature shifted its weight, sliding further down her left arm towards the still-open flask. Lina shifted it into her other hand. The scryn cried out, and stretched after it.

"None of that now," said Lina. "Terrible stuff. Probably eat your innards out."

"*Chirr*," it said, insistently. The scryn constricted around her arm painfully. It reared up to hiss, jaw unhinged, rows of needle-teeth displayed within. Four barbed tongues waved on the air, musky spittle dropping down to sizzle on the iron exhaust-pipes. The hump behind its head unfolded, spreading to reveal a wide flat body like that of a manta ray, the mandibles really hooked claws at either end. The patterns glowing across the underbelly flared into strange, hypnotic arrangements.

Lina gave a surprised shout. Then she grabbed the tail-end of the scryn with her free hand and swung it down like a whip at the exhaust-pipe. The creature banged against the heated steel, ringing it like a bell. The scryn yowled in pain.

Lina didn't give it time to recover. She looked about for the closest weapon at hand and only found the flask. *Why not?* She jammed the open end of the drink into the hissing, spitting maw of the sky-ray. It struggled, but Lina held it tight, pinned against the exhaust-pipe by the upended flask. It uncoiled from her arm, flailing hard to get away. She let go, throwing herself from the flying monster. Hitting the deck she scrabbled backward, to where Andrea and Ryan stood with their blades drawn.

The scryn struggled to right itself atop the pipe. It reared back, blinking. Looking at the pirates, it reared up to show them its belly. The red patterns were intermittent, confused. The creature wavered in the air, gave a weak hiss, and fell abruptly over. It slapped against the pipe again and rose up, head shaking, body weaving. Then it fell over again.

"Stone me," said Andrea. "I think it's drunk."

"*Chirr*," said the scryn, rising again. It looked at Lina with eyes like the bottom of a well, then threw itself over the side of the ship.

She climbed to her feet and pulled herself up over the pipe to look past the gunwales. The Atalian Sea shone blue down below, sunlight shimmering on its waves. The scryn dropped through the air, not at all gracefully, seeming to wriggle and coast as it flew below the ship out of sight.

Lina turned back, breathing heavy. The pleasant buzz from the drink was gone, cold shock and realization replacing it. *Goddess above, what was I thinking?*

Lina looked over to see her friends staring at her. The two pirates broke out into laughter. Ryan fell to his knees, Andrea wiped at the tears dampening her face. Lina giggled. Then she hiccupped.

As others came over to see about the noise, Lina learned that scryn were uncommon creatures, but widely hated and feared by pirates of all sorts on this side of the Atalian Sea. Though many strange creatures lived in and around the Yulan Continent, scryn were among the most obnoxious, extremely territorial of the rocky hive-clusters they tended to prefer. The rest of the crew were all amused by the tale Ryan told about Lina, and more than a little impressed. In short time Lina made easy acquaintance with several others.

Time passed and by mid-afternoon Lina found herself desiring quiet, a little nauseous as her body found equilibrium with the drink. She made her way up to the bow, which was momentarily empty. Without a forecastle or even a prow, the bow was more of an observation deck, a place to watch the world go by. Andrea told her that the lookouts were up above on the gasbag frame, a place Lina had yet to go.

The Atalian Sea rolled beneath them. The water was deep blue and clear for a dozen feet beneath the surface. Through it she spied great schools of silver fish and the hard gray lines of sharks on the hunt. Salt scent tickled her nose, mixing with the smell of the oil that was used to weather the deck. Through her feet she felt the faint vibration of the steam-furnace, ever present. High overhead the sky was clear, a few puffy clouds scudding high across the heavens. Lina hadn't seen land since she'd gone off-shift the night before, and it felt strange. The airship just seemed to hang, a fixed point in space surrounded by cerulean.

Something caught at her attention on the horizon. Lina watched it until it resolved; a heavy cloudbank dead ahead where the ocean met the sky. It was thick and heavy, but not dark like the herald of some storm or sudden squall.

Lina frowned. *What's this?* Considering the recent event with the scryn, she turned back down the ship to look for someone to fill her in on what was undoubtedly some other piece of common knowledge she lacked. Henry Smalls stood nearby, examining one of the stanchions attaching the deck of the ship to its gas-bag frame overhead. Lina walked over.

"Mr. Smalls?"

Henry looked up, brightening on seeing her. "Miss Stone. You're looking well. I heard the tale about the scryn."

Lina coughed.

"Daresay I wouldn't have acted as quickly as you." He looked thoughtful for a moment. "Though I probably wouldn't have let it crawl onto my arm either. Anyway, what can I do for you?"

Lina pointed out past the bow. "I saw something strange on the horizon. Odd clouds. Not sure if I should tell someone?"

Henry walked up to the bow, peering beyond. "Already? Those *are* good sails. We're making excellent time."

"That's expected?"

"Oh yes." He pointed. "That, young miss, is Engmann's Maelstrom."

Lina blinked. "What?"

"A perpetual storm, of sorts. Though a calm one. Come, let's go inform Lucian and the Captain." He bustled off.

Captain Fengel, Lina thought to herself. She frowned then, acutely aware of her knife-hacked hair and rough hands. *No. Stop it.* Lina started after the steward, following him down the length of the deck. She glanced at the other pirates of the day-watch as they lazed about. Lucian and Fengel stood at the helm near the stern, dark-haired Maxim at the wheel as before. The aetherite was smiling slightly.

"All I'm saying," complained Lucian, "is that a man's trousers should be sacrosanct. I mean, really. Powdered peppers? That's a paltry sort of jape. And stop smiling Maxim. I *know* it was you. Oh, hullo Henry."

The three turned to face Lina and the steward. Lucian had been restored to his usual dashing self, while the captain was redoubtable as always. When he looked her way, Lina averted her eyes.

"Miss Stone sighted the Maelstrom off the bow ahead," said the steward.

Lucian frowned. "I knew this ship was fast, but damnation. We're only a day from the Continent and the Stormwall then. Hm. If she saw it from the bow, the lookouts above should have called out first. Hey there!"

The first mate called out to a passing pirate. Ryan Gae stopped. "Sir?"

"Go up above and yell at the lookouts for a bit. I'll be up to do the job proper shortly."

"Sir," said Ryan, running for the ratlines up to the gasbag frame and beyond.

Lucian started walking up the length of the deck, calling out orders and rousting the crew. They jumped to attention, rushing about to tighten slack lines and lock away loose objects.

"Sir," Lina asked Fengel. "What is the Maelstrom?"

The captain looked up from the dials studding the gearbox. He held her with his eyes, so striking and green. "Engmann's Maelstrom? A permanent storm of sorts." He smiled, fatherly. "Do not worry, Miss Stone. It's not a real storm, and in a ship like this we'll be just fine. Maxim? Could you explain it a bit better?"

The navigator nodded cheerfully. "You see," he began. "There is a substance that surrounds us, that binds the world—"

"Aether?" interrupted Lina.

Maxim frowned. "Yes. Well, it is not as unordered as the other elements. Aether runs in great—"

"Yes, big curvy paths called aetherlines that we can ride a bit. Got that too."

The navigator glared at her. "Well. Sometimes there are great disturbances in the aetherlines, where two of them meet, or where a powerful daemon is trapped along its length. This causes the aetherline to churn and whorl. Did you know that?"

Lina thought about it a moment. "So it's a permanent maelstrom made out of aether. Why didn't you say so?"

Maxim blinked, opened his mouth to say something, then turned away with a disgusted sound.

Fengel smiled at her. "That's pretty much the gist of it. Clouds gather around it for some reason, and there are rocks below. But it's not a real storm, so I wouldn't worry overmuch about it. We'll keep the skysails out, and use them to tack around the edges of the Maelstrom without losing any momentum. Otherwise we'd drop half a day getting back up to speed." He patted her shoulder like a fond parent and moved past to speak with Lucian. Lina blushed at the touch and hid her face.

Once he was gone she looked up to see if Maxim had noticed. He hadn't. Lina made her way back up the deck amidships where one of the delicate skysails fluttered beyond the hull of the ship.

The Maelstrom grew closer. Though she couldn't see the aether, the bank of swirling, churning clouds ahead was visible enough. It was odd, watching them roil. There was almost no wind at the moment and the day was warm and easy.

Small islets appeared just below the perpetual storm. As Fengel had said, they were a collection of rocky crags jutting up out of the water. They weren't big enough to land on or even shaped for it, being barely two dozen feet across with sharp, knife-blade peaks rising up some fifty feet from the water. White dung coated them, with small sprigs of greenery growing hardscrabble from the cracks and crannies.

The *Dawnhawk* sped closer. Lina thought she spied the eye of the storm through the swirling clouds. The crew shouted reports back to the helm, where the captain and his officers conferred. Alongside the ship the skysails stretched and rippled, pulled tight by the invisible force of the aether. They were speeding up.

Lina watched in fascination. She felt herself grinning like a little girl. *This is amazing.* Her attention was split between the strange, stately roil of the Maelstrom, the airship itself as the crew raced about, and the knife-like rocks below. People couldn't live on them, but maybe there were other things, seabirds and such. She took another quick glance at the rocks, the first of which they were just passing above.

Dark shapes wriggled beneath the foliage as the shadow of the ship fell over the islets. Lina frowned, bending farther over the gunwales to get a better look. Beside her the skysail flapped and rippled.

A shudder shook the front of the ship. Lina glanced back up toward the bow reflexively. The Maelstrom loomed hugely now. All about the clouds swirled, a giant vortex hanging in the sky. She could see its eye through the mist, a hole in the quiet fury of the vortex. Another shudder shook the ship as the *Dawnhawk* picked up speed. They were being sucked in. Their prow touched the edge of the vortex and the skysails there went taut like an umbrella caught in a strong wind. The whole ship shifted, almost violently. They were listing a bit to starboard.

"Hard to port!" cried Captain Fengel. "Take us hard to port. Skirt the edge of the eye or we'll never get out!"

A raucous cry rang out from below the ship. Lina glanced back over the side. Below, the creatures on the rocks were taking flight, bursting out from under the foliage and flinging themselves into the air. They stretched, unwrapping to reveal wide sinuous tails and thick, manta-ray bodies.

Scryn.

Others joined them. Dozens and dozens of the things emerged from the cracks and crannies of their roost. The rocks below were covered with the creatures. "Scryn!" she cried out, turning back out to the deck. "The rocks are covered in scryn!"

The crew nearest her glanced up, too focused on dealing with the Maelstrom to understand quickly. Their looks of confusion turned to startled comprehension, just as the first of the flying creatures swooped up over the gunwales onto the deck.

Shouts of alarm rang out. The crew drew daggers and swords. The scryn didn't seem to care. They descended in an angry flock, hissing and spitting poison at whichever pirates were nearest. Their bellies blazed red like the one Lina had fought earlier, illuminating the normally shadowed deck with an infernal glow.

Lina ducked down low behind the gunwales and took cover below the exhaust-pipe as the ship gave another shudder. The flying monsters aboard were larger than the one she'd seen earlier that day. Her daggers wouldn't do a thing to protect her. Lina looked about for something better.

The airship listed again, shaken the other way now by the churning of the Maelstrom. Forced away by the furious swarm of scryn, crewmen and officers left their posts. Without their guidance the ship was whirling, shaking, and spinning like a toy boat going down the drain. Through the cloud of black monsters, Lina spied the skysails at either side of the ship. They rippled and shook, their armatures groaning and twanging. If something wasn't done soon they'd be torn away.

Nearby a pirate stumbled, the usually silent Geoffrey Lords. He cursed and lashed wildly about with a saber. That earned him a brief respite, just long enough to notice another scryn swooping up from behind. The pirate whirled to defend against it and slammed up against the exhaust-pipes. Something broke free of his belt and clattered against the deck next to her.

A hip flask.

The Cure-all. Her scryn had been extremely attracted to it and Ryan said he'd found two barrels of the stuff. They'd be in the cargo deck below, where she hadn't been yet. But pirates were sailors first, and if she knew sailors, then Ryan would probably have kept some somewhere personal. An idea took root in her mind.

Lina waited for a break in the action, then bolted down the deck toward the rear hatch. She ducked and weaved past screaming scryn and yelling pirates. Sharp cracks sounded as those with pistols fired them, sending plumes of smoke billowing about a deck that pitched and rolled.

Lina reached the hatch. Past it near the helm, Fengel and Lucian stood back to back, fending off scryn while Maxim fought against the swarm with caustic light. She paused, breath caught in her throat.

Maxim's magic was impressive, but the captain was an elegant blur. His saber flashed through the air, neatly separating the wing of a scryn before whipping about to skewer another. He stood with his back stiff, his off hand neatly held behind him in a classic fencer's pose.

"This must be a new colony," cried Lucian as he swatted at another of the flying creatures. "Territorial little bastards! I should have known when that new girl saw one of them earlier!"

"Keep fighting," said Fengel, loud yet calm. "Keep them off long enough to get us through the Maelstrom!"

They don't see the real danger. They had to get control of the ship again, and soon, before the sails were torn away. But there were just too many scryn. She had to get rid of those first.

Lina dove down the aft hatch. Darkness enclosed her and the sounds of the strife on the deck above became muted and distant. Down the short hall she found herself in the crew room again, hammocks swaying in the air.

She moved through them, pulling out sea chests and upending sailor's bags. Knickknacks, weapons, bent cards and spare clothing went flying across the room. Lina looked for something, anything, that would hold a drink or three. Shoved into a corner beneath a hammock, hidden underneath a pile of blankets she found a keg. *Would Ryan have just grabbed the whole thing?*

Lina threw the blankets aside and hefted the cask. It was heavy, and sloshed when she pulled it out into the room. It was already breached, a cork now plugging the hole. She drew a dagger and wedged it out. A pungent stink immediately wafted from it to fill the room. Lina fell back, choking. This was Corsair's Cure-all, all right.

She held her face away and hoisted the keg. Lina grit her teeth and moved on, making her way back to the stair and tottering up it to through the hatch onto the deck.

Pandemonium still reigned. She did he best to ignore it, the cry of battle and the groaning of the ship. Lina took as straight a path as she dared to the starboard-side. There she shifted the cask to sit atop the exhaust-pipes and peered over the rail. The islets were still there, though they were just passing the last of them. It was large, and flat at the top like a pillar.

Groaning, Lina lifted the cask up to balance on the rail. She made sure to splash Cure-all out of the open bung onto the hot metal pipes. The air filled with the pungent, acidic scent of the stuff.

The scryn nearest stopped their screaming to look in her direction. Lina dropped to the deck, curling into a ball, and wedged herself under the exhaust-pipe as much as she could. The air above her filled with cacophony as the scryn swarmed, irresistibly attracted to the alcohol. They screeched and squabbled, fighting to be first. Lina heard the cask scrape against the wooden railing as the mass of creatures shoved it overboard. The red glow along the deck all about her darkened.

Lina look up. The massed scryn were gone, though she heard them just out of sight. A few still fought, though most of those were circling around her and the place where the Cure-all had spilled. She scrabbled away, climbing to her feet. The crew had the upper hand now, and quickly dispatched the remaining sky-rays.

Fengel moved up beside her, blade dripping black scryn ichors. "What happened?" he asked. "What did you do?"

"No time," she cried. "The Maelstrom is ripping us apart!"

Captain Fengel blinked at her. Then he looked up at the Maelstrom around them and cursed, taking notice of the groaning cries of his ship. "Hard to port!" he yelled, whirling back to face the helm. "Maxim! We've gained too much velocity! Get us turned hard to port and ride the wind!"

Those crew unwounded scrambled back to their stations. She glanced at the Maelstrom, at the skysails. *No. That won't work.* They had to pull the sails *in.*

The ship shook violently, first to one side and then the other. It swayed like a drunken horse. She opened her mouth to yell back to the captain. *No. Not enough time.* She had to do it herself.

Lina raced up the deck to the bow. She reached the first skysail along the starboard-side and the chain linkage that controlled it. A series of pulleys ran fine cord out from the mechanism to the skysail, attached to the linkage by a spool mounted on an axle, like the reel of a fishing rod. The cords hummed, taut against the invisible pressure of the Maelstrom. The thin metal armatures that suspended the sails squealed at the stress.

She placed her hands upon the reel and twisted. It gave only a little. Lina threw herself at it. The reel wound a little bit, and the skysail moved inward slightly. Bit by bit, swearing under her breath, she pulled it in. Finished, she stepped back to view it. The skysail wriggled and twisted, even folded up. But it would hold.

The ship still shook. There were five more sails to go.

Through the yelling of the captain and the frantic movement of the crew, Lina raced unnoticed. One by one she pulled them in, the second, third, fourth, and fifth. The ship shook less, leveled out. She was working on the sixth, near the helm in the stern, when a hand landed on her shoulder, spinning her about.

Lucian Thorne stood before her, Captain Fengel and Henry Smalls just behind. Smalls looked confused and the captain impassive, like stone. Maxim, stood at the helm past them, staring at the eye of the Maelstrom, as if seeing nothing else.

"What are you *doing*, girl?" The first mate glared down at her, furious. "We need to tack around the edge of the storm!"

Lina wanted to wince, to shrink away. "It was too late!" she said. "We were already caught up in the Maelstrom, and the skysails were tearing away!"

"The skysails would have been fine!" shouted Lucian. The dashing, easygoing man she'd seen was gone, replaced by the rough second-in-command of a crew of brigands and rogues. "We've taken them through aetherstorms like this just fine. You think you know better? We're going to be stuck in the eye now until we can fire up the furnace again and propel our way out! We've lost hours of travel because of you!"

"The girl is correct." Everyone turned at the harsh, almost mechanical voice. The Mechanist stalked over from the mouth of the rear hatchway, moving like a machine. "This ship is not your *Flittergrasp*. You presume too much about her capabilities." He turned to Captain Fengel. "The skysails installed upon the *Dawnhawk* are light, and will speed you more efficiently than any built by the Brotherhood so far. But they are fragile. You should have consulted me before adopting this tactic. A penalty will be applied to the fee after the voyage, as well as costs to repair the skysails, should they prove necessary."

Dismay flashed across Fengel's face. Whether at the fee or the possible damage to the ship, Lina could not say. Her captain visibly regained his composure, then nodded stiffly at the Mechanist. "My apologies, sir. The Brothers of the Cog know their own equipment best, of course." He glanced over to Lucian and Lina. "Miss Stone," he said, changing the subject. "What was it you did to lure away the scryn?"

Lina blinked in surprise. "Corsair's Cure-all," she said. "It's how I got rid of the one from earlier."

Captain Fengel raised an eyebrow. Then he moved to the rail to peer overboard. Lina shrugged off Lucian's hand and took a step back, glancing over the gunwales as well. Below them flew the cloud of scryn. They swarmed around the last islet where the cask had fallen and shattered. The creatures screeched and fought, but ignored the *Dawnhawk* in favor of the spilled liquor.

Fengel turned back to face them. "I see," he said. "Lucian. It appears that Miss Stone has acted both quickly and cleverly. She is to be commended. Sir Mechanist, please bring up the furnace, if you would, before beginning your inspection."

Lina released a breath she hadn't realized she'd been holding. The Mechanist glared at them all, but gave a nod and moved away belowdecks to comply. Lucian sighed and shook his head. He turned away to shout orders at the pirate crew scattered about. Fengel made to move back to the helm where Maxim stood. He paused.

"Miss Stone?" he said, half-turning. His green eyes pinned her, not pleasantly.

Lina swallowed. "Sir?"

"Initiative is prized. But in the future, I would appreciate it if you would notify me of such intentions before acting upon them."

Lina blushed. "I would have, sir. But there wasn't time. We'd have lost the skysails, at the least."

"Duly noted." The captain walked away, shouting orders for the wounded to be taken below and the ship to be seen to.

Lina frowned, not sure what to think or how to feel. She realized that one person still stood at her side. Henry Smalls leaned in. "How did you know we wouldn't be becalmed?" he asked.

Lina looked at him blankly. "We're on an *airship*. There isn't even any wind trapping us here. It's just the aether, right?" She looked after Lucian, and the captain, suddenly worried. "Should I...?"

"No. Just give them a bit. You did the right thing, twice over. Lucian just feels guilty he didn't solve the problems, and the Captain didn't like you going against his orders. Still, he commended you. And if he said it, he meant it; I know the man. Maybe just...find somewhere unobtrusive for a bit, eh?"

The steward patted her shoulder and followed his captain. Lina sighed, then moved back to where she wouldn't be in the way. The ship no longer shook. Rather, it seemed unnaturally calm for the roiling Maelstrom they were passing through. The eye of the storm was just off the port-side now, an empty hole in the cloudbank. Lina stared at it, and she almost, almost thought she saw something in the middle, perhaps a long shadow against the clouds where none should be. Andrea's talk of daemons came back to her and she shuddered, looking back to Maxim at the helm. The man stared at the empty space as well, pale and shaking, tears rolling down his face. Captain Fengel was pulling him quietly away from the helm, letting Henry Smalls step in to take his place. Lina shook her head at the strangeness of the world.

Something landed with a thump on the exhaust-pipes beside her. Lina whirled to see a scryn only inches away. She opened her mouth to yell warning, then paused. It was a runty creature, the small one she'd met earlier today.

"Chirr!" The patterns on its belly lit up in dancing, drunken whorls. It coiled, ready to leap forward at her arm.

It suddenly belched, then fell down behind the exhaust-pipe with a thud.

CHAPTER EIGHT

FENGEL REMOVED HIS MONOCLE. He wiped at it with the cuff of his sleeve, trying to clean away the thick, black ichors coating it. The glass fogged as he rubbed, smearing. Scryn blood was foul stuff, sticky and rank. With a sigh, he gave up for the moment and replaced his eye-piece, making a mental note to give it a more thorough washing later.

Groans echoed down to him from the rest of the deck. His crew lay about in the aftermath of the attack, resting and looking over their wounds. Lucian moved among them, looking for anything serious enough to need real attention. Fengel's heart went out to them, and he cursed himself again for missing the danger until it was too late. He glanced over at the helm where his gray-haired steward stood, keeping them on course for the moment.

"Henry." The little man glanced over at him. Fengel gestured toward the bow. "I'll take the wheel for a bit. Get some bandages and go help with the wounded."

"You sure, sir?"

"Aye. I misspoke to the Mechanist. I'm going to bring us out of the Maelstrom, then to a full stop. We're already losing our momentum. We might as well see to the injured and take stock, be certain that nothing was seriously damaged." He looked over to the port-side railing where Maxim stood, silent and paler than usual, staring up at the empty eye of the windless storm. "Take Maxim with you."

Henry looked to their navigator and gave a nod. He passed the wheel to Fengel and walked over to the man. Maxim started when Henry touched his elbow, but went along when the steward pulled him up the deck. Fengel set himself behind the helm and took quick stock of the console of the gearbox, the wavering needles of the compass, altimeter, and barometer.

Fengel glanced at the great open space within the middle of the storm, now rolling past them on the starboard-side. Supposedly a daemon sat in its middle, unheard and unseen, trapped in its center like a fly caught in amber. Or so Maxim swore. Fengel had never seen it himself; he hadn't a lick of the strange inborn ability that revealed such hidden mysteries. On the whole, he appreciated that. The world was a very strange place sometimes, and he had more than enough to worry about on his own.

The *Dawnhawk* finished skirting the eye. Fengel spun the wheel, using their latent momentum and the small head of steam built up in the furnace beneath his feet to push them away from its whorl. The roiling cloudbank washed over the bow of the ship, enclosing them in misty gloom. Fengel checked the gearbox instruments again. They were still on course. Minutes passed, and the churning fog of the Maelstrom brightened. Bit by bit it thinned, then finally parted as his vessel emerged from the perpetual storm and back into bright blue skies. The Atalian Sea spread out beneath them again, empty and white-capped. Thick, puffy clouds scudded low across the sky, far more than had been on the other side of the Maelstrom. This was common, for some reason, in the places so close to the Yulan. Fengel never understood why. He and the crew preferred the west, but a few adventures had brought him this way over the years. Each time the seas nearby were cloudy, and he had never heard of it being otherwise.

The sun sat low in the west, below the layer of heavy cloud. It illuminated the deck of the *Dawnhawk*, highlighting the disorder and filth from their recent travails, rendering them stark and apparent. Fengel frowned at the state of the ship. She deserved better.

It was definitely time for a bit of a break. Fengel wondered if he'd pushed too hard to get this far. Their brazen theft had warranted a quick escape, but he had to admit to himself that they'd gotten clean away, and it was simple eagerness that drove him now. No one chased after them. The other airship spied this morning had given him a start; his fear then was pursuit by Natasha. But the other vessel had quickly fallen behind, its course aimed elsewhere. Fengel had put it out of his mind.

He checked the wide expanse all about the ship. Nothing gave him pause. In the distance, leagues ahead, he thought he saw a dark stain on the horizon. That would be the Continent and the Stormwall, still a day's worth of travel at their current rate. He called out to the lookouts at their stations. Their answering cries came back a few moments later. The ocean was free of nearby islets that might harbor more scryn.

As good a place as any. He looked again to the gearbox, where a brass tube emerged from its top. Earlier, the Mechanist had informed him that it would allow vocal communication down to the furnace-room where he resided. Fengel cleared his throat, leaned forward and spoke clearly. "Cool engines. Full stop."

He waited for acknowledgement. There was no reply. Fengel frowned and leaned in closer, wondering if he'd been heard. The Mechanist would be irritated, having just gotten the furnace fired up again. He opened his mouth to speak again and a shrill cacophony erupted from the tube. Fengel jerked back in startlement, his ears suddenly ringing.

Apparently it worked. The rhythm of the furnace below changed, its constant low vibration slowed. He glanced back to the stern to see the steam-pipe exhaust dwindling, the chain-driven propellers halting in their spin.

Fengel waved down a passing crew-woman, Andrea Holt. He gave her the wheel and told her to keep it steady, then walked up to listen to Lucian's reports on the state of ship and crew. His first mate stood up near the bow. Fengel started to make his way up, but stopped a short distance from the helm. The new girl, Miss Stone, crouched furtively near the port-side gunwales.

Lucky, indeed, to have you along. The incident with the skysails was embarrassing, but losing them entirely would have been disastrous. Not to mention expensive. As well, though, her quick thinking with the scryn-swarm would have her firmly in the crew's good-books, raising him again in their eyes as well for letting her aboard. Who knew that a Triskelion doxy would prove so useful? "Miss Stone?" he asked. "Are you well?"

Lina whirled in surprise. She clutched a hip flask in one hand, white-knuckled. "Yes!" she cried, over-loud. "I'm fine! Perfectly fine." She smiled, leaning back against the exhaust-pipe. "How are you?"

Fengel paused for a moment to consider the question. He felt tired from the stress and the strain of their recent exertions. Mistakes had just been made, and they were his to own. Abruptly an acute pang of loneliness washed over him. In times past there would have been someone else to prop him up, help check his blind spots and poor decisions. His wife...

He blinked, surprised at the feeling. He shoved it aside as a pointless and treacherous line of thought. *I've been better, but also a lot worse.* Fengel smiled at Lina. "Capital," he said, "thanks in no small part to you." A caustic stench tickled his nose, making him sneeze. Only one thing smelled like that. The flask in her hand must be filled with Cure-all. "Good Goddess above." He waved a hand to disperse the stink. "You're not actually drinking that stuff, are you?"

Lina appeared to notice the flask in her hand for the first time. She jerked it behind her back. "No! No, I—" She quieted, calculation in her eyes. Then she pulled the flask back around, staring at it. "Yes," she continued, voice now deadpan. "Yes, that is what I am doing." She glanced down at the flask, and then back up again at him, as if trying to decide whether to take a swig from it, and really hoping not to.

Fengel frowned. Miss Stone was acting decidedly suspicious. Then it came to him. "It's all right," he said with a smile. "We're pirates, not Perinese sailors, Miss Stone. It's fine, so long as you're not drunk on watch." Everyone dealt with the stress of battle differently. And she had been through a lot today, not including getting reprimanded by Lucian awhile before. "You're not the first to calm their nerves with drink after a bit of a scuff."

"*Chirr.*"

Miss Stone went pale as a sheet. Fengel raised an eyebrow. "I'm sorry?"

Lina coughed, fist to her mouth. "Um, *hrm*. Excuse me. That was... ah. That was me." She glanced around like a cornered animal. "I may have overdone it? I'm a little drunk?"

Fengel nodded. "Perfectly understandable. But as I said, please remember that your watch is on in several hours." He leaned in. "Personally, if you want some advice, you're going to want something that takes the edge off but doesn't put you under too much. Cure-all is something I would probably stay away from."

Lina stared at him. Then she nodded eagerly. "Yes, sir. Thank you, sir." She glanced back up the deck toward the bow. "I'd, ah, I'd best get below for a bit. Henry said I should avoid Mr. Thorne for a little while to come."

Fengel looked up to the bow where his first mate stood. "Don't worry yourself overmuch, Miss Stone. You surprised us all at first when we realized what you were doing; we didn't understand. That's forgiven, though. We're not some Navy ship, ready to punish quick thinking. Lucian's just upset now that he didn't catch that detail about our lovely new vessel. Still, maybe you should head down below, if only to find something else to drink."

Lina smiled, bright and brittle. "Yes, sir. Thank you, sir." The young woman turned back to the gunwales and pulled a hempen sack up and out from between it and the exhaust-pipes. "Chirr," she seemed to say again. Glancing furtively about, she bowed to him and ran for the aft hatch belowdecks.

Fengel watched her go, then shook his head. "Strange girl," he muttered.

He examined the ship as he made his way up to the bow. Blood smeared the boards, most of it the black ichors of the scryn. Fengel swore another curse at the horrible creatures under his breath. They really were vile things, and one of several reasons he didn't fly much in this direction. Though he'd never seen it himself, there were horror stories of scryn-swarms burrowing into the frames of the airship gasbags, attracted to the smell of light-air gas. Inevitably such stricken vessels crashed into the ocean with no survivors. Fengel did have to wonder at that last bit, though. If no one survived, how did anyone know about it?

The crew took notice of him as he passed, calling greetings. Fengel returned the favor, and commended those who'd fought well. His men and women were all skilled and confident in their abilites, he knew, but, like everyone else, they liked it to be noticed. Fengel made sure that he did; it was one of the many carefully orchestrated reasons they all stayed so loyal to him.

Up near the bow, he finally found Lucian. The first mate was eyeing a stanchion connecting an anchor line to the gas-bag above. "The little vermin will chew on anything," he muttered at Fengel's approach.

"Did they go after anything else?" asked Fengel.

Lucian turned to his captain. "No, thankfully. The new girl got rid of them before they had a chance to really run wild. As for the ship herself; we knew she was a beauty, guess that means she's a bit more delicate than we thought too. I chatted with the Mechanist."

Fengel raised an eyebrow. "Chatted?"

His first mate grimaced. "Was lectured by, rather. These skysails will give us a higher consistent motivation along the aetherlines, apparently. But we can't subject them to the kind of pressure we're used to in places like the Maelstrom." He sighed. "Yet another thing that girl caught that I didn't."

If Lucian had any faults, Fengel knew, it was a tendency towards perfectionism. He was much like his old nemesis Mordecai Wright in that respect. It also meant that Lucian tended to dwell on failure. Both of them knew it, though, and Fengel was careful not to prod at it any further. "And the crew?" he said, changing the subject.

Lucian shook his head. "Could have been a lot worse. Mostly cuts and bruises. A few got stung. That's going to hurt. Scryn-poison is painful stuff, but not usually deadly. We're going do be down a few more on day-watch while they recover."

Fengel rested his hands on the bow railing. "Well, we should be right enough. It's good that it's not any worse." He watched the horizon, then gestured at the distant, dark stain of the sky. "The course was correct. That's the Stormwall, if I guess correctly. And thus, the Yulan Continent." He smiled at his first mate. "Payday is almost here."

Lucian nodded. "We'll have to find the Silverpenny River. I went over the maps, and it should be somewhere south of the Engmann's Run terminus.

Not far, but the place was only seen once before by a Perinese survey team. We'll have a day, a day and a half maybe, to get things back in order." He turned to his captain. "Looks like you were right this time."

Fengel grimaced. "I've been wrong enough lately that I think I'm due. It's good to get a break once in awhile."

"Ship ahoy!"

They both turned back down the deck. One of the lookouts, a skinny youth by the name of Jonas, had scrabbled down the ratlines from up above. He pointed out and upwards. "Ship ahoy! Dropping fast on us from above, starboard-side!"

Fengel met Lucian's gaze. Then both of them ran for the starboard gunwales. Reaching it, Fengel leapt up onto the rail and grabbed at the mesh of the ratlines leading up to the gas-bag frame and above.

The dark, bulbous shape of an airship was falling fast on them from up above, using only propellers and steam. She was on a direct bearing; there was no mistaking her intent.

It can't be. Fengel fumbled in his jacket for his spyglass. *It can't be.* Yet he already knew who it was. He brought out his spyglass and extended it, peering into the sky. The distant skyship resolved into a black-hulled vessel, ancient and makeshift. He let out a soft, but heartfelt, curse.

"What?" asked Lucian. "Who is that?" Fengel said nothing, instead passing the spyglass wordlessly to his mate. Lucian looked through it and uttered an exclamation. "The *Copper Queen*?" he cried. "Euron himself is bearing down on us?"

"No," said Fengel. "Natasha." He knew it to be true. The ship from earlier *had* been her. If she'd moved quickly enough from Haventown she could have just made it to Engmann's Maelstrom. But it would have been close. Fengel had an epiphany. He dropped back down to the deck. "She knew. She *knew* about the skysails. That was her earlier, Lucian. She wasn't chasing because she knew she could lay an ambush here, knew we'd have lost the sails if it hadn't been for Miss Stone. She'd have had to go at full speed to make it. Blast it, how did she know?" he turned to the deck and bellowed through cupped hands. "Everyone to stations! Heft open the weapons lockers! Arm the wounded and call everyone up on deck!"

Fengel raced back to the helm without looking at the crew. Andrea Holt made to relinquish the helm and he waved her back to it. Instead, he leaned in towards the speaking-tube atop the helmsman's gearbox. "Furnace to full!" he cried.

Silence. Fengel felt Andrea's gaze on him and turned back to her. She shrugged, watching him curiously. *Did the Mechanist hear me?* He leaned farther in. "I say, are you down there? Get that furnace stoked up—"

A discordant screech exploded from the tube. Fengel jumped back, cursing and rubbing at his ear. The tube fell silent, only to erupt again in an unintelligible cacophony.

"Dash it all," muttered Fengel. He turned back to the helm. "Andrea, get down to the Mechanist and—"

"No time sir," said the piratess, pointing. She shook her head, dark locks of hair splaying about. Fengel followed her gesture. Up the deck the crew moved frantically, grabbing weapons from hastily opened lockers while others climbed up from the hatches belowdecks. Past them, the black hull of the *Copper Queen* was just visible, descending two hundred feet away to come level alongside.

Sarah Lome clambered up from the aft hatch and took in the situation at a glance. She immediately moved amidships to the weapons locker. Fengel nodded to Andrea and moved up the deck to where the massive piratess stood. His gunnery mistress nodded at him as she picked up a heavy axe and belted on a brace of pistols. Lucian and Henry Smalls joined them.

"Evening, Captain," said Sarah. She turned to Lucian. "Mister Thorne, what have you let happen on your watch? I'm told we got attacked by scryn too."

Lucian glowered. "Well, not all of us can sleep the day away—"

"Belay all that," ordered Fengel. His officers immediately quieted. He gestured them away so that the crew could keep arming themselves. "We're going to be boarded. If things go poorly, though, I'll call for quarter."

Henry frowned at the other airship. "Think she'll use a broadside to soften us up?" Most modern airships had a few cannons along the lowest decks, to bombard seagoing vessels. With it's traditional layout, Old Euron's ship was ironically better suited to attacking the *Dawnhawk* than any modern airship.

Fengel shook his head. "No. She won't want to damage the *Dawnhawk*. Still, if she came all this way in that old wreck..."

He trailed off as the other airship approached. It was close enough that he could pick out the individual crewmen on the other side, all shouting and waiving cutlasses high. A few overeager musket-shots rang out, too far away to be even close to effective, the plumes of gun smoke puffing away on the wind. Natasha stood on the foredeck, blade held in the air. Up on the aftcastle he spied Mordecai, a dark figure standing quietly.

Fengel hardened his heart and drew his blade. "This is *our* ship," he said, quietly, dangerously. "We stole it, fair and square. And that besotted slattern is *not* going to take it back from us. Lucian, give the order."

His first mate nodded and turned to face the deck. "Stand ready to repel borders!" he cried. The crew readied their weapons and pushed up against the rails, swords raised and axes readied to hack away boarding-ropes. Lucian looked back to his captain.

Fengel met their gazes in turn and then smiled. He drew the saber at his hip and stuck it point down in the deck. "Well then, me hearties, let's be about it."

His officers turned to the starboard-side, and the enemy airship, with a wordless yell.

CHAPTER NINE

They were closing in on their prey.

The *Dawnhawk* lay dead ahead. Even adrift, its skysails presumably damaged, the airship appeared mighty. Her long, clean lines were magnificent in the late afternoon sun. The sight of his ship relieved Mordecai, just as it enraged him to see her in the grip of her captors. Fengel's Men scurried about its deck in alarm, moving like cockroaches startled by a sudden light. Mordecai allowed himself a smile.

Raucous cries echoed about the deck of the *Queen*. Natasha's crew of brigands all massed on the port-side gunwales. Eclectically armed, they loaded pistols and brandished axes, or just waved their swords in the air, howling for plunder and blood. The old scow listed dangerously. Thankfully, though, the Mechanist had done his job, solving the wild steering problems from earlier. Mordecai found he didn't care much. They'd burned through most of their coal stores to make it to the Maelstrom on time. Now they were mere moments away from taking back their ship, their real ship. Whatever came afterward for the *Queen* was worth less than a worry to him. The makeshift airship could go to the bottom of the sea, so long as it got them to their prize first.

An overeager pirate fired his musket. They were still a hundred feet off from the other ship; the ball wouldn't have hit a thing. Mordecai frowned. Unruly and bloodthirsty though they were, his crew knew better than to waste shot. He took a step toward the ladder down from the aftcastle deck, ready to discipline the man.

"Save yer fight!" yelled Natasha. The pirate princess stood up on the bow, gorgeous and wicked. Gone was the cranky, frustrated woman he'd had to put up with over the last two days. Now she stood like something out of a painting or a boy's penny-paper. Her hair was bound by a bandana, the free ends dancing in the wind. She smiled, a crooked, dangerous thing that held ugly promises for whomever it was aimed at. A bandolier strapped a brace of pistols to her chest, wrapped snugly under a blouse cut low to cause distraction.

"You won't hit a damned thing at this distance," she said, voice mocking, chiding. Mordecai's captain turned back to face the aftcastle deck, where Mordecai stood next to Konrad at the wheel. "So let's remedy that! Bring us in, Mordecai!" She addressed her men, raising her sword high. "Get up the hooks! Get ready for blood! Get ready to take our ship back!"

The assembled buccaneers all roared. Despite Natasha's rebuke, a few more pistol shots rang out. Those nearest the rail picked up the boarding-ropes. These were a standard tool of the trade, thick rope attached to a chain with a grapple. Normally they were thrown into the rigging or rails of merchant ships from up above to preclude any thought of flight. But the grapples would suit here well enough.

The *Copper Queen* closed on the *Dawnhawk*. Fengel's Men had organized, muskets arrayed along the rail, hatchet-men standing by to repel the grapples. Mordecai raised an appraising eyebrow. That was one thing he'd give Fengel; the man knew how to organize his people.

One hundred feet shrank to fifty, then twenty-five. Mordecai spied Captain Fengel standing back from the action where he could see and be seen by his men. The pirate captain drew his saber and raised it high, shouting a command. Those with muskets along the rail fired, a staccato racket that echoed in the space between ships. Two of Mordecai's crew fell and he heard the whip-hiss of a ball as it sailed through the air near his head, a miss, but close.

"That all you've got?" Natasha cried. She howled laughter and gestured at the *Dawnhawk* with her sword. The crew on the deck below her roared. Muskets and pistols returned fire, and those with grapples let fly. The hooks shone in the fading light, like captive birds of bright metal trailing thick leashes behind them.

Some of the heavy hooks fell short, bouncing off the hull. Some went too far, braining those in the enemy crew at the rear. But enough fell just right, catching on the railings and behind the gunwales, connecting the ship almost bow-to-bow, like a pair of sky-borne animals nuzzling.

Natasha's men knew their work. The first wave of pirates up against the rails grabbed the ropes and heaved, pulling them tight and taut before the defenders could unhook them. The second wave knelt, preparing to clamber over.

Fengel's hatchet-crew hacked at the hooks, severing a few even through the chain. Mordecai watched in irritation as Sarah Lome, Fengel's giantess, reached over the rails to grab a rope in each hand. She yanked and six of Mordecai's men, three to a rope each, jerked forward against the rails, releasing their grip before they plunged down between the airships. Sarah then took up the slack and unhooked the grapples, throwing them overboard before reaching for another pair.

Mordecai frowned. He held out his hand to Konrad. "Gun," he said. The aetherite passed a pistol into his hand. Mordecai cocked it, took aim, and fired at the giant piratess. The ball just missed, scarring the wooden railing near her hand. Sarah Lome cursed and fell back. A hit would have been nice, but that was good enough.

The ships slammed together. Roaring their bloodlust, Natasha's crew clambered at the rails of the *Dawnhawk*. Fengel's Men fought back, forming a hedge of swords, axes, and pistols that flung the assailants repeatedly back onto the *Copper Queen*. Mordecai watched in irritation.

"Shall I throw in, Mordecai?"

Konrad watched the battle, fingers grasping, eager to join it. Mordecai shook his head. "No. Save your magics. It's too uncertain, still." He put his fingers to his lips and whistled up at the gas-bag frame above them.

Ten carefully picked pirates swung down from the far side of the gasbag, their ropes anchored up above the melee. They flew over the deck and up past their brethren, letting go at the apex of their arc to land on the *Dawnhawk* behind the defenders. A few stumbled, but most landed well, turning back to harry Fengel's Men from behind. Mordecai sighed in vexation, despite the success. He and Natasha had argued long over this particularly ludicrous trick.

The surprise attack threw the defenders into disarray. Bit by bit Natasha's men drove them back and forced their way onto the *Dawnhawk*. Natasha followed her crew over, yelling for blood at the top of her lungs. Mordecai nodded at Konrad and drew his own blade; it was time.

Calmly, he descended to the main deck and made his way over to the press. "Out of the way, you laggards," he roared. Even in their zeal, the crew obeyed him. Those closest opened up a path. Mordecai leapt up onto the gunwales, then over to the other ship. For a moment he had the brief sensation of being weightless, unsupported by anything at all as he moved through space with only the momentum of his jump. His boot touched onto the *Dawnhawk's* railing and Mordecai clambered down to the deck, stepping onto the familiar exhaust-pipes and the polished wood of the ship herself.

Pandemonium reigned. Natasha's pirates drove Fengel's Men back, individual fights spreading out across the length and breadth of the airship. They gained ground, and quickly. Something struck Mordecai as odd; resistance was fierce, but the fight was going easier than he and Natasha had expected. Had his trick with the topmen been that surprising? No. Fengel's Men were wounded, many sported fresh bandages and cuts across their faces, and semi-fresh ichors stained the deck. They had been in a fight recently.

All the better, then. Mordecai dove into the fray. A gap-toothed pirate appeared before him with a cutlass. Mordecai contemptuously parried a blow and gutted him as he pushed past. Then a short woman with boarding axe hacked at him. He ducked it and ran her through.

Something exploded near his head. The charm in his ear warmed to almost scorching, and he felt the faint pressure as the pistol ball deflected away. Mordecai turned to face an unfamiliar woman with a scar across her lips. She stared at him, the flintlock pistol in her hands trailing smoke from its barrel. Mordecai smiled contemptuously and raised his sword.

He broke out in a cold sweat. In seconds he was soaked, teeth chattering in a biting chill that stole the breath from his lungs and the warmth from his skin. As he watched, hoarfrost broke out over his sword arm where his shirt was damp all the way through, growing with each passing moment until his arm and his ribs were coated with ice. He fell to his knees under its weight, panting, now desperate for water. He fought to lift his weapon back to a defensive stance.

A man in a half-cloak with dark, shoulder-length hair appeared through the melee a short distance away. His blew out over his cupped hands, guiding his breath at Mordecai. It was Fengel's aetherite, Maxim.

Mordecai felt a wild current of unaccustomed fear. He'd yet to find his equal with a blade. And the charm in his ear kept his opponents from equalizing things with a gun. But against the Workings of an aetherite he had nothing. When pressed an aetherite could conjure hungry and living fire, turn your weapons to rust and your friends into enemies. Only their extreme reticence at expending their power balanced this; Worked magic was hard to come by even for an aetherite, and they paid for each hex dearly.

Maxim grew red in the face as if winded, and his skin were chapped by the cold. Still he blew, and Mordecai's ears ached with the bite of a sorcerous wind that forced the sweat from his pores and then froze it in place. The eyes of the other man were dancing; he was going to kill the infamous Mordecai Wright.

Liquid light splashed across Maxim. The aetherite recoiled with a yell. Konrad stood a short distance away, hands wrapped around a luminous orb that seeped between his fingers. Its spill landed on the deck, spattering and sizzling. Natasha's foreign navigator swung his fists out at Fengel's aetherite, casting the droplets in a luminescent spray.

Maxim cursed and fell back again. His clothing smoldered where the liquid light touched it, the fabric abruptly rotting away. He brought up his wind-burned hands and clapped them once at his rival. Konrad flinched, then yelled as those closest to him, both friend and foe, fell on him in screaming, inchoate rage.

Mordecai left the aetherites to their duel. At worst they would keep each other occupied. And who knew? Maybe Konrad would come out on top, kill his opponent, and turn his powers to help the raid.

Grunting with effort, Mordecai hefted his arm. Ice covered it, and his hand was already numb from the cold. He lifted his arm with his other hand. Then he swung it down at the deck. The impact travelled from his fist to his shoulder, seeming to shake his bones all along the way. Chips of dirty ice flew free, going rotten and melted without its sorcerous creator present. Mordecai grit his teeth and swung, again and again until he was free.

He climbed back to his feet. His limb ached, and he felt almost withered, his mouth like it was filled with balls of cotton. One of Fengel's Men appeared and hacked down at him with a hatchet. Mordecai brought his blade up and parried the blow against the haft of his assailant's weapon. The movement was sloppy, and he felt the grip of his sword slip almost out between his fingers. Mordecai cursed and stumbled back. The pirate grinned and raised his axe overhead with both hands.

Foolish. Even numbed as he was, he was far from helpless. Mordecai stepped forward, too close to use the blade of his cutlass, the blade out at an angle. He rammed the basket hilt of his sword up into the other man's face. The fellow's nose broke and he yelled as blood flew on the air. Workmanlike, Mordecai drew his sword down and back, cutting the pirate's throat. Mordecai turned away, flexing his hand on the grip of his blade and working the blood back into his fingers. He looked about, first for threats, then to take in the battle raging about him.

Natasha's crew was savage, but Fengel's Men fought well. The two pirate crews raged back and forth, individual duels swirling into a great clatter of squealing swords and the howls of the wounded. Near the helm he spied Captain Fengel, neatly holding off a pair of Natasha's Reavers. Mordecai frowned and began moving in that direction. He avoided further engagements, only lashing out with his blade in opportunity, as much to restore his blade arm as to help his crew. But halfway to Fengel, Mordecai spied Natasha jumping into the fray against her husband.

"I told you you'd pay for this!" she laughed at him, hacking out with her cutlass.

Fengel parried the blow neatly, turning his saber to catch an opportunistic thrust by her crewman, a vicious woman by the name of Reaver Jane. "I assure you, darling" he replied calmly. "Listening again to the chalkboard screech of your voice is punishment enough." The pirate captain stepped sideways, bringing the bound blades directly into the path of his third assailant's strike. Fengel disengaged and then lashed downward, stabbing Jane in the foot. She howled, dropping her sword and falling to the deck, hands grasping at her.

Natasha shoved her crewmate aside and brought her blade up, thrusting at her husband. Fengel stepped to the side to avoid the blow and cut upward, slicing through the bandolier she wore and the front of her blouse. Natasha ducked backward, clasping at her blouse, yelping.

"Come, now," said Fengel, green eyes flashing, smiling slightly as he turned to the remaining pirate. "Surely there's nothing there that your crew hasn't seen, especially during your many, many, drunken adventures."

The last pirate stared at Fengel, eyes wide, aware that he was outmatched. Fengel dispatched him with a flourish, barely turning in time to parry the wild blow that Natasha had launched at him from behind. The pirate princess fought with abandon, hate in her eyes, careless of the disarray her clothing hung in. "Is it any wonder?" She yelled at him. Fengel lost his smile, concentrating on deflecting her wild blows. "Marriage to you would drive a saint to drink!" She hacked at him again. "You and your pompous, arrogant, holier-than-thou attitude. You wear a *monocle,* for Her sake. Why? Your vision is perfectly fine!"

Fengel sniffed. "A gentleman of breeding maintains a specific standard of—"

"Ha!" cackled Natasha. "You're even more baseborn than I am. You just never got over that Perinese press-ganging of yours, being passed up for every promotion. So now you play pirate, pretending to be the gentleman officer you never were!"

Fengel growled, composure cracked. He parried her blows and then went on the offensive, a blurred wall of steel that licked around her defenses. Natasha's eyes widened and she took a step back, then two. She shut up, all her attention focused on keeping the man before her at bay.

Mordecai stepped in from behind. Quick as an eel, he thrust squarely at Fengel's back. The pirate captain wheeled, knocking the blade away at the last second. Mordecai blinked, surprised. Fengel must have noticed his approach, but how, he could not say.

Fengel quickly backed away, putting both of them within his field of vision. "Oh, basely done," he said, disgustedly. "Is that this excellent skill that I keep hearing of?"

"So long as it works," replied Mordecai, voice more even than he felt. His arm still ached from the ice. He raised his sword back into guard position. Fengel did as well, a fencer's stance, body narrowed, facing them both, off hand tucked behind his back. Natasha moved apart from him, circling around, attempting to split Fengel's attention.

Mordecai struck first, a low-quarter blow to test his opponent's defenses. Fengel parried, playing along, not revealing a single weakness of form. Natasha tried to take advantage. Fengel wheeled about, parrying, binding her blade, and giving her a nick along the back of her hand in one smooth motion. She hissed and fell back, shaking her arm.

Fengel wasn't done. Before Mordecai could even rally for another blow the other pirate was back, beating on his own blade. Shock travelled down the hilt, into his numbed fingers and forearm. Mordecai gave ground, step after step, as Captain Fengel fought them both back.

This isn't going to work. The thought was galling. Fengel really *was* a skilled swordsman, as good as him or better. But the aetherite's Working had him in poor condition; even with Natasha's help, maybe even with half a dozen more men, they would not be able to subdue the pirate captain.

He spat at Fengel's eyes. The other man drew back, automatically bringing up his guard just long enough to blink. Mordecai didn't bother to follow up. He turned and fled, moving back into the press of the crowd. Fengel took a step after him, then turned as Natasha entered the fray again.

The fight dragged on. A quick glance about the deck told Mordecai that things were still evenly matched between the two airship crews. *So maybe it's time to make things* un-*even.* Fengel may have been peerless, but everyone knew he had one particular weakness.

Mordecai glanced at the crowd for a handy victim. Lucian Thorne moved about the far end of the deck, flailing away while the giant piratess Lome bulled her way through Natasha's crew. *No, someone else.* He spied a lithe young woman, the one Fengel had brought to the Bleeding Teeth several nights ago. She jabbed a dagger in a pirate's shoulder, then ducked around as he screamed to cut his throat. Mordecai took a step toward her, but quick as a cat she looked up at him, checked herself, and ducked between two others fighting. *Not her then, either.*

Another of Fengel's Men stood nearby, hard pressed against two of Natasha's pirates. Mordecai smiled in recognition. *This one.* He stepped up neatly behind the man, catching him roughly by the back of his collar with his free hand, sliding his blade up against his victim's throat during a break in the action. Mordecai glared at his crewmen, who paused at the sight of their first mate. Then he smiled down at the figure he clasped.

"Hullo, Henry Smalls," said Mordecai.

"Mordecai!" growled the figure. "Let me go, you lickspittle dog! I'll—"

"Help me do whatever I want, I think," replied Mordecai. "This way. Smartly, now." He nodded for his men to cover him, and whirled the steward around, marching him back to where Fengel and Natasha fenced near the helm. Natasha was backed up against the gearbox. Two more of her men lay at her feet, wounded and groaning.

"Once again," said Fengel calmly, "you are outmatched. Give in now and save some face."

"Never," gasped Natasha. "If you could have shown this kind of stamina somewhere else but swordplay, you'd have found another woman by now."

"Enough!" called Mordecai. The others turned to look at him. "Captain Fengel. Drop your weapon and order your men to stand down, or I slit your steward's throat this instant."

Fengel stared. "You dog! You dishonorable—"

"Call for quarter, or this fellow gets it in the neck."

Henry fought. "Don't do it, Captain!"

Fengel stared at them, at the fight raging up the rest of the deck, and then back to Mordecai. He glared at Natasha, who smiled sweetly. He turned back to Mordecai.

"Face me fairly," growled Fengel. "You hull-sucking worm. Fight me fairly!"

Mordecai raised an eyebrow and pulled his blade tighter. Henry Smalls gasped in pain. Fengel chewed his lip and then tossed his saber to the deck. "Damn you," he hissed to his wife. "Quarter!" he called to the deck at large. "Stand down, men! Stand down!"

Mordecai glanced around. Fengel's Crew were pausing, uncertain, pulling back to stare disbelievingly over at their captain. The fighting slowed, then stopped. Natasha's Reavers moved to take immediate advantage, disarming the losers and herding them together.

Mordecai let Henry go as more of Natasha's men moved up to take the captain and the steward captive.

"Curse you," hissed Fengel. "You dishonorable dog. You can't beat me in a fair fight—"

"Which is why we don't fight fair," said Natasha. She gestured and two of her men grabbed Fengel, wrapping his arms around behind him. She reached up to pinch his cheek. "We're pirates, after all." She laughed as her husband jerked away.

Mordecai glanced around the deck again. They'd won. "Let's get rid of him, now," he said to his captain. "Clear them all off the ship to feed the sharks. We can be under way and at the treasure wreck by tomorrow night."

Fengel started. "What? You can't! I've called for quarter!"

Mordecai smiled. "I think I can, and I will."

"No." Natasha tapped her lower lip with one finger, smiling.

Mordecai frowned. Of all the times for *this* to come into play. "That's foolishness. Let's kill him and be done with it."

"I think not."

He sighed. "Captain, you yourself suggested it just the other night! He took the damned ship! Just off him and be done with it, and whatever miserable latent feelings—"

"Enough," said Natasha, voice low and deadly. "Remember Mordecai, who is in charge here. I'm sure you do. Why don't you tell me?"

Mordecai ground his teeth. "You are. Captain."

"And don't you forget it." She turned back to her husband, golden eyes flashing. "But you. You did steal my ship. And made me a laughingstock back in port." She grinned. "I think I'm going to have a little fun. Don't worry, Mordecai, they'll pay." She turned back to her crew. "Bind them. And someone find a net from down in the cargo bay."

Mordecai watched, angry, his arm aching, as the men scurried to obey her orders.

CHAPTER TEN

THE WORLD TURNED.

Lina watched it spin through the rope mesh of the cargo net. At the back of her head swelled a throbbing goose egg, a constant reminder of their struggle and loss. She'd *thought* she'd been quick enough, clever enough, to avoid getting hit. She had been wrong.

"Harridan!" yelled Captain Fengel. Lina winced at his voice, strident and close. She felt him shift directly below her in the pile, pulling himself up against the net they were all balled into. He thrust an arm through the mesh and shook his fist at the dimly visible shape of the *Dawnhawk*, fast retreating on the horizon. "Slattern!" he continued. "You besotted, hair-brained wench!"

Lina realized that in other circumstances she would feel giddy. Fengel was just below her, she could smell his sweat and cologne and feel the hard lines of his officer's coat. But she was weary, she ached, and there was a hollow in the pit of her stomach. Her new home was gone, along with her knives, her new pet, and even some of her new friends. *Why? Why did we surrender? Were things really going that badly?*

She lay atop the pile of pirates, dangling out over the ocean in a cargo net hung from the bow of the *Copper Queen*. The dark ship sagged above them, creaking and groaning, an uncertain anchor in the sky. Below them roared the ocean, its susurrus backdrop to the groaning and grumbling of her crewmates. Their mood was low. Some had lost crewmates, some were wounded. Many wondered aloud why Fengel had called for quarter.

Lina had just stowed her new pet belowdecks when she'd heard the call to arms. She'd raced out of the storage lockers near the furnace-room and armed herself, coming back up to the deck just in time to see Natasha's crew close in. Then the battle was joined, and she'd been gratified to find that in the press and fury she didn't back down; in fact, Lina found she *liked* it.

Things were going well then. So well that when she'd heard Fengel's call Lina had been confused. Only when it became clear what was going on had she been afraid. Fengel's harpy of a wife herded them all atop a cargo net laid out on the deck and Lina's fear had turned to sick terror when they'd been forced at gunpoint to fling themselves over the edge. Embarrassingly, she'd lost her lunch. It was then that they'd found that drowning wasn't their fate. At least not right away. The cargo net was tied by a heavy rope to the other airship, the *Copper Queen*. Natasha's men flew away laughing, leaving them to dangle over the Atalian sea.

Goddess above. What a bitch.

Fengel quieted, panting, as the twilight glimmer on the horizon faded. Lina tried to get comfortable. She lay at an awkward angle, atop both her captain and a knot of muscle and hair that she deduced to be Henry Smalls.

"Miss Stone," said Fengel. "You are an *excessively bony* individual."

"Sir!" cried Henry.

Her captain fell silent. "My apologies, Miss Stone," he said. "I find myself somewhat vexed at the moment."

"It's all right, sir," she said.

"I am *rather* upset. And being stuck in this net is not helping my disposition."

"I've got my knife still, sir," said Henry Smalls.

Captain Fengel made a disgusted sound. "And what would we do with it? We cut this miserable net too much and we all run the risk of being dumped into the ocean."

"Aye sir. But we could make a small cut near the top. Miss Stone's up top, and she could probably slip through and shimmy up to the ship. She's small enough." The groaning and rustle of the massed crew beneath her fell silent. Lina couldn't see them, but she could almost feel their gazes turn upward.

"She puked on me!" cried Oscar Pleasant, voice muffled and echoing up from somewhere below.

"That'll only improve how you smell," said Andrea Holt. Despite their mood, several pirates chuckled.

Fengel cleared his voice. "Well?" he asked. "What do you think, Miss Stone?"

Lina looked up at the *Copper Queen*. The makeshift airship hung like a black moon above them. The rope supporting them climbed up to the prow, suddenly all too thin a thing to ascend. The idea was madness. *But let's consider my options. I could refuse and end up starving over the ocean with a bunch of scurvy brigands. Again. It's rather a long drop, and the water sounds very cold, but what more have I got to lose?*

Lina eyed the net around her. It tented above them, rising sharply to meet the rope they dangled from. The mesh was tight, tough, and narrow. But if she cut *there,* and *there...* "Yeah," she said eventually. "I think I can fit through this, if I'm careful. Give me the knife."

The crew below her grew silent, stifling their groans and curses, waiting to see if she could escape. Someone shoved something hard up past her rump, which Lina might have taken exception to in other circumstances.

"Here," said Fengel, muffled, arm pinned against the net by her thigh. He pressed a heavy knife, sheath and all, to her. Lina felt a glimmer of the butterflies. She took it, drawing the blade free. It was a heavy thing, meant for both utility and fighting, bigger than the duelist's cutters she'd lost.

The ambient twilight faded with every passing moment. Lina took a breath and sat up, moving until she hunkered in the little hollow where the mesh of the net came together.

Lina took the rope in one hand and bent to work. The tough fibers split beneath the sawing of her blade, first only a few and then in bunches. With a jerk that shook their whole net, the rope split. The pirates gasped, likely staring at the ocean below. Lina couldn't see it, but she could hear it in the dark. Somewhere below the waves crashed and roared as they were pushed onto each other by the wind.

In quick succession she cut through another two pieces of mesh, the net jerking and swaying. "Captain," called Lucian from somewhere below. "Perhaps we should think up another plan?"

"This'll do," said Lina, fingering the hole. It was just barely wide enough for her to squeeze through. She replaced the knife in its sheath. "Captain," she said, looking down below. "What am I supposed to do once I get up there?"

Silence. She felt Fengel beneath her, and dimly spied the shape of his hat crushed against the net. "Improvise," he replied after a moment. "Look for a winch, perhaps."

Lina nodded. She tucked the sheath into her shirt and parted the hole in the net. Taking a breath, she pushed herself through to her waist and twisted to grab at the upper part of the mesh. Slowly, carefully, she pulled herself out to half-stand on her fellows. The whole thing swayed. Lina cursed and closed her eyes, fighting off the vertigo and the sudden awareness that nothing, nothing at all, would keep her from falling.

Below, pirates swore. Sarah Lome loudly retched, Oscar Pleasant complaining immediately. By feel, Lina pulled herself up to where the net hung from the rope. She opened her eyes and stared up that rope, rising into darkness, the hull of the *Copper Queen* even blacker than the night sky above. Lina couldn't tell how far down they dangled, how far she had to climb. *Oh well. Sink or swim.*

"Here I go," she said to those below.

Lina started her climb, pushing off from the mesh of the net, grabbing higher with her other hand. Bit by bit she pulled herself up. When the mesh ran out she took the brunt of her weight with her arms, grunting at the strain, while she wrapped her thighs around the rope. Stretching, she grabbed a higher span and pulled up before clamping with her legs again in a jerking inchworm ascension.

The rope spun, a trick of the wind, or the momentum of those below her. The pirates groaned and cursed. Lina put them out of her mind. She climbed, until her arms burned and her legs cramped. Ten feet felt like a hundred. Twenty felt like a thousand. Lina paused for short rests, stopping more and more often. *I can't keep this up.* Cold fear settled in her stomach. She would fall, maybe bouncing off of the heavy net below before splashing down to her death in the wine-dark sea.

After an eternity, Lina reached up again and felt hard wood brush the back of her hand. Peering up, she saw the prow of the ship and let out a relieved gasp. She climbed a little further, just a little higher, until she could grab onto the gunwales. With an undignified shimmy she scrabbled over its edge and collapsed on the bow deck in exhaustion.

Panting, her limbs aching, Lina lay still and recovered from the climb. When she could breathe normally again she put a hand out to the deck and sat upright, fumbling the awkward, uncomfortable knife sheath out from her shirt. Taking a look around the deck, she decided she probably wouldn't need it.

The *Copper Queen* was a ghost ship. The forecastle deck spread out before her, widening until it dropped abruptly down to the main deck. That tier was wide and flat, a single large cargo hatch covering its center with ropes dangling onto it from the gasbag frame above. Along both the port and starboard gunwales were a row of light cannons, notches cut beneath them so that they could be aimed at targets below the ship. To the rear rose the aftcastle deck, a pair of stairs leading to the ship's helm at the top. This vessel was old, the dark wood chipped and scuffed. Equipment lay about the deck carelessly, forgotten in the excitement of the attack. Natasha obviously hadn't taken care of it in the little time she'd been aboard, not the way that either crew had cared for the *Dawnhawk*.

Lina picked herself up and stretched. *Well. What now?*

The rope that dangled her crewmates from the bow was not tied to the prow, or even up here on the bow. Instead, it stretched taut down the length of the ship, running all the way back to the aftcastle deck. There it terminated past the helm and out of her sight.

Lina turned back to the prow. She bent to inspect the rope, rubbing against the prow and the wood of the gunwales. The fibers were tough, and did not seem *too* damaged; they would hold for awhile.

She leaned over the edge. Dimly she spied the crew, still hanging, the net a bulbous outline against the sea.

"I made it up," she yelled.

"Excellent," replied Fengel. Faint, halfhearted cheers echoed him.

"I'm not sure how to get you up," shouted Lina. "There's no winch here I can see. Ship's deserted, though. I'm going to take a look around."

"Right then," Fengel called back. "See if you can find a ladder. If not, then improvise!"

A ladder. Right. She turned back to the ship and made her way over to the edge of the forecastle deck. A small, steep set of steps led down to the deck. Quickly but carefully she descended.

Lina followed the rope supporting the net full of pirates down the length of the deck. Maybe there was a winch in the stern? If she could just see how it terminated, maybe she could figure something out. She certainly wasn't seeing any rolled-up rope ladder anywhere.

She climbed up to the aftcastle deck, and her heart almost fell into her stomach. The rope suspending her crewmates stretched back past the helm to the very stern rails of the ship. There it was tied in a heavy, but simple knot. Already the wood of the rails was splintered and cracked, some of the spindles dangling free. The anchor point was uncertain, and would not last. Natasha *had* meant to kill them.

Lina glanced about for some other way to anchor the rope. Nothing made itself apparent. She ran back down the stair and back up to the bow, cursing under her breath.

"Captain?" she cried, leaning over the gunwales.

"Yes?" came Fengel's reply.

"It would be a really, really good idea if you lot down there could move as little as possible."

Silence greeted her statement.

"We will endeavor not to," said Fengel at last, both in reply to Lina and as an order to the wordless crew.

Lina turned back to the ship. There had to be something she could do. *Improvise, improvise. Forget that. There's got to be rope ladders* somewhere *on board.* Or more ropes, at least. If she found one she could anchor it to something properly, buying more time if—when—the railing snapped free.

She descended back to the deck. Where would they keep spare rope or ladders? There weren't anything like the neat equipment lockers aboard the *Dawnhawk.* Lina cursed, stopping as she glanced at the forecastle behind her. Up above was the bow deck, but here below it was open. Once, comparing bedding arrangements with a client in her former line of work, she'd heard that sometimes sailors slept there where they could access ready gear quickly. Lina took a step toward it, when a sound caught at her ear.

It was a sob.

Lina stopped. All around her the airship creaked, groaning and complaining in its dotage. Had she misheard? No. It had been the sound of a grown man crying; she'd heard it far too often to mistake it for anything else.

She drew the loaned knife from its sheath. When she'd thought herself alone, the ship hadn't seemed at all dangerous. Ancient and rattletrap maybe, but not dangerous. Now though she knew better, and her heart raced.

The sound came again, a thick choking sob echoing from the aftcastle deck. There, the door of the captain's cabin was slightly ajar. She had not noticed it until now, too focused on the predicament at hand. Lina crept to the door, knife held at the ready, peered within.

The cabin was a mess. It smelled of old mold and alcohol. The window-hangings above the box-bed at the rear of the room were moth-eaten and pulled shut. A lone figure crouched in the far corner on the floor, a tiny nub of candle his only illumination. It was a young, red-headed man in the rumpled greatcoat of a Mechanist. Several bottles of cheap rum lay at his feet. Lina pushed her way inside. The Mechanist didn't seem to notice. Softly forward she crept until she crouched just before him.

"Who are you?" she whispered, knife held at the ready.

The Mechanist started. He leapt backwards with a yelp and banged his head on the rear timbers of the cabin. "You didn't leave me!" he cried, rubbing at his head. Freckles covered his face. "You came back for—" He looked up at Lina and blinked in confusion. "You're not Miss Blackheart," he said. "Who are you?"

"Lina Stone," she said. "Are you the ship's Mechanist? Are you alone?"

He sniffed, nodding. "They left me on board when they abandoned the *Queen* for their old ship. I tried to come with, but the first mate just kicked me down and laughed. I can't pilot this thing by myself—it's barely aloft as it is! I'm going to die here, just like the others dangling off the bow." The Mechanist covered his face with his hands, weeping again.

Lina sighed, all her wariness gone. This was an oddity, but it didn't change anything. She still had to get Fengel and the others aboard, and needed help to do that. She appraised the youth before her. He really was very young, and didn't seem worth much. *But needs must.* "Hey now," she said, voice soft. "It's going to be all right."

"What?" blubbered the Mechanist. "Wait. Where did you even come from?" His eyes widened and he shrank back. "Please don't hurt me! I didn't have anything to do with what they did!"

You could have helped after they'd left, rather than hiding up here and sobbing your guts out. Lina hid her thoughts behind a smile. "I'm not going to do anything to you. But I want to get my friends up on board, and I can't do that alone." She sat demurely, working to make herself look less threatening. "Why don't you help me out, and then I'll make sure they aren't angry at you, all right? Afterward we can fly back to port, and everything'll be fine."

The Mechanist looked at her like a deer about to bolt. He sniffed, and Lina couldn't help but stare at the bubble of snot that shrank from one nostril. She kept her smile small and placid though, and eventually the young man nodded.

"There," she said. "Not so hard, eh? Come on." Lina stood, grabbing the Mechanist by the hand. He started, reflexively trying to pull from her grip. He couldn't. The Mechanist's hands were soft and un-callused. Lina's could crack walnuts. Acting as sweet as she dared, Lina pulled him to his feet, then tugged him out from the captain's cabin and onto the deck.

The rope holding the pirates off the bow was still taut. Faintly, she heard the sounds of the rail anchoring it strain. Lina looked back at the Mechanist.

"What's your name?" she asked, fighting to keep calm herself.

The youth gawked. "My name? I...I'm Allen," he said. He blanched, as if suddenly remembering he wasn't supposed to have one anymore.

"All right, Allen. Where can we find a ladder?"

"Nowhere," Allen mumbled. "I mean they're all up top. We had to use some of them to replace the ratlines and rigging, and to get the starboard rudders shored up. We could get one down, but it'll take another pair of hands than just us two."

Lina cursed. "All right then. Improvisation it is. Where can we find some rope?"

That, he could provide. The Mechanist led her belowdecks to the engine room he stayed in. It was nothing like the one aboard the *Dawnhawk*, more an equipment locker than a place for proper engineering. A little cast-iron stove squatted in one corner, banked low. A coal-ladder to the store somewhere deeper in the ship opened next to it, but it was largely empty, black dust staining it heavily. Lina grabbed a heavy coil of rope, and with Allen's help hauled it back up to the deck. They anchored it to a heavy steel cleat just below the aft deck, one connecting the gasbag frame above to the ship. Then she ran the other end up to the bow.

"Here," she cried at the pirates below. Fengel looked back up at her, his monocle winking in the moonlight. She threw down her end of the rope, and held it until someone grabbed it from within the net. "Tie that off so's you don't fall in the meantime. And don't move too much. I don't trust my knot-work up here." Without waiting for a reply she turned back to the ship.

Problem One, improvised. That took care of any immediate mishaps that might occur. *Now to see about Problem Two.* There was still issue of getting the crew back up on board, and she had no idea how to go about it.

"Do you have a winch?" Lina asked. They stood amidships, looking up at the rope. Allen stood beside her, eyes down and subservient.

The young Mechanist flinched. "No," he said with a shake of his head. "We're not even close to being properly supplied. I tried to tell them, but Captain Blackheart just hit me. They were in such a hurry to get aloft! I tried to tell them that the *Copper Queen* wasn't ready yet. We ended up just drifting for a day and a half after we went up. The linkage and turning system wasn't even close to being usable."

Lina frowned. *Well, I'm not going to be able to pull them back up. And with wrists like that, Allen here isn't going to either.*

The ship lurched, pushed by a strong wind. A stray belaying pin rolled down the deck toward them, then reversed and rolled the other way as the *Copper Queen* settled. Lina watched it, then looked up at the taut rope above them. An idea occurred to her. "What about something really heavy?"

Allen blinked. "Like what?"

Lina held out her hands. "We need something really heavy. Like, I don't know, a bunch of water barrels or something."

The young Mechanist gave her a funny look. He pointed to the port-side gunwales. "Like those?"

Lina followed his gesture. The light cannons sat upon their mountings, pointing out from the ship. They were carronades, almost solid iron, with handles cast into their thick bodies, one on either side of the barrel. And they were very, very heavy. Lina tapped her lip thoughtfully. "I think they just might, at that."

With Allen's help, Lina unlocked one of the carronades from its wooden mounts. Then they rolled it off onto the deck where it landed with a deafening thump that echoed up and down the length of the ship. Inclined as the ship was, the artillery-piece slid down to a stop against the forecastle. Lina cursed. She hadn't thought this entirely through.

Taking a spare piece of rope, she tied it through the errant weapon and gave one end to Allen. Cursing and swearing, they dragged the thing back up to the aftcastle and tied it in place.

"Okay," she said, panting. "Now we've just got to get this up to the helm. Think you can push it up if I pull from the top of the stair?"

The young Mechanist stared at her. "No."

Lina cursed. "Damnation. You'll have to pull."

Allen shook his head. "I don't think that will work either."

Lina sat down with a scowl. They had to get the cannon up, or her plan wouldn't work. She glanced at Allen; the Mechanist wasn't looking at her though. Instead he stared at the complex system of steerage pulleys and cabling that hung from the gasbag frame above.

"What've you got on your mind?" she asked.

Allen started, looked at her, then examined his feet. "Nothing."

She wanted to sigh, but held back. *I still need him.* "No, go on, tell me."

He shrugged. "Well, it's just, *I* couldn't pull that up those steps. But if we change the pulleys up there, we could hang a rope from it, and the two of us together could pull one up."

Lina eyed the mechanisms. "All right, then. Let's get to work."

With a little coaxing, Lina found Allen to be a fairly clever fellow, though still incredibly bashful and uncertain of himself. If he'd had any initiative, life with Natasha's crew must have beaten it out of him.

At her urging the young Mechanist grabbed an iron gaff-pole and clambered up to prod at the steering mechanisms. Once he started, Lina found the idea easy enough to follow; he was disengaging several of the pulley systems so that they could feed the rope on the carronade on through. Between the two of them the work went quickly. Clambering up onto the aftcastle deck, they raised the artillery-piece up, and guided it back past the helm. It wasn't easy, but it was possible.

They moved six more. Hours passed. "There," Lina said when they were finally done. She collapsed, shaking, onto the pile of iron weapons. Only a few remained onboard in their original positions now. Her muscles quivered and she was drenched in sweat. Allen fell to the deck beside her, doing worse than her. They both lay there a moment, gasping for breath.

"What next?" croaked the young Mechanist.

Lina eyed the railing. "We go get a rope, thread it through the handles on these cannons, then tie it to this other rope attached to the rail there." She stopped. "Oh. And find me a sword." The back railing anchoring her crewmates was splintered and cracked; it wouldn't last much longer now.

Allen went back down below while she rested. Once back he worked at her directions, running the rope through the wrought-iron handles of the cannon and tying a knot to each before moving onto the next. When they were secure, Lina and Allen tied the rope to the one running back across the ship and over the bow. By the time they finished, the moon had risen, crossed the sky, and was about to set.

"All right," said Lina, standing and stretching. She would sleep for a week when this was all done. "Now we just shove this whole mess over."

"I don't know if I have the strength," said Allen plaintively.

"Nonsense," replied Lina. "You just start small."

Spitting into her palms, she grabbed the top-most cannon on the pile and shoved it. The weapon rocked, unwilling to budge, until she grit her teeth, set her feet and went at it again. It abruptly rolled down, bounced off the cannon below it with a clang to fall up against the splintered wooden railing, punching through.

Everything happened at once.

The cannon fell overboard, pulling the second one after it. Then the third, and fourth, and fifth. At the same time, the rail disintegrated and the rope supporting the cargo net hanging from the bow flew forward. Shards of wood flew through the air, pelting the two of them.

The two weights fought, pulling the rope back and forth. More cannons fell overboard, turning the tide and teasing the rope in their direction. As Lina had hoped, the weight of the cannons was greater than the whole of the crew. She ran back down to the deck, ignoring Allen's shouts, drawing the heavy cutlass he'd found for her.

Faint cries echoed up from over the bow. They grew in strength with every passing second until the cargo net full of pirates appeared. It rose up over the bow like a catch of so many screaming fish, flinging up over the gunwales to land on the forecastle deck. The pirates within all grunted at the impact, then yelled as they tumbled en masse down to the main deck. The guide-rope Lina had attached earlier for security pulled taut in the other direction now, bringing the crew to a halt and giving the whole ship a mighty jerk. Lina raised the cutlass and brought it down, severing the rope stretching from the cannons to her crewmates. It parted with a snap, and the stanchion holding the guide-rope parted from the deck with a wrenching squeal, whipping down the deck, past Allen, and off into the sky.

Silence stretched across the deck; most of the crew were stunned. *And that's Problem Two.* She ran forward, drawing her borrowed knife again. She knelt at the net and started sawing at its fibers. Allen was there in a moment, helping.

Coincidentally, Captain Fengel lay before her. He looked up blearily at her through the mesh. "Miss Stone?" he asked in confusion. "What in the Goddess' name did you do?"

Lina paused, sat up. "I," she said proudly, "have improvised."

CHAPTER ELEVEN

Fengel spun the wheel of the *Copper Queen*, despondent. It turned free, disengaged for the moment from the rudder. *That's it. There's the thing exactly. I am utterly rudderless.*

The primitive airship drifted through the night. His crew moved about its decks, cleaning up the mess left behind by Miss Stone's impromptu engineering. Ropes, cannons, and stray oddments like loading rammers and iron gaff-poles were being packed back out of the way. Lucian called out for reports while Henry saw to the wounded. Sarah Lome, Maxim, and a few others searched the lower decks for further surprises left by his wife. Fengel was weary now that his ire had run its course. He stood by the helm, not doing anything of worth.

And if he could, then what? The crew kept their eyes down, stayed out of his way. He didn't blame them. The battle aboard the *Dawnhawk* had been lost before the tide had even turned, and all because of him. But what should he have done? His men knew the risks; they were pirates, and there was no shame in falling to honorable combat. Yet for Henry, or any of his crew to be blithely executed while he watched? No. He could not, would not let that happen while he had the power to stop it.

Of course, that meant they'd lost the fight. And their ship. And more than a little of his pride. Natasha had won, leaving a hole that only revenge could fill. But she was long gone; that solace was lost to him.

The wheel still spun. Fengel put out a hand and stopped it. Through its spokes he spied Maxim ascending to the aftcastle deck. The aetherite looked disheveled; his clothes were burnt and his skin blackened in places. His duel with Konrad had unleashed strange, otherworldly energies. For all that, it was the exhaustion on his face that spoke his pain the loudest. Fengel must have looked even worse.

"We're secure for the moment, sir," said Maxim. He turned to mutter something to his shoulder, then turned back to his captain. "Let me take the wheel. You should head below and get some rest."

Fengel thought of arguing. *What's the point?* Where were they going to go? If he returned to Haventown without the treasure, there would be no safe place to haven from Mr. Grey. That, and they were in the *Copper Queen*. Euron's ship. That would not go over well.

But what else was left to them? Not piracy. The airship was a scow. A fantastic, impractical thing cobbled together a long time ago on a daring dream and not a little recklessness. Its raiding days were done.

He didn't know what to do. In sweeter times there would have been someone he could turn to. The crew all idolized him, though he didn't dare confide in them. But Natasha...Fengel felt his mouth twist as the incongruity met him head on; his horrible wife was *responsible* for their situation. Fengel spat and shoved the thought aside. With a nod to his navigator he made his way down to the main deck. Lucian and Henry Smalls conferred nearby, looking up as he passed them.

"Captain," said his first mate. "We're all aboard and relatively shipshape. I've broken us up into a skeleton crew for the moment; we're organizing and taking stock. We should be as ready as we can be by dawn."

Fengel nodded at his officers, then sighed. "That's good. Carry on." He turned away, toward the door to the captain's cabin.

"Captain," said Henry. Fengel glanced back over his shoulder at his steward. "Is something wrong?"

Fengel wanted to laugh, a dry, black chuckle from deep within in his chest. "No, Henry. Nothing at all." He couldn't quite keep the sarcasm from coloring his voice. "Take stock of our provisions, I'll decide where we're going to sail in the morning."

From the corner of his eye he saw his steward and first mate share a look. "We're going after Natasha," said Lucian, a hard edge to his voice. "Right, sir?"

"What's the point?" Fengel all but shouted. "She got us!" He threw his arms wide. "And she got us well! She was the better pirate. She was the better captain! I stole her ship, but she not only found it again, but took it back and repaid us in full!" He shook his head.

He looked back up at his officers. Sarah Lome joined them, her thick braid swaying as she walked up. Maxim watched from the helm up above. Several of the crew watched from nearby. All shared the same look of concern.

"Just...take stock of our provisions," Fengel continued. He turned and strode through the door into the captain's cabin.

A funk permeated the air, the scent of rum, mold, and dust. A box-bed sat just below a wide window at the rear of the space, heavy curtains drawn over rumpled bedding. Fengel blinked. The room was spacious and dark, just as he'd remembered it. Memories rose to the fore at the sight of the bed, of happier times when he and Natasha had been almost-strangers and still blind to the flaws of each other. Euron's ship had been a great hiding place back then; no one but Natasha dared board it. A hollow pang bit at him. Fengel shook his head with a snort and ignored it. He yanked the coverlet free and curled up in a corner, next to an extinguished candle nub and several bottles of rum. There were *far* too many memories still laying in that bed.

A knocking at the cabin door woke him. Fengel opened his eyes, surprised at how easily he had fallen asleep. The sound continued, someone gently tapping. He blinked and sat up cross-legged, a groan escaping his lips. His back hurt and his mouth tasted horrible. Thick fuzz coated his teeth. "Come in," he said with a yawn, reaching for one of the unopened bottles of rum.

The door cracked wide and Henry Smalls stuck his head in. Seeing Fengel he entered, Lucian sauntering behind. Before they shut the portal Fengel spied the light of an early dawn out on the deck. His first mate glanced about as they approached him. "Goddess," he said. "This place stinks."

"Captain's cabin," replied Fengel. "Natasha would have slept here recently. She was never much for cleaning up." He still felt aimless, though less weary.

"Faugh. It stinks of rum and mildew. Are you sure? How could anyone live in this?"

"There are fresh obscenities carved into the floor by the bed," said Fengel. Lucian and Henry craned their heads to look. Fengel ignored them and picked up a bottle. He swallowed a mouthful of rum, breathing out as it burned its way down his throat and filled his chest with warmth.

Henry turned back to him. "We're holding stable, Captain. You'll want to say a few words later for those we lost, but the crew is as good as can be expected. The ship's a wreck, but she...should serve. Our coal stores are fairly low. Natasha must have burned through most of it to beat us to the Maelstrom. We've...maybe enough to get back to Haventown. I've got Geoffrey Lords downstairs scavenging what he can for breakfast for you. I'll bring it right up."

Fengel sighed. "No need. I'll get something later. I think I'll just sleep a bit more."

Lucian frowned. Henry blinked. "Well, let's at least get your shave, sir."

Automatically his hand went to his chin. A thick patch of whiskers sprouted there. Fengel sighed and shook his head. "No. We'll take care of that later."

His officers stared at each other in alarm. Fengel ignored it. "I mean, what's the point?" he continued angrily. "She got me. I tried to pull one over on her, but she caught up. I've lost us our ship twice now, old and new." He looked down at the bottle in his hands.

Henry walked over and knelt next to him. "Captain, come on now. Things haven't been great lately. But we've still got a ship. Of sorts." The steward frowned. "Never mind. Let me go get you an egg from the kitchens. You always like a good hard-boiled egg."

Fengel shook his head silently.

"Or how about we go up atop the bag? I'll clear everyone off, so you can read your poetry in peace." He frowned again. "Um. Though I think your kit bag is still back aboard the *Dawnhawk*. But ah, you've got your favorites memorized, right? That's *like* reading them. We'll make a morning of it."

Fengel shook his head silently.

"Well," said Lucian. The first mate walked over and sat on the edge of the bed. He held a thick folio in one hand, battered and stained by travel. "I hate to interrupt a good bit o' self-pity. But there may be a chance we're not done yet." He smiled like he knew a secret, then cracked the book wide and shoved it into Fengel's face. "Take a look at this."

The tome was a journal. Its left page was a scribbled shorthand, a collection of notes, measurements, and geographical datum. The right was what looked like a map, a carefully sketched bit of coastline around a river mouth, and the boundaries of the river for several miles inland.

"What's this?" asked Fengel.

"This," said Lucian with a flourish, "is the original survey logbook from the expedition that found the Silverpenny River. Really, it's full of all sorts of interesting notes. I don't know who Natasha beat up to get her hands on it, but they left it behind when they retook the *Dawnhawk*."

Fengel felt a glimmer of interest. It was obvious what Lucian wanted. Fengel wanted it too. But why even bother? "Interesting. But we know where she's going. There's no way we can catch up to her in time with this old scow, even if her skysails are damaged."

"That's true," said Lucian. "At least as far as it goes. But as I was reading through this book, I noticed something interesting." He tapped the mouth of the river, where a series of notes had been scrawled. "The Silverpenny apparently has a number of rocks at its mouth, and according to the original survey, an unusually strong tidal draw, matched with a very deep riverbed."

Henry made a small, curious noise. "So the *H.M.S. Albatross* got sucked over and ran aground as it was passing by?"

"Likely so. But it's been almost a week now. A week of constant tidal draw."

"Which could have sucked the wreck farther upriver," said Fengel, understanding. He pointed at the map. "Probably there, where the survey noticed a shallow draft. But how does that help us?"

Lucian placed his finger beyond the map. "Engmann's Run comes up at the river from an oblique southern angle. It's fast, but goes around in a curve." He moved his hand up onto the page, north of the river mouth. "I estimate we're somewhere here. Natasha's got a head start, but if we move quickly, in a straight line, we might be able to meet them there. Same way they got us. We're so damned dependant on the aetherlines that we never think to go *straight*."

Henry blanched. "We'd have to go overland and cross the Stormwall. There wouldn't be enough coal for the return trip."

Fengel blinked. Slowly it came to him; Lucian was right. If they went in a straight line, and the maps were accurate, then there was still a chance. He could beat his wife to the treasure. Fengel saw Natasha in the eye of his mind. She was laughing at him, laughing herself sick at having taken his ship and his treasure to boot. But slowly her visage changed to one of stunned incomprehension, and then the mask of inchoate rage that would come when she got to the wreck and realized that he had beaten her again.

He threw aside the coverlet and shot to his feet. "Lucian!" he cried. "I want two watches, evenly distributed. Get the Mechanist, Lina Stone, and one other assigned to patching up this wreck. Take stores and inventory, I want to know what weapons we've got, and what supplies. Henry! Go down to the kitchens and get me an egg, then meet me atop the wheelhouse. Bring a razor; I'll want a shave."

Fengel strode to the cabin door and threw it open without a further glance at his officers. The sun was rising in the east, casting long shadows across the deck. Chains, ropes, and other equipment were piled up neatly along the wooden surface as his crew took inventory. A light breeze blew, tousling his hair. Fengel straightened his monocle and climbed up atop the wheelhouse. Maxim stood there, eyes red, his exhaustion apparent.

"Navigator," said Fengel. "You are relieved. Go get something to eat and then get some rest. I want you fit and prepared for the next watch. Prepare some Workings."

Maxim started back in surprise at his captain's fervor. Fengel stepped in and took the wheel, spinning it. Without instruction, the navigator had kept their heading north by northeast, fortunately. Slowly, Fengel oriented the ship toward the cloudy eastern horizon.

"Captain," said Maxim. "Where are we going?" Lucian and Henry ran out onto the deck, looking up at him. The pirates nearest paused in their tasks to listen as well.

"Why, Maxim," said Fengel with a grin. "We're pirates. We're going to *steal* something." *And we'll show that drunken wench a thing or two.*

Fengel's mood spread throughout the ship like a drop of oil on a calm pool of water. Those crew closest to the helm moved with renewed confidence and enthusiasm. The lingering, hang-dog depression over their circumstances faded. Those he'd heard complaining about the surrender quieted, bending to their tasks more readily. In short order the ship was alive again and bustling.

Fengel flew them as hard and fast as they would go, aimed dead ahead for the cloudy horizon, where the Stormwall bordered the strange eastern shore of the Yulan. Their speed wasn't much. The *Copper Queen* lacked skysails, and even if it did they'd never catch the *Dawnhawk* now; with their stores, Natasha could simply outrun them. So instead he kept them pointed dead east at the Stormwall. Fengel trusted to the weak propellers of the airship and caught the wind as best he could.

The sun rose to mid-morning, then high overhead at noon, before sinking back down again in the mid-afternoon. Their stores of fuel grew smaller. Maxim returned and insisted on taking the helm again. Fengel reluctantly let him, moving down onto the deck and eyeing the state of the ship. He called for more anchorage to the gas-bag frame and reinforcements to weak sections of railing. Several times he came across Miss Stone carrying a long iron gaff-pole. Ryan Gae and the Mechanist moved with her, making minor repairs to the steering systems she'd changed to get them all aboard. Fengel wasn't certain who led whom; Miss Stone seemed just as canny and far more confident than the young Brother of the Cog she'd found.

Fengel made certain to compliment her. His opinion of the little waif only seemed to rise. She was constantly pulling them from one dire problem or another on this voyage. The only oddity was her bashfulness whenever he approached her. This time she listened to him, blushed furiously, and then scurried off to see to a pulley assembly, her crewmates following after her in confusion. *Ah well. She'll relax at some point.*

When he was sure that things were running smoothly, Fengel descended to the kitchens for a bit of lunch. Not much was to be had, aside from a haunch of salt pork and wormy ship's biscuit. But it would suffice. He took his meager meal up to the bow and watched as the churning Stormwall grew closer. *Faster. We need to go faster.* The sun sank into late afternoon just as tall rocky islets appeared in the distance, the precursor to the shores of the Yulan. Their journey was almost over; they had reached the far continent.

The Stormwall was aptly named. It was just like he remembered; a roiling, churning cloudbank that stretched along the coastline as far as he could see. It towered, the upper end rising out of sight where lightning crackled in its reaches. The only consistent point of weakness was Breachtown, more than a day's journey north. A few other places were rumored, like the river mouth they'd sought. Unlike the Maelstrom though, this storm was real. Already its winds brushed at his hair and jolted the airship.

Fengel returned to his post at the rear of the ship and its helm. Lucian climbed up to stand beside him. They watched in silence as they approached the churning black wall dead ahead. "That doesn't look pleasant," said his first mate.

"That it does not," replied Fengel. He smiled. They'd all heard the rumors of the Stormwall, and seen it from afar. But this was the first time they were going to *enter* it. There might be the chance that they could fly over it. He'd never heard of anyone trying it though, and with the furious bolts shooting through the heights, he had no intention of trying to. Fire was a sky-pirate's greatest fear; the light-air gas was very, very flammable.

So, straight through it was. *I* will *pull this off. That treasure's mine.* It wasn't so much even his debt anymore. He just didn't want Natasha to get it.

His first mate stared at the Stormwall. "You know, there is entirely too much bad weather in this region."

Fengel smiled. "That's why no one ever comes out here."

They quieted. Maxim kept their course true and they flew at the continent and its storm. Beneath them the surface of the sea grew choppy and foamy. The strong breeze grew into a buffeting wind. The airship moved past the islets and now he spied the sand of the coastline, a thin, grey stretch of land lashed by rain. Past that everything was occluded by the rage of the storm.

Lucian called for all hands to stations. The pirates scurried about, binding themselves to the gunwales and ratlines. Hatches were battened down and loose gear stowed as best it could be. Then the storm was upon them.

It towered, a violent wall. Rain lashed the deck and drummed the gas-bag frame. The sun disappeared, blotted out by churning clouds. Beneath them the deck heaved and shook, swaying like a drunkard about to collapse. Lucian shouted something at their navigator. Fengel could not hear him, and neither could Maxim from the shake of his head. The first mate grabbed his half-cloak and thrust out a hand clutching a small compass. The needle swung back and forth, rocking its way clockwise. The storm was trying to turn them around.

Fengel understood. The initial surveyors had been amazed at the perpetual nature of the Stormwall, but even more confused by how thin it was. According to the logbook, as well as rumors Fengel had heard from Breachtown, the Stormwall was only several hundred feet deep. So long as they could stay on course they would punch right through.

But the Stormwall fought. It twisted, pushed, and pulled. Maxim wrenched the wheel back and forth, twisting the rudder assembly and the sails it was attached to as best he could. The steam-driven propellers pushed, moving them slowly, slowly forward.

A brilliant spear of light illuminated the deck. The lightning bolt licked out from the storm to strike at the port-side gunwales. The railings blew apart, burning flinders flying up and past Fengel and his officers.

Fengel's shut his eyes til they passed, then watched as more jagged bolts tore across the sky, increasing in frequency. He fought his way to the port-side rail and leaned over. They whirled, and clouds streamed *down* past them. The ship was rising, buoyed by the mad currents of air and right to where the storm-bolts played.

Another lambent blast cast stark illumination across the deck. The thunder that followed was deafening. Fengel clapped his ears while Lucian and Maxim dropped to their knees. Fengel threw himself at the wheel, catching it before they lost their course. The wood was slick between his fingers though, and fought.

The ship swayed violently. Maxim slid away, rolling up against the starboard gunwales. Fengel reached down and grabbed Lucian. "Take the wheel!" he shouted.

His first mate climbed to his feet and grabbed the ship's wheel, more to anchor himself than out of duty. "What?" he yelled, sandy hair flying in the wind. "What are you going to do?"

The answer was obvious. "If those blasts catch the gas-bag alight," said Fengel, "we're done for. We need a rod!"

Lucian shook his head. "I didn't see one on board! Where are you going to find one?"

Fengel glanced about the deck. Tools and equipment rolled all about, knocked free from their lockers or not packed entirely away in the first place. There had to be something he could do.

"I'll figure something out," he said to Lucian. "Don't worry about that, just get us through this storm!"

He left his first mate to the wheel and descended to the deck. The ship swayed as he climbed, the wood of the stepladder slippery from rain. Fengel took a breath and shimmied nimbly down. He'd been through worse as a sailor.

The deck was chaos. Storm clouds obscured everything beyond the ship. The crew clung to anchor points and railings, a few dangling from cables they'd tied themselves to. The cannons were locked in place still, thankfully. More than once had he seen artillery slide free from its mount during a squall to crush some hapless bystander.

A wailing gust slammed into the airship. The deck beneath them swayed madly, tilting up almost thirty degrees. Buckets, ropes, and tools slid past him to go flying overboard. One, the long metal gaff-pole that Miss Stone had been using, caught at the hem of his jacket. Lightning blasted again, this bolt connecting with the wooden railing beside him. The spindles exploded, pelting him with burning flinders.

Fengel blinked away the afterimages as the ship settled again. *Of course,* he realized. He grabbed up the gaff-pole before it could fly overboard. There was his lightning rod. *Now I just need somewhere to anchor it properly.* He glanced about the deck and his eyes alighted on the cannon there. *Perfect.*

This wasn't a job for just one man though. Several pirates tumbled about the deck nearby. Sarah Lome, Miss Stone, and Oscar Pleasant being closest. "You three!" he barked. "Attend me!" He waited for the ship to level out again and then strode confidently up the deck. The three pirates scrambled after him.

Fengel knocked his catch-pole against the middle-most cannon in the row. "Gunny, Oscar, get this fat bastard unmoored. I need it pointed out and up." He turned to the waif. "Miss Stone, get me a rammer and a length of chain. I see two rolling around against the gunwales opposite us."

The three stared at him, bewildered. "But Captain," said Pleasant. "What are we doing—"

Fengel rounded on him. "Do you want to live? Get to work!" The crewman ducked his head. Sarah shrugged and bent to unlock the cannon. Miss Stone scrabbled off across the deck.

The gunnery mistress unshipped the cannon, her braid swinging in the storm as she worked. At Fengel's direction she lifted the cannon up to rest on the wooden rail. The wood complained, but held. He had Oscar secure it in place with a rope. It wouldn't hold for long, but maybe long enough.

Miss Stone returned with a rammer for loading cannon and the length of chain. He had her hold it steady while he bound the gaff-pole to the wooden rod, chain dangling down its length. Now came the hard part.

"Get back, all of you." He stepped towards the edge of the deck. Lightning crackled by, a thunderous blast that scorched the canvas of the gas-bag frame above.

Sarah Lome's eyes widened. "Sir," she said. "You can't mean—"

"Stay back, Gunny," said Fengel. Swallowing, he stepped up to the rail. Then he quickly thrust the rod out, trying to get it placed to slide down the barrel. The iron gaff-pole was heavy, and unwieldy, loosening already against the chain that bound it. Then the small hairs on the backs of his hands stood painfully straight. Fengel tasted something coppery.

The end of the rammer fit into the cannon bore. Fengel forced it down and then threw himself back at the deck. Lightning flashed, bright and actinic and impossibly close. Distantly, he felt his right arm go numb. When he hit the water-slick wood of the deck the world seemed to cave in with a rumbling crack that almost drove the sense from him.

The numbness faded to an unpleasant tingle. Someone grabbed him by the shoulder and rolled him over. For a second, madly, he thought it was Natasha. But no, it was Miss Stone, looking down at him with wide, frightened eyes. Fengel realized he was smoldering.

Sarah Lome crawled over to him. "Captain," she said. "Are you—"

Another crackling blast impacted nearby, followed by a thunderous roar. Fengel flinched, then looked over to the makeshift lightning rod.

It worked. The wood was charring all around the cannon, its metal glowing dull red and hot. The iron gaff-pole was almost white, the metal hook on its end drooping like a piece of string. As they watched, another blast licked out from the storm, only to twist mid-course towards the rod.

Fengel laughed. He ached, and his sword had fallen free to skitter along the deck at his fall. But he felt wonderful. "Just capital!" he cried to his gunnery mistress. "Absolutely capital." He climbed to his feet. "Now let's do it again on the other side. Quickly now, before we all get blown to smithereens."

They hastily performed the same maneuver on the starboard-side, again just narrowly avoiding electrocution. Once done, Fengel ran up to the bow to laugh and shake his fist at the storm. The crew all stared at him in awe.

Bolt after bolt exploded throughout the cloud of the storm. The rains lashed the deck, and the winds pummeled them. The crew clung for dear life, offering up prayers, promises, curses, and whatever else they thought might convince the Goddess to let them live through the raging fury they flew upon.

And then they were through.

The Stormwall parted before them. Green jungle spread out beneath the *Copper Queen*, twisting and rolling as far as Fengel could see. Distant mountains rose up through the haze of the horizon, and rivers shone like silver under the late afternoon sun. Clouds scudded across the sky, pushed down and out to the base of the Stormwall on this side, but further inland the skies were clear.

Fengel turned back to the ship and let out a yell. The crew, bedraggled and soaked, looked up at him. They took up the cry after a moment, sounding amazed to be alive. As he watched, the makeshift lightning rods collapsed, the wooden rammers crumbling away to ashen flinders that blew away in the strong gale so close to the Stormwall. The cannons still glowed red-hot, charring the wood of their mountings.

Lucian made his way up to the bow, along with Sarah Lome and Miss Stone. Henry Smalls appeared, looking soaked. The little steward stared at the cannons, shaking his head. Lucian gave his captain a smile. "I cannot believe you did that."

Fengel straightened his monocle. "I only did what was needed," he replied in his most authoritative voice. "Lucian, take stock and make sure no one was unduly injured. Also, get aloft and make doubly certain that we don't have any fires." The ship was listing slightly, more so than usual. "I'm not worried," he continued, "but better safe than sorry. Check on the lookouts. Now, it's a slim chance, but let's get out that logbook. We need to discern where that wreck should be, if it did in fact float upriver."

"No need, Captain," said Lina. "Look."

The pirates all turned to follow her gesture. She pointed starboard, south of the ship. There flowed a thick river like a lazy snake, wide and argent in the light of the sun. Clouds from the Stormwall obscured it, but a wrecked sail ship was clearly visible at a wide bend in the river several hundred feet below them. The vessel lay on its side, caught between a sandbar and the shore. Past the bend on its opposite side an airship floated just a dozen feet above the river: the *Dawnhawk*.

Fengel made a small, animal noise in his throat. *It worked. It worked, and I have you.* He almost cackled with glee. Instead he spoke over his shoulder at the crew. "Lucian, get back up to Maxim, see if he can conjure us more clouds, or at least a concealing mist. Henry, get out all the spare ropes we have. I want ladders, drop-lines, anything that'll help us take them from above. Gunny Lome, get everyone armed." He patted his hip, then frowned. "Miss Stone?"

The waif looked up. "Yes?"

"Fetch me my sword."

CHAPTER TWELVE

"FIFTEEN DEGREES STARBOARD," cried the lookout up on the bow.

"Fifteen degrees, aye," acknowledged Konrad. He spun the helm wheel until the bow of the *Dawnhawk* shifted to follow the bend in the river.

Mordecai watched Natasha. The pirate captain stood proudly by the helm, smiling, golden eyes bright. She called out orders to the lookouts, having them check every wake below the water to see if it were really wreckage. They prodded at the water with long wooden gaff-poles, so far finding only submerged rocks and startled crocodiles. The *Dawnhawk* floated a dozen feet above the Silverpenny River. They kept a slow pace, moving as little as possible as they hunted for the wreck of the *Albatross*. It was not easy work. Strong gusts from the Stormwall pushed at the ship from the rear, driving it off their course toward the northwest bank and the thick jungle there.

The last day had gone surpassingly well. They had regained their ship and taught a lesson to the thieves who'd dared to take it. The particulars of that lesson had deeply irritated Mordecai at first; were it up to him, they would have just cut the throats of Fengel's Men and been done with it. Natasha's insistence on leaving them alive was foolish. Still though, even that poor choice could not dim the pleasure he felt at being back in his proper place. And, he supposed, in the end the results would be the same; there was no way that Fengel would worm his way out of his predicament. In time the ship would lower enough to drown them all, if simple exposure didn't finish them.

After regaining the *Dawnhawk,* Mordecai and Natasha had conferred with each other, for once finding that they were in complete agreement. His appalling thievery aside, Fengel's lead was a good one. A whole frigate stuffed to bursting with foreign treasure, ripe for the plucking. So why not find and take it for themselves?

They took stock of supplies and damages to the ship. Finding the former ample and the latter minor they had flown on, coasting along the slight curve of Engmann's Run. By the time the dawn rose they'd reached the Yulan coast. From there it had been most of the effort of a day to locate the mouth of the Silverpenny River.

It was rare for any pirate, water or sky, to come this close to the strange eastern land; there simply wasn't anything worth taking. Mordecai found that the rumors of the place were understated, if anything. The Stormwall raged and wailed, pushing them away with violent winds only to create cross-drafts that sucked them back in again. They had spent hours just trying to approach the perpetual storm without plunging straight into it, repeatedly skirting around the edge of it, close enough to examine the mouth of the river.

Because the mouth of the Silverpenny River was empty. No tall ship lay among the rocks scattering the small bay, and no wreckage was visible on the nearby beach below the storm. Ultimately Natasha decided that the *H.M.S. Albatross* must have been sucked upriver by the tidal flow, and Mordecai was forced to agree.

They'd come too far to give up now, and so with great trepidation had entered the Stormwall. Or at least, somewhat. Over the river mouth it weakened, almost opening. Moving carefully they were able to just slip beneath the unnatural weather, the ship itself so low that when a strong gust caught them wrong the *Dawnhawk* brushed the choppy froth of the river. Rain drummed the gas-bag frame, and they lost two men up among the ratlines, blown clean off and lost to the storm. But before long they'd pushed through to the other side. Now they drifted, hunting for treasure with the raging wall of wind at their backs and the Yulan Interior spread out before them.

"Portside," shouted Natasha. "Three yards off. Check it."

The land was strange. Little things all about the airship reminded Mordecai that this was an old continent and an alien one as well. The waters of the river below them were mostly clear, though it shone argent in the light of the setting sun. The banks on either side were made of fine grey sand, so unlike the clean white of the Copper Isles. Beyond that lay jungle, thick and dark. Gibbons and brightly colored lizards hung from the trees. One of the latter took flight, spreading wide wings to flap across the river past the stern of the *Dawnhawk*. Mordecai blinked in surprise as the creature passed on by. Scents of citrus and rich earth wafted out from the jungle, mixing with the ozone smell of the Stormwall behind them. The whole place made Mordecai feel uneasy.

"Just another crocodile," shouted Guye Farrel from the portside ratlines.

"Then keep looking," snarled Natasha.

The new pirate glowered, but turned back to the river before he thought they could see him. Mordecai was amused. The man had been beaten, berated, and all around battered since joining their crew. His once well-groomed brown hair was limp and oily. Life as one of Natasha's Reavers was likely not turning out the way he thought it would have. During the fight with Fengel's Men he had acquitted himself well enough, though he had lost a pair of fingers to Lucian's sword. Yesterday, well after the fight, he had appeared from down belowdecks with an ugly red boil swelling on the side of his neck. Farrel claimed that he had been attacked by an angry beast down in the bowels of the ship's storage. Mordecai thought it far more likely that he was drinking something unusual that Fengel's crew had left behind.

"Dead ahead," called the bow lookout as the airship rounded a bend in the river. "Wreckage dead ahead!"

Mordecai met Natasha's eyes. She turned and strode up the deck eagerly. "Bring us in slow," he said to Konrad. Their navigator nodded and Mordecai moved to follow his captain.

They passed the Mechanist on their way up to the bow. The Brother of the Cog was oblivious to their journey, only mildly interested in the strange new continent. Of far greater concern to him was the care of his ship. He moved along the skysail mounts with two press-ganged pirates in tow, examining the damage wrought by the Stormwall and by Fengel's crew back at the Maelstrom. This man was made of different stuff than the milksop youngling they'd had back on the *Copper Queen*, and it pleased Mordecai.

Natasha slowed her pace toward the front of the ship. "How go the repairs?" she asked the Brother of the Cog.

The older man paused. "You are continually pushing this vessel beyond its designed capacity."

"Our apologies," said Mordecai. "But it was necessary to breach the Stormwall."

The Mechanist grunted. "I do not refer solely to that. This entire excursion has exceeded the recommended equipment margins that you agreed to upon taking ownership of this vessel. A penalty shall be applied once we return to the Yards."

Mordecai glowered. "Now see here—"

"It appears I misspoke," said the Mechanist, cutting him off. "A *larger* penalty shall now be applied once we return to the Yards. Do not force me to increase that number." With that, the Mechanist turned and stalked off. Natasha glanced at him and shook her head. Her meaning was clear; the Mechanist was stodgy, and not worth irritating further for the sake of pride.

Mordecai and his captain reached the bow just as the whole ship rounded the bend. The river continued more northeasterly from here, wide and flat. But it was bisected directly ahead by a sandbar. On it lay a warship.

The *H.M.S. Albatross* was a newer vessel, a steam frigate. It was long and heavy, made of dark seasoned oak. Like any sailing vessel it had three masts hosting a magnificent array of sails. But amidships were two massive paddlewheels with armored housings. Cannons poked their stubby noses out in regular intervals along the top deck and those below. She had been recently painted and was a pretty vessel indeed.

Well, almost. The Perinese warship lay beached on its port-side, a gaping hole in its belly open to the river. One mast was broken and its sails dangled from the others, their rigging torn and tangled. Shattered wood, rope, and other flotsam floated in the water at the base of the hulk, where the sandbar made a small tidal pool.

"Yes," hissed Natasha in pleasure. She flashed Mordecai a feral, wicked grin and turned back to the ship. "Everyone on deck!" she yelled. "Get the holds open, and prepare to go ashore! Konrad, bring us in to a holding pattern."

Mordecai caught her eye. "We should arm." His captain raised an eyebrow and he continued. "According to our sources, that vessel only wrecked on the rocks a week ago. There's bound to be someone left aboard, even if the tide sucked her up here past the Stormwall."

"You don't think they went back to Breachtown?"

He nodded. "Certainly they sent someone. But this is a Perinese ship. Her captain wouldn't have dared risk losing all that gold and silver; he'd be strung up, or cashiered at the very least."

Natasha nodded. "Wise." She raised her voice again down the deck and gave the order to bring blades and guns to hand.

They approached the wreck. The crew assumed their customary positions, ready to throw ropes from either side of the deck and quickly rappel down. Konrad was uncharacteristically quiet, and brought them in slow and steady. The Mechanist disappeared back to his warrens. Mordecai stood with Natasha at the bow, a hand-picked crew of five others ready to join them in descending to the treasure-ship.

A thousand feet became five hundred, then two hundred and fifty. "Close enough," said Natasha. She let out a cry and it echoed about the deck. Ropes were thrown over the side and the pirate captain went first, leather gloves letting her slide down to the sand below.

Mordecai shoved the others toward the line. As first mate it fell to him to be more calculated, more reasonable. If Perinese sailors were waiting, he needed to be able to call out warning from his higher vantage.

No one arose on the wreck of the *Albatross*. Heads didn't poke up from behind the gunwales or from beneath the forecastle. No crewmen ducked out in alarm at the noise on the beach. Natasha hit the sand followed by the others in the first wave, seeming for all the world the only ones around.

Mordecai frowned at the lack of reaction and took the bow-rope in his own gloved hands. He slid down it, shoulder aching still from the arcane attack he'd suffered during the fight with Fengel's Men. He touched the sand of the beach with a thump and drew his sword.

The crew were faltering in their charge. No one rose up to fight them off; they weren't certain how to proceed. Mordecai ran up to Natasha, walking now at the lead. His captain had quieted as well, wary and watching still for defenders or sudden ambush.

The *Albatross* merely sat there. Long shadows cast by the setting sun fell down from the rigging onto the argent river. The only noises to be heard were the raspy calls of the flying lizards in the trees, the whirr of the *Dawnhawk's* propellers, and the occasional hoot of a gibbon.

Natasha came to a stop three dozen feet from the broken hull. "Where are all the sailors?" she asked.

Mordecai glanced about. "There *should* be a few here."

"Maybe I was right."

He shook his head. "No. They wouldn't have left this all alone, and they couldn't carry all the treasure on foot, not all the way to Breachtown."

Natasha smiled. "Well then. A mystery." She turned back to her crewmen on the beach. "All right, lads! Get aboard and search it out!" She looked at Mordecai. "I never had much patience for mysteries. Let's see if Fengel's information was good."

The crew threw ropes and grapples up onto the gunwales to climb aboard. Mordecai picked four of the ablest standing nearby, and followed Natasha up to the breach in the hull. The opening was just past the sandbar, where the waters of the river formed a large tidal pool. Ropes, broken wood, and other junk floated just beneath it. Whatever rock had cracked the ship had done its job well. The breach in the hull was as wide as three men.

Mordecai gestured for two men to go ahead. They splashed down into the pool and waded over to the breach, cutlasses out and at the ready. Nothing jumped out at them, so Natasha waded over as well, then clambered up into the hole. She was silent a moment, then let loose a long low whistle. The pair of pirates beneath her began laughing and hooting.

"Get over here Mordecai," said his captain. "You're going to want to see this.

Mordecai sheathed his blade and moved across the pool, and then up into the breach to stand beside Natasha. The cargo hold was like many other seagoing vessels he'd seen. It was long and tall, extending all the way up to a hatch in the upper-deck. And it was crammed full. Crates, chests, coffers, and urns packed it from one end to the other, stern to bow and port to starboard. These had all shifted during the rough journey, and several were cracked and broken open to the fading light of day. In the shadows Mordecai spied gold bars, thick silver coins and casks of jewels.

A pirate splashed down next to them, out of breath. It was Guye Farrel. "Captain, first mate," he said. As he gasped the boil on his neck visibly throbbed. Mordecai tried in vain to ignore it. "There's no one aboard the rest of the ship. Found signs of life, though, and there are tracks leading into the jungle."

Mordecai caught Natasha's eye and jumped down out of the hold. "Show me," he said to the pirate.

Farrel led him back around to the far side of the ship. Cook-fire pits, lean-tos, and crates of salvaged goods all huddled under the masts and torn rigging. The sand was kicked all about, dark patches staining it liberally. There were no corpses, or live sailors from the *Albatross*.

Reaver Jane appeared from beneath a bit of sailcloth. She moved with only a slight limp, a gift from Fengel. That was good; she was one of Natasha's more trustworthy lieutenants. "Signs of struggle, sir," she said. "Maybe twenty people, some injured. Taken by surprise, looks like. Two days old or so, by the blood."

Mordecai frowned. "Where are the bodies? Who attacked them?" *And why would they have left the treasure?*

Jane shook her head. "Dunno, sir. Bodies are all gone, sailors or attackers alike. There's tracks leading off into the jungle." She gestured. "Don't look human, though."

The first mate raised an eyebrow. "Not human? Ogres?" That fit. He'd heard tales of a few tribes within reach of Breachtown. Such savages wouldn't have any need for the gold and silver in the hold, but plenty for the meat of the crewmen.

Jane shrugged. "Dunno, sir. Something else kind of odd." She gripped the hilt of the knife at her belt, as if nervous.

"Show me."

Jane led Mordecai up from the wreckage towards the tree line of the jungle. It rose up, thick and green and smelling strongly of plant life. Away from the wreckage of the *Albatross*, tracks could be made out. Mordecai knelt to take a closer look at them. They were strange, longer than that of a man by several inches, and not booted in any way. There were three toes, long and claw-tipped, with the heel ending in a fourth talon. Mordecai looked up at the jungle and narrowed his eyes. These didn't belong to ogres. But as far as he was concerned, the result was probably the same.

"You've heard the rumors," he said, turning back to Jane and those crew who had followed. "All manner of strange creatures inhabit this land. Looks like they got the Perinese sailors." He smiled. "But apparently, they lack a taste for gold."

He stood and looked back at the *Dawnhawk*. It floated golden in the light of the setting sun, dramatic against the backdrop of the Stormwall. Thick clouds roiled out of the unnatural barrier, some of them almost right overhead. In fact, it was growing darker all around them, and not just from the setting sun. Wispy clouds were forming overhead, split off from the fury of the perpetual storm and heading right for them.

"Jane," said Mordecai. "Get back aboard and have Konrad come in close. Get the ship anchored to this wreck and start moving the treasure aboard." He pointed at another pirate. "Kevyn, take a detachment of ten or so and keep watch on this jungle. *Don't* let anyone go in by themselves, and if you hear or see something strange, *raise the Goddess-damned alarm*. I don't plan to be taken by surprise the way those last poor bastards were. And all of you, get a move on, I don't like the look of those clouds coming in. Last thing I want to have to do is work in the rain."

The pirates all scurried off to their tasks. Guye Farrel stood, looking stupid, waiting for orders. Mordecai ignored him and returned to his captain.

The *Dawnhawk* came in closer. Lines were dropped and tied off to the rigging of the *Albatross*. Exuberant pirates swarmed over the wreck, grabbing everything of value and everything not nailed down. Mordecai worked with Natasha in the hold.

The crew aboard their airship threw down more ropes, along with wide cargo nets. Mordecai arranged a system for packing up the loot and moving it to the ship while Natasha took stock in the hold. Before long a steady stream of treasure was moving from the hold, over the tide pool, and onto the sand to be lifted up. He almost wanted to smile. They had taken some good hauls in their time, but this was ridiculous. Instead, he kept a careful eye out. Natasha's crew was well trained, but they *were* pirates. Stealing from the take was a known death sentence, but there was always someone who thought they could get away with it.

Aside from the gold and silver, there was still much worth taking. Logbooks, maps, and equipment stores abounded on the Perinese warship. Mordecai left the hold to review it, then ordered it all packed up. None were worth even a fraction of the take in the holds, but the Perinese vessel was a modern one. Everything aboard had value to someone.

The sun sank lower as they worked. Finished overseeing the sack of the officer's cabins, Mordecai returned to the hold and Natasha. There he found Guye Farrel standing near her with a wine bottle. Mordecai yelled at him and sent him scurrying off to move the crates. Natasha raised an eyebrow at him; apparently she had ordered the man to attend her. He shrugged. There were more important things to worry about. Namely, that they had not found the fabled Governor's gemstone anywhere aboard. She spoke first.

"You know," said Natasha. "I almost want to thank Fengel for stealing the *Dawnhawk*. I've never seen so much loot in my life. We've had to pull down some of the provisions and spare light-air canisters to make room for it all." She wore a silver crown, thirteen golden chain necklaces, and drank the wine Farrel had poured from a tall golden chalice they'd found amongst the treasure.

Mordecai frowned. "We'd have heard about this wreck soon enough. And it isn't as if this trip hasn't cost us."

"Yes," she replied with a snort. "Fengel's a silly bastard. But he always manages to make more trouble for me." Her visage darkened, and the knuckles of her fingers went white around her goblet. "I had to ask my father, Mordecai. I had to *ask* my *father* to take that rattletrap garbage scow of his. And he was so proud."

Mordecai rolled his eyes. *Oh, here we go.*

His captain curled a lip in irritation. She was looking past him now, somewhen distant. "He'll be upset that the *Queen* is gone, but you know what? Euron will be so damned happy it all worked out that I doubt he'll notice much. He will be able to say that I couldn't have done it without him. And in his eyes it'll be more confirmation that I'm not any *better* than he was in his heyday." Natasha fell silent, surrounded by a fortune, brooding into her goblet.

Mordecai glowered, irritated by her old complaint. "Well," he said. "That's a problem for later. As for Fengel, he's paid. The man is either drowned in the Sea or is well on his way to starvation."

Natasha frowned abruptly and looked up at him, dismay cutting through her black mood. Mordecai felt a small, petty pleasure at the sight. He knew she still cared for her husband, at least a little. Maybe this would shake her out of it. He turned away to help move another chest of gold.

The work continued as the sun set below the horizon. They didn't even have twilight to work with; the scattered rainclouds he feared dropped onto them faster than the light could fade. Fortunately, by then most of the treasure had been hoisted, or was on its way up. Konrad and the other crew aboard the *Dawnhawk* had quieted. At first they had called excited queries at those in the hold below, whooping in excitement as they brought the first loads aboard. But even the richest treasure lost its luster when compared to the monotony of moving it.

Mordecai jumped down from the breach in the *Albatross* to the pool. He walked around the laboring pirates and past the current pile being assembled in a cargo net for transport, the last one for the night. He made his way to the beach and then up the sand past the stern of the wrecked ship. Beyond, the jungle loomed, dark and impenetrable. The strange lizards had quieted and the gibbons fallen silent. Reaver Jane's picket stood, lackadaisical and unhappy at their task.

They need a thrashing, he thought. Bored guards were useless guards. But more importantly, they needed light. The thick jungle, and the heavy clouds just above them were drowning them in darkness. Much longer and they wouldn't be able to see their hands before their faces, and that would be the perfect time for an ambush.

Torches. There should be plenty aboard. Or at least lanterns. The Mechanist should be able to whip up—

Something was wrong. His instincts sang out. He had noticed something, out of the corner of his eye mayhap. Something that didn't belong...

Mordecai turned back to look down at the beach and the airship there. The crew worked busily below it, tying up the latest cargo net of treasure for their mates above to hoist to safety. The *Dawnhawk* floated at anchor three dozen feet above, lower in the air than when they'd started. Thick grey rainclouds crowned the gas-bag frame of their airship. But seen from out here, they were incomplete, thin things. More of a mist than real clouds. Through them, he glimpsed something else entirely.

Another airship.

The *Copper Queen* floated just above the *Dawnhawk*, cloaked by the unnatural clouds just beneath it. It looked terrible, black hull scorched and smoking in places, the gas-bag frame sagging on one side. Ropes and chains hung loose, frayed or broken from their moorings. It looked like it had fought a war and lost.

That wasn't the worst, however. Figures were rappelling quietly down on dropped ropes, presumably landing atop the hidden gasbag of the *Dawnhawk*. None of his lookouts atop the ship called out.

"Alarm!" he yelled at the top of his lungs. "Boarders atop the *Dawnhawk*! Get back aboard, get back aboard!"

He drew his sword and dashed back down the beach. The crew all about him stared stupidly. Natasha stuck her head out from the hold of the *Albatross*. They all looked around wildly at the sound of gunshots ringing out from the deck of the airship above them.

"Blades at hand!" cried Natasha. She stared past him at the gloom of the tree line. "Pull back to the wreck!"

Mordecai snarled in frustration. "No! Above! We're being attacked from above!"

Natasha stared at him. "What? Who? How?"

"It's your damned husband!"

Gunshots rang out from the deck of the airship above. Mordecai ignored them. He ran down to the cargo net full of treasure, tied and connected to the ship by a rope. He sheathed his sword and leapt onto the cable, climbing up toward the *Dawnhawk*.

A strange howl arose from the ship above him. Mordecai saw a flash of light back near the helm and a pirate flew off the deck of the ship, yelling in Greisheim. *Damn you, Konrad,* he thought. He had been counting on the aetherite's help once he got aboard. The rope jerked beneath him; others were climbing now and following his lead.

The deck above grew ominously silent. Figures appeared, peeking over the gunwales. Directly above, Mordecai spied the waif he'd seen on Fengel's crew. She moved out of sight, then returned with a boarding hatchet in her hands.

No. "Don't you dare," he grunted. She raised the hatchet, and he saw a flash of pearly teeth in the dark. "No, no, no, no—" The hatchet swung down.

The rope parted with a snap and suddenly, horribly, he was falling. He landed in a tangle of pirates that fell back onto the treasure on the beach, bouncing and landing and rolling painfully down to the waterline in the sand. Mordecai put his pain to the back of his mind. He pushed himself up from the sand and clambered to his feet, looking for another means of getting back to the ship.

All around him the others were falling as well. Natasha landed with a yelp as the rope she'd been climbing was cut, and the other mooring lines were falling away, the pirates upon them landing on the wreckage of the *Albatross* or splashing into the river. The *Dawnhawk* started rising.

"Get back here!" shouted Mordecai at the retreating airship. "Get back down here and face me, you cowards!"

Light bloomed up above. Lanterns on the unseen deck illuminated the ribbed gas-bag frame. A tall figure in an officer's coat leaned over the rail amidships. "Hallo the beach!" he cried.

One of Natasha's crew, Reaver Jane, took an enterprising shot with a pistol. It went wide. Two more figures leaned over the railing, each with an oil-lantern. Mordecai recognized Sarah Lome and the waif. Fengel's monocle reflected their light.

Natasha picked herself out from the pile of pirates she'd collapsed into. "You're alive!" she yelled in surprise.

"So sorry to disappoint," replied Fengel.

"Get down here!" cried Mordecai. "Get down here and fight me!"

Fengel rubbed his chin. "Now, why would I do that? I have *my* new ship back, and a hold full of treasure to boot! No, I think we'll be flying away now. Enjoy the beach." He made to turn away.

"Fight me fairly!" snarled Mordecai. He drew his blade and shook it at the airship as it lifted away. "Come back and fight me fairly, you dog!"

Fengel paused, and looked back down at the snarling pirates below him. "Now, Mordecai. What was it that you said?" The pirate captain made a show of rubbing his chin, as if he were having trouble remembering something. Then he snapped his fingers. "Ah. That's it. We're *pirates*, after all. Yes." He moved out of sight as braying, mocking laughter echoed out from the unseen deck above. The waif waved down at him and disappeared.

"Shoot them!" screamed Mordecai. "Get aboard, kill them!"

A few shots rang out. None of them hit an important mark. Natasha and her pirates ran frantically around, uncertain what to do. Mordecai raged. But it wouldn't do any good, he knew. Fengel and his Men moved out from under the *Copper Queen*, rising higher and higher as the raincloud above them disappeared.

A wind picked up, sending the *Copper Queen* drifting southward. The *Dawnhawk* flew away, with all their treasure aboard. And there was nothing he could do.

CHAPTER THIRTEEN

"AGAIN," SAID ALLEN. "Thanks for not leaving me behind."

Lina moved another barrel aside. "Mmhmm."

"I really do appreciate it.

The storeroom was dark and cluttered. Sealed casks filled it almost to the ceiling of the deck above them. They held provisions like salt pork and fresh water. Other objects were jammed in there as well: ropes, spare lumber, boxes of nails. Small spaces threaded between the piles to form a twisty, winding maze that Lina could just squeeze through. At the door behind her stood Allen, the Mechanist-in-training. He held up an oil lantern scavenged from the stocks. It threw odd shadows about the confines of the space.

Three hours had passed since the retaking of the *Dawnhawk*. It had been absurdly easy. Fueled by their anger, Fengel's Men had overpowered the skeleton crew left aboard the ship, even continuing to pull up the loot that Natasha's Reavers thought they were recovering. Once they'd been discovered, Fengel had Sarah Lome cut all the mooring lines. The airship floated up and away into the night, leaving the *Copper Queen* drifting the other way, and his foul harpy of a wife screaming epithets from the sandy beach she and most of her crew were marooned upon. In all, Lina thought they'd let her go easy.

But she couldn't argue with results. There were eight captives aboard, and Fengel and Lucian were seeing to them now. She'd scurried about with the crew, making sure they were shipshape and that there hadn't been any surprises arranged since last they'd been aboard. The Mechanist took the change in command impassively, grabbing Allen by the ear and lecturing him all the way down to the boiler room. Things had quieted, and now they hovered over the jungles of the Yulan, heading for Breachtown and its break in the Stormwall with a hold full of silver and gold. Lina had begged off as soon as she could, and now scoured the dark corners of the ship belowdecks after finding Allen out on some task for the Mechanist.

The room was of a fair size. Someone, or something could hide fairly well back here a long time before being noticed. With the recent activity in the hold she doubted that her missing pet would be there, or even on the same deck. Back here though, with pork, water, and plenty of dark crannies to hide in, she thought there was a fairly good chance of finding him. At least she hoped so. Lina wasn't particularly fond of the idea of searching the coal-stores, which was the next place on her list.

She hadn't meant to keep the thing. Especially with how badly off they'd been in the aftermath of the scryn attack. But there was just something so...innocent about the runty little creature. It reminded her of herself, in a way; both of them were small and deeply out of their element. It hadn't tried to attack her after it returned, and seemed almost affectionate. Though admittedly that might have been the drink. So she gave it a tipple to knock it out, shoved it in a bag, and took it down below to her hammock. As soon as they'd come aboard again she'd gone down to the bunks; her few meager possessions had been gone through, but the sack was still there. It was split open however and covered in blood. Human, though. Someone had obviously found the little scryn. Maybe they had even killed it. But she hoped not. *I should at least have a look around.*

Lina slipped the hip flask from her belt. Ryan had given it to her after rescuing everyone in thanks. She'd refilled it from his cask. Now she uncorked it, holding the open end out in front of her, away from her face. The pungent scent brought instant tears to her eyes.

"Pfaugh!" cried Allen. "What is that stink?"

"Pet food," said Lina absentmindedly.

"Gah. Smells like rotten apples." The young Mechanist spoke overloud, as if trying to comfort himself in the dark room. "Lina, you don't think your captain will take us through the Stormwall again, do you?" He shuddered.

"No," replied Lina. "I overheard him talking with Lucian. We're bound for Breachtown as fast as the propellers can take us. There's an opening there we can use to get out to the Atalian Sea, and then back home. *Dawnhawk's* a good ship. No need to threaten her in that mess, aye? Especially since we don't have to worry about being chased anymore. No way Natasha will get after us again, and the *Queen* is pretty much done for."

The Mechanist digested this, then he nodded. "Well ... good. But there aren't any aetherlines that run up toward Breachtown. It's going to take a few days trip, and there are still all sorts of weird, dangerous creature out here." He shuddered. "I've heard tales."

Lina ignored him. She crept between the stacked barrels, sloshing the container of Cure-all back and forth.

Something made a noise.

Lina paused. She shook the hip flask, sending a pungent vapor of liquor wafting about. "Hey, there. Hey there you runty little monster. Are you back here?"

The noise came again, from the far side of the room. There the casks met the rounded walls of the airships hull to make a small space. Lina crept up softly toward it. She made soft but obvious sounds and kept up a constant stream of low-grade baby talk.

Lina walked up to the last row of barrels and stopped. The shuffling noise echoed out from behind the barrels. A thousand thoughts raced through her mind. *This is madness. Worse, it's stupid. How do I know it won't just attack me?* The scryn had actually done that, until she'd gotten it drunk. She took a breath. Ah well. Nothing ventured, nothing gained. And the creature *really* seemed to like the Corsair's Cure-all. She turned the corner, smiling.

A pirate stared back at her.

He was only average height, but bulky. A round gut strained beneath his sweat-stained shirt, open down to the middle of his chest. His beard was thin and his hair long and wild. He stared at her like a cornered animal.

The pirate leapt at her with a snarl. Surprised, Lina yelled. She pulled instinctively back as the man rammed into the casks to her right. His outstretched hand grabbed at her shoulder and just missed, still slamming her hard enough to spin her around as she dodged. Lina fell to the wooden floor.

"What's going on?" asked Allen plaintively. "What was that noise?"

"Get help!" yelled Lina. She didn't recognize the pirate. He must have been one of Natasha's Reavers, hidden belowdecks when they'd taken the ship.

"Shut up!" snarled the pirate. "Shut yer yap, you whore!"

He leapt at her from where he'd fallen. His bulk landed on her legs, trapping her feet while he grabbed at her head. She yelled out again and blocked him.

"I'm coming, Lina!" yelled Allen. The light at the back of the room grew momentarily brighter, then stopped, shaking madly as he got caught in the first path back through the barrels. The young Mechanist cursed.

Allen would be useless in a fight. *No, you idiot. Go get help!*

The pirate was crawling on top of her, still grabbing at her face. He aimed clumsy blows at her head, but she was quick. Even though she was trapped, she ducked and weaved and bucked away from them. Lina knew she couldn't keep that up for long though.

She needed a weapon. The way he flailed, she couldn't risk grabbing for the heavy dagger at her belt, one she'd yet to return to Henry Smalls. Worse, it was trapped between her hip and the wooden decking. She realized she still held the hip flask in one hand. The contents splashed everywhere, mostly on the pirate.

Metal's metal. Lina ducked a clumsy blow and went on the offensive. She grabbed the pirate around one forearm and pulled it aside, just enough so that she could lash out at his head with her impromptu weapon. It landed with a *thunk* that jarred her arm and cut his eyebrow. She lost her grip on the flask and it fell, splashing Cure-all everywhere. The pirate screamed as the burning liquor seeped into his eyes. He scrabbled backwards, clutching at his face.

Lina moved, too. She crawled away from him, between the barrels and back toward Allen. The pirate growled behind her and she whirled, sitting up, drawing her dagger in a smooth motion and holding it before her.

Natasha's Reaver had his back to the hull, facing her. He pressed the palms of his hands to his eyes, groaning. Pulling them away, he glared blearily at her. The skin around his eyes was swollen and puffy. Blood seeped down his face in a steady stream from the cut on his eyebrow.

"You bitch," he gasped. A dark look came over his features. He sat up to kneel, growling low in his throat. Lina swallowed; before, he wanted to quiet her. Now their fight had changed.

A red light bloomed from atop the barrels above them. It shifted slowly, illuminating Lina and the pirate before her. She looked up to see the wide underbelly of a scryn.

The creature leapt. It screamed as it landed on the pirate, its manta-wings wrapping around his forehead. The man yelled and threw up his hands. It did no good. The scryn wrapped itself tight and lashed out with the sting on its tail whenever the pirate tried to grab it.

Behind her the barrels shifted. Some fell down in the paths off to the side. Warm yellow light illuminated the scene as Allen bulled through to stand above Lina.

"Lina! Oh good Goddess above!"

The enemy pirate stilled, his arms swollen from the poison of the scryn. Abruptly, the creature released him and he curled into a sobbing, bleeding ball. The serpentine creature flapped back from him to land on the deck between Lina and the pirate. It was covered in blood. The thing curled its wings around its body and sat upright.

"Chirr!" it said, happily. It flowed forward onto Lina's legs, then her chest and back. She held herself very still as it wrapped itself around her again, snuffling greedily at the hand that had held the flask.

Moving slowly, she picked the metal container up from the floor where it had fallen. The scryn perked up and she tipped the opening towards it. The scryn latched on greedily, like a baby with a bottle.

"Runt," she said quietly.

"What?" said Allen. The Brother of the Cog was almost beside himself in horror.

"I'm going to name him Runt," she said.

The pirate was still alive, amazingly. Runt calmed, drunk immediately off of the dregs of the flask and what it had sucked off of Natasha's Reaver. Lina sent Allen out to find the first crewmember he could. A few minutes later he returned with Ryan Gae.

Her friend leapt back in the doorway, fumbling at the cutlass at his side. "Lina! Get away from that!"

Lina held up her free hand. Runt was laying across her shoulders again, rumbling like a cat in contentment. "No, Ryan," she said. "This is the one from earlier, remember?" She beamed. "I'm keeping him. I named him Runt."

Ryan stared at her. His mouth pursed beneath his scruffy black beard. "Lina, you saw what happened. Those little monsters are dangerous."

Lina sighed. "Look, it's docile at the moment, and that's not why I had Allen go find you." She stepped aside so that he could see the unconscious, wounded pirate. "This fellow attacked me. I think he's one of Natasha's Reavers."

Ryan quieted immediately. "Stay right here," he said quietly. "I'm going to go get the gunnery mistress. You too, Mechanist."

Her friend drew his cutlass and shoved Allen into the small room, then left to go get more help. Sarah Lome arrived with him a few minutes later, and from the shouts up the hall it sounded like searches were being made of the remaining storerooms on this level. The huge piratess said nothing, only hoisted the Reaver over her shoulder and hauled him up to the deck. Lina followed, rubbing her pet on its sinuous neck just behind its head. The creature seemed to like the gesture, and belched contentedly now and again.

The *Dawnhawk* floated across the night sky of the Yulan. Darkness encompassed them, broken only by the pinprick lights of the stars and the few low lanterns lit on the deck of the ship. The Stormwall was somewhere to the west, the wreck of the *Albatross* hours to the south. The moon had yet to rise. It was warm here; each little breeze was more pleasant and cooling than it had been out over the sea. It smelled different, not briny, but instead carrying a rich scent of earth from the impenetrable jungle below. So many little things told them they were strangers here, tourists in this land.

Crewmen moved quietly about the ship. A few low gas-lamps had been lit in standing braziers along the centerline of the ship. Both shifts were out; having recaptured the *Dawnhawk,* any sense of urgency was lost. Those without obvious duties were belowdecks in the hold, counting the treasure from the *Albatross.*

Ryan, Sarah Lome, and two others hauled the stung Reaver up towards the captain at the bow of the ship. The three of them kept stealing looks back at her and her new pet; Gunny Lome shoved their captive forward. This might damage her standing with the crew a little, but Lina didn't particularly care. Runt was hers.

They reached the bow. Fengel stood there leaning over the gunwales and peering at something down below. Henry Smalls stood by, Fengel's faithful right hand, as always. Three stout pirates stood nearby, hands on a set of ropes tied off to a cleat down on the deck. The ropes ran over the bow. Lina heard faint yelling from that direction.

"Now, now," said Fengel in exasperation. "Don't all shout at once. What, are you a howling mob of ruffians and cut-throats? Let's start again. How much of that loot was left behind? What happened to the survivors of the *Albatross?*"

Sarah Lome dumped the pirate from below onto the deck with a thump. Fengel glanced over his shoulder at her. She threw her thick red braid back over her shoulder, then raised an eyebrow at him.

"What are you doing, Captain?"

"Just interrogating our prisoners," replied Fengel. "I was quite curious how they'd gotten through the Stormwall without trouble; apparently hugging the Silverpenny was much less problematic than our own entrance." He paused and touched his chin, looking thoughtful. "Also, I am engaging in a bit of extracurricular catharsis. But so it goes. What have you got here?" He turned to take in the moaning, shuddering pirate at their feet. "Who is this poor devil? And what in the Goddess's good name has happened to him?"

"One of Natasha's Reavers. Miss Stone surprised him down below and... took care of him."

"Took care of him how? This man looks like he's been attacked by scryn. Or an angry Haventown prostitute."

For the first time she'd known Sarah, the big gunnery mistress looked at a loss for words. "Ah, there, sir." She gestured at Lina. Arriving in the storeroom below, Sarah had only asked Lina if she had it under control, though she'd had a strange expression on her face.

Fengel looked up, noticing Lina for the first time. His eyes widened and he went for the saber at his side. "Stone! Hold still!"

Runt raised its head at the noise. "*Chirr?*" it said.

Lina held up a hand. "It's fine, Captain. Runt's safe," she lied. "Helped me with this fellow."

"That's a *scryn*, Miss Stone. Don't you remember what happened last time? Hold still so we can get it off of you."

"I *do* remember," said Lina defensively. "This one's fine. I've got it drunk on Corsair's Cure-all."

She met his gaze and held it. He owed her for the scryn attack and her quick thinking at Engmann's Maelstrom. And he knew she knew that.

Fengel appeared to come to a decision. He relaxed, moving his hand away from his saber. The look he gave her was obvious. *Fine then,* it seemed to say. *Its messes are your own though, and keep it out of trouble.* "Well," said her captain. "So long as it's *under control,*" he stressed, "that should be all right then."

He turned back to the pirate at their feet with a frown. "Henry, go tell Lucian, then take care of this fellow here. Tie him up and then see if we have any antivenin left. Gunny Lome, round up some men and search this vessel from top to bottom. Get the Mechanist and move the light-air cells in the frame around if you have to. I find I am tiring of surprises this evening."

Both rushed off to their tasks. Those that Sarah didn't take with her glanced at Runt and found reasons to be elsewhere. She hadn't been ordered away, so Lina moved up to the gunwales to peer over the edge. The ropes descended over the railing to somewhere below the bow. Several pirates were outlined by the backdrop of the jungle, the captive Reavers all tied up and suspended upside down. Some moaned, some pleaded, others cursed.

Fengel sidled slightly away from her. Lina looked up to him; he quickly glanced away from her and the serpentine creature on her shoulders.

"So," she asked hesitantly. "What have you found out?"

Captain Fengel raised an eyebrow at her. Then he shrugged. "Not much of import, really. Apparently the *Albatross* was deserted when they got there. Strange, but it could be that most of the crew decided to make their way on foot back up to Breachtown. Moreover though, we didn't get quite *all* the treasure aboard, and I want to know how much we left behind. Looks like just a few chests of coins." He gestured at the bow gunwales. "From what these fellows tell me, the Lantern wasn't in them."

Lina had peeked down in the hold. The amount of loot they'd taken was enormous. "Does that matter? We've got a ton of treasure down below. That gemstone your Sindicato friend wants has got to be in there somewhere."

Fengel snorted. "The thought of leaving my harpy of a wife anything worthwhile chaps my hide somewhat fiercely."

Lina considered that fact, and agreed that it was somewhat irksome.

"Still," she said. "We're golden. You pay off that debt, you've got a new airship, and we're all rich now." Lina smiled. "And you've left Natasha marooned in a strange jungle filled with Goddess-knows-what, with a hundred-league march back to civilization."

Her captain nodded slowly. "That's true."

"She's probably wanted in Breachtown. I mean, we *are* pirates, right?"

Fengel brightened. "True! They'd confiscate everything she has and lock her in the dungeon. I hadn't thought of that."

"Don't sell her short. If Breachtown is like Triskelion, they'll have her head off inside a week."

He frowned. "That may be going a bit too—" Fengel trailed off as Lucian came stomping up the deck to them. They turned to face the first mate.

Lucian was dirty. Grime covered his face and clothes. He was, however, wearing ten golden rings, four silver necklaces, and a pair of diamond-studded earrings. "Finished the count Captain," he said.

Fengel smiled. "And?"

"Quite a haul. We're good to pay that debt off and then some with just the lucre below."

"Capital. But I'd prefer we hand over the Lantern and keep the loot."

Lucian shook his head. "Plenty of lesser gemstones. Diamonds in particular. But nothing like the description we've heard."

Fengel stared. "Then where is it?" At Lucian's shrug he bent back over the gunwales toward their captives. "Hoy! You lot *sure* you never saw a glowing diamond, big as two fists?" The pirates below answered him in the negative. He turned back to face them. "We need that gem. Grey won't leave me alone without it, and I would *really* like to keep the rest of the treasure."

Lucian held up his hands. "It's not up here, Captain. And from what we know, it's not back there with Natasha."

Fengel clenched his fists at his side. "Then where *is* it?"

The first mate could only shake his head.

CHAPTER FOURTEEN

Fengel paced the deck. The moon was rising on the eastern horizon, just high enough now to be seen over the port-side gunwales. It spread pale illumination out over the deck, removing the need for lanterns. The rigging, gas-bag frame above, and the crewmen were all ghost-colored. Were he to look overboard, Fengel knew the jungle canopy would be visible as a silver carpet spreading out for miles in every direction.

Maxim had the helm. The aetherite growled something into his shoulder, then smiled at Fengel's approach, trying to catch his captain's eyes. It was obvious he wanted someone to talk to. Maxim was normally a solitary man, though not by choice—the constant mean-spirited pranks he played on the crew in order to retain his power were responsible. He'd once told Fengel that the daemon on his shoulder nattered constantly, and on occasion he felt the need to converse with anyone else.

Fengel didn't feel like talking at the moment. Just before he would have had to politely acknowledge the helmsman and become trapped in banal discourse, he turned on his heel to march back up the deck. At the far end of the bow, Lucian and several crewmen were pulling up their captives. Once they'd been wrung of anything useful, and then hung a little extra to teach them manners, Fengel had ordered them stowed somewhere they wouldn't cause trouble. They could be dropped off somewhere relatively safe in time.

He turned his mind back to his quandary. Lucian had not lied. After the incident with Miss Stone and her troubling new pet, his first mate had brought up the final tally from the holds, less a few small pieces that would go "missing" only to turn up as "longtime family heirlooms." Fengel let a little pilfering slide amongst the crew so long as it wasn't excessive. Even with such considerations, the treasure in the hold was ridiculous. It was estimated at some three hundred thousand sovereigns' worth of gold, silver, and precious gemstones. That would pay the two-hundred-and-forty-thousand sovereign debt to Mr. Grey and the Sindicato, with a decent amount left over to divvy up amongst the crew and to resupply the airship.

The problem was, Fengel really wanted to keep it all.

Unfortunately, he didn't think that he'd be able to. Grey wanted the Lantern, but the gemstone wasn't in the plunder that had been loaded aboard. Fengel had ordered another search and gone down himself, but nothing he could find came close to fitting the description. Also, he'd interrogated their captives again; there was the chance that Natasha and her Reavers simply hadn't found the Lantern aboard the *Albatross*. That was unlikely, however. His wife wasn't the kind of woman to miss any plunder of worth, especially considering the brass fixtures and old pots that Fengel found in the loot. There existed a small chance that she'd found the thing and hidden it. Fengel dismissed the idea almost instantly: the action was wholly out of character. Natasha was as subtle as a cannonball to the head.

Ah well. We've still come out of this mess a damn sight better than we entered it. They didn't have the Lantern for Mr. Grey, but there was no way that the financier would turn down good gold and silver toward his loans. Still. Fengel tried to force himself to be happy; his debt would be paid, he'd won out against his harpy wife, and he had his brand new skyship back beneath his feet.

But still. It wasn't *quite* perfect.

Fengel stopped his pacing and turned toward the starboard rails. He spied Miss Stone a few dozen paces away, back to the gunwales, playing with her new pet. The young woman seemed to be teaching it to sit up, the scryn making odd little leaps at the open flask in her hands. Fengel shuddered and forced himself to put her out of his mind. If she wanted to keep the little monster, then he wouldn't stop her. She'd made it plain to him that this was what she wanted for rescuing the ship in the Maelstrom. If the beast went rabid they'd kill it. If she actually trained the thing, what she did with it didn't really matter.

He gazed out at the jungle canopy. It stretched below them into the horizon, only broken here and there by the swell of hills bulging up to form lonesome and craggy cliffs. As far as he knew, he might very well be the first civilized person to set eyes on them. The initial surveyors had never made it this far into the Interior.

The thought struck him then. Below him lay a strange new world. Wondrous and ancient, and he had all the freedom to explore it at his whim.

But what he really wanted was someone to *show* it to. Someone to hold beneath the shining moon, someone he could confide in...

Fengel snorted. He pushed the thoughts aside and gazed out at the jungles of the Yulan. *Maybe I should write a journal? A memoir?* People back on the Western Continent bought up air pirate stories like mad. Why shouldn't he be involved in that? And there were the Perinese explorers' clubs. What would they pay for an account of the Stormwall and the Yulan Interior viewed from the air? *Captain Fengel,* he mused, *The Adventurer.* The title certainly made him sound more dashing. Even if there wasn't much money to be had, there would be renown. And that was just as good.

Henry Smalls approached, grey hair ghostly in the moonlight. He likely wanted to hint that Fengel should retire to the captain's cabin below. Fengel was far too interested in his own idea, however, and struck first. "Mister Smalls," he said with a smile.

The little steward paused. "Yes, sir?"

"Go give Maxim a new heading. Slightly north by northeast. Then, take a hand or two and bring up a chair, writing table, and implements. By the bow, I think."

Henry stared for a moment. Then he nodded. "Sir."

A short time later Fengel was seated by the bow railings. He held a quill in hand and stared out at the evening sky. *Let's see. There we were, deep in the stinking jungles of the Yulan Interior. My treacherous harpy of a wife...* He penned a few more lines. Reaching the end of the page, he paused to re-examine his work. It took all of two seconds to decide that they were rubbish. Fengel tried again, reordering his thoughts.

It didn't work. Time and again he tried to jot down an exciting opening line for the memoir. But upon review he found them tawdry, banal, or downright silly. The moon rose higher and Fengel decided to take a break, his hand cramped from holding the feather quill. He pushed the chair back and stood to stretch. Leaning on the gunwales, he pondered the ghostly jungle below. Weird hoots and strange cries echoed up from it. He smelled overripe citrus and odder scents on the air. The evening breeze here was pleasant, but the air itself was warm and muggy.

Something caught his eye. A light twinkled in the jungle canopy far off to the east, just below the horizon. It was probably just the moonlight on a lake, or even the headwaters of the Silverpenny River they had left behind.

Curious, he retrieved his spyglass from within his coat. Extending it, he placed the device to his eye and peered out at the light. It resolved a little, but was still too far away to ascertain. It wasn't a river or lake, of that he was certain. The color was off as well. It burned orange and yellow, not the silver of reflected moonlight.

A campfire?

Henry Smalls approached the bow. He stopped beside his captain, waiting quietly.

"Here," said Fengel. He passed the spyglass to his steward. "What do you see out there?"

Mr. Smalls took the glass deftly and peered where Fengel indicated. "Is that a...campfire?"

Fengel nodded. "That's what I'd thought. But out here? We're still at least three days out from Breachtown, and that's as the dragon flies. Natasha and crew are directly behind us now, and a goodly distance away."

Henry passed back the spyglass. "Could be another expedition. Or something else. It's not entirely empty out here, from what I've heard."

The Yulan Interior was a strange, mysterious place. But Henry wasn't wrong. Tribal savages had been discovered by the Breachtown Colony, and were regularly traded with. Rumors circulated of other things as well, tribes of ogres that lived in the deep jungle and even sightings of dragons against the horizon. Such creatures were either nigh extinct on the Western Continent or driven to the deepest, darkest places in which to hide. The Yulan, however, was virgin territory.

"Still, though," mused Fengel. "Interesting. At any rate, you have a look about you that says you've something to say. What is it?"

"The hour's late," said his steward. "You need rest, sir. We've got everything in hand here, and it looks like smooth flying ahead."

Fengel *was* tired. And his literary endeavors were going nowhere. Worse than that, he was getting unacceptably scruffy as well. His steward had a point. "Very well," he acceded.

He turned away from the rail and walked down the deck, stopping where Miss Stone sat against the starboard-side exhaust-pipe. The scryn was looped around her shoulders, chirping to itself softly. She looked up at his approach.

"Miss Stone," said Fengel.

"Sir?" Her expression was haggard. It had been a busy night.

He gestured up to the bow. "Pack my things up and bring them down below." He took a step away, then paused. "Oh," he added. "Don't read any of it, either."

They moved down to the aft hatch. Fengel nodded at Maxim and descended belowdecks, Henry following obediently behind. The musky air of the jungle was replaced by the smell of oiled wood, burning coal, and sweat. Oil lanterns mounted to the walls were lit, lighting the wooden hall below the stair in warm, golden tones. The captain's cabin was below the stern deck of the ship, as was traditional. It sat on a level with the ship's equipment stores. In an emergency both could be accessed in a minimum of time. The stairwell continued downward to the bunks, mess, and the engine room of the Mechanist.

Lucian was leaning against the wooden arch of Fengel's doorway. His first mate looked tired, and no longer wore the jewelry plundered from the treasure in their holds. He smiled though, like a cat that had just caught a mouse. A heavy, leather-bound tome was cradled in his hands.

"I know where the Lantern went," he said.

Fengel perked up. *Pay the debt and keep the treasure.* "Inside," he said, quietly, insistently. Lucian opened the door with a grin. Fengel and Henry followed him.

The captain's cabin was sumptuously spaced, yet strangely utilitarian and empty— at least now that he'd thrown most of Natasha's junk overboard. Each wall was twenty feet wide, stretching from the port-side of the ship to the starboard. Windows of reinforced glass looked out from three of the four sides, set above and between numerous cubbies and cabinets worked into the walls. A wide table was bolted down in the middle of the floor, big enough to host several people at a meal. A simple box-bed unfolded from one corner, capable of fitting two people at the least.

Knowing Natasha, Fengel had been surprised at first. He had expected thick carpets made from some rare beast's hide to cover the floor, maybe gaudy, cloth-of-gold draperies over the windows. Instead, all he'd found was her clothing and a few personal effects. Though, admittedly, there were three full liquor cabinets cleverly hidden in the cupboards.

Henry closed the door behind them. Fengel removed his hat and jacket and threw them to his steward. He moved to the main chair behind the table and sat, picking up his legs one at a time so that Henry could remove his boots.

"All right, Lucian," he said. "What have you got for me?"

The first mate held up his hands. "Well now, sir. Don't get your hopes up. Knowing what happened to it doesn't mean we can even get at it, or that we should try."

Fengel rolled his eyes. "Yes, yes. Your missed calling in theater is duly noted."

Lucian raised an eyebrow. He set the tome in his hands onto the table and then turned to one of the liquor cabinets. Fengel picked the book up.

It was a leather bound ship's log, much like a thousand others he'd seen over the years.

Lucian brought a jug of wine and three glasses to the table. He spoke as he poured. "What you hold in your hands is the log of the *H.M.S. Albatross,* penned by one Captain Everett Homme. I found it when I was completing my inventory of the holds. Your lovely wife took everything that wasn't nailed down, and, being as it wasn't gold or silver, I didn't notice it until the last."

He paused to pass filled glasses to Fengel and Henry. Then he waited expectantly. Fengel realized what was wanted and took his glass, raising it high. "Cheers to a theft well done," he said.

"Cheers," said Lucian and Henry at the same time. They all drank. "At any rate," continued the first mate, "I went through it over dinner. The tale is quite amazing, really." He gestured at his captain. "Go ahead."

Fengel put down his glass and picked the logbook back up. He opened it to the first page and read aloud:

> *Fifteenth of Marchwater. Eighth bell. Two days out of Triskelion, and the itching has started. A curse on all the poxy dockside whores in that abhorrent city.*

Fengel fell silent. Henry coughed.
"A little farther in," said Lucian. "Ten pages or so."
Fengel flipped to the aforementioned location and started again.

> *Twenty-second of Marchwater. Sixth bell. We have reached the Breachtown Colony only to discover that chaos and anarchy reign. Fires rage through the city. The cries of battle and the reports of gunfire can be heard throughout. Ships at anchor along the quay fight both pillagers and locals desperate to get away, themselves unable to pull out.*
>
> *I have ordered anchor dropped farther out in the bay, still within sight of the city. Guns are prepared and the Marine contingent is on alert. Rationing has been instituted, should we have to return across the Sea to friendly lands without resupply.*

"Hmm," said Henry. "It sounds like things were worse than we'd heard during the rebellion."

Fengel nodded. "The timing is right. This would have been two weeks ago." He bent back over the logbook and read on.

Twenty-second of Marchwater. Eighth Bell. While discussing the situation with my officers, a dinghy approached from the city. Several had done so in the hours since our arrival, manned by people desiring to escape the issues ashore. Every time so far we were able to warn them off without bloodshed, but my heart still leapt in my throat; it would only be a matter of time until we were forced to open fire.

Fortunately, this time we were not approached by refugees. A lone soldier from the local barracks had rowed out to hail us, on behalf of the Governor's Secretary, one Joshua Vrey. It seems that the Colony was in open rebellion, and this man Vrey was even now attempting to restore order. He begged our assistance and stated that he wished to meet at the Governor's House within the city.

There were too many questions that the soldier could not, or would not, answer. Where was the Governor? How had such things come to pass? After conferring internally, a decision was reached. Leaving Mr. Marley in charge, we lowered a longboat and went ashore, taking all but one contingent of Marines to form a beachhead.

Conditins were even worse up close. On our way to the Governor's House, we witnessed much chaos. The city is very much like something out of the Realms Below at this moment; fires, illness, and starvation.

The House itself was a stately building on a hill overlooking the Colony. It made an impressive sight, built with the Stormwall to the rear of its grounds and recently fortified against assault. Within, we met the haggard Mr. Vrey, and learned a most disturbing story. Apparently the Governor had taken complete and utter leave of his senses and declared the Colony independent from the Empire. Just prior he had imprisoned the Major of the local Marine contingent. The rest he captured with his own men, and shipped them all off west in a commandeered merchant cog to inform the King of his declaration. Shortly thereafter, the city descended into civil war.

Fortunately, Mr. Vrey had retained the good sense which seems to have fled the erstwhile Governor. He imprisoned the man, took control of the loyalists, and was in the process of restoring order. With the local Marines either untrustworthy or largely dead, he begged our aid, and swore to fill our holds with all manner of treasure to return to the King in reparations.

Well, we know our duty, even if these colonials are utterly confused by it. I have given my commands. Tomorrow we begin a two-pronged attack, restoring order to the streets and buildings that may be saved, and bombarding the redoubts of those scurrilous rebels that are not worth saving.

"What a charmer," said Henry Smalls.

"Duty, King, Goddess," said Fengel. "And a whole lot of misery and murder for anyone who stands in the way. Or might be in the wrong place at the wrong time. That is the Perinese Royal Navy that we all know and love."

"Ain't that the truth," said Lucian darkly.

Twenty-fourth of Marchwater. Noon. The rebellion was easily quelled and order is now restored. At the sight of the bluecoats, many rebels surrendered immediately. Their leaders are being put to trial and will be summarily executed. A few malcontent strongholds were too heavily defended to risk our loyal Marines on. I ordered them shelled from offshore. While those buildings were demolished, there was a certain amount of unfortunate collateral damage; the local hospital and a series of tenements were annihilated as well. However, the folk within were poor rabble of no consequence, and the fires were halted when they tried to spread to the nearby counting houses.

The former Governor himself has gone missing, under extremely mysterious circumstances. As the highest local authority of the Crown, I have named Joshua Vrey acting Governor. I will say this for the man, he moves quickly. Already all manner of gold and silver taken from the local ruins and savages flow into the hold of the Albatross. We will depart on the evening tide. Mr. Vrey hopes that we will be able to beat the exiled Marines back to the Kingdom, to appease His Majesty before their news can reach him. It should be a matter of no real consequence, but we will make haste anyway. Returning with such a bounty as now sits in our holds is easily worth a lordship to the man in charge of the operation, not to mention being the driving force behind quelling a colonial rebellion.

Supplemental Entry: We are now an hour under sail, catching the Stormwall wind headed directly west. A curious addition must be mentioned. Mr. Vrey arrived at the pier just before we were about to set sail. He had a manservant in tow, a plebian of the lower classes who had obviously suffered grave misfortune during the recent troubles. Acting-Governor Vrey was sweating, and seemed to be under intense distress, highly at odds with his recent satisfied attitude. The manservant held a small chest made of expensive woods, such as those used to store fine jewelry.

The Acting-Governor insisted that I take the chest and its contents as additional restitution. Our holds already loaded, I assured him that the treasure already given over would suffice. Vrey would not be appeased however, until we had taken the box. He then departed posthaste.

Within, my officers and I discovered a single, massive gemstone. It is quite unlike any I have ever seen, big as two fists and rough-cut of some luminous material. It is capable of lighting a darkened room as well as any lantern and shines brilliantly. The stone is a fortune by itself.

I wonder now at Acting-Governor Vrey's insistence. He could have easily kept the gem, with us none the wiser. Most curiously, I recall now that Vrey was very careful to never handle the box directly himself. How odd.

"So that's that," said Fengel. He paused to sip his wine. "I hope we get to the meat of the matter shortly?"

"Keep reading," said Lucian.

Fengel bent back over the tome.

Twenty-sixth of Marchwater. Eighth bell. Poor weather has assailed us since leaving the Colony. The winds have carried us south along the coast and show no sign of relenting. My officers are flummoxed, and insist on fighting the weather to continue bearing west. While we've enough coal on board to work the paddlewheels, I have had another idea. We will go with the winds until we are south of the Copper Isles' latitudinal. By then the weather should let up, and we can sail west without depleting our stores excessively. On another note, I have had Vrey's gemstone, the 'Lantern,' brought up to me. I must admit that it is a fascinating specimen, and I am quite taken by it.

Twenty-seventh of Marchwater. Second bell. Crew unhappy. Apparently a rumor has spread amongst the seamen from their time on the Colony. The Lantern is apparently somewhat infamous (unsurprising), and rumor holds that it is cursed. I will not have such superstition aboard my ship, and have ordered any man caught speaking of such matters flogged. On another note, Mr. Marley is becoming rather agitated about our course. I reminded him of his need to trust me. I do hope he is not becoming unreliable. It would be a shame for him to cut his promising career short.

Twenty-eighth. Marchwater. Lantern a fascinating piece of gemology. I do not have the tools to verify, but I rather suspect that it is singing to me. Could it be a Worked jewel? That would be something out of a storybook, almost. But not unheard of. Have decided that I shall keep it for myself. His Majesty will neither know nor care; I have stricken it from the audit, and arranged to have the common men who know of it flogged for insubordination concerning these crass rumors spreading about the ship.

Twenty-ninth. Have had abrupt discussion with Marley. Have apparently missed our bearing to turn west. Unimportant.

First of Highwing. Third bell? Fourth? Storm last night. As well as attempted mutiny. Marley led them against me. After all I'd done for him. Things were not going well, when we ran suddenly aground on some rocks just off the coast. Stormwall high above. Temporary truce. Taking command. Keeping Lantern on self at all times; they want to take it from me.

Third of Highwing. Ship has come to rest again, past the Stormwall and up the river. Had Marley and his mutineers killed after rescuing the ship. Handful left. No matter. I have had an epiphany. The Lantern does sing. It calls to me, and is on the very verge of revealing a wondrous secret. But not yet, not yet. It needs to go home. Then it may speak.

Fourth of Highwing. Crew morale low. Fires spied in the night, in the jungle beyond. Sent some scouts; they did not return. Hear drums. See eyes in the jungle. Not human.

Fifth of Highwing. They are coming. The Lantern must go home. The men struggle. It is of no import. The Keepers are here for me, for the Lantern. To bring it home. Home to their worship-fires. Home to the Tomb of the Voorn.

Their leader is before me now. He holds out his hand. I must carry the Lantern home, to Old Yrinium.

The account ended abruptly, but not, as Fengel had suspected it would, with a dramatic splash of blood or ink. He leaned back in his chair, sipping from his glass.

"Well," said Henry. "That puts paid to that. The thing is cursed. Good riddance to it."

"What a tale," said Lucian. "We're better off without it."

Fengel sighed. "I don't know. That gemstone would make us all rich. And we'd get to keep the treasure in the holds." He sighed internally. He *really* wanted to keep that treasure. And more than that, what if Natasha got her hands on the gem? It was unlikely, but possible. He had left her on the same beach that the Perinese sailors had ended up on.

The more he thought about it, the more the idea preyed upon him. He had her ship, but what if she got the gem? What if *she* was the one to bring it back to Grey? She'd be able to afford another airship at the least. She would come for him.

Lucian shook his head "No, we're definitely better off without it. Just thought you'd like to know." He stood. "Evening then, sir. I'll go make sure Lome is settled, then hit the sack myself."

Henry put away the wine bottle. Then he moved to prepare his captain's bedding for him.

"Worship fires," muttered Fengel. He sat upright as it came to him. "Lucian, give Maxim a new heading. Dead east. Watch for anything unusual. Skeleton crew: I want everyone rested and fed."

His first mate paused at the door. "Sir?"

"I saw something on the horizon to the east just before we came down here. Henry did as well. Now that I think about it, it simply *must* be one of those tribal worship fires the mad captain described." Fengel stood from his chair, removed his boots, and moved to the bed. His officers sputtered, the both of them trying to dissuade him at the same time.

"Enough!" he said with the iron voice of command. "We'll have our cake and eat it too, and make sure that Natasha won't get a slice at all. Wake me when we see something. We've got a gemstone to find."

CHAPTER FIFTEEN

MORDECAI SWUNG HIS CUTLASS AT THE THICK FOLIAGE. Four of the tightly packed nettles fell, brushing against his unprotected forearms. Pain bloomed where they touched him, his skin feeling like it had caught fire. He clenched his jaw to keep from making any sound, yet a strained grunt pushed itself from his lips.

Morning sunlight illuminated the jungle in shades of pink and blue, though it was still too low to cast any real light in the clearing through which they forged. And the clearing was anything but. Nettles grew thickly in the space, shooting up to head height from the rich earth beneath their feet. Encompassing the clearing was the jungle; dark, dangerous, and impenetrable. To their right hung the Stormwall, close enough to shake the jungle canopy with its gusts and breezes. Directly ahead to the south rose a rocky crag, jutting up from the jungle canopy maybe a league farther on. Up above it hung their prize. The ragged form of the *Copper Queen* dangled in the breeze, somehow snagged in such a way to halt its aimless drifting.

Natasha followed on his heels, widening the path with her own blade and muttering a constant low-grade stream of invective against her husband, the jungle, and the baser attributes of the Goddess herself. Mordecai heard her gasping breaths between each curse. She was getting tired, finally.

Behind them followed the crew, or what remained of it. Their march had been forced, pushing through the night in desperation after the drifting airship. They followed it across the Silverpenny River and into the jungle on the southern bank. Through thick foliage, poisonous creepers, and surprise quicksand they ran. Numerous obstacles presented themselves. Sometime around midnight, after the second aerial attack by the aggressive, venomous spiders living in the lower branches of the surrounding trees, some of the men decided to make a stand. They refused to go any further without rest. Natasha accommodated them, leaving their corpses to feed the rich earth of the jungle floor.

Fengel had won again. Somehow he had escaped the predicament they had left him and his men in, gotten back aboard the *Queen*, made it through the Stormwall, and then crept up on them, taking Natasha's Reavers utterly by surprise. But *how?*

It was an academic question. Without another airship they'd be stranded in the jungle, at the mercy of whatever had killed the crew of the *Albatross*. They'd also miss any chance of getting the treasure back. Or any chance at revenge.

Oh, yes. Especially revenge.

Mordecai let his rage burn slowly, the fuel that kept him going. After a few more minutes they reached the edge of the clearing, skin blistered and swollen from the sting of the nettles. Natasha again took the lead and he fell back to rest his arm. He followed her back into the grip of the jungle.

Darkness enclosed them again. Beneath the upper canopy it almost seemed another world. The earth at their feet was rich and dark, thick ferns growing wild. Here and there lay deadfall trees, but there was surprisingly little dead foliage. Overhead grew the banyan and baobabs, all laced together and fighting for sunlight. The air was musty and sweet, like fruit set out for too long and gone to rot. Branches swayed overhead as the pirates moved, a sign of the monkeys and lemurs that leapt from branch to branch, spying on them from high above. Mordecai kept a wary eye about. Last evening they had been attacked by poisonous snakes, jungle cats, and unnaturally large spiders.

Natasha's Reavers trudged onward. The cracks in the canopy grew brighter as the morning went on, but precious little light spilled down into the gloom they moved through. Though there were no more nettles, Natasha still hacked at any overgrown fronds or thick vines that dared to be in her way.

The ground grew steeper. Beneath them the loamy earth slanted sharply upward until they were forced to climb on hands and knees up a slope. They had reached the craggy hill. Hopefully, the *Queen* was still caught at its summit.

Mordecai stopped to rest against the trunk of a banyan, panting heavily. The incline rose even more sharply just up ahead. Rocks protruded from the hill to form a network of minor cliffs. Natasha started to ascend. Mordecai shot out an arm. "Wait," he gasped. "We need rest before we can climb that."

His captain gave him an ugly look. Her eyes were sunken and bruised from exhaustion. The skin along her jaw was swollen from the touch of some venomous plant. "Got to catch the *Queen*," she snarled. "Stay here and have a bit of a sit for yourself if you want to."

She shrugged his hand away and threw herself into the ascent. A spasm of anger coursed through Mordecai. He forced himself to calm, or at least to somewhere calmer, then followed.

The trees were shorter and thicker here, not having to grow so high for nourishment. That also meant that there was more undergrowth. Between the rocks and the branches, Mordecai needed both hands free. He sheathed his sword. All too soon he wished he'd had it back. Branches that Natasha pushed aside whipped back at him, and his fine, soft gloves were going to tatters where he grabbed at the sharp rocks. Gradually, the gloom brightened. The way became easier, and the foliage less thick. The rocks leveled out back to an incline rather than a set of cliffs. Mordecai ducked under one last low-hanging banyan limb and stepped out into daylight.

And then he stared.

The top of the hill flattened, stretching out into a broad overhang that extended above the jungle below. It was grassy and level with the canopy of the trees growing from the flanks of the hill. The *Copper Queen* was caught on the jutting outcrop of rock by some rope that dangled from its bow, the deck being only a little higher than the rocky outcrop. Past it, the Yulan Jungle stretched for hundreds of miles, brilliant and emerald green in the morning sunlight. His captain stood only a few feet ahead.

The ship looked even worse in the daylight than when he'd seen it last. The bag was sagging, the hull was scorched through in places, and the ratlines and rigging were a tangled mess. Cannons had either broken free or unmoored themselves and lay scattered about. All in all, Euron's ship was not destined to fly for very much longer, if at all.

Also, there were apes.

They were large and white furred, shorter than a man by a foot, but thick and powerfully built. Heavy tusks poked up from their lower jaws, gleaming white in the sunlight. The apes, fifty or so, crawled about the deck, hooting and gibbering.

"Well," said Natasha after a moment.

Mordecai glanced at the outcrop and the uncertain footing of the deck. In both places they'd be at a disadvantage. And while the apes would die like anything else, there were quite a lot of them. "We should wait them out," he said after a moment. "Maybe somewhere down below."

"No."

Mordecai caught her eye and held it. "We're exhausted, and I don't think these brutes will cow easily." He grimaced back at their own ragged line of crew still making their way up the hill. "Unlike our own. There's nothing we can really do at the moment."

Natasha snarled. "You're wrong, Mordecai. There is one thing we can do; we take that damned ship back."

She hefted her blade and marched across the outcrop to where the rigging had snared. *Senseless wench,* Mordecai cursed to himself. He glanced back at the crew stretched behind him. They were just as rag-tag and exhausted as he'd said. Reaver Jane looked dead on her feet, and Guye Farrel was a swollen mass of stings and bug-bites. The Wiley brothers were gasping and cursing. Everyone else either stared at him dumbly, or had taken the opportunity to sit. Mordecai hissed a command at them, voice hoarse from weariness and pain. Those closest started and shambled forward, while those sitting climbed wearily to their feet. He made sure they were all moving before stalking over to his captain himself.

He caught up with her just below the ship where the snared rigging created a convenient ladder up to the slanting bow. Hoots and grunts echoed off the ship, and a single white ape clung to the ropes before them, jumping up and down. It noticed Natasha approach and stopped. As Mordecai walked up to her, the creature bared its fangs and hissed in warning. Some of the other apes clambering about up above peeked over the bow, curious at the noise. They stared at the pirates.

Mordecai glared back at the row of inhuman faces. He kept still, but readied his grip on his blade. Glancing over at Natasha, he wasn't surprised to see that she only looked peeved. *Well, my idiot captain, now what?*

Natasha held out a hand to him. "Mordecai?" she said in bored tones. "Gun."

He looked at her incredulously. She met his stare when he didn't act immediately, then shook her open hand at him. Her request brooked no refusal. Uncertain, he drew his pistol and passed it over, barrel first. Natasha was unpredictable, vicious, and short-sighted. But surely even she wouldn't be so reckless as to fire into the beasts.

He was wrong.

Natasha gave him a disgusted look and twirled the flintlock around to grip it. The she took a smart step forward, pointed the barrel of the gun right between the eyes of the ape before them, and pulled the trigger.

Smoke erupted from the gun and the report echoed across the hilltop. The ape sagged and fell at their feet, face shattered by the weapon. For a moment everything was frozen. The pirates watched fearfully; Natasha stood with her arm outraised. The apes cringed back from the noise. Then the creatures spied the corpse of their fellow. As one they bellowed, eyes bulging. Those closest above flung themselves from the Copper Queen down at the hilltop, the others behind following suit.

The battle was joined. Mordecai and Natasha tried to hold their ground, swinging their blades and firing shot after shot from the pistols at their belts. Still, they fell back before the charge. For a moment Mordecai thought they were lost; clubbing fists and gaping jaws filled his vision. He felt a sudden, powerful loathing for his captain. Her recklessness had brought them to ruin.

Reaver Jane appeared, a long knife in each hand. She ducked past Mordecai's offhand side to jab her long knives into the face of an ape. His crew joined the fray as well, their cries barely heard over the roar of the jungle creatures.

Mordecai fought like he'd never fought before in his life. He thrust, ducked, and cut. He whirled right, hacking at a neck, slashing at a pair of eyes. Blood flew through the air. The howls of their enemy were deafening. But it wasn't enough. The beasts weighed at least half as much again as a man, and were hideously strong and savage. White-furred limbs crashed down at him, heedless of his blade and how much damage they might take. Mordecai was battered, beaten. Hoary talons tore at his side, his arms, his face. Their nightmare trek through the jungle was nothing compared to this.

Then something changed. The flow of the battle shifted, and the apes were less furious, less numerous. Mordecai sensed the chance for victory and threw himself at it, as a drowning man might grasp at a piece of driftwood just out of reach.

An ape before him reared up. It raised both arms, intending to clobber him into the ground. Mordecai ducked forward and to the side. He lashed out at the creature's inner thigh, felt his blade bite into the thick fur and muscle there. The ape screamed and hammered down as he darted away, blood spraying from a new wound. Mordecai regained his footing, then threw himself at his foe, turning now to face him. He brought his cutlass up and hacked with a two-handed blow at the face of the ape. It bit and the creature screamed.

The struggle ended. The ape before him backed away, clutching at the bleeding ruin of its face, trying to leave. Mordecai let it. Warily, he looked to the rest of the hilltop. The apes were fleeing, nursing wounds, or hooting in pain as they descending down into the tree line. Pirates stood dumbfounded, three-fourths as many as they had reached the hilltop with. The wounded and dying groaned from where they lay on the earth.

Natasha stood nearby. She was bruised and bloody, but alive. Putting one foot on the corpse of a foe, she raised her sword up high and yelled victoriously. Amazingly, the cry carried, the crew roaring after the retreating white apes.

Mordecai staggered over to her. "What," he gasped, "were you *thinking?*"

Natasha did not reply at first, or even look at him. She panted, calmed, and then wiped her blade on the fur of an ape. Only then did she look to her first mate. "I suppose I thought the noise would frighten them off. It appears I was wrong." She shrugged. "No matter."

Mordecai stared incredulously at her. "Look at us! We've just lost a quarter our number!"

Natasha raised an eye at him. "Then those that are still alive had better get aboard, unless they've grown fond of these jungles." She turned away from him and marched up to the *Copper Queen.*

Mordecai spat in frustration and turned back to the crew. The damage wasn't as bad as it seemed. Many nursed broken ribs, sprained limbs. They were battered, cut, and torn. But they would serve, and live to serve another day. Some eight of their number were dead or dying, necks broken or wounded beyond survival. Mordecai ran a tally. All in all, they were still within an acceptable number of losses.

And yet, it had been completely unnecessary. *She didn't have to fire.* They could have waited out the apes, or at least rested before the attack. Mordecai understood Natasha's hurry; should the *Queen* free its tangled rigging from the outcrop, they'd lose their only method of transport. But it had lasted throughout the day; it was likely to hold here a little longer.

He ordered the dead stripped, the dying put down, and then moved the crew onto the airship. Thankfully, they were too tired or injured to feel resentment; Mordecai himself didn't have much left in him to deal with such trifles.

The *Copper Queen* looked just as bad on the inside as it did on the out. The apes hadn't helped. Detritus, tools, and rigging were strung everywhere. Above them the gasbag frame bulged at the stern, and the whole deck slanted dangerously toward the bow.

Natasha was already waiting for them. She stood amidships, clinging to a support line anchoring the deck to the frame. "About time," she said, voice flat but pitched to carry. "Reaver Jane, you alive? Good. Take the Wiley Brothers and Farrel up above. Get the light-air cells in the frame rebalanced. Have a care, I think there's still an ape or two up there. Skinny Tom, get yerself and five others to cleaning up this mess. Toss anything we don't need and won't burn; it's just ballast. Something happened to the cannons.

They look melted, I don't know. Get rid of all but one. Keep the powder. Mordecai, get us cut free from this damned rock, and see if you can get that furnace going; we're going to need the propellers."

Their captain turned back and began the climb to the aftcastle deck. Mordecai stared at her, then looked at the others. They stared after Natasha wearily.

He had to retain order. "You heard her," he snapped. "Get moving."

Mordecai waited until the crew were busy, then rushed up the deck after his captain. He found her glaring up at the propeller system. The old propellers had long rusted away to disuse; these had been hurriedly fitted back in Haventown, and only kept going thanks to the bungling Mechanist youth they'd acquired.

"Looks like it should work still," said Natasha. "Have Tom keep anything that'll burn. Attend to it now, though, we haven't a lot of time."

"What," asked Mordecai, "is the hurry? We're aboard now, the apes are gone. The crew are going to mutiny if we keep up at this rate."

Natasha gave him a cold look. "That is what I keep *you* around for. Besides, you exaggerate. They're all so dead tired they can barely get moving. Which isn't enough, damn it. We need to hurry."

"Again, why?"

"We're going to need to swing back to the *Albatross* wreckage. There's that last bit of treasure, and those canisters of light-air gas we replaced from the *Dawnhawk*. We need the latter, and I am *not* leaving the former behind. There's also some wreckage we can burn for fuel."

Mordecai relaxed a little. That was sound. "Of course not. But we can afford to wait a Goddess-damned bit. We just lost eight crew, ten if you count last night. We've got the ship. This thing is a wreck as it is. Let's take it easy back to Haventown. We cut our losses carefully—"

Natasha broke into wild, angry laughter. Her face was manic when she finished. "Cut our losses?" she said with a smile. "Head back to Haventown? You're confused, Mordecai. We aren't going home. We're going after the *Dawnhawk*."

Mordecai started. He shook his head. "We've lost it already. He's leagues and leagues away by now."

"I don't care," said Natasha, quietly, dangerously. "He's stolen my ship twice now. He's stolen my treasure, made me a laughingstock." She took a step towards Mordecai. "I will hunt Fengel to the ends of the earth, and teach him a lesson he won't soon forget."

She held his gaze. It was terrible. Mordecai turned away first. When he looked back up he saw that she had turned her own attention away, back to the deck to shout orders down to the crew. Mordecai stared at the back of her head, rage and frustration almost overwhelming him.

He suddenly had an epiphany. It washed over him in a moment of crystal clarity. *She's going crazy. This whole mess is driving her mad.* He would have to do something about that, he realized. Soon.

And Mordecai was nothing if not a conscientious first mate.

CHAPTER SIXTEEN

LINA WAVED A CHUNK OF HARDTACK. Runt lurched up in an attempt to snag it from her.

"Beg," she said to it. "Go on. Beg for it."

Early evening sunlight filled the deck. She sat with the scryn in her favorite place, up against the port-side exhaust-pipe. Almost a full day had passed since the retaking of the *Dawnhawk*. Lina preferred not to think about that; they weren't nearly as far away from the wreck of the *Albatross* as she would have liked.

Footsteps approached where she sat. Lina looked up to see Oscar Pleasant moving past her toward the bow with a coil of rope slung over one shoulder. The two of them had been on separate watches ever since she'd dropped him over the side of the ship. They had otherwise avoided each other, but for the frantic times when all hands were needed on deck.

Oscar stopped a few feet away. He sniffed, wriggling his long, ratlike nose. His lip curled in revulsion as he peered down at her. "You're crazy," he said. "That thing is going to kill you. Or someone else."

Lina didn't bother meeting his gaze. "Captain said it was all right," she replied. Runt coiled and stretched for the hard-tack. She'd found that the scryn would eat or drink just about anything, though it still preferred hard liquor. Inspection of its mouth revealed fangs like a snake and a triple row of crushing molars all the way back where its throat began.

"Captain's crazy too," replied Oscar sullenly.

She rolled her eyes. "Nonsense. Look. I've been teaching him tricks. He's really very smart." Lina held up the chunk of ship's biscuit. "Sit!" she commanded. Runt stilled, coiling neatly at her feet. She wiggled the biscuit in the air. "Beg!" Runt lurched up as high as it comfortably could. Then Lina pointed the hardtack at Oscar, and lowered her voice. "Now, Runt. *Kill.*"

Her pet turned toward Oscar and hissed. Venomous spittle flew from its open maw to spatter across the deck. It unfolded its wings and mad red light danced across his face. The pirate screamed and backed frantically away. He tripped over an equipment locker halfway across the deck and tumbled into a pile. Other crewmembers looked up at the disturbance. A few laughed.

Lina rubbed Runt along the back of its head. "*Good* monster. Who's a good little monster?"

"*Chirr!*" replied the scryn.

Lina tossed it the biscuit. Runt caught it neatly and coiled down to devour it. Another pair of footsteps sounded an approach, and Lina looked up to where Andrea Holt and Ryan Gae stopped a few feet away. Her friends watched her pet in apprehension.

"Don't worry," Lina said with a smile. "He's safe enough. Have a seat." She gestured.

The two pirates looked at each other, then took up their customary positions to one side. Ryan, she noticed, kept his dagger-hand free.

"What are you getting up to over here?" asked Andrea.

"Waiting," she said. "Shift's on soon."

"We didn't see you down in the mess."

"I ate up here. People were uncomfortable when I came in."

"Now there's an understatement," said Ryan darkly.

Lina shrugged. "They'll get used to it in time. Runt's harmless." She paused. "At least, I think."

Andrea rubbed her forehead. "Your new pet is awful, yes, but that's not what's got everyone upset."

Lina looked up at her friend. "Oh?"

"It's this...detour."

"Oh, that. Yeah, I wanted to see Breachtown, too. I've only ever heard of it. And I wish we'd get farther away from Natasha's Reavers. What if they catch up to us again? Still, we've plenty of coal."

"Lina," said Ryan as he rubbed his forehead. "That's all part of it. But you really mean to tell me you haven't heard of the Lantern? That's why Captain changed course. He thinks these weird fires will lead us to where it is."

"Oh, is that it?" She leaned back against the pipe. It was warm. "Seems a lot of work when we've already got the treasure down below."

"Aren't you worried about the curse?" asked Andrea.

Lina looked over at her friend. She saw the worry there, and it dawned on her what the problem was. "Wait. You're telling me that everyone's worried about a curse?" Lina shook her head. "There's no such thing."

"Of course there is," said Ryan. "This one time I saw Maxim—"

"*Magic*, sure, of course. But a curse? I'm more worried about that bitch wife of the Captain's."

"Anyway," said Andrea. "You're right, curse or no, it's a little silly to linger here when we've got a hold full of loot. And the fires are probably just locals. Ogres or savages or some such. There are all sorts of weird creatures out here, from what I hear." She shook her finger. "Mark my words. Following them is a terrible idea."

"Well," said Lina. "The treasure will probably all go toward his debt before anything. Or, a big chunk of it. That's probably why he wants that gemstone so badly." She paused. "He must think the locals took the gem from the *Albatross*. Though I can't imagine how the Captain would figure that out."

Andrea and Ryan looked at each other. "What debt?" they asked simultaneously.

"Fire four degrees off the starboard bow. And a city!"

A lookout atop the gas-bag had climbed down to yell from the ratlines. He pointed up ahead. Lina looked to the others and stood. The fires were mysterious, but nothing special. They'd been following them for most of a day now. But a city?

She grabbed Runt by its coils and slung it over her shoulder like a rope. The scryn chirped in indignation. Lina waited a moment for her friends and then made her way up to the bow. A mob had formed out of other crew just as curious as she. Lina pushed her way through them using Runt to surprise and dismay the bigger crewmates.

The jungle stretched out below them, a carpet of broad leaves and reaching branches that occluded any vision of the forest floor. Only the little dips and rises in the canopy hinted at differences in the terrain, hidden ravines or covered hills. Distantly she spied a thin column of smoke, maybe half an hour away at their current rate.

Lina knew what to expect. When they'd reached that first fire the night before, the captain had ordered a team down. Lina hadn't gone along, but from the deck of the airship she could see the site. It was empty, whoever had lit the fire long since gone, leaving not even tracks into the forest. Every fire since had resulted in the same, and she didn't expect this one to be any different.

There was something else, though. Past the fire and a little to its left stood a pyramid. It wasn't large. The structure just barely broke the canopy. Thick vines and foliage covered it. But in the light of the setting sun, the pale, golden stone and the cut of its stair-step shape was obvious.

Captain Fengel pushed his way through to the bow. Henry Smalls, Sarah Lome, and Lucian Thorne followed. The first mate glanced down at Lina and then jerked away with a curse. The captain produced a spyglass and extended it. He raised it up to peer at the jungle below for a long while before saying anything.

"Another fire, all right. And what looks like a ruined pyramid. More than that, there are other structures past it on the horizon. Lower to the ground. They're either smaller, or built lower than the surrounding landscape. Beneath a cliff, perhaps."

Fengel lowered the glass and tapped it against the bow rail. Lucian leaned over to get his attention. "Sir," he said. "This is obviously a trap. Whoever's lighting those fires is leading us straight to this place. We're not going to find anything at all worthwhile at that fire."

"Of course we're not," said Fengel with a smile. "But, unless I miss my guess, that's where the Lantern is." He turned back to the ship and the crew. "All hands to stations. Prepare for a fight. Miss Lome, prepare a shore party, myself included. Aah!"

Captain Fengel jerked back upon noticing Lina. And her pet. Runt uncurled and rose up to peer drunkenly at the pirate captain. "Chirr?" it asked, wavering a little.

Fengel regained his composure and glared at the scryn. "Miss Stone. I think that you shall accompany us too. Perhaps that creature of yours might be of help in an ambush."

He moved brusquely past. Lina's heart sank in her chest. Runt was not popular with the crew, and Captain Fengel had behaved oddly toward her since letting her keep it.

All hands meant everyone. Lina rolled Runt over her shoulders and took up her station beside the starboard rail. The crew bustled to find their own places. Equipment and arms lockers were thrown open. Muskets and pistols were passed to the best shots. Lina didn't get one, but that was just as well; she had only the barest idea of how to fire a gun.

Then came the waiting. The *Dawnhawk* floated through the air, quiet but for the creak of the ship and the whir of its propellers. The crew was watchful at first, taut with expectation. As minutes passed their tension faded. Hissed queries and suppositions went up and down the deck, quiet conversations about what they'd find, who built the ruins, and how they'd react to the pirates' presence. Lina joined in a little, but mostly kept a wary eye to the jungle down below, especially when the first mate stalked past her up the deck. He checked the stanchions and boarding-ropes, then ordered the idle chatter quiet. Lucian seemed on edge lately, frustrated about something. Lina kept her peace.

The smoke plume grew closer, a white, streaming beacon spiraling up through the canopy of the jungle. With each passing minute it thickened until, finally, they were almost over it. The airship slowed to a halt as terse orders rang out to the crew. Sarah Lome moved up the deck toward the bow. She paused by Lina and gestured for her to follow. Lina stood and followed obediently to where Captain Fengel, Henry Smalls, and several others waited.

This wasn't the first time they'd investigated one of the fires. The officers conferred and apparently saw nothing immediately alarming. Lina watched as Sarah hefted a sky-anchor and threw it down to catch the canopy below. Maxim came forward, along with Lucian. The aetherite was going ashore as well, though Lucian, as first mate, would likely stay behind, watching and ready to get them all aloft again in a hurry.

Andrea Holt tossed a coiled rope ladder over the rail. Fengel clambered immediately overboard. The others followed suit and shortly it was Lina's turn to go.

She glanced over the rail to the ground below. They were close enough to the smoke column that errant winds wafted the plume to brush against the ship. It smelled of burning wood and pungent sap. Its origin was a small clearing with a fire pit built in the center. It was otherwise unoccupied.

Lina checked the knives at her belt and gripped the ladder. She clambered over the gunwales and tried to ignore how it swung as she began her descent. Instead, she focused on the east, past the clearing and the nearby pyramid. Like the captain had said, there were other ruins. From her vantage they seemed to poke up from a space on the horizon several miles away, where the canopy disappeared down a ravine or past a cliff face.

The ruins were of the same stepped-pyramid design as the one nearby. They were wider, though, and unless the jungle played some trick, much, much larger. There was something about them, the way they were built, that plucked at the back of her brain. Lina felt as if she knew something, some distant memory, and it just wasn't coming to thought.

She descended down past the canopy of the jungle. The space darkened almost instantly, lit only by the flickering flames of a burning bonfire. Lina reached the bottom of the ladder where it hung a few feet off the ground.

She dropped, moved aside, and turned to survey the area with her dagger at hand.

The clearing was not wide. Maybe three dozen feet across, most of it was dominated by the fire pit and the stacked bonfire that burned within it. Unlike the others they'd come across, this one was still live. The sky-pirates spread out, weapons drawn.

"Fire's still burning, Captain," said Sarah Lome.

"Your perception is keen as always," said Fengel. Their captain hefted his sword and gazed about the space. "No one here, but I do not think that they have gone too far this time. Keep a wary eye about for the locals. I still suspect a trap."

Runt rolled around Lina's shoulder, curious. She was suddenly, acutely aware of just how far she was from anywhere civilized, and how vulnerable they were in the small space of the clearing. The wood smoke of the fire covered the jungle smells she'd grown used to, and in the fading light she couldn't see more than a foot or two. Something howled, far off in the distance. Aside from the fire pit, there was nothing to indicate anyone had been here. No food, tools, or even a cleared space for a tent or suchlike. *Lucian was right. This is a trap.*

Something caught her eye near the edge of the clearing. It was a mark, pressed into the loamy earth. Lina crept forward and examined it.

"Captain," she called. "I've found something."

The others quickly joined her.

"That looks like a footprint," said Henry Smalls.

It did. Though not like any that Lina had ever seen. It was smaller than that of a man and had only three long toes, almost like that of a bird, or a lizard. There were divots in the soil at the tip of each toe, as if they were clawed as well.

"Gunny Lome," said Captain Fengel. "It may be wise to get everyone back aboard the ship."

"Too late, sir," said the gunnery mistress.

Something in her voice raised the hairs on the back of Lina's neck. She whirled along with the other pirates to see the huge woman hefting her cutlass towards the opposite end of the clearing.

They were no longer alone.

A figure stood there, man-shaped but inhuman, just within the far edge of the clearing. It was shorter than a man, thin and wiry. Fine green scales covered it from the tip of its sinuous tail up to the lizard-like maw of its face. Lighter-colored scales covered the skin around its eyes, almost like a mask. Its hands had only three long fingers with a thumb, but long talons grew in place of fingernails. Its legs were backward-canted below the knee, and terminated in the long-toed feet that likely made the footprint she had found. The creature wore a loincloth, and a golden torque around its neck. It carried a simple wooden spear in one hand, tipped by sharpened crystal.

"Blades up, lads," cried Fengel. "Miss Stone, you're up the ladder first, everyone else cover the retreat!"

The lizard-creature held up a hand. Then it spoke. "Stay your blades, manlings," it said, voice raspy and unused to the cadence of human tongues. "I have been waiting for you." It took a step forward, lowering its spear in a non-threatening posture. "I have a great need, and only you may save my people from destruction."

Lina blinked.

Fengel stared at the reptilian creature. Too late he remembered his composure. Fortunately, the rest of the crew were surprised as well. *Never let them see you stumble.*

"Capital," he said, forcing his voice to calm. The lizard-creature appeared to be alone. Gambling with an assurance he didn't feel, Fengel sheathed his sword in one smooth motion. Thankfully, the monster didn't scream and charge. It didn't snarl and throw its spear. Instead it crossed its arms over its chest and bowed down low at the waist.

"Rastalak," it said. "Of the Mauvengy Tribe." The creature's voice was sibilant, hissing as it spoke.

He nodded to it. "Captain Fengel, of the good ship *Dawnhawk*," he replied. Fengel gestured around at his crew. "These are my Men. Their names aren't important right now."

The others glanced over at him. Henry Smalls raised an eyebrow. Fengel ignored them, concentrating instead on their strange visitor. It watched them in silence. The awkward moment stretched out to a minute and then on to two. Beside them the fire crackled and burned. Something hooted in the depths of the jungle.

"Well, then," continued Fengel. "I assume that you're behind these signal fires we've been following? What is your purpose? Who are you, and what are you on about?"

Rastalak nodded slowly. "It was I who lit these prayer fires. It was I who spied your sky-barge to the west and hoped to lure you closer." Rastalak planted the butt of its spear in the ground and leaned on it. "My people are the Draykin. My tribe, the Mauvengy, are in danger. I think that only your kind can help them." It shook its head sorrowfully. "Again are we under the accursed thrall of Burning Eye. I had thought it gone forever, but the stone has returned itself. I beg of you to take it away once more."

Fengel paused. *I have no idea what the little monster is talking about.*

The crew muttered amongst themselves. Maxim took a step forward. "What's this 'Burning Eye?'" he asked.

Rastalak knelt. It placed its spear aside and scratched at the ground with a long talon. A rough oval took shape, cross-hatched like a faceted egg. Or a cut gemstone. "Like this," said Rastalak. It then held both hands together, closed into fists. "And so."

"The Governor's Lantern!" exclaimed Fengel.

His heart was leaping in his chest. This was better than he could have hoped. He'd just known, *known*, that following the fires would lead him to the Lantern. Fengel took a calming breath and forcibly regained his composure. "Excuse me. But let me see if I understand you aright. You have the gemstone, this 'Burning Eye,' and you want us to take it away?"

The little Draykin nodded. Fengel felt a stupid grin crawl its way onto his face. He covered it with a cough into his fist. "Well," he said. "It's been a little out of our way, but I think we can accommodate you."

Rastalak pulled back the skin of its jaw in a strange smile and nodded furiously. It stood, grabbing up its spear. "This is most good," it said. "Come. The way will be difficult, and my people most hostile. But if we move quickly, and quietly, we will succeed."

The Draykin turned back to the jungle. Fengel blinked in confusion. He raised a hand to stop it.

"Sir," said Henry Smalls. "I don't think he has it on him."

Fengel scowled at his steward. "Hold on there," he said to Rastalak, waving his hands at the creature. "Hold on. I may have been hasty. Where *is* the Lantern at? And what did you mean by your people being 'most hostile?'"

The lizard-creature glanced back. It waved a claw at the eastward jungle. "The Burning Eye is ensconced again in its place, within the greatest temple-manse of Old Yrinium. The way is not far. But my people would resist its removal with claw and spear. They are under its sway, and the power of the Burning Eye is a fell one. We must be cunning, and quick. We sneak in, steal the Burning Eye, and you fly off never to return, yes?"

Rastalak eyed Fengel speculatively. Fengel knew a sales pitch when he heard one, even if it came from an upright lizard. Still. He'd *known* that the Lantern was close. And now it was; the solution to so many of his problems. *And then I'll have truly beaten Natasha.*

"How many people are your tribe?" he asked.

Rastalak shrugged, shook his head. "Not many."

"How many is many?" asked Maxim.

"Not so much," said Rastalak. "Few hundred."

The pirates all clamored dissent. Rastalak held out his talons. "Please to be quieting! Some of them might hear you."

That got their attention. "Wait," said Henry Smalls. "There are more of your hostile tribe nearby?

Rastalak gave them a flat look. "Your wondrous sky-barge is to be seen many, many, many leagues distant on clear day. Signal fires are also to be seen. Most of the Mauvengy are back in Yrinium, celebrating the return of the Burning Eye with new sacrifices. But hunters and scouts remain in the jungle. Fires could be worship fires, as lit on the path of the Burning Eye during its return from the wrecked water-barge. The sky-barge? Not so much. We must be going, and going quickly."

Maxim turned to Fengel. "This is madness, Captain. Let's get back aboard and get clear. I don't know what these Draykin are, but they don't sound friendly. And do we really need that gemstone?"

Fengel considered, tapping his chin. "Right you are. The locals don't sound very friendly at all. And here I am, going to do them a service, even." He turned back to Lina Stone. The young woman stood with her awful pet a short distance away watching the proceedings. "Miss Stone. Get back up aboard. Bring a message to Lucian."

She blinked at him. "Captain?"

"Mister Smalls, Gunny Lome, Oscar Pleasant, Geoffrey Lords, and Maxim are all with me and this Rastalak. We'll make our way over to the city on foot during the dark of this evening. A small group is less conspicuous. Tell Lucian to get aloft and drift on over to the city, this Yrinium. Do it as quickly as you can, then hold position. Be showy about it. I want all these Draykin busy watching you, and not us. Once we've got the Lantern in hand, we'll return here and light a fire. Then just swing back and pick us up." He rubbed his hands together. "We've plenty of coal still in our stores. It's a perfect plan. Utterly foolproof."

Henry Smalls stared at him in dismay. "Sir, you can't mean to do this. That gem is cursed, and held by a bunch of angry, violent savages. We've already got a hold full of treasure, and the *Dawnhawk*. Why are we even considering this?"

"There's no such thing as curses," said Fengel. "And this order is not open to debate. I mean to have that gem. Miss Stone, get back aloft. We should have the stone by noontime tomorrow."

The steward stared at him. Then he shook his head.

"Captain," said Lina. "Why can't I go? Me and Runt—"

Fengel held up a hand. He was fond of Miss Stone and she had proven useful in a pinch. But this was going to be truly dangerous work. That, and her new pet revolted him. "I've no room in the party. And docile though that thing may be, we cannot risk it. Better it be left aboard, and as it is your responsibility to look after it, you must stay aloft too." He turned back to Rastalak without meeting her eyes. "Now. You say that time is of the essence? Let us move on."

The Draykin nodded. It turned to the press of greenery and disappeared. Fengel gave one final nod to his steward and moved to follow. Out of the corner of his eye, he saw Miss Stone. She glared at him, then muttered under her breath and started the long climb back up to the *Dawnhawk*. It was for the best, really.

The ferns warding the jungle were a green wall into darkness. Fengel took a breath and pressed through. They brushed his face and caught at his jacket for a moment before giving way to a space where the last vestiges of twilight disappeared entirely. Thick underbrush fought with low-hanging creepers for space, and the wide trunks of trees stood like silent sentinels, their columns supporting the green canopy high above.

Rastalak moved like a ghost ahead of him. Its small form and scaly hide was perfect camouflage. It walked at a good speed, neither talking nor looking back at the pirates. Fengel chased after it while his crewmen followed, almost blindly. Sometimes he lost it entirely in the gloom. He would then all but run into it, waiting patiently for the humans behind to catch up.

Fengel didn't entirely trust the creature. It had lured him to their meeting via trickery and subterfuge, and with its reptilian mannerisms, he found he couldn't read the thing like he could a normal man. It was an iconoclast, though, if not an outright criminal, apparently going against the wishes of its tribe. Still, it knew where the Lantern was, and more so, wanted his help in stealing it away. Fengel was happy to oblige.

The Governor's Lantern had preyed much on his mind of late. All the night before he had dreamed of it. Today he'd had Lucian recount all that he'd heard of its initial appearance, and had then spent most of the afternoon shut in his room with the logbook. Fengel could almost see it in his mind's eye; larger than an apple, egg-shaped, milky light shining from its facets. *Maybe I could sell all the treasure, and just keep the gem?*

He tripped on a fallen log and almost went sprawling. Fengel regained his balance with a curse, made sure his hat was on properly, then called out to their guide. "I say. It's getting to the point I can barely see my hand in front of my face. Haven't you a torch we can light?" *Maybe we should go back and gather lanterns?*

Their Draykin guide paused only half a moment. "No. Too easily seen." It half-turned back to face him. "Can you not move more quietly? Your noise is great."

Before he could reply it turned back and moved onward. Fengel glared at the little creature until someone behind him stumbled. Looking back, he spied Henry Smalls cursing in the dirt.

Fengel offered a hand and hoisted his steward to his feet. "Thanks, Captain," said the little man. As he brushed himself clean of the dirt, Fengel made to turn back for their guide. Henry grabbed his elbow. "Captain?"

Fengel looked back. "Yes, Mister Smalls?"

The gloom of the nighttime jungle made it difficult, but he saw the concern on Henry's face. "Are you feeling all right, sir?"

Fengel frowned at the other man. *What an odd question.* "Pardon? I'm feeling perfectly fine, Mister Smalls. Why do you ask?"

Henry shrugged, uneasy. "Well sir, you have to admit this is a little odd. Do we really need that gemstone so badly?"

Fengel stiffened. "I have made my orders clear, Mister Smalls. You may either help carry them out, or return to the *Dawnhawk*."

The little man sighed. "Yes, sir. Never mind, sir." He peered into the gloom ahead. "But...do you trust this creature?"

Fengel followed his gaze. "I have never heard of its kind before, these Draykin. But we all know the rumors; strange things populate this land. To answer your question, Mister Smalls: as much as I need to. It speaks Perinese, and wants to help us steal the Lantern. That is enough for now."

Sarah Lome tripped on the log and let out a curse. Henry turned back to help her up. Fengel moved on ahead to catch up with Rastalak. Their odd guide waited impatiently ahead. Without a word it led them deeper into the jungle.

Night reigned. The space beneath the canopy lightened a little as the moon came out, silver shafts of needle-thin luminescence descending to the loamy forest floor. What had seemed a strange and alien world changed yet again. The plant life seemed to writhe with their passing. Hanging vines were mistaken for snakes, and hanging snakes for vines. Insects chirped a singsong rhythm, falling quiet as the pirates passed them. A big cat growled, eyes flashing gold in the undergrowth for only half a moment before it slunk away.

Rastalak led them onward. The creature would move quickly through the jungle, pausing to wait impatiently as Fengel and his Men caught up.

Other times Fengel would stumble over the Draykin, stopped somewhere ahead, squatting on its haunches and listening quietly to their surroundings.

That was how he found it now. Fengel pushed aside the last of the fronds between them and halted, panting. The air down here was thick and muggy, deeply contrasting with the cool breezes blowing above the jungle.

"What are you listening to now?" he asked.

The Draykin held up a hand for quiet. It cocked its head, as if straining to catch a sound. Fengel quieted, listening as well. The only noises he heard were his crew, swearing and stomping through the jungle after him.

"What?" he asked. "What do you hear this time?"

"Please to be quiet," said Rastalak. It listened a moment longer, then shook its head. "Nothing. Thought I heard something. But no, nothing." It straightened. "Please ask your men to be speaking little."

Fengel frowned. "I don't understand. Do you think we've been noticed?"

"No," said Rastalak after a moment. "But we have come to a sacred place."

It pressed into the greenery. Fengel frowned and hissed a call for quiet behind him. Then he pushed after their guide.

To his surprise the ferns parted to reveal a wide, rectangular space. The canopy above opened to a starry sky and a gibbous moon rising in the west. Moonlight shone down on old ruins, the remnants of a squat, pyramidal building dominating the clearing. Its peak had long ago fallen in, and most of the walls along with it. What was left were four partial walls slanted toward the open center, a stretch of flat earth both bereft of foliage and weirdly smooth.

"Follow," hissed Rastalak.

Their Draykin guide avoided entering the ruins, turning to the left to follow the exterior wall. Regretfully, Fengel did as instructed. Though the clear floor of the ruin was free of jungle, the exterior was not. The ferns brushed him, the ground was full of unstable roots, and bugs fell to crawl in his hair or along his jacket. Low-hanging vines constantly plucked at his hat. In all, it was annoying.

Rastalak turned to follow the wall up its western side. Fengel did as well, almost tripping over an especially thick root that seemed to grab at his boots. He cursed under his breath and fought for his balance before moving on. Grumbles and startled yelps echoed up from behind as the others met it.

Fengel thought to turn back, say something to bolster their morale, but stopped. A noise had sounded out in the jungle to their left, out beyond the immediate border. It was unclear— he noticed it only because of how out of place it was.

"Confound this!"

He whirled back to his crew. Henry Smalls stood behind him, sweating and exhausted. Past him stood Gunny Lome. Past her lay Oscar Pleasant, face-down on the earth, having been tripped by the root.

"Enough of this traipsing," growled Oscar. "We want to cross to the other side right? Well then, we're just wasting energy by going around!" He climbed to his feet and clambered over the wall.

Fengel didn't like Oscar. The man was boorish, crude, and perpetually disheveled. There was something almost... ratlike about him. Still, he was a member of the crew, and had been almost since the beginning. "Mister Pleasant. Get back in line this—"

Oscar took three steps into the open ruin. He glanced back at the tone in Fengel's voice, then sank. The smooth ground beneath his feet turned liquid as the pirate fell *into* it, splashing murky water all about. Oscar yelled out in surprise.

Fengel cursed. He called a halt behind them. Then he moved up to the wall and put his hands on it. "Quit thrashing around, you fool," he hissed. "It's quicksand." Breachtown tales abounded about this sort of threat; Fengel was mildly interested. He had never expected to see it in real life.

"But I'm *sinking*," wailed Oscar.

"Yes," replied Fengel, "that's the point. Now hold still while I figure this out."

His crewman stilled, panic written across his face. He had sunk to his waist and as Fengel watched, slipped an inch in the course of a minute. The problem wasn't unsolvable, however. His pirate was only a few feet past the crumbled wall.

Fengel directed Lome and Henry Smalls to cut free a long vine to use as a rope, and then ordered him pulled out. They bent to the task while Fengel stood back to watch. Rastalak appeared beside him from out of the jungle. Only long practice kept Fengel from starting in surprise.

"This noise gives us away," hissed their guide.

"Yes," admitted Fengel curtly. "Oscar is an idiot." He was vexed. The actions of a crew reflected upon the captain. "But frankly, it's surprising that something like this hasn't happened before now. We are not exactly locals."

"I have been keeping us out of most trouble," said Rastalak.

"Hmm."

They watched the rescue process. Lome found what looked like a suitable vine, only for it to rear up and reveal itself as a long snake. Calmly, Sarah broke its neck, shrugged, and then tossed the other end over the wall at Pleasant. The trapped pirate screamed.

Rastalak sighed beside Fengel. Fengel winced. He turned to the Draykin. "So," he said casually. "I have been wondering. How did you come to lose the Lantern originally?"

The guide was quiet a moment. "Your kind exist in these lands. Your tribes war and trade with the Draykin, each to their own. I have wandered far from Yrinium, to escape the effects of the Burning Eye, and to seek a solution. It was not long ago that I came across other men, from a tribe much different, a tribe such as yours.

"I followed them for a time, learning this tongue. They were travelers, scouts. Their chief was a man called Silas of the Thorn, and they were strangers to all in this land. They sought treasures, to return them to their tribe beyond the Curtain of Winds. I was gladdened; they were perfect. I approached Silas of the Thorn. After some...misgivings...we came to an agreement. In the dead of night we crept into the great temple-manse of Yrinium, and stole out with the gem. Silas of the Thorn fled back to where he had come, and I thought that the end of it."

Rastalak covered his face with one hand. "Woe! The curse of the Great Masters has proven strong, however. The Burning Eye has corrupted those hands I trusted, bringing itself back to blight my people."

The Draykin guide quieted. Fengel frowned. A kernel of discouragement had taken root as Rastalak spoke. Fengel shook his head, clearing it. *Silas Thorn stole in and took it away without a hitch. No reason why we can't do the same.* And then he'd have it, and Natasha wouldn't. Though these Draykin would likely be more alert this time. He shrugged away the concern.

His crew recovered their companion. Fengel forbore from a withering chastisement. They were short on time and his disapproving stare should have to prove sufficient for now. With Rastalak leading the way again, they were back into the jungle, a seemingly endless expanse of thick foliage, biting insects, and creeping vines.

The moon rose high, and then sank low again. They encountered several more ruins along the way. Rastalak steered them around each time. Now properly warned, Fengel and his crew encountered no further issues. The Draykin treated each ruin oddly. It requested quiet as they passed, be they monolith, ruins, or simple statue. Fengel thought at first it was simple prudence, avoiding detection by the others of his tribe who would be presumably angered at their approach. It occurred to him that the cause might be something different, however; Rastalak hissed in displeasure when they would touch the stones, even just by accident.

It was obvious to Fengel that the ruins were not built by Rastalak's people. The Draykin was short, but there was something else. The dimensions were too strange, the archways too tall, the stairs too deep. Bas-relief decorations could be half made out, and though weathered and shrouded by the dark, the beings they depicted were unlike any other people he had ever seen or heard of. For all its obvious inhumanity, Rastalak was closer to man that whatever odd race were responsible for the construction of these monuments. He wondered what their relation was, these builders and the Draykin.

The answer came quite unexpectedly.

During their travel the sky had darkened to blackest night; now it lightened again into the rosy glow of pre-dawn. As they walked the jungle became lighter and more sparse, both easier to see and traverse. Though they'd walked all night, Fengel was filled with a kind of restless energy. The gem, the Lantern, was nearby. Soon it would be his.

The underbrush thinned. Fengel moved across flat, warm ground after their guide, his trousers soaked by sweat and condensation. Up ahead Rastalak stopped at a thick banyan tree, beyond which Fengel didn't see any others, or any other growth, for that matter.

Fengel caught up to their guide. He climbed up on a high root beside the Draykin. "What is it?" he asked. "Why have we stopped?"

Rastalak was staring out past the tree. Fengel followed his gaze and his jaw dropped.

There were no trees and no undergrowth, because there was nowhere for it to grow. The earth abruptly gave way to a cliff wall that dropped down three hundred feet to a valley floor. The valley was a mile wide and roughly two miles long, encompassed on all sides by sheer stony cliffs.

The valley was not empty. Stair-stepped pyramids, low, wide houses, and towers constructed in strange unreal whorls filled the space, separated by broad thoroughfares of paving stones. The tips of the tallest buildings towered hundreds of feet above the ground, just below the lip of the chasm, higher than any building Fengel had ever seen, even those back in the old cities of the Western Continent. The stonework of each structure was a soft gold in color, shot through here and there with silvery lines that seemed to almost shine. Flying lizards and the eel-like scryn swooped from niches in the upper structures to fight, hunt, and play.

It was the city they'd seen the evening before from the *Dawnhawk*. Fengel felt a moment's incredulity. They'd walked all night but barely covered a few miles.

"Behold," said Rastalak with reverence. "Yrinium. Ancient seat of the Great Masters."

"The Voorn," said Fengel in realization. "These are Voornish ruins. That's who made all this." Artifacts and ruins from the old race were found occasionally back on Edrus, bits and pieces of the civilization that had come before those of man. But nothing like the city down below. He was possibly the first living man to gaze upon this place. *I wish Natasha could see this.* Immediately, he quashed the errant thought.

"Voornehai," nodded Rastalak. "The Great—"

Their guide broke off. It twisted its head suddenly, as if hearing a sound. It looked back the way they'd came and hissed. Fengel turned, hand automatically to his saber. The rest of the crew were crawling along, obviously exhausted. Henry Smalls led their way toward him, Gunny Lome at the rear. Fengel spied something past her, hiding in the bushes only a dozen paces at her back. A face, reptilian and long-muzzled. Just like Rastalak.

Their Draykin guide hissed something in its own tongue. Fengel didn't understand, but the meaning was clear. "Alarm!" he cried. "Sarah, at your back!"

Gunny Lome was a warrior born. She whirled, drawing her cutlass as she did so. The hiding Draykin leapt from the bushes, a spear upraised and ready to throw. Sarah took in the threat and squared herself, ready to dive aside.

A spear flew through the air. It caught Henry Smalls in the back and he went down, eyes wide, still trying to understand the danger. Fengel shouted in denial and drew his blade.

Draykin appeared, seeming to rise out of the very earth itself. There were dozens of the short reptiles. They hissed and screamed, and then the battle was on.

CHAPTER EIGHTEEN

I REALLY HATE THIS SHIP.

The *Copper Queen* lumbered through the air like a pregnant cow. It swayed, not always with the movement of the wind. The light-air cells were a third depleted and the others rolled around loosely within the gasbag frame. As if that weren't enough, the support struts and cables stringing the ship itself to the 'bag were on the verge of giving way. Several had already torn and been rapidly replaced.

Mordecai had just woken for his shift, yet still felt exhausted. The last eighteen hours had almost killed him. He felt like murdering someone in turn for having had to live through them. First had been the repair of the *Queen,* as mishap after mishap revealed the little life left in the craft. Then they'd returned to the wreck of the *Albatross* to load aboard the lingering treasure, supplies, light-air canisters, and anything that would burn for fuel. After that, Mordecai would have been glad to put the whole sorry adventure behind them, to return to Haventown if they could, or simply to Breachtown where they could scuttle the ship and make their way home via smuggler's routes.

But no.

Mordecai hated Fengel and wanted him dead. Yet this desire paled beside that of Natasha. His captain was driven, almost manic. At several points he'd thought to sway her from her mad course. Every attempt had been met with withering scorn. Still. He thought he'd almost had her. Until they'd seen smoke on the horizon, and then a distant, shining dirigible in the light of the setting sun. There'd been no choice then, though still he tried. It galled him to watch Fengel go, but the *Queen* would never catch the *Dawnhawk* now. They had just enough coal and burnable fuel scavenged up for a return to Haventown. *That* was their best bet at the moment. Go home. Set a trap. Fengel's Men would have to return sometime.

That wasn't happening. Natasha lashed them onward. Mordecai had spent all night keeping their haphazard vessel aloft and chasing their prey. On the verge of passing out, he'd slipped down below to rest for an hour or two, and had only just now been kicked awake by his captain, her face grim, preparing herself for a fight that he knew would not happen.

The pre-dawn twilight set the eastern sky afire and the canopy below them a softer shade of blue. They flew lower than Mordecai would have liked, but that could not be helped. To the northeast hung the *Dawnhawk*, a speck against the horizon, just barely visible.

He yawned, just as a spring popped free from the rudder linkage overhead. It shot out past where his head had been a moment before, across the deck, whistling over the tired and edgy crew up to the bow, where Guye Farrel was coiling rope. It pelted the man hard across the back of the neck and Mordecai watched him topple, momentarily stunned. He hit the deck, then shot up, swearing and yelling at the ship, the men around him, and the more notable aspects of the Goddess. Other members of the crew started to mutter, either at the rattletrap airship they all worked to keep afloat, at Farrel, or just at their situation.

Mordecai knew a tipping point in the making when he saw one. He didn't intend to let it even form. The crew hurriedly bent back to their tasks as he stalked down from the aftcastle deck, yelling orders and cursing them aloud. He stalked up to where Farrel was ranting and quieted the man with a glower, until Farrel looked away to sullenly coil rope again. Mordecai turned and strode back down the deck, sighing under his breath.

Sad thought it was, he missed their Mechanist. Well, not really. But the youth's skills would have been invaluable now. Mordecai somewhat regretted leaving him behind.

The sun finally rose above the horizon to spill gold across the jungle below them. Mordecai marveled for a moment, caught by the view. The Yulan was amazingly clear, its clouds high and distant. He could see for miles and miles in every direction, even to the omnipresent Stormwall bordering them distantly to the west. Even the *Dawnhawk* looked clearer, its magnificent frame shining, the skysails along its side all but glowing.

Mordecai frowned. He stalked back up to the bow. Guye Farrel flinched at his approach; Mordecai paid him no mind and drew out his spyglass instead. Through it, the *Dawnhawk* resolved, far clearer than it should have been. They were gaining ground.

Fengel had to see them. The clear skies of the strange jungle continent worked both ways. It was possible that the *Queen* hadn't been spotted during the night. *Possible, but not plausible.* Mordecai had been working under the assumption that they were making a pursuit they couldn't possibly win.

So why were they catching up?

He strode back down to the aftcastle. He took in the status of the ship as he went and ordered crewmen to tighten ropes here, loosen the rigging there. Back near the captain's cabin their lone cannon lay lashed to the deck. He ordered five crew to free it and secure it up on the bow. Then he ascended to the helm.

Konrad had the ship's wheel in hand. The aetherite was muttering to himself, probably arguing with the invisible daemon on his shoulder. The man hadn't dealt well with their recent troubles. During the last surprise attack and theft of the *Dawnhawk*, his counterpart Maxim had unleashed some apparently extremely unpleasant hex upon the man.

"Navigator," said Mordecai. "Bring us over six degrees. See if you can get us some height."

Konrad started at his voice. He turned tired blue eyes toward Mordecai. "What is the point?" he asked in his thick accent.

"We're gaining on our prey."

The ship's navigator stared at him, then nodded slowly. Mordecai turned away and descended back to the deck, where the door to the captain's cabin was shut. He rapped on it, waited, and went to rap again. Before he could knock a second time, however, the portal opened wide and Natasha glared at him, eyes bloodshot and baggy. She couldn't have been asleep for more than an hour. For a wonder, she didn't stink of booze.

"What?" she asked, voice tight.

His captain looked half-mad. Mordecai wondered whether he should tell her. But duty won over in the end. "The *Dawnhawk* is dead ahead," he said.

She scowled. "Tell me something I don't know," she said, disappointment coloring her voice.

"We're gaining."

Natasha stared at him. Then she threw open the door and sauntered out onto the deck, brushing past him. She was still dressed, though her shirt was un-tucked and both her boots were missing.

The pirate captain strode up to the bow. Mordecai followed quietly as she stared out at the world. Natasha hissed suddenly, like a cat. She slapped the barrel of the carronade that the five crewmen struggled with.

"Get this mounted," she ordered them. "Dead ahead. Cut open the old gun ports in the bow again if you have to." She turned to Mordecai. "We've plenty of powder and shot left?"

He nodded. "I only dropped about half of what was in the magazine. We could fire all day if you really want to. But they have to see us. They know we want them dead. There's no way they'll let us catch up close enough."

"I don't care," said Natasha. She was almost vibrating with excitement, and her smile was ugly. "Get us closer, Mordecai. Get us back on top of our ship."

He returned to the helm and ordered the crew, keeping his thoughts suppressed. The sun rose, revealing more of the world around them. To his surprise the lookouts called out again; there were buildings ahead, just below where the *Dawnhawk* was hovering. *What's this? Could they have found something?*

Mordecai waited impatiently as the distance shrank between the two airships. He saw their prey clearly now, even spied the little figures running about on the deck. Anger, thick and raw, surged up in his breast, surprising him. Fengel had stolen his ship. Twice now. It was galling and incredible at the same time. Occasionally spats did arise between pirate captains. But never before had Natasha's Reavers come out the worse in these exchanges. Natasha herself fought harder and more ruthlessly than anyone Mordecai had ever known, desperate to move out from under her father's shadow. And until that tussle with Fengel aboard the *Dawnhawk* he had never found his match with a blade. This chase was no longer a futile desire of his captain's. He looked forward to the impending struggle. He would *relish* it.

Yet something was off. They were indeed catching up. With each passing minute they grew closer and closer. That shouldn't have been the case. Mordecai wondered what had happened. *Had they sustained damage? Did something happen to them?* It was obvious from the frantic scurrying that the enemy crew was aware of their presence. Why weren't they moving off?

Natasha gasped in surprise. Mordecai looked up at her, then walked to the portside rail and followed her gaze. His captain looked not at the *Dawnhawk*, but to the jungle down below. Peering down, he found himself blinking in surprise.

The jungle ahead of them fell completely away to reveal a wide valley with sheer cliff walls. Between those lay a city, the source of the ruins his lookouts had seen. Mordecai had never spied anything like it. It was massive, alien, and very strange. And far from empty. Figures moved about it, sized like human children, though odd in shape. They clustered in the streets below the *Dawnhawk*, hovering over the center of the city, and Mordecai heard the cry of their voices. Scryn, those dangerous flying nuisances, soared over the streets in agitation at the noise.

"What is this?" he wondered aloud.

His captain stared. Then she shook her head, narrowed her eyes and cast her gaze back at the airship off their bow. "It doesn't matter. We'll find out later, after we take our ship back."

The figures on the *Dawnhawk* moved frantically about. Fengel turned his airship about. Mordecai frowned. What had they been waiting for? There was still a chance at escape, the *Queen* was a wreck, but it was a slim one. Natasha growled as the *Dawnhawk* tacked ponderously into the wind and let it carry them to the far side of the valley.

"Damnation," she hissed. "Blast it!"

"We can't catch them," agreed Mordecai flatly. They were down to burning doors and cabinets scavenged from the interior for fuel.

They watched the airship pick up speed. Then, amazingly, it stopped. The *Dawnhawk* reached the northern wall of the valley, but rather than pass over it, she turned her nose eastward, following the cliff-line.

Natasha and Mordecai shared a look. They didn't waste time in wonderment, though—something was very odd here. Mordecai called out orders to the helm to give chase.

So it went. The *Dawnhawk* would fly ahead, the *Copper Queen* would chase doggedly behind. The stolen airship refused to leave the valley. But though she was faster and more refined, the *Dawnhawk* was still a dirigible, with limited maneuverability. Bit by bit they closed upon her.

Finally, they caught up. The *Dawnhawk* had performed a full circuit of the valley, back to where it had started on the west-most cliff, only a dozen feet above the canopy. But now Natasha's Reavers were only a hundred yards away. Fengel made to turn her west. Natasha ordered the cannon fired across their bow. The report was thunderous, and made the whole *Queen* groan and creak alarmingly. Yet the message was clearly understood.

Mordecai moved back to the helm, his place for the moment. He ordered the crew armed and ready for boarding. Hooks and grapnels were brought out. A barrel of powder was brought up from the magazine for those with muskets and pistols. Natasha moved to the starboard rails, ready to lead the action, hungry for it.

The defenders did what they could. Muskets were brought out and potshots fired, doing little damage. Lines were formed to repel the assailants. Mordecai saw Lucian striding back and forth, shouting orders and calling for discipline. But nowhere did he see the tricorn hat or shining monocle of their captain.

Fifty yards left. Then forty, then thirty. The grapnels were thrown and muskets fired. Mordecai watched a number of his men fall. Natasha herself flinched aside as a ball cut her cheek. The losses were more than acceptable.

The airships ran together with a crunch.

Natasha howled a bloodthirsty cry and leapt over the gunwales. Her men followed her, blades in hand and murder on their minds. Even the white ape went, leaping over to the *Dawnhawk's* gas-bag. Fengel's crew were prepared, though. Muskets fired at point blank range. Boarding axes hacked at the ropes while their mates covered them from above.

There was no clever distraction this time, no crewmen waiting to swing across and catch the defenders from the rear. It was a struggle in the old way, with blood staining both decks and sulfurous gun smoke tainting the air. The defenders slew a few of the boarders, those not quick enough or skilled enough to hold their own against so many on so many sides. Natasha though, held her own.

The piratess hacked about her with reckless abandon, anger giving her the ferocity she needed. Natasha wasn't nearly as skilled as Mordecai, but she was no one to ignore. She slashed with her cutlass back and forth, and when someone tried for her blind spot, she calmly drew a pistol and fired it.

Reaver Jane dropped down beside her. The skinny woman was a wire-whip, deadly and vicious with her long knives. Between the two of them, they formed a bridgehead that allowed another crewman to come over. Bit by bit, they made the boarding.

Mordecai took another look at the deck. He didn't see the giant gunnery mistress, Sarah Lome. Nor did he see Captain Fengel, or the ever-present Henry Smalls. *Where in the Realms are they?*

He had no more time to worry about it. The pressure was mounting on Natasha. It was time for him to join the fray.

Mordecai moved to the press of yelling men and women on their side of the struggle, and with curses and back-handed blows, made his way to the front. He drew his cutlass and went over, fighting beside Natasha, Reaver Jane, and three others.

It felt good to wield his sword. The fight against the white apes had been too surprising and desperate to enjoy. There was also a catharsis to be had. The foes before him now had wronged him. They had stolen his ship, shamed him before his crew and captain. It felt good to lay them out.

Mordecai hacked forward into the face of the man before him. His opponent fought in the new style, and brought an off-hand dagger up to block the blow. Mordecai ignored the sword he held; the quarters were too close for his opponent to really use both. He pressed forward, sliding the blade back and ramming the man in the face with the basket hilt of his own blade. Cartilage crunched and blood flew on the air. His opponent screamed as his nose was broken, pulling instinctively back and giving up more room.

Using the time and space just bought, Mordecai drew the blade back sideways, across the bare neck of a man fighting Natasha. Blood sprayed from a cut artery. Mordecai ignored it, turning back to his original foe and lunging into the now-open space, running him through. The man gasped and fell to the deck. Mordecai freed his blade and moved on.

Mordecai slew efficiently, workmanlike. Pressed at the back by the others on his crew, he scythed through the defenders with deadly efficiency. A few blades licked out at him, a few lucky blows were struck. It was inevitable, with quarters so close and the fighting so furious. But nothing was lethal or even really much of an inconvenience. Pistols were fired at him, but the charm in his ear warmed and the bullets whizzed past, deflected by its aether-wrought magic.

The press cleared. The defenders fell back and spread out, no longer united, two-dozen individual duels springing up as they fought for their lives. Mordecai moved to a free part of the deck and took a moment to search for the leaders. Fengel, Lome, Smalls, Maxim: none of them did he see about the deck. Only Lucian, at the far end of the ship now, barking out commands and holding his own against two other men.

Mordecai frowned. *Where in the Realms Below are they?* Without the others in the fight, things were going poorly. Fengel's men fought well, but Natasha's Reavers were angry, and desperate, and bloodthirsty.

Time to end this. If Lucian was the only one in command, then that was where he needed to be. Mordecai moved to make his way down the deck.

A short, boyish form landed right before him on the deck. It was a girl, a waif with blond knife-hacked hair, ill-fitting clothing, and leather gloves. She'd leapt out from one fight to his left, ducking under someone's legs, and rolled to a stop. She looked up at him in surprise. Mordecai recognized her. She was the one who had cut the rope he was climbing back near the *Albatross*.

He narrowed his eyes. "You," he snarled.

"Oh, no," she said. "You."

Mordecai raised his cutlass. But the waif was quick. She was on her feet as the blade came down at her. She backed away, bare inches from the edge, and brought a single heavy dagger up to guard herself with.

Mordecai advanced. He lashed out again, testing her. The young woman yelped and threw her weapon up to block the blow. His heavy blade crashed into it and sent her back. Mordecai brought his cutlass back into guard and raised an eyebrow at her.

Something dark flew at his head, screaming. Mordecai ducked and drew back. Raising his eyes he saw a wide, serpentine shape winding through the air, red light emanating from its belly to reflect upon the deck. To his amazement, the scryn circled around and landed on the waif, who held up her now-empty arm to it. The creature landed and wrapped itself around her shoulders.

"Chirr!"

"No! Not now Runt. Get off, you're too heavy!" She struggled with the thing, trying to dislodge it. For its own part, the scryn didn't want to be removed, and used its muscular length to grip onto her even tighter.

Mordecai stared a moment, then shook his head. He wasn't the sort to give up an opportunity. He raised his blade and stepped forward.

The waif looked up at him, eyes wide. She threw out one scryn-wrapped arm at him. "Runt! Kill!"

The creature turned to him, rising up. It flared its body wide, shining hellish red light at him. The scryn opened its jaws, mandibles flexing, and hissed. Poisoned spittle flew everywhere.

Mordecai raised his blade instinctively and fell back. The poison spattered across his arm and blade. Where it touched his bared wrist the skin instantly went numb. Thankfully, though, he'd been quick enough, and his face was unmarred.

Some sixth sense warned him just in time. He ducked, and the scryn flew overhead, tail whipping down to jab its stinger at his eyes. It missed by a hair's breadth. Mordecai cursed and leapt forward, hacking with his sword. He had to keep the waif on the defensive, before she could use the distraction for those knives, or before her pet could wheel back around.

The blade passed through empty air. He glanced up; she was gone, running away towards the starboard gunwales. Mordecai leapt after her with a snarl.

She heard him. Reaching the rail and the exhaust-pipe there, she wheeled around to face him, half-stumbling on a coil of rope tied to a stanchion up on the rail. Her eyes were wide and uncertain, though she did not appear frightened. For some reason, that angered him.

"Nowhere to go, girl," he said, slowing. "Now I'm going to—"

Her eyes warned him. He turned and punched out with the basket hilt of his sword. It caught the scryn in mid-flight. He felt its muscular, ropy body impact and deflect, knocked away and back into the melee.

"Runt!" the young woman yelled.

Mordecai turned back to her, an ugly smile on his lips. She looked left and right for help. None was coming. She was trapped. Mordecai decided he would take his time finishing her; he owed her a debt from the scene at the beach.

"Don't think I'll give you quarter, girl," he said.

She narrowed her eyes and sheathed the dagger on her hip. "I wasn't about to ask you for it," she said.

Quick as a cat she grabbed up the coil of rope at her feet and threw it overboard. Then she danced up the exhaust-pipe, took some of the length in her hands, and jumped overboard.

Mordecai stared. Then he leapt forward, lashing out with his blade. It missed, biting into the wood of the gunwale instead. He yanked it free and then bent out over the gunwale.

She was falling, halfway already to the green canopy of the jungle a dozen feet below her. He couldn't reach her. It might as well have been a hundred. She was escaping. The young woman looked up at him as her part of the rope went taut. Her eyes were merry and she laughed at him.

Mordecai growled. *Oh, no you don't.* He hefted his cutlass again and hacked out, this time at the knot around the metal stanchion on the gunwale. It parted and went flying away. He leaned out again over the rail just in time to see her plunge into the canopy, eyes wide in surprise and sudden fear. Mordecai leaned back with a smile, darkly amused.

He threw himself back into the fight, working his way back to the helm where Lucian fought with Natasha. They were evenly matched, the two of them. And just versed enough in dirty trickery enough to counter the other.

Lucian spied Mordecai's approach. He cursed and gave ground, trying to fight his duel and command the crew at the same time. Natasha pressed her attack and Mordecai moved in on her flank. *I must have pleased someone. Things seem to be going my way today.*

Fengel's first mate put up a valiant effort, but it wasn't enough. Mordecai put his counterpart's blade into a bind and then disarmed him, sending Lucian's sword flying away. He then punched the man with the hilt of his cutlass—Lucian, and satisfyingly, some of his teeth, went sprawling. He recovered quickly and made to stand, but paused when Natasha lowered the tip of her blade to his throat.

"What," asked Mordecai. "No clever escape this time?" He moved closer. "No witty repartee?" He felt pleasure at the dark glower of the other mate. *How does it feel now, you little shit?*

Lucian said nothing. He peered past his captors at the battle on the deck. Without his guidance, it was going poorly. He looked up at Natasha. "Spare the crew. I ask for quarter."

"Well, you're not going to get it," snarled Mordecai. "You and Fengel have been an irritant long enough—"

Natasha held out her free hand, cutting him off. Mordecai glanced up at her. His captain affected the cool amusement that was her usual attitude. "Mordecai's view has merit," she said. "But there's something I don't understand here. You will answer it for me." She leaned in a little, pressing her blade down to bite at his throat. "Where is Fengel? What happened here?"

Mordecai's curiosity quelled his irritation. If the missing pirates were still on the ship, they would have joined the fray by now.

Lucian licked his lips. "Will you give quarter?" he asked.

"It will be taken into consideration," replied Natasha. Behind her, two Reavers cut down one of Fengel's Men.

The first mate closed his eyes. "They're not on the ship. They're in the city below."

Natasha raised an eyebrow. She shared a questioning glance at Mordecai. "What? Why? Whatever is that fool doing now?"

Lucian grimaced. "We found the Governor's Lantern."

Mordecai blinked in surprise. "It wasn't in the treasure you'd stolen?"

Fengel's first mate shook his head, sandy hair swaying. "No. The ships log hinted that it had been taken from the *Albatross* before either of us had even gotten to these shores. We tracked it back here, to the city below. Captain's become obsessed with it. We didn't leave because there was trouble on the ground, just as you'd arrived."

Natasha looked bewildered. "But why? Why come here? Why not flee? You had to know we'd be coming after you. Why not make your escape? There's a fortune in the holds below already!"

Lucian looked up, held her gaze. "Because he wanted to make sure that *you* couldn't get the gem."

Mordecai's captain went very still. She didn't move, didn't speak, only stood there with the tip of her blade against Lucian's throat. Behind and around them came the cries of those still fighting, mixed in with gunshot reports and the groans of the wounded.

When she spoke her voice was low and dangerous. There was something in it that Mordecai couldn't identify. "Tell your crew to lay down arms."

"You'll give us quarter?"

"Tell your crew to lay down arms."

Lucian stared up at her a long moment, then turned his head to the side and called out. "Quarter! We ask for quarter! Stand down, Fengel's Men!"

He repeated the call a few times, and slowly, sporadically, the fighting slowed to a stop. Fengel's Men were quickly disarmed and herded into the middle of the deck.

"Excellent," said Mordecai. "Now we'll cut their throats and dump them over the side, and put this whole sorry mess behind us." He smiled.

Lucian started from the deck. Only the blade at his neck kept him from rising. "You can't! We've called for quarter, you miserable son of a bitch!"

Mordecai smiled down at him. "We never said we'd give it."

Natasha pulled back her blade. "Have no fear, Mister Thorne. You'll have quarter."

Mordecai turned to frown at her. "This is foolish. Haven't you learned? They're all too dangerous to be left alive. Kill them and be done with it."

Natasha sheathed her cutlass. She tapped her chin thoughtfully, staring out past the deck of the ship, back toward the *Copper Queen.* "I think not." She caught Mordecai's gaze. "Round them up, tie them into a cargo net, and move them back to the *Queen.*"

Mordecai stared. "Again? Again? This is madness! Euron never would have let this go on so long!"

He knew he'd gone too far. Natasha looked over at him with eyes like ice. She stepped up and slapped him. She wasn't some dockside prostitute or pampered mistress. The blow had the full force of her arm behind it, an arm that was used to wielding a sword. Mordecai reeled back, vision blurring.

"Tie Lucian and his crew up in a cargo net," she snarled. "Secure it tightly to somewhere on the *Queen.* Dump them over the bow and cut us free. Those are my orders. Will you obey them, or do I have to find someone who will?"

Mordecai flushed. He straightened and met her fierce gaze. "No. Captain."

"Good. Get moving. Once you're finished, come see me in the cabin. We need to go over that logbook, and prepare a shore party."

The first mate raised an eyebrow. "What? Why?"

"Because *we* are going to find the Lantern first."

She turned on her heel and stalked off. Mordecai stared at her in confusion. One of his nearby crewman coughed. He flushed as he realized that the whole scene had been public. Snarling, Mordecai gave the orders.

He saw Lucian and Fengel's Men bundled over to the *Copper Queen.* Lucian especially, he treated roughly, taking out his frustrations. The man took it all in good charm, smiling whenever he knew Mordecai was watching. It was infuriating.

It's a game, he realized. A cold shock ran through him at the epiphany. Fengel's Men were tied up in their cargo net, the latter being anchored to a stanchion on the deck of the *Queen*. A few crew he'd kept to this task. The rest were retaking the *Dawnhawk* and checking her over.

They hate each other, but never stopped caring, either. Mordecai's anger grew with each passing moment. That was why they danced around each other so, why Natasha refused to kill off her husband. The two played a constant game of one-upmanship, always seeking to come out on top. All other considerations were secondary.

Cold certainty mixed with his anger. He glanced back at the deck of the *Dawnhawk*. His captain was nowhere to be seen.

Guye Farrel trudged past with a length of rope. Mordecai reached out and caught him by the arm. "Come with me," he ordered. The other pirate winced at his voice, but nodded. The journey had not been kind to Farrel. His face was scarred and swollen and he had a limp.

Mordecai led the way belowdecks. Shortly they found themselves in the magazine. Though half-emptied, there were still enough casks of black powder left to do the job. *I'm putting an end to this madness.* He pulled down a cask and with Farrel's help breached it.

"There," he said. "Pour a trail back up to the deck. Be very careful that it is unbroken. Tell no one. Understand?"

The man nodded, eyes wide. Mordecai was certain that he'd make a trail. The bigger question was whether or not he could keep his mouth shut. If he didn't, however, he was easily dealt with. That was why Mordecai had chosen him, after all.

Mordecai returned to the deck and walked to the bow. There, his crew were herding Fengel's Men over the edge of the ship. Mordecai called a stop, then moved around to where Lucian stood within the net.

"Hello, Mordie," said Lucian cheerfully. "It appears that you got one over on me, finally. I suppose anything's possible in a world such as ours, yes?"

Mordecai met his smile with one of his own. "Keep thinking that," he said to the rogue. "Keep thinking that, after I send you off to the Realms Below."

Lucian lost his smile. Mordecai turned away. He ordered Fengel's Men pushed overboard. His crew complied, goading with cutlass and long knife. The net went over the edge, Fengel's surviving Men screaming. They fell until the anchor-rope went taut.

Mordecai ordered his crew back aboard the *Dawnhawk*. Then he waited. In a few minutes, Guye Farrel reappeared, and completed his trail. Mordecai ordered him aboard the other ship, walking over to the thick line of black powder.

He drew a pistol and turned one last time to gaze about the floating wreck. *I really hate this ship.*

Mordecai knelt and cocked the empty weapon. He placed the pan next to the powder and pulled the trigger. The flintlock snapped close and sparks flew. Some landed on the dark line, instantly catching it. He walked briskly back to the *Dawnhawk* and boarded. At the snap of his fingers, crewmen cut the last line tethering the old airship to the new.

An order to Konrad and they were moving speedily away.

CHAPTER NINETEEN

LINA HUNG UPSIDE DOWN. She dangled, holding onto the branch with both feet, praying it was strong enough. It was a thin one though, and brittle. Lina didn't dare reach up to grab at it with her hands.

The jungle canopy was a world all its own, even viewed upside down. Long branches covered in thick green leaves surrounded her on every side. Both the dark ground and the blue sky were hidden by dancing foliage that shook with the wind and the passing of the lighter jungle creatures. Should Lina be set adrift to float free, like an airship, she thought she might quickly lose all sense of direction.

Unfortunately, that wasn't the case. The direction *down* was very emphatically insisting on its presence.

If I can just find a strong one. Lina glanced about slowly, carefully. There were a few branches within reach, but they seemed too supple to bear her weight.

She swayed. A crack sounded from above. Heart leaping in her breast, Lina glanced back up at the limb she hung from.

A monkey peered down at her from next to her boots. It was small and black, not even half of Runt's size, maybe as large as a parrot. The little creature watched her curiously, eyes black and beady in its wizened face.

Oh no, no, no. Get away you pest. Shoo! Even something as small as the monkey was already stressing her branch beyond its tolerance.

Lina waved her hand at it in a shooing gesture, trying to move as little as possible. The branch made another loud cracking sound. She froze.

The monkey peered at her curiously. Then it hooted and clapped its hands together. It made the shooing gesture at her in turn.

Lina wanted to throttle the thing. "No," she hissed. "Go away!"

The monkey shooed her again. Then it jumped, up and down in excitement.

The branched snapped clean in half. Lina yelled as she suddenly plummeted. The monkey leapt away with a surprised scream.

Branches and leaves brushed her head, face, arms. She reached out with desperate hands, trying to grab onto something, anything that might save her or slow her descent. Lina caught a branch. It held for half a second, then snapped. Five feet down she hooked her leg around another... only for it to bend, creak, then snap.

Lina fell through the open air. The ground rushed up to meet her, dark, loamy earth dotted here and there by ferns and other undergrowth. Then she landed with a bone-jarring thump. Dimly, she felt the length of rope from the *Dawnhawk* land heavily on her back, knocking the wind out of her.

Sense came back. Lina gasped. She hurt, her left arm and shoulder especially. Also, her right foot was bare. She felt the rich, black dirt of the jungle between her toes. *Great,* she thought, groaning aloud. *I've lost a boot.* Gingerly, she checked to make sure nothing was broken. Lina reached back with her good arm and pulled the rope off her back. It twisted in her hands, strangely slick and smooth. She brought it around and found herself staring face-to-face with a long black snake.

The creature hissed and reared up. But before Lina could yell, or the serpent strike, something fell from above, clobbering it.

Her boot.

She threw the snake, forgetting her hurts for the moment. It landed a dozen paces away, a long black line at least four feet in length. It didn't move after landing. Lina watched it for a moment, then sat up. She quickly checked her arms, legs, and shoulder. Nothing was broken, thankfully, though she would hurt for awhile to come. *That was lucky,* she thought, looking up at the trees above. That last fall had been at least ten feet.

The jungle stretched out around her. It was strangely bare down at ground level. The underbrush was not thick, starved by the trees high above. She had no idea which direction was north, or which led back to the valley and its alien city.

I have to find the Captain. He's got to be told what happened. Though, last she'd seen, Fengel had had troubles of his own.

She'd been angry when Fengel sent her back to the *Dawnhawk* the night before. But over time worry and boredom dulled her irritation. She spent the night's shift drowsing and watching the jungle and the strange alien city of Yrinium. The inhabitants, these Draykin, lit fires all throughout the temples. It was amazing to see from the air. Only the depth of their valley kept the fires from being seen from hundreds of miles around.

Lucian and the others had seen the approaching *Copper Queen* long before dawn. The question had been what to do about it. At first, the thought had been to simply avoid it, move off and pick the Captain back up later. But just as the sun rose, they'd seen Fengel's party again, under attack by native Draykin.

Time and again Lucian had tried to bring them in to assist. But by then it was too late. Natasha's damnable skyship had hounded them all about the valley before finally closing.

Lina grimaced. The fight for the airship hadn't been going well when she'd fled. *I hope Runt is all right.*

She glanced around. The question now was what to do. Sounds of the fight had faded while she was trapped in the canopy above; the airships must have moved off. Should she try to run after them? No. Even if Lucian won out, at best they'd drive Natasha back to her ship. They were outnumbered, and he'd probably use the greater speed of the *Dawnhawk* to move off. In worst case, Natasha had won the day, and Lina would be shot or captured on sight.

Fengel needed to know. She was still irritated with him, but he could do something about this mess. She was confident that he'd pulled through the ambush he'd encountered; Sarah Lome and Maxim were with him, and he was no slouch himself in a fight.

Lina put her boot back on. Then she stood and brushed the dirt away from her trousers. Glancing around the jungle, she encountered a new problem. Which way to go? The canopy diffused the light of the rising sun. It filtered down to twilight near the ground, but Lina thought one side looked stronger. *That'll be east.* Last she recalled, the *Dawnhawk* was just west of Fengel's struggle when they'd been attacked. So, east it was. Lina nodded to herself, feeling pleased at this deduction. Then she struck out.

She didn't get far before the jungle thickened. The sparse ferns grew more common, appearing in clumps of twos and threes. Before long Lina was pushing her way through the things, their long and feathery leaves catching at her clothing and chafing her skin. Spores from the plants filled the air, and Lina found herself sneezing wildly. When she finished, she stood back up straight, sniffling, her eyes watering and red.

She wasn't alone.

One of the pygmy lizard-men, the Draykin, stood before her. Its scales were a soft green, and its maw was filled with dozens of needle teeth. It wore a loincloth and carried a spear tipped with a gleaming bronze point. It held a weighted cord in its other hand.

Lina started, then she relaxed. The Draykin was strange, but that was normal, right? There were still sightings of ogres back on Edrus, and all the tales talked about the bizarre things that lived on this strange continent. "Rastalak, right? You scared me."

"*Yamana!*" it growled in reply. "*Cobar hastracki!*"

"You are not Rastalak," she said. Too late, she remembered the fine 'mask' of green scales that the other lizard-creature bore. Lina realized that she had just made a terrible mistake.

The creature hissed, long, low, threateningly. Lina turned and ran. She only had one dagger, the Draykin had a spear. And though smaller than a man, the Draykin wasn't far from her size. She pressed through the ferns at a flat run, her boots pounding the earth beneath her feet. Behind, she heard the Draykin cry out and give chase.

She struck out at random and regretted it almost immediately. The ferns thickened, keeping her from running all out. The tall trees grew more closely together this way, spreading thick roots across the jungle floor that threatened to trip and doom her. Vines dangled. Still, Lina ducked, dodged and leapt as best she could to avoid these obstacles, driven on by the bloodthirsty cries of the savage creature behind her, and by the hammering of her heart in her throat.

Something whistled past her head. Lina had the impression of a dark shape whipping only inches past to crack against a tree just up ahead. Three stones connected by thin cord fell down out of sight, having dented the bark.

Lina paled. It was *throwing things* at her! She ran more desperately, ducking under a thick clumps of hanging vines and dodging to put the big trees behind her as soon as she'd cleared them. The Draykin howled in frustration and anger.

She made for a heavy banyan tree, with root-branches growing to a thick maze. Some of the paths would easily hide her, or give her the advantage for a moment. Something sailed past her to impact the nearest root-entrance and stuck, quivering. The hunter's spear now blocked her way. Lina cursed and dove left into another thick bunch of ferns.

The canopy ahead opened wide. Lina took it in at a glance, getting the impression of a towering pile of stones open to the sky. The ferns parted and she found herself at the cusp of a clearing past a thick tree. A temple ruin dominated the space. It was a stair-stepped pyramid, crumbling in places and vine-shrouded. Light underbrush surrounded it.

A wide and slick stretch of very flat earth was the only thing between the underbrush of the clearing and Lina. Instinctively, she didn't trust it. She pulled a great breath into her already tortured lungs and leapt from the highest root before her. Lina sailed over the bare patch, arms flailing like a windmill. She landed roughly, tumbling to the ground just beyond it.

A wet splash sounded just behind her as she came to a stop, and the outraged howls of the Draykin hunter. Lina glanced back to see the creature floundering in the bare space, the small bog revealed for what it was.

She thought to draw her knife, take the advantage. *No.* The Draykin thrashed in the muddy earth, but it was only surprised. Soon enough it would be back on its feet, and it looked both stronger and faster than she was. She turned her attention back to the ruin and looked for an escape.

The structure rose several stories high. Weird carvings of strange creatures and peoples covered the bare flat surfaces. Most were too eroded or hidden by foliage to easily make out. Up above, about the third story, large cracks and openings appeared. There was no other entrance on this face.

Her lungs were burned raw from the chase. She had to go to ground. Lina scrabbled to her feet and sprinted for the ruin. She climbed from one step to another, glancing back to spy the Draykin free of the muck and preparing to give chase again. As it crossed the clearing she made it to the third level of the ruin, where a crack maybe just large enough to fit through was hidden by the jungle vines.

She was desperate. Lina pulled the foliage aside, revealing the space a little more. It was small. A dog might fit, but just barely. *Nothing for it then.* Giving up a heartfelt prayer to the Goddess, Lina threw herself at it and crawled within. The rough stone caught her shoulders, brushed her hair. But barely, just barely, she fit. Before her the crack continued, a small crawlspace going deeper into the ruin. She wriggled, writhed, and scrabbled. Head, shoulders, then chest and waist, she pulled inside. Her floundering hand felt an edge ahead, where the passage opened into something wider. Lina pulled an arm through, felt a shelf or some other surface a few inches below the lip. Her head poked into the space, then she pulled her other arm through.

The Draykin caught her foot.

It howled triumphantly on the outside of the structure. Its voice was weirdly muffled, but the terror Lina felt was clear. She cried out, then kicked and scrabbled and fought. Her head, chest, arms and shoulders were all inside the temple, in an open space too dimly lit to make out the details. Her legs were trapped by the close confines, too small to even bend them all the way.

The creature yanked at her, and Lina slid back deeper into the crawlspace. Her chest brushed painfully against the stone of the lip. She cried out fearfully. The she grit her teeth, growled, and kicked her boots down against the stone. The Draykin outside yowled. She did it again, and again. The creature fought, though, yanking and pulling in turn.

Abruptly she was free. Her boot, the same she'd lost in the canopy, slipped off. Lina reacted instantly, pulling and heaving with her arms, kicking and pushing with her legs until she was out of the small passage and fully within the temple. Outside, the Draykin hunter roared in frustration.

Lina drew her knife and waited. Sunlight through the crawlspace was a white glow, impeded by the clutching arm of the Draykin. Thankfully, it could not reach her now. Lina's pursuer snarled and hissed and spit. It growled at her in its language. Lina kept her dagger ready, waiting to strike should it reach in far enough.

The Draykin pulled back. Sunlight illuminated the crawlspace. Then there was a rumble and the space went dark but for a few thin cracks of light. *It blocked the space with a stone. I'm trapped.* Lina turned around to stare at the interior of her prison.

The ruin was mostly hollow, she realized as her eyes adjusted. Its stair-step pyramid shape was visible from within, continuing another two dozen feet to a point above. The ceiling had fallen in there, and diffuse morning sunlight shone in through the vines and creepers that covered that opening. Lina lay on a wide ledge about halfway up the space, looking down onto a floor strewn with rubble and debris. Statues of strange, half-formed things adorned the ledge, like squat fat children carved of heavy stone. Sunlight shone onto the floor of the ruin from the near end, where the wall was carved open to form an entryway high enough for a man.

Lina let out a sigh of relief. *Not trapped, then.* Opposite from her, the vines in the ceiling had grown down to wreathe the statues, then continued a short way to the floor. She rose to hands and knees and crept that way, moving quickly.

The Draykin hunter appeared in the entryway. Lina froze. It crept within, long muzzle casting about, hunched and ready to spring. It did not carry its spear, but the long talons on its outstretched fingers were more than enough to rip her to pieces.

The creature peered up at the ledge she was on. Evidently it did not see her, yet. Lina shrank back until the stone of the ruin pressed against her shoulder blades.

"*Hastrack*i," said the Draykin. "*Muweilo guyvalla.*"

It crept forward into the open. Lina hefted the dagger in her hands and thought about throwing it. She thought better. *There has to be something I can do.* Then her eye caught on one of the nearby idols.

The Draykin crept about the floor again. It called out to her in its gibberish language, softly, menacingly. The words were opaque to her, but the intent was clear. Lina pulled off her other boot, positioned herself, and then dropped it to the floor of the ruin.

It landed with a thump, overloud, it seemed, in the roomy space. The Draykin twitched at the sound and leapt forward, running and landing on the rubble where her boot had fallen. It peered about, looking for somewhere nearby Lina could be hiding. Then it looked up.

Lina put her back to the idol and shoved with her legs. It was lighter than she thought it would be and fell free from the ledge with a loud scrape. Lina caught herself from going over the edge and rolled back. There was the crunch of an impact, and a wet thud.

She peered over the ledge. Her pursuer was crumbled in a heap on the rubble of the floor. Its head was a ruined mess. The idol lay nearby, bloodied.

Lina sighed in relief. She spent a few moments getting her breath back, then crawled over to the vines and made her way down. She threw a few rocks to make sure the bloodthirsty Draykin was dead, then retrieved her boot. Shielding her eyes from the light, she left the ruin through the ground entrance.

The valley yawned wide before her. This face of the pyramid opened onto the cliff only a dozen paces from its edge. Ruined flagstones led along the face, back around to the jungle and the clearing she'd run into. A short distance away, a switchback stair was carved into the cliff face, one of many leading down. Below her the city rose, massive and strange in its architecture.

Completely coincidentally, she'd gotten where she wanted to go. *Maybe someone heard my prayers after all?*

Movement down below caught her attention. She moved to the ledge and peered downward. It was Draykin, hundreds of them, moving in a massive procession toward the large pyramid at the center of the city. Their raucous cries echoed back up to her, and as they moved it seemed that those in the middle were carrying something. Or someone.

A light glinted from the middle of the crowd. Like a monocle just catching the sun.

Lina cursed. The more she watched the more she was certain. Captain Fengel was caught, him and some others, tied together and being marched through the city of bloodthirsty lizard-men.

She cast about above, looking for the *Dawnhawk*. There. It circled to the west, following the lip of the valley. The *Copper Queen* drifted a distance away. A full cargo net hung from the bow by a long cable.

Lina closed her eyes. Lucian had lost. Thankfully though, it looked like Natasha had left them alive again.

She took a deep breath. Nothing for it, then. It looked like it was all up to her to rescue her crewmates, and her captain. But first, she had to go find her boot. And maybe check its laces.

CHAPTER TWENTY

Fengel swung from a wooden pole. It was really rather uncomfortable. He was tied by his hands and feet, like a pig caught during a hunt. Four of the Draykin carried him, two in front and two from behind. Their diminutive height was a problem; when they stumbled, he was drug along the ground. To his left Sarah Lome hung similarly, though her eight carriers struggled more than a little. On his right hung Maxim. Fengel was worried about the aetherite. He'd taken a hard knock to the head during the battle, and had yet to awaken.

"Henry," Fengel called. "Are the others still alive back there?"

"Yes," replied his steward. Henry Smalls hung from a pole somewhere behind him, just out of sight. Fengel had been worried at first, but the thrown spear had only gouged his man's shoulder. And not *too* deeply.

"Excellent," he said. "Well then. We're doing a lot better than I expected. Capital."

"Yes, sir," replied his steward after a moment.

The ambush had gone poorly for the pirates. Fengel had his men put up a ferocious defense, and for a moment it looked as if they might win out. Lome was ferocious, hacking the lizard-pygmies to pieces, and laying them out with one blow from her free hand. Maxim exhausted his remaining Workings, calling up caustic fire to wield against the Draykin. Fengel fought over Henry while the little steward recovered, and his other crew had made a similarly spirited show.

There were too many, however. They were outnumbered at least six to one. Fengel wondered, as he was tackled to the ground, how long Rastalak's people had been following them. He wondered, as well, if their guide was responsible for the current strife. It had disappeared during the struggle, and he did not see it among their captors.

Ferociously subdued, they were, all of them, bound. The Draykin saw to their own wounded and then moved with their new prisoners down one of the long stairways carved into the valley wall. His memory of the trip was imprecise; a blow to the head had left him groggy. By the time he fully recovered, they were down at the base of the steps, being carried by their captors through the streets of an alien city.

The sun hung at high noon, casting no shadows and illuminating the structures about them brilliantly. Past the bodies and serpentine faces of the Draykin, Fengel spied spiraling towers and weird ziggurats. Their angles were odd, curving and swooping like the shells of a sea-creature, yet obviously cut of crafted stone. Creeping vines wrapped them, all the way to their cracked and crumbling tops. Some of the buildings held balconies, archways, and windows. Others were smooth monoliths unblemished by any visible openings. Both of these towered over cruder, squat stair-step pyramids, lacking the artistry of their neighbors. These were covered in bas-reliefs and stone idols. It was as if two peoples inhabited Yrinium. An older race, and a much younger, more primitive one attempting to ape its grandeur.

Fengel glanced around at his Draykin captors. *Oh.* The reptilian pygmies were not the builders here.

The rest of the city was similar. Each building was a block all its own, separated by long, wide thoroughfares. These lanes were mosaics formed of polished white stones, the designs and mandalas they created too large and strange for him to identify from his vantage, though the heat they radiated made sweat pop out beneath his arms and across his brow.

The Draykin moved as a group. Of the three-score that had joined in the ambush, maybe twenty remained. They walked through the city with the pride of successful hunters, though, hissing and growling at each other in their savage tongue. As they moved Fengel spied others, carrying baskets, sharpening weapons, or simply sunning themselves on the steps of the low pyramids. He still couldn't tell their sex apart, but Fengel did see a child, no bigger than a dog. When the procession passed, some of these others ran up to query and chat with the hunters, falling in behind to peer at the captive pirates. Before long they had quite the escort.

I need to consider an escape plan. Unfortunately, nothing came to mind. Ultimately, he simply needed to watch for the proper moment, and be ready to seize it. Weirdly, Fengel realized he wasn't afraid. Being captured was vexing, and the state of his crew was worrisome. But the Draykin had expended much effort to bring them all alive. And if Rastalak had been true, they were bringing him straight to the Governor's Lantern in the temple at the center of the city. He lay back, and decided to try and enjoy the ride.

The procession turned a corner. Fengel could only look up with any ease. Yet up above, just as they passed the curve of a spiraling tower, appeared a lumbering blimp-shape over the far western edge of the valley.

It was the *Copper Queen*.

Euron's airship looked much the worse for wear. Worse even than the shape he'd left it in last. The gas-bag frame was broken and slumped, most of the light-air gas cells bulging out of the stern-end of the bag, distending it like fish eggs in a cloth sack. Below it the deck of the vessel itself pitched downward, the bowsprit poking down at the ground at almost forty-five degrees. The hull was blackened and scorched. Ratlines and support cables dangled free. No cannons poked their fat noses out from the gunwales.

The angle was such that Fengel couldn't see well onto the deck; his captors and the cityscape got in the way. He didn't see any movement, though. And if the ship were crewed then there should have been the lithe shapes of the lookouts atop the gas-bag, if nothing else.

Some of the Draykin in the streets called out and pointed to the flying wreck. The procession slowed as others noticed, gabbling amongst themselves.

"Mister Smalls?" Fengel called.

"Aye, sir?" replied the steward.

"I can see the *Queen*. She looks abandoned. What do you think she's doing up here?"

"We left her drifting, sir. It's possible, I suppose, that she's here coincidentally. But I doubt it, were I being honest."

"And you are the soul of honesty indeed." *Too far, too fast.* Natasha had to be involved. "Can you see the *Dawnhawk* anywhere?"

"Aye sir, just a moment ago. The northern edge of the valley."

"Curious and more curious," he muttered to himself. "I sincerely hope that Lucian hasn't—"

He was interrupted by a massive explosion that flared into the life above them. The noise deafened him, echoing and reverberating down the city streets. His captors yowled in surprise and dropped him. Fengel landed with a grunt on the paved stones of the wide street beneath them. He rolled back to look, still tied to the long pole they carried him upon. Up above, the *Copper Queen* was gone. Where it had floated, a cloud of spreading debris rained down onto the city.

He stared. Only one thing could have happened. It was every sailor's fear, sea-borne and sky.

Fengel glanced back at the procession. His crew had been similarly dropped, the Draykin all cowering and gabbing at each other for the moment. Henry, Sarah, Oscar, and Geoffrey were all awake and looking around. Even Maxim stirred a bit, for which Fengel was thankful. Unfortunately, their bonds were still tight; now was not the time to escape.

He caught his steward's eye. "Powder magazine," he said.

Smalls nodded. "Or the gas-bag. Captain, I saw a rope, I think. Hanging off the bow. You don't think Natasha..." He trailed off, and Fengel understood his fear.

Their captors recovered from their surprise. They hoisted the sky-pirates and again moved on their way, if a little slower and more distracted than before. Up above, the explosion of the *Queen* had disturbed the nesting birds and sky-creatures that lived in the ruined upper towers. They soared and flew, calling out to each other in raucous, screeching cries.

As they moved along, Fengel came to a realization that knocked him out of his worries. *Those are scryn.* More took to the skies with every passing moment. Whole flocks of the repulsive creatures roosted in the upper bounds of the city. Fengel shuddered, glad that they didn't seem interested in coming below to harry the Draykin.

The street opened onto a wide plaza, the massive temple-manse they'd seen at its center. The building was huge, like almost everything else here. Unlike the others, it bore the marks of both the old style of architecture and the newer, more primitive ones. It seemed almost remade, or repurposed. The stair-step pyramid shape was evident in its lines, but more elegantly constructed than the others in Yrinium. *Replicas*, Fengel realized. The smaller pyramids were of Draykin construction; this was what they were copying.

The pyramid was at least ten stories tall. Its peak was a sharp point, sloping down to the next terrace, which stretched, then sloped down to the terrace below it. At its apex, an archway opened into the interior, and a long, wide stair was carved up the side of the structure to meet it. Strange, crude statues carved by the Draykin dotted each terrace, and were spaced through most of the plaza below.

Fengel eyed a few of these as they moved past. Larger and heavier than a man, they depicted humanoid figures, different from the Draykin. Their clothing and dress was certainly odd. But they almost appeared human, otherwise.

Their captors brought the pirates to the temple. Fengel watched as the Draykin hauled them up the stair, climbing up above the city to the entrance of the massive pyramid. Trepidation filled him, paired with the cold uncertainty about his crew, and what had happened with the *Copper*

Queen. The Draykin had wanted them alive, and he was about to find out why.

The stair ended at a wide landing. Behind it the archway entrance to the temple yawned, a gaping mouth of stone. To either side stood a pair of metal braziers, burning brightly even at noonday.

A single Draykin stood in the middle of the landing. It was older, its scales dulled, its posture stooped. It wore a headdress of gold and precious gemstones that Fengel recognized from the statues below. The creature leaned on a staff of pale wood topped in wrought gold.

The Draykin procession came to a halt before the older figure. They knelt before it, lowering Fengel and his crew to the ground. It was obviously a chieftain or priest, a figure of importance. Fengel assumed the former.

The old creature hissed something and two of Fengel's bearers stood. They cut him free of his bonds and stood him up roughly. Fengel resisted the urge to curse; blood pumped painfully back into his numbed fingers. His bearers each reached out to grab him. Fengel shook their grip away violently. They jumped back, immediately wary and on edge, moments away from grappling him.

Fengel forced himself to calm. *Never let them see you stumble.* He glanced back at the procession. All eyes were on him, though most still knelt. He and his crew were easily outnumbered fifty to one at this point, and he had no clue where their weapons were.

Still.

His crew watched in concern, still tied like hogs bound for the spit. Fengel winked at Henry Smalls and then slowly, carefully, reach up to replace his monocle. Before the guards could grab him again he moved forward to the chieftain, slowly and without threat.

The *Dawnhawk* came into view just above the temple. Its shadow cast the landing into darkness. The assembled Draykin gasped and muttered to themselves, pointing up at the sky-vessel. Fengel didn't know who was on board or in control, but they couldn't have appeared at a better time. *Perfect.*

He raised his most imperious eyebrow at the Draykin chieftain. Up close, he was easily two feet taller than the thing. "What," he demanded, "is the meaning of this?"

Gasps echoed from the landing behind him, the indrawn breath of his crew, and the startled hissing of the lizard-men.

"Sir," stage-whispered Smalls. "What are you doing?"

"Mind your tongue, Henry Smalls," he replied without glancing back. Fengel glowered at the chieftain. "Now. I believe I asked you a question."

The old Draykin stared back at him, eyes wide in surprise. *Perfect,* thought Fengel. He had the old lizard on the defensive.

"*Ra,*" it said. "*Stalki-haio.*"

"I," said Fengel, "do not care."

It seemed Rastalak, friend or foe, was unique. The chieftain didn't speak civilized Perinese, and from what he'd heard while moving through the city, neither did any of the other Draykin. Still, some things were universal. The body language of the lizard-men was easy enough to read. Fengel bulled onward.

"We have been rather rudely assailed," he said, slashing at the air. "Then captured, and paraded through the streets of your stinking city like hogs meant for a feast-day! I demand you answer me. What is your purpose? How dare you treat a noble group of civilized adventurers so?" He gestured up at the *Dawnhawk* above them. "My ship floats above, ready to deliver retribution upon your primitive heads at any moment. Now, I demand you answer for these...these insults!"

Fengel had let himself grow more incensed. He put years of authority and every pound of overwrought pomposity he could into each word, until the guards were standing back, and the chieftain stared wide-eyed and uncertain.

He pushed the advantage. "How dare you," Fengel hissed.

Smartly, Fengel stepped forward, lashing out. The chieftain's headdress went flying through the air. It landed with a clang, then skidded off the side of the pyramid. All assembled listened to it clatter down the side of the building.

The mood in the air changed. Surprise and awe evaporated, replaced by outrage. The Chieftain narrowed its eyes. The Draykin around them hissed, low and angry.

Fengel reconsidered his position. "Mister Smalls," he said calmly.

"Yes, sir?"

"It appears that I might have been just a tad too bold."

His steward sighed. "I know, sir."

"*Korvachi,*" shrieked the chieftain, spittle landing on the shirt of Fengel's breast. "*Korvachi hailo!*"

The two guards at his side leapt forward and seized him painfully. He tried to struggle, but they had him in grips of iron. Two more jumped forward to help subdue him.

"*Te Salaas Voorn!*" yelled the chieftain. It raised its staff up and pointed at the opening to the temple.

"*Te Salaas Voorn!*" echoed the guards. They hoisted Fengel and hauled him forward, the chieftain stepping aside. Others behind them took up the cry, until it echoed throughout the plaza. The Draykin hauled the sky-pirates into the dark of the ancient temple.

Through his panic and his fear, Fengel thought he spied a light in the depths ahead, burning like the glow of a lantern.

CHAPTER TWENTY-ONE

MORDECAI WAS GETTING ANGRY.

"I specifically ordered you not to kill them!" shouted Natasha. Her golden eyes flashed.

"The ship exploded. You saw what condition it was in. It's a miracle it got this far. We stocked it far too full of powder before we set off on this little trip. It could have been anything. A leftover candle burning down in the magazine, or a spark in the gas-bag frame."

They hovered over the strange city of the lizard-men and the large temple in its central plaza. The inhabitants watched them float above in awe. Of far more concern to Mordecai were the swarms of scryn soaring about. The death of the *Copper Queen* had agitated them, revealing their presence. There were far more of the vermin in this city than Mordecai had thought even existed.

The crew were on edge. They had taken their airship back, but rather than fleeing with the treasure in their hold, they'd stayed. Now scryn surrounded them, hostile natives swarmed below, and their captain and first mate were arguing in the stern near the helm.

Mordecai thought he'd be able to convince Natasha to move on. Yet once they'd spied Fengel and the procession below, she'd ordered them to draw closer. Then the *Queen* had exploded. They had been arguing vehemently since.

"Do you think me a halfwit?" snarled his captain. Natasha narrowed her eyes and let her hand fall to her sword. She paced back and forth. "You wanted them all dead. Especially Lucian. You never quite got over what he did to you, and you finally broke rank to take your chance, deliberately ignoring my order!"

His composure evaporated. "That is *not* why I killed them!" Mordecai hissed. "You want the truth? Fine! I blew up the *Queen*. I had a long trail drawn back to the powder room and lit off as we departed. And you know what? I would do it again in a *heartbeat*."

Natasha grinned fiercely as she caught him out. Mordecai ignored it and went on, stabbing a finger at her to punctuate every sentence. "You should have dumped Fengel in the ocean the minute we got our ship back the first time. None of this ever would have happened then. But no. You had to get soft. You had to play *games*. I did what was necessary. I did what you should have done a week ago. You're soft around him, and it'll be the doom of us all!"

Mordecai quieted, panting. Natasha glowered, now outraged. "You forget your place, first mate," she hissed.

"No," he replied. "*I* know my duty. One of us has to think with something other than their loins."

Natasha glared daggers, then she smiled sweetly. "No worries there for you, eh Mordecai? Tell me, when was the last time you were able to hook up with someone you didn't pay?" She tapped a finger to her chin and glanced away, looking puzzled. "I truly can't remember."

Mordecai opened his mouth to reply. He shut it and turned to stalk up the deck. "You aren't a worthy captain," he snarled at her over his shoulder.

Konrad at the helm was staring resolutely ahead. The navigator wisely said nothing as he stalked past. Others in the crew close enough to overhear were abruptly busy elsewhere. Mordecai noted this distantly, and approved. They feared him, which was good. That they were wise enough to avoid him meant they'd grown some sense, against all odds. Which was also good. Mordecai wanted very badly to kill someone right now.

He stalked up to the bow, thoughts blacker than jet. Mordecai tried to think back to the first time he'd met Natasha. It was a number of years ago, just after old Euron had stepped down and given her a ship. Mordecai had served with the old pirate shortly before, and apparently the man had been impressed with his ruthlessness. Natasha asked for him by name, and after a short interview, he'd been given his posting.

At first he had been reticent. She'd seemed wild, chaotic, truly her father's daughter. Quickly enough he realized she had a hard edge to her, and was capable of surprising shrewdness. He'd thought that over time maybe he could channel or curb her worst excesses, which often threatened her,

her crew, and everyone else around. Mordecai suspected that he had been wrong.

But what could he do? She was his captain, and he didn't dare quit his post. Once word got out, he'd be lucky to find another berth in Haventown at all, much less one on a skyship. Euron still had quite a bit of sway, and Natasha wasn't one to *ever* forgive a slight. Mordecai thought dark thoughts and watched the jungle horizon.

Boot steps brought him back to the present. Guye Farrel was approaching him rapidly. Mordecai felt a small moment of glee at the prospect; the greenhorn pirate was the perfect outlet for his frustrations. He turned to snarl at the man, and paused.

Farrel was a wreck. Bandages covered his neck and lower jaw. He moved with a limp. Hair was missing in rough patches and wherever skin showed, he was covered in bruises.

"What in the Realms Below happened to you?" asked Mordecai.

The other pirate paused to take a labored breath. "The white ape. We killed one, but there was another hiding inside the frame."

"And it got you before it died?"

Farrel shook his head. "No, it drove us away. It's moved in up there now. The lookout has some sort of truce with it. I think it's eating the seabirds that land atop the frame."

Mordecai growled in exasperation. "Well then, what are you doing down here? Get back up there with some men and kill the thing!"

Guye Farrel winced. "Sir, lookout sent me to ask you to the bow. Fengel and his Men are being hauled into that temple."

Mordecai blinked. *And what in the Realms Below do I care?* But no. He glanced back to the helm. Natasha had already received the message, and she was striding up to the bow. He had to check her, keep her from doing something ruinous.

"Fine, then," he growled. He stalked off, hoping to make his way to the vantage point first.

Natasha beat him to it. Cursing silently to himself, Mordecai moved up beside her and the lookout, Farrel limping behind.

The lizard-creatures still gathered in the plaza below to point and jabber at the *Dawnhawk*. Above them, on top of the temple stair, a few others were still gathered, though the procession was making its way inside. Mordecai caught a glance of only one of the prisoners, a huge woman that could only be Sarah Lome.

They watched the last of Fengel's Men disappear inside, along with their captors. A single lizard-pygmy ran after them, having gathered up a shining golden object from one of the temple terraces.

"Well," Mordecai said. "That's that, then." He felt a little relief. Out of sight, out of mind.

Natasha drummed her fingers on the rail. "We should do something."

Mordecai turned to stare at her. His captain looked pensive. She stared down at the entrance to the temple and the lizard-creatures there. A small frown twisted her lips. He knew the look; she felt guilty.

"We could drop a lit keg into the temple. Or some other distraction. That should be more than enough an opportunity for him and his crew to use. I don't want to have to mount a rescue. That would be going a little far."

"What?" said Mordecai, aghast. "What are you...why are you even *considering* such actions?"

Natasha looked at him, almost surprised to find him there. Her face hardened, but the feelings underneath were visible. "Fengel knows where the Lantern is. If we leave him to his fate, we will never find the thing."

"To the Realms Below with the Governor's Lantern!" Mordecai almost yelled. "No. No! This is enough and more than enough! He's dead, or as good enough to us to be. Move on. Let's just go! Bury whatever wretched sensitivities you have for that fool and his stupid monocle, and just move on! We're pirates, after all!"

Natasha glared at him. "Mordecai. I have heard all that I care to hear from you. Go audit our food stores for the return trip."

"What? Don't be daft, woman—"

"*I*," she hissed, "am captain on this ship. *I* decide what ultimately needs to be done. Make yourself scarce, and that's an order. By the Goddess above, I'd be better served making that white ape first mate, I'm beginning to think."

Mordecai flushed. He stared at Natasha for a long moment. She met his gaze, daring him to defy her. "Very well, then," he said. Mordecai turned away woodenly, and strode down the deck.

She's well and truly gone. More than that, he could read the writing on the wall; he had no place at her side anymore.

The thought filled him with inchoate rage. Years, *years* he'd spent propping her up, slaying her foes, and maintaining her ship. The *Dawnhawk*, and the *Cloud King* before it. And just like that, it was at an end.

Or was it? Mordecai stopped halfway down the deck. A thought occurred to him. He had been willingly subversive for days now, always for the good of ship and crew. But *why* did they let Natasha lead them? Pirate crews were a mix of democracy and brute thuggery. Nominally, captains only held their position by confidence of the crew. In reality the most vicious, ruthless, capable people got voted up, and stayed up through both threats and persuasion. Natasha was capable enough, and the crew loyal, but her father's name put the most weight behind her. That was why she was always so desperate to be out from under the old man's shadow.

Mordecai looked around the deck of the ship. He looked to the crew at the bow, the stern, and those moving around on the gasbag frame above. The faces he saw were tired, and on edge. None of them wanted to be here.

More than that, he saw the ship. The *Dawnhawk*. He had spent countless hours cleaning it, navigating it, and making sure the crew wouldn't be an embarrassment to it. *It's my ship, far more than hers.*

He was surprised to realize that his decision was already made. It had been for days. *Very well, then.* If he was going to stage a coup, he had to do it the right way. First he needed to sound out the crew, find who would back him. There were optimum choices here. Once a specific few were convinced, the others would fall in line. Though it had never been done before on this ship, calling a Crewman's Vote was a time honored tradition.

Mordecai thought for a moment, then stalked back to the ship's helm. Konrad stood there, alone as usual, glowering at the city beyond the railings. The aetherite nodded to Mordecai but said nothing. Unusually, he seemed sensitive to Mordecai's mood. The argument with Natasha hadn't happened long ago.

"How is our course?" he asked the navigator, voice curt.

"Steady as she goes," replied Konrad. "We're still partway down in the valley, even up here. No crosswinds to toss us all around. We can hold here awhile, if you want."

Softly, softly. "What I want is unimportant," said Mordecai. "Natasha wants us here, to keep tabs on her husband and his poxy crew." He let a little of his bitterness seep into his voice, and watched the aetherite from out of the corner of his eye. He was gratified to see the other man scowl.

"It's madness," said Konrad bluntly. "We shouldn't be here. This place isn't ... isn't meant for us." He turned to growl into his shoulder at the daemon riding there. "No, I don't care how comfortable it feels to you." Konrad looked back at Mordecai. "We can't stay here."

Excellent, thought Mordecai. Konrad had been his first choice for two reasons. As an aetherite, the rest of the crew walked softly around him. Also, because of that, the man wasn't usually afraid to speak his mind.

Mordecai shrugged, looking pained. He let a bit of worry seep into his voice. "I don't have any say in that. As long as Natasha is captain, what she says, goes." He gazed up the deck, where she was giving orders at the bow.

"If we keep to this course, though, I don't think we're all going to make it out alive."

Konrad scowled. "We should call a Vote. That'll make her look around."

Better than I could have asked for. The aetherite was more on edge than he had believed. Still, he had to go carefully.

Mordecai turned a disbelieving stare at the man. Konrad, for his part, looked embarrassed, and suddenly a little worried. Mordecai looked frankly at him for a long moment, then cast his gaze back up the deck. "I think you might be right," he said, at last.

The other man visibly relaxed. "Others are unhappy," said Konrad, as if Mordecai was unaware. "Reaver Jane, the Wiley Brothers, and that Farrel kid, among others. And it's not as if we'd be displacing her. Just...airing our grievances, right? That'll make her turn us around, leave this place."

Actually, it'll make her more obstinate, and there'd be blood all over the decks to boot. Mordecai nodded, keeping his thoughts hidden. "Say nothing. I will take care of it."

He moved down belowdecks. Fortunately, almost everyone was up above. He found Reaver Jane in the cargo with another hand, not counting the loot, but hauling up a powder keg they'd kept from the *Queen.*

She frowned at Mordecai's approach. "No need to chap my arse," she said. "Just found the thing. I'll be getting it up to her queenship shortly."

Mordecai kept his face impassive. The other pirate was Hans Droicker, a simple man with brutish tastes, but no real connections amongst the rest of the crew. Reaver Jane had been there since the beginning, though, and everyone knew she was steadfast and loyal. For a pirate, at least.

"Something on your mind, Jane?" he asked her.

The piratess frowned. She bent back to the keg to pick it up. Her short red ponytail fell over her shoulder, hiding her face. "S'nothing, sir," she said.

Mordecai put his boot on the small keg. "It doesn't look like 'nothing,' Jane. Out with it."

She looked up at Mordecai with a glower. Taking his tone for a challenge, she stood up straight and faced him. "Fine then. I don't like this. And you can take that straight to her ladyship. She wants to drop a lit keg on those lizard-devils outside...what's next? Assaulting them outright? And for what?" She gestured at the rest of the hold. "We've already got the treasure! We've already got our ship back!" Reaver Jane shook her head. "I'll do as ordered. I'm no scrub. But I think this is madness. Someone needs to make her sit up and notice, but all she can see is Fengel down in the city below. And I don't care if you tell her that, sir."

Mordecai smiled wryly. "You know very well that I recently did just that." He pulled back his boot and turned for the stair up from the hold. "You should know that Konrad intends to call a Crewman's Vote. He doesn't really mean it, but he thinks that's what it'll take to make Natasha see the light." He glanced back to see Jane and Hans staring at him in surprise. "And I have no intention of stopping him," he said. Then he turned and climbed back up the stair.

And so he moved down his list. He sought out the Wiley twins, Berringer, Lazy Tom, and others with pull among the crew. All had grievances of some sort; pirates always did. But, perhaps surprisingly, all were still mostly loyal. They pounced on the idea of a Crewman's Vote when he brought it up. Some meant it, most just wanted their captain to take notice. Mordecai kept himself strictly impassive, seemingly impartial. He let them know that he was irritated as well, and would let the Vote happen, but not what he thought of it. Lastly, he sought out Guye Farrel.

The beleaguered crewman was amidships, coiling rope. He mumbled and muttered in irritation to himself, staying as much under the shadow of the gas-bag as he could. Mordecai moved quietly up, and then waited to be noticed.

Farrel paused when he caught a glimpse of the first mate, then, slowly, he stood, ready and at attention. Mordecai noted the barely concealed hate that the man had for him. He would have been irritated not to see it; he'd worked hard to put it there, after all.

"Sir?" asked Farrel.

Mordecai let a bit of unaccustomed warmth into his voice. "This voyage hasn't been what you'd thought it would be, has it Farrel?"

The other man looked at him warily. Farrel seemed uncertain how to answer. "No," he said after a moment.

Mordecai turned aside. He paced slowly around the pirate. "No, it hasn't, has it? *I* know better. But I can imagine what you thought when you approached Natasha. Let me see." He held up his hands theatrically. "A gorgeous and ruthless pirate captain, heir to Pirate King himself. And she was no mere ocean-going scallywag at that, but a sky-pirate, mistress of one of the wondrous Brotherhood airships. You, being a young and dashing man, capable with both pistol and blade, would make an excellent addition to her crew. From there you would carve yourself glory and renown, win the heart of the gorgeous pirate princess, and even take up the role of captain once all saw your able skill and expertise. Yes?"

Farrel looked sullen, and did not reply.

"But, obviously, you know now that real life doesn't work like a penny paper. I imagine that you started to realize that the moment she shot you." He stopped, faced Farrel, and met his gaze. "Answer me."

"Yes," said the pirate, voice small.

"Since then, you've been beaten, stabbed, bruised, bit, bashed, and treated to the same drudgery that occurs on an ocean-going ship, just at a different altitude. And now, because your gorgeous captain is crazy, you're going to meet some improbable doom in some alien city, trapped on a jungle continent where you couldn't hope to survive."

Farrel nodded slowly.

Mordecai stepped closer and leaned in. "Well. It appears I've got some good news for you. You can't have everything you wanted. But you *can* have a little bit of it, and maybe save your life in the process. Look there."

Mordecai jerked his head back down near the helm. All the crew he'd spoken with were gathered near Konrad. They talked excitedly amongst themselves, working up their courage and nerve. It wouldn't be long before Natasha noticed.

"You aren't alone. This whole trip has been one mess after another. The crew have decided to call a Crewman's Vote. You know what that is?"

Farrel nodded, surprise clear on his marred face.

"Though we disagree, I am loyal to my captain. I only inform you of all this because you have a right to know. Someone needs to bring the Vote to the captain, and none of that lot have the sand for it." He snorted. "Cowards. Still, if you want a better lot, and a bit of that glory you imagined, now's the time for it. Things don't work like that in real life, s'true, but sometimes they get *close*, you follow? Sometimes opportunities arise to lift you up, but only if you've got the gumption for it."

Farrel was looking at the assembled crew. The mob was bustling now, and started forward in ones and twos. That seemed to be a sign, and soon the whole assemblage was moving up. It wasn't the whole crew, but a good chunk of it, twenty or so. Enough for the Vote to work.

Mordecai stepped back, giving the pirate next to him a significant look.

Farrel looked indecisive. Then he frowned fiercely. He threw down the rope he'd been coiling and stood up straight. As the first of the crew came close he turned and stalked up the deck with them at his back. The young man Mordecai saw back in Haventown marched up toward Natasha.

Mordecai smiled. *Perfect.*

The crew passed him by. Mordecai moved around their edge, staying close to the gunwales. He moved up where he could easily see the bow, and what was about to happen there.

Natasha was alone at the bow railing. She peered down at the temple, not even noticing the approach of the crew. Once the assembled pirates came to a halt, she still didn't seem to notice.

Guye Farrel stood at their lead. He stepped forward dramatically. "Captain," he said. "Your attention is required."

Natasha straightened and turned around. "What now?" she asked, irritated. "What—?"

The captain of the *Dawnhawk* fell silent as she saw the assembled pirates. "What is this?" she asked.

"I speak for the crew," said Farrel. "We've had enough. Turn this ship back to Haventown, or we'll call a Crewman's Vote."

The pirate princess stared at him. "You're not serious." She shook her head at the assemblage. "Enough tomfoolery. I've decided that we're going to send down a shore party—"

An immediate cry rose up. "This is madness!" yelled someone at the back of the crowd. "We've already got the treasure, let's leave!"

"Aye!" shouted another. "We've barely enough coal to make it home as it is."

Konrad pushed to the front. "Captain," he said. "We are not meant to be in this city. There is something here, something powerful and hexed. We must go."

"Oh, quiet, all of you," said Natasha. "The Governor's Lantern is worth a fortune by itself, and it's somewhere in the city below. I mean to have my cake and eat it too." She smiled. "Let Fengel do better than *that.*"

Farrel stepped defiantly forward. "No. No more, pirate princess. You've had your fun, had your play at captain. But you're not old Euron Blackheart, and never will be. We're calling a Vote."

The mob quieted. Even Mordecai blinked in surprise. He hadn't expected the fool to go *that* far.

Natasha narrowed her eyes. In one smooth motion she dropped a hand to her cutlass, drew it, and struck. The steel of her blade sang out against the leather sheath before landing with a meaty thud. Farrel didn't even have time to scream. The greenhorn pirate fell to the deck, hands twitching up at the blade buried in his neck. Natasha hadn't decapitated him. Not quite.

The pirate captain put her boot on his chest and yanked her blade free. "To have a Vote," she hissed, "you've got to have someone else who can replace me. Now get back to your posts before I—"

The moment couldn't have been timed more perfectly. Farrel's murder shocked the crew. Not because they cared about him, or were surprised at his death; Mordecai had slain more than a few recalcitrant crewmen. But because Natasha was so obviously ignoring them all.

"I volunteer," Mordecai said, stepping into the small space at the front of the bow. He turned and spoke out to the crowd. "I'll get us back to home port safely, with no more of this foolishness." The assembled crew stared at him in surprise. Mordecai was Natasha's right-hand-man, her loyal dog.

"You treacherous snake," hissed Natasha. "You'd go this far?" She hefted her blade again.

Quick as a flash Mordecai had his own sword in hand. "See how far she's gone? We have to do this. Back me, and I'll portion out her share among the rest of you when you're back in port."

"I'll see you dead for this," Natasha snarled.

The pirate captain raised her blade and came at him with a hacking blow. Mordecai parried it and stepped aside. The crowd pressed back to give them room.

No need to drag this out. He needed to remind the crew that he was confident and capable. *Short and brutal then.*

Mordecai stepped forward and lashed out. Natasha parried the blow returned it. Mordecai caught the blade with his own and then whirled down and around, binding her blade and then disarming her in a smooth motion. Natasha's sword went sailing over the edge of the rails.

She stepped back, eyes wide. He held the tip of his sword to her throat. Natasha put her hands up, glaring daggers at him.

"There," he said to the crew at large. "You see how she is. Unfit to lead. I call for a Crewmen's Vote! All displeased by the captaincy of Natasha Blackheart vote aye."

A chorus of 'ayes' rang out. It was obvious to him that some didn't want to depose their captain. But they were carried along by the events, too caught up in the action.

"I believe you are deposed," he said to Natasha.

She glared at him. "I got my ship back from Fengel," she snarled. "I'll sure as sin get it back from *you*. I may have pushed them too far, but you'll only have them hoodwinked for so long—"

"And all those in favor of my taking the captaincy, even temporarily, say 'aye!'"

A number of the crew, no doubt motivated by the now-free share, called out in favor. Their voices spread as others took up the chant. Most voiced a little half-heartedly, but, seeing no better option, went with their crewmates. In moments, enough of the crew had affirmed the vote.

"That's that then," said Captain Mordecai Wright. "First order of business: seize her."

Two pirates came close and grabbed Natasha. She fought them, but they held her. "What shall be done with her, sir?" asked one.

Mordecai sheathed his blade. "My first order: bind her well, then tie her to a rope. If she wants to go after her husband so badly, she can do just that. For my second order, you've all earned a reprieve. Bring up drink from the holds; we'll share a toast, and then put this repugnant place behind us!"

The crew cheered and scurried off belowdecks. Others stood and watched while a long rope was tied to the bow with Natasha bound to one end of it. She spat and yelled and cursed them all, biting at those who came near her. Mordecai smiled in grim satisfaction as she was set over the gunwales and lowered down by three of the crew. He leaned over to watch with everyone else as she reached the top of the temple-manse where a mob of the lizard-creatures were waiting. Unfortunately, they did not kill her. Instead they cut her free and hauled her inside, still screaming epithets.

Mordecai had the rope cut before the lizard-creatures could climb up, then he stalked down to the middle of the deck where overeager crewmen were hoisting up caskets of ale and rum from the stores belowdecks. Mugs were brought out and passed around expectantly. Mordecai took one small keg in hand and set it atop another. Then he drew his sword and stoved in the bung with his pommel. The crew cheered as he held it up, pouring it for the first man to shove his mug beneath the flowing liquor.

"Let this be a celebration," he called out. "Let's mark this moment as the moment that we of the *Dawnhawk* became stronger, and more free. We of the Copper Isles are free men and women, who brook no tyranny. We— *pfuagh*. Goddess above...what is this?"

The liquor flowed down over and into mugs, spilling onto the deck. It had a horrible, caustic scent to it. Those with pewter or steel mugs jerked back, dropping them. The liquor inside was fizzing, eating at the bottoms. Mordecai tipped the cask back, kept from pouring it anymore.

"Corsair's Cure-all, sir," said Reaver Jane. She looked glum and tired. "S'terrible stuff. Maybe something else?"

Something fell at them from overhead the gas-bag overhead. It screamed at them as it fell, hellish red light shining down on the pirates. The men and women ducked and swore, dropping their mugs. Cure-all spilled out onto the deck, stinking horribly.

The scryn banked at the last second, whipping the stinger of its tail out to catch someone across the face. The pirate screamed and fell. It whirled around, a smallish, runty creature, and came at them again. The pirates scattered, and Mordecai saw the thing coming straight for him. He didn't have time to draw a weapon, instead he held up the cask, blocking the whip-tail of the creature as it struck for his head. The wood of the cask resounded with a thump, cracking slightly.

Mordecai threw it aside as the creature flew past. The cask rolled, dumping the liquid inside across the deck. He kicked it away to free up his footing, drew a pistol and took up a stance. He fired, smoke and thunder billowing out, but at the last second the creature jerked upward.

Others had recovered from the surprise. Shouts rang out and weapons were drawn. The scryn, perhaps sensing its danger, disappeared over the starboard gunwales and did not rise again.

Mordecai looked up at the gas-bag where the thing had come from. No more of the flying vermin could be seen, though up near the starboard ratline he did see a face, white-furred and simian, watching them.

Blast, damnation, and other diverse curses. His triumphant morale-building speech had been ruined. *Enough tomfoolery. I am captain now.*

"Enough of this," he shouted. "It was just one of those little monsters. Everyone back to your posts. We're putting this place behind us. Konrad! To the helm. Reaver Jane! Go tell the Mechanist about our change of heading, and make sure he's ready to help us make all speed. And could someone get up aloft and kill that damned ape?"

"Captain!" came a cry from the starboard gunwales. A frightened looking pirate was pointing frantically overboard.

What now? he wondered. Anger rising, he stalked over to the man. "What is it? I've got more important things to do than—"

The city was gone. It was obscured by a black cloud of shifting, soaring creatures. Hundreds upon hundreds of scryn were rising up, bathing the ship in crimson light.

CHAPTER TWENTY-TWO

Lina crouched down lower behind a bush. The two Draykin stood on the other side, hissing and spitting at each other in their guttural tongue. Lina was close enough to touch one, if she wanted.

The sun hung just a little after noon. Its light peeked down past the towers to reflect off of the wide, paved streets. Up above the valley, the jungle air was hot and humid and Lina had had to work for each breath she took. Down here it was dry, almost baking. That was probably why the reptilian Draykin liked it so much.

She had descended into the valley by way of the thinly carved stair in the southern cliff. It had been almost two hundred feet, dizzyingly high above the ground. Back aboard the *Dawnhawk*, Lina had never had the chance to be up on the gas-bag frame. She wondered, after that climb, if she would ever do so, given the chance.

Once on the ground she'd found herself in the streets of the city, and far from alone. The Draykin seemed hostile, at least all of them so far, barring the mysterious Rastalak. And she wasn't even sure about him yet. So she had hidden herself and crept after the procession carrying her friends and captain.

That was easier said than done. The streets of the city were wide enough to allow five wagons to pass abreast. Between the streets sat wide green spaces where the great towers arose. Most of those spaces were filled with foliage, either gardens cultivated by the Draykin, or spots the jungle had reclaimed. These would be ideal for sneaking, but for one problem. Most of these lots were bordered by low stone walls scrawled with bas-reliefs. Sneaking parallel worked well enough, but every time she came to a side-street or junction,

Lina was forced to scramble madly over a wall, dash out into the open, and then climb over another into the shrubbery.

Amazingly, it had worked fairly well so far. The denizens of the city were either following the procession, or pointing up at the sky between their buildings at the airship overhead. Lina had gotten a good quarter-mile before getting stuck in one place.

She lay down now on soft grass beneath a thick fern, moving as little as possible. Behind her lay a jumbled ruin of the same cunningly worked stone as all of the older, larger structures. The lot around it was overgrown, spilling out into the street through the likewise-broken wall. Lina smelled jungle smells here, and something else. An overpowering and pungent scent that rankled her nose and made her breath through her mouth.

The two Draykin had appeared just as she was running through the brush. She'd caught sight of them quickly enough and had thrown herself prone. Unfortunately, they'd continued walking the grounds of the strangely verdant ruin until they were right above her.

Huh. They wear jewelry. From where she lay, Lina spied the legs of the nearest. It wore anklets made of brass or gold, but was otherwise barefooted. She hadn't noticed at the time if the one she'd killed had worn anything special.

The lizard-creatures jabbered on. *Oh just get* on *with it.* Why were they even in here? As far as she could see, the grounds of the ruin was just that, of no value to anyone. Were they lovers? Or conspirators? Whatever their goal, they could have picked a better place to chat. This one *stank.*

Just as Lina was about to try something drastic, one of the Draykin left. She wanted to sigh, but the other didn't move to follow its friend. Instead it squatted down, pushing its tail back through the fern until the tip was above her head.

Then it relieved itself with a grunt.

The pungent stench assailed her. Lina gagged and rolled away, not caring if she was heard. She scrabbled through the grass and ran blindly until she reached the next wall. Lina was mortified. *No wonder this place stinks.* The ruin was a communal toilet.

From the grunts echoing up behind her, the Draykin hadn't even noticed her flight. As well, it was likely sick. Lina glared at the foliage around her head and brushed her hands on her pants. Then she peered out through the nearest crumbled section of the wall.

She'd made it closer to the center of the city. The ancient towers around her seemed to stop a short distance ahead. Unfortunately, she had lost the procession. That was all right, though. If she had to guess, they were heading straight for the large pyramid that dominated the city. That gave her a goal. Though, she was worried. Not about Fengel, though the thought of something happening to him made her stomach twist. No, she'd seen him being carried through the streets along with the others.

It was her friends on the airship she was worried about, and whatever had happened in the skies above. A short time ago she'd been scrambling after the procession when something up in the sky had exploded. She hadn't seen what, but the noise had been thunderous. The *Dawnhawk* she could still see now and again past the towers. But not the *Copper Queen*. Lina feared the worst.

Through the crumbled wall Lina spied another lot. Rather than by a tower or ancient ruin, it was occupied by one of the wide, low pyramids that were obviously of Draykin make. Small statues were clustered on its terraces. More foliage surrounded the building, but this was tended and well grown, a garden of sorts. A single, wide opening allowed access from the side facing the main thoroughfare to her right. There was no adjacent wall surrounding the space.

Five Draykin stood before the opening to the pyramid. All of them were armed with spears. They argued excitedly until one turned back to the opening and stood before it. The others jogged out from the garden and onto the main street, running toward the center of the city. The one left behind crouched down and hissed something into the interior of the pyramid behind.

Lina glanced to her right. The main thoroughfare was too wide, too open to sneak across. Irregularly, more Draykin came running up it toward the center of the city. To her left, the side street continued until it met another just like it, similarly busy. Her only way through was forward.

She took a breath, regretted it, and then darted out from behind the ruined wall and over the side street, taking refuge behind a fern just before the pyramid. It hid her from the lone sentry left to guard the squat structure, but from nowhere else. Lina felt horribly exposed.

The Draykin guard stayed where it was, squatting on its haunches, spear held in its claws. It looked toward the center of the city, only periodically turning to hiss threateningly back into the pyramid it sat before.

Two sounds caught at her attention. From somewhere near she heard an intermittent popping noise, like the echoed reports of gunfire. Much closer she heard more of the hissing, spitting Draykin language. Those noises came from the entrance to the pyramid, pitched higher than the voice of the guard out front.

Lina thought furiously. She couldn't stay hidden here for long. Sooner or later someone out in the street would notice her. But if she moved through the garden path, the guard would see her. What to do?

No time to be clever. Small stones surrounded the lot, remnants of a low wall that had once stood there. She picked up the nearest one she could without moving too much, then threw it off into the brush toward the wide main street. It landed with a rustling of leaves and branches.

The guardian Draykin perked up at the noise. It peered at the brush toward the main street, obviously wondering if it had misheard. Lina picked up another stone and threw it in the same general area.

The Draykin guard called out. "*Randache?*" It sat up, peering at the greenery ahead of it. Lina threw another stone. The creature hissed and stood. It gripped the spear in its hands more threateningly. Cautiously, it crept forward.

Lina stood and sidled over to the front of the pyramid. There was no covering brush here, and the guard had only taken half a dozen steps or so. It peered back and forth, took another step. Lina snuck along the wall, hoping, praying that it didn't turn around and see her.

The guard pushed forward into a bush where she'd thrown her stones. It jabbed about with its spear. Lina took the opportunity move up to the opening and then past it. As she stood in the threshold she spied movement within, out of the corner of her eye. Half-panicked, Lina turned.

The low pyramid was hollow. Its entrance opened into a wide, open room, similar to the ruin she'd crept in on the outskirts of the strange city. This one was not dark, however. Nor was it empty.

Torches glowed from little nooks cut into the interior wall. Carpets of woven hemp covered the floor, along with bowls, baskets, and other minutiae. Small, diminutive Draykin clustered around the interior entrance. They were obviously children, the source of the high-pitched noises she had heard.

All of them were staring at Lina.

One of them pointed a finger at her. "*Hristala!*" it squealed in excitement.

Lina glanced back. The guard turned at the noise, saw her, stared. It opened its mouth to bellow a warning. Lina didn't bother staying around long enough to listen.

She fled. Across the front of the pyramid, out through some fruiting bushes, into the street beyond. A low wall appeared before her. She vaulted it. Beyond she found a small pen, filled with small, squealing, pig-like creatures. They oinked and hooted in alarm at her appearance. Lina danced, pushed, and kicked her way through them until she reached the other side. A hissing cry and more alarm from the pigs told her that the guard was chasing after her, hot on her heels. She didn't bother looking back, and vaulted the next wall.

The street beyond was empty of other Draykin, thankfully. But the irregular gunfire sounded louder now. Up ahead lay another ruin, toppled and tangled, yet still bearing something of its original form. The foliage grew over it thickly, but not thick enough to hide its doors and windows. Tall, spiraling towers framed it at either side. Beyond, she saw no more structures; she had likely almost reached the plaza at the center of the city.

Lina dashed across the street and into the foliage. The cries of the Draykin guard grew closer, and she was only halfway across the street when she heard claws scrabbling on stone and the muffled thump of two feet landing on the street. Her back itched, and she wondered if she'd feel the jab of a thrown spear at any moment. The ferns and vines of the overgrowth pushed at her, impeding her progress. Cold, desperate fear welled in Lina's belly.

"*Astarche!*"

Claws grabbed at her shoulder and at her shirt. Lina yelped and struggled. The creature was smaller than her, but stronger. She half-turned as she was yanked back. Lina grabbed desperately for her dagger. Grinning jaws in a long, fierce muzzle filled her vision. The breath of the creature stank like overripe fruit.

Something screamed overhead. Lurid red light illuminated the face of the Draykin who held her. It blinked in startlement just before a long, serpentine form landed on it, a wide hood covering its head and muffling its cries. The guard let go of Lina.

She didn't pause to wonder or give thanks at the reprieve. Lina shot off for the nearest opening in the ruin, a half-collapsed entryway at the ground level. She pushed through the fern that mostly covered it and into the dark space beyond. After a short tunnel it widened into a low room with a stairwell leading downward.

Lina scrabbled around the interior entryway, taking cover behind it and peering back outside. Inhuman screams and guttural, hissing cries echoed. The scryn that saved her flashed into view, flying into the entryway tunnel and past her head. Lina froze.

The guard appeared in the light of the tunnel. It peered inward, then up, then past the entrance toward the plaza. Blood oozed from numerous small scratches and bites. It quested, sniffing, peering, hunting for Lina still, or the creature that had attacked it. After staring into the dark for a moment, it grunted and moved past. Lina closed her eyes and relaxed, taking a deep, shuddering breath.

Something slithered over the rubble and cold stone floor behind her. Lina twitched back, hands going for the dagger she'd never had time to draw. The scryn reared up, spreading its hood. Mad light danced from its pale belly.

"Chirr!" it cried.

Lina paused. "Runt?"

"Chirr," said the serpentine monster. It leapt onto her arm and writhed up over her shoulders to its accustomed place.

Lina was beside herself. She almost wanted to cry. In all the excitement, the strangeness and all the near-misses, she'd almost forgotten about her new pet. "What are you doing here?" she whispered.

The creature nuzzled at her cheek, then went questing for the flask she usually held at her hip. It froze suddenly, rearing up. The shift in weight threw Lina off-balance.

"What?" grunted Lina. "Runt, don't—" It hissed, threatening at something in the room behind her, illuminating its belly in warning. Lina glanced over her shoulder.

A long muzzle filled with needle-teeth filled her vision, the eyes above it black and beady in the hellish glow of the scryn.

She cried out and picked up the nearest rock at hand. Lina lashed out at the Draykin behind her. The angle was awkward, but the blow still connected, cracking the creature across the mouth.

It fell back with a hiss. Lina followed through. She turned and leapt onto the creature, raising the rock up high for a two-handed blow.

The Draykin held up its hands. "No!" it said in Perinese. "Wait, human!"

Lina paused. Runt still hissed and spit and writhed. His weight pulled her back and off balance. "Rastalak?" she asked. "Is that you?" In the dark she couldn't tell. She could barely remember what the semi-civilized Draykin looked like, just the green eye-scales. It *was* the only one to speak Perinese, at least so far.

The creature nodded. "Yes. It is I. Stay your hand, and quiet your voice. The matron is still outside, hunting."

Lina moved off of it. She lowered the rock, but kept a grip on it. Runt still hissed. She reached up absentmindedly and scratched him where he liked, on the plates behind his head, until he calmed. Without the bioluminescence of her pet, the interior of the ruin was dark again, ambient light from cracks above and the entryway casting everything into hard-edged shadows.

"But what are you doing here?" she asked. "Where have you been? Did you see what's happened?" Lina narrowed her eyes. "Did you lure everyone into a trap?"

Rastalak sat up. "No," it said, holding up its hands again, as if to stay her wrath. "No trap. But your kind make noise, too much noise! I had thought you like the hunter, the Silas Thorn. But your Fengel and his people, they trudge through jungle like razor-boars in heat! Even still, I had thought to avoid the sentries, but alas, I was wrong."

"Well, we have to get them free."

The Draykin nodded. "The High Priest has ordered all outsiders, Draykin or not, to be held for sacrifice. My people believe that such offerings given directly to the accursed gemstone bring them directly to our gods, the Great Ones."

Lina stared. "What? They're going to be sacrificed? We've got to do something!"

Rastalak made a kind of shrug. "Yes. That is the desire. With your people dead, my hope dies as well, the Burning Eye will tighten its hold upon my people. I, outcast that I am, have hidden here to try to devise a rescue. But the city is alarmed. Many of my people of gather in the Plaza of the Great Ones. They watch the wonder of your sky-vessel, and await the sacrifice before the Eye, that they may give up their prayers. Also, they watch the swarms of scryn native to the city as they attack your sky-vessel. I should have mentioned that first, perhaps."

"Chirr!" said Runt eagerly.

Lina blinked. "What? That's what's going on? Show me!"

The Draykin shrugged again. It turned and moved deeper into the ruin. Lina followed it around a collapsed chunk of the ceiling, which led upward to another story. Here shafts of sunlight illuminated a space through cracks in the four wide walls.

Butterflies churned her stomach. She had seen hundreds, thousands of Runt's kin flitting about the towers outside. If her friends were up on the *Dawnhawk,* and not on the *Queen,* they could be in deep trouble. And Fengel and the others were apparently going to be executed by the natives.

The lizard-creature scrabbled up the incline to a wide hole in one wall. Lina stopped, nonplussed. She tried to think of something to say in reply, then cast the thought aside as Rastalak gestured at the hole. She moved up to the wall and peered out. Then she caught her breath.

This side of the ruin looked out onto the pyramid at the center of the city, as well as the wide Plaza of the Gods that it dominated. Hundreds and hundreds of the Draykin were gathered below the temple steps, focused not on that building, but on the *Dawnhawk* hanging low in the skies above. They pointed and hooted at each other, watching the strangeness of the show.

The airship was blanketed. A writhing black cloud of scryn swooped in and out, driven to frenzy by something aboard. Pistol shots and battle-cries echoed down from the vessel. Ghastly red light set the deck and the gas-bag frame aglow.

"That is new."

Lina followed the pointing finger of the creature. It gestured at the high temple steps. There, a small procession of guards were carrying something. A woman, bound. She kicked and screamed and even over the din of the conflict above Lina recognized the voice.

Natasha. Lina felt a sinking feeling in her stomach. If she was here, then the ship above must have been under her command. Except...what was she doing down here, and not up above?

She turned to face the Draykin beside her. "There has to be something we can do," said Lina.

Rastalak raised its hands. "I can think of nothing simple," it replied.

Lina shook her head. "I don't care how brazen, how unlikely. I have to rescue my captain." And then maybe he could get them all out of this mess.

The Draykin eyed her. It stopped, as if caught by an idea. "There may be something that we can do," it said slowly. Then it gestured all around them. "I did not choose this ruin at random. Before my exile, I was Lorekeeper-in-training. The Lorekeepers are given to study the holy secrets that the Great Ones left behind. But what I have in mind may not be enough."

"You let me worry about that," said Lina. "Just tell me what you're thinking."

Rastalak told her its plan.

Lina decided she needed to worry about it.

CHAPTER TWENTY-THREE

Fengel examined his fingernails. They were getting rather long.

"Mister Smalls," he said. "Lend me your knife."

The little steward glanced up from the corner of their cage he was sawing at. Henry looked perplexed. The Draykin had taken all their weapons, but Henry had managed to keep a little paring knife hidden in the waistband of his trousers. Wordlessly, he handed it up. Fengel took the blade and trimmed his index nails, then handed it back. His steward gave him a flat look before bending back to his task.

Their cage was surprisingly spacious. Twenty paces by twenty, and a full ten feet high. Its bars were formed of some dense native wood, bound by gut and twine. The right and rear sides were flush up against the stone walls of this corner of the temple. Beneath the bars under their feet was a flat, stone surface. All of his crew were here; Sarah Lome, Maxim, Henry Smalls, Oscar Pleasant, and Geoffrey Lords. Each were either tending to their wounds or working on some method of escape. Fengel stood in the middle of the cage, supervising.

The great temple-manse was mostly hollow. In its depths a pool of lava seethed, overheating the air and illuminating the interior with a lurid red glow. The entryway high above led onto a wide ledge only a few dozen feet below the roof of the great space. Stairways at either side led down to a catwalk ledge on a lower level that extended all the way around the interior, meeting with the ledge on its opposite side.

It was at this lower level that Fengel and his crew were caged. At regular places the walk widened out from the wall to support more of the strange stone idols he'd seen throughout the city. From the four widest spaces extended a rope bridge with wooden slats. These connected to the large structure at the center of the pyramid, a spiraling tower of stone rising up from the molten depths below.

Wide stairs were carved into the tower. They circled upward from where the rope-bridges were anchored, to a wide platform at the top. There, on an altar carved like a pair of stone hands, sat the Governor's Lantern.

Strangely, Fengel felt a little underwhelmed by the gem. The Lantern was a luminescent orb maybe a little larger than his fist. From where it was ensconced up above it shone with a shifting, opalescent brilliance, like a tiny multicolored star. It was *pretty*, that much was certain. But after all the fuss and fury, it didn't seem to live up to its reputation. He felt no waves of madness, nor any immaterial sense of power. He still wanted it, very, very badly. But that felt like nothing more than simple greed, and the desire to tweak his wife a little further. He certainly felt no sense of devotion toward the thing, unlike the Draykin who had genuflected on the platform before it. The guards and their chieftain had returned outside a short time ago, just as a great racket rose up. Fengel was curious about that. The noise sounded like pistol shots.

Fengel shrugged and turned away. He moved to where Sarah Lome was watching over Maxim. The aetherite had not reawakened after their imprisonment. That was worrying. His magic would be undoubtedly helpful. More than that though, he was a crew member.

"How is he?" asked Fengel.

Lome looked up at him. She shrugged, her broad, placid face giving nothing away. "Can't say, Captain. He took a good hard knock during that ambush. Ain't bleeding anymore. Pulse feels strong."

Fengel frowned. He leaned down to look his navigator over. The aetherite was pallid and his skin waxy with perspiration. His dark hair lay in a tangled cloud beneath his head. Minor cuts and bruises covered him, but nothing serious. Fengel reached out to feel his brow. It wasn't aflame, there was no fever. "Maybe I can beg some medicine from our captors." They still didn't know what the Draykin proposed to do with them. The cage was obviously a general-use item, not intended specifically for pirates.

Lome gave him a flat look. "Captain. Maybe someone else should handle any negotiating?"

Fengel raised an eyebrow at her. "Gunny Lome. While our initial diplomatic endeavors did not turn out as best could be hoped, I strongly feel that I've the beginnings of a rapport with their chieftain. Shaman. Whatever."

Sarah Lome blinked. She opened her mouth to reply.

"Let me go, you cockless eunuchs! I've eaten snake and lizard before, don't think that I won't do the same to you. Unhand me!"

The voice was shrill and high pitched. It came from another human captive supported between ten Draykin guards. The chieftain walked behind them, glowering. It was missing its headdress.

The captive was a woman, that much was obvious. But Fengel knew who it was before she was hauled close enough to their cage to see. Only one person could hit those high, ear-shattering notes with her voice alone. Only one person possessed such a library of the basest and vilest insults known to man, ogre, and dragon alike. Only one person set his teeth on edge whenever she walked into the room.

His wife.

The Draykin hauled their captive kicking, screaming, and biting up to the cage. One of their number opened it. Fengel caught glances from his Men, wanting to know if this was their chance, if they should try to free themselves. He didn't respond to them, one way or the other, only glared in irritation and frustration at their newest companion.

Natasha was thrown into the cage. She landed hard on the wooden slats, bouncing back to her feet to throw herself at the opening. The Draykin slammed the cage door shut in the pirate princess's face. She fell back with a curse and one of the guards made a strange croaking sound, what must have been a laugh. Fengel knew how he felt.

The Draykin chieftain returned to his platform at the center of the temple. The guards moved to stand before the doorways, two of them close enough to watch the prisoners. Natasha yelled at them for awhile before pausing to catch her breath. She seemed to wilt. Her hands gripped the wooden bars of the door high up to support her weight. But her knuckles were white. She took a deep breath, stood, and turned to face her fellow captives.

Even in defeat Natasha looked as she always did. Stunning. There was nothing elegant or refined about her, however. She wasn't lovely or picturesque. Instead she was sensual, vibrant. His wife always reminded Fengel of a panther or some other great cat. Nervous anticipation twisted his stomach even now at the sight of her crooked smile, just like when she'd taken the *Dawnhawk* back, just like when he'd seen her in the Bleeding Teeth at the start of all this. His heart always ignored his head and the many other, extremely negative, emotions she woke in him.

"Well," said the pirate princess. "Fancy meeting you lot here."

Not really. I'm right where I want to be. You're just bad luck. Fengel went over the insult a few times and found it lacking. Then the moment had passed. *Ah well.* He turned and faced his crew, who were all glaring at Natasha with undisguised loathing.

"Headcount," he said. "What's our status?"

Henry Smalls coughed. "Back hurts from that scratch," he said. "But I'm good. Sorry, sir, this knife isn't doing much. Maybe if we're here awhile."

"I'm fine," grunted Gunny Lome. "Was doing better, until that batty whore showed up."

"Oh," sighed Natasha sarcastically. "Why, I do believe I've been insulted. By a seven foot cow with no neck and wrists bigger than her teats."

Sarah Lome glared at her.

"I…I think I'm okay," said Oscar Pleasant. "But I haven't walked right since that Lina girl—"

"Geoffrey Lords?" interrupted Fengel.

The pirate spat, then grinned, revealing teeth filed down to points. Geoffrey rarely spoke. He looked up from where he'd been testing the strength of each bar. The grin meant that he hadn't found anything yet. Or that he was hungry. Or something. Fengel nodded in awkward reply.

"Well," said Fengel. "Nothing for it, then. Let's keep up our tasks. Once the moment strikes, we'll make our move. If only Maxim—"

"Here, sir," came a croak from the floor.

Fengel was there in an instant, Gunny Lome back to cradling their aetherite's head. Maxim looked terrible still, but his eyes were wide and peered at the cage around them.

"Hello, there," said Fengel. He grinned. "I worried that we were losing you."

"Shut up." Maxim groaned. Then he blinked at Fengel's face. "Sorry, sir. I didn't mean you. Just him." He tipped his head toward his left shoulder. "My head pounds, but I am alive. Please help me up. Where are we?"

Fengel stood back to allow him room. Gunny Lome supported his weight, but Maxim got his own hands under himself and sat up. He looked around at his crewmates, the cage, and then Natasha. He blinked in surprise and narrowed his eyes. The aetherite opened his mouth to say something, then lowered his eyebrows, as if puzzled. He stared, gibbered a scream, and scuttled back away from the front of the cage, into Sarah's ample grasp. Maxim kicked and pushed and fought, desperate to get away from something near the cage door.

"Cute," said Natasha.

Fengel frowned. His navigator was terrified of something, and it wasn't his wife. He peered back out the cage. The temple had not changed. Some of the nearest guards watched them in interest, but had come no closer. The lava below was terrifying, yes, but it couldn't be seen directly from where they were kept prisoner. The only other thing of interest was the chieftain, near the Lantern atop its pillar.

He turned back to Maxim. "What's wrong? What are you seeing?" Aetherites could see the immaterial, daemons and the curving aetherlines of the world. "Is it a daemon?" Fengel remembered the creature at the eye of Engmann's Maelstrom. For him it had been invisible, unfelt. But it had deeply impacted Maxim.

"Oh, Goddess," said Maxim in an awful voice. "It's cursed. *Cursed.* It warps the very air. It tarnishes the aether with its very presence."

Fengel peered back at the center of the temple. "What, the chieftain?"

Maxim caught his gaze when he looked back at the aetherite. "No, Captain. The gemstone. The Lantern. Oh, don't touch it. If we even just touch it we're doomed."

Fengel pursed his lips. Everyone and their brother had been trying to tell him the Lantern was cursed. And now it really was. That was quite vexing.

"Well," he said. "We'll just have to be careful. I seem to recall that in Breachtown they put it in a box. Maybe we can find a rope or something."

His crew were staring at him. Henry raised his eyebrows in surprise, and not a little admiration.

"Typical," said Natasha. "You come all this way, lose so much, for a Worked gemstone that just happens to be cursed."

Fengel didn't bother to reply. Henry Smalls did, however. "Why are you even here?" he asked, glaring at her.

Natasha glowered. "Really. Did you think I'd let you steal *my* ship? Again? And just get away scot-free?" She smiled and folded her arms. "I swore to make you pay for that little jape. And now I have. The *Dawnhawk* is mine again."

Dismay echoed around the cage. Fengel turned to face her, to demand answers. But the smugness on her lips was too much. He shut his mouth, teeth clicking audibly.

"You bitch," grunted Sarah Lome. She frowned. "Wait. But if that's so, why'd you get captured by yourself? Where's your lackey? That snake, Mordecai."

Natasha frowned. She looked away from the big gunnery mistress. "He's...occupied. Busy. We got separated." She set her shoulders and met their gazes. "My crew will come for me."

Footsteps and hissing growls interrupted them. Draykin were approaching the cage, a group of twelve. Half were guards, the others wore ornaments like the chieftain, his acolytes or under-priests. One carried cloth bundles in hand, and another a bowl filled with something that stank. Fengel caught his crew glancing at him, wondering if this was the time. He shook his head in negation. Their captors were watching carefully, and still had spears.

The Draykin opened the cage and fanned out, herding the group into one corner with short jabs from their weapons. The one with the cloth bundles threw it down at their feet. "*Raktass*," it said with a gesture. "*Raktass*." It pointed at them, and then at the bundle.

Fengel frowned and picked up the bundle. It fell apart, a stack of folded loincloths, similar to what the Draykin themselves wore. He snorted. "I think not."

Their captors didn't speak Perinese, but it seemed his message was clear enough. Two guards jabbed him with their spears. Fengel cursed and jumped back. They pointed at the loincloths again.

"Sir," said Henry. "I think they want—"

"I know what they want," growled Fengel. "I'm still not going to do it. A gentleman should dress like—" One of the Draykin poked him with a spear again. "Ouch! Damnation! Fine!" He tore off his jacket and shirt, waving them back at the guard with the spear to ward him off.

Face burning, he removed his clothing until he was stark naked. After a bit of trouble, and some humiliating suggestions from the crew, he managed to put on the loincloth. However, in defiance of his captors, he replaced his hat, and wedged his monocle firmly over his eye.

Natasha snickered. "You look like an utter fool." One of the guards jabbed her with a spear. "Stop that!" she ordered. They jabbed her again and pointed at the pile of loincloths. "Not a chance in the Realms Below," she told them.

One guard looked at another. It shrugged. It whistled, and four of them moved together, herding Natasha into a corner. They restrained her and began tearing off her blouse. She yelped, snarled, and swung at them. Fengel glanced at his crew. Now might be a good time to move...but, no. They were all watching Natasha's treatment with savage glee, not looking remotely concerned. *Ah well.* He went back to enjoying the show himself.

In moments Natasha was released, now clad in only a thin loincloth. She glared daggers at the Draykin, who moved back to threaten the other pirates. She snagged another loincloth from the pile and used it to bind her breasts. "Go on," she snarled at Fengel. "Enjoy the show. It's all you're going to get outside of some Haventown doxy." She smiled. "Actually, you probably don't even need it; I bet that stick up yer arse gives you all the pleasure you want."

Fengel fought to keep his mouth flat. He turned away to face the Draykin with the bowl, who now approached him warily. There was some red ichor in it, and a brush.

Out of the corner of his eye, he saw Natasha turn her head slightly at him, as if seeing something for the first time. She stared. "Oh my *Goddess*," she snarled at him. "You're trying to *ignore* me. You have been since these stupid reptiles brought me here. You are such a childish idiot!"

Fengel ignored her. The Draykin with the bowl pulled out a brush and hissed something at him. It was clear he was supposed to stand still. Fengel took a step back.

"You never got over your little impressment adventure," continued Natasha. "You spend so much time trying to be something you're not. That hat. The monocle. You're no different from a kid playing dress-up with his father's clothes."

Fengel had had enough. He whirled, the Draykin acolytes falling back with a cry of alarm. "Well, at least I'm not so afraid of *being* my father that I turned myself into a brazen hussy and raging alcoholic!"

Natasha stared at him, mouth agape. "How dare you!" she hissed. "I am my own—"

"Oh, save it," said Fengel. "You've been running out from Euron's shadow ever since you could put one foot in front of the other. Everything you've ever done has been an attempt to be someone different." He took a step toward her. "But you know what? With every step you take, you turn out to be a little more like him." Fengel grinned nastily.

His wife went white. The fists she made at her side trembled with suppressed rage. "*You're* the one who's running away," she hissed, voice thick with contempt. "Do your crewmates here even know the truth? The one you've been hiding all these years?"

His crew turned to look at him curiously. Fengel felt the blood drain away from his face. "You wouldn't," he said, voice small.

"Oh, yes. Yes, I would." She turned to the little steward, the big gunnery mistress. "Do you know even his first name?"

"Don't," said Fengel.

"What?" She put a hand to her throat in mock surprise. "You mean you haven't told them? But *Ashley*, why ever not?"

Silence filled the cage. Not even the Draykin moved. Distantly, he could hear the rumble of the boiling lava at the bottom of the temple.

"You horrible bitch!" screamed Ashley Fengel at the top of his lungs. He threw himself at her, hands stretched out to strangle. "You slut! You scheming, backstabbing harpy!"

"As if you don't deserve it!" she howled back, fending him off. "You started this whole mess! It's your fault your crew are dead!"

Fengel paused, shocked. Natasha threw him back. "What?" he asked. All the crew were on their feet now, eyes widening.

Natasha waved a hand. "We retook the *Dawnhawk* using that wreck you'd discarded. Fairly bloodlessly, too. I tied them all up and sent them overboard again as a lark." She shrugged. "Unfortunately the powder magazine or something went up. The whole thing exploded out to the northwest of the city. Wouldn't have been any survivors."

Fengel felt a cold weight settle into his belly. He turned away from his wife, his crew, even their Draykin captors, watching their interaction in alarmed confusion. The Governor's Lantern gleamed at him from its pedestal in the center of the temple. *Dead,* he thought mutely. *They're all dead.*

"You bitch!"

He glanced back to see Sarah Lome leap at his wife, ham-hock fists swinging. Natasha leapt contemptuously aside, grabbed the big woman by the head, and rammed her into the wooden bars that were at her back. The whole cage shook, and the Draykin gave a fluting cry of alarm.

The rest of his crew wasn't done. Henry Smalls leapt at her with his paring knife. She kicked him in the stomach, pulled the blade from between his fingers, and threw it at Maxim, who was raising his hands to invoke a Working at the back of the cage.

"Enough!" cried Fengel. "Back, all of you! I'll deal—"

Wooden spear hafts rammed into the back of his legs. Fengel went down to the floor of the cage. Glancing up, he saw that the Draykin were moving in to restrain him. Their captors had had enough.

He was hauled out from the cage, along with Natasha. Fengel thought about fighting...but, no. His wife, however, didn't realize the futility yet. She bit, fought, screamed.

The two of them were pulled up the stairs and out of the temple entrance. Outside, the sun was bright, heading on into mid-afternoon. The plaza was filled with the Draykin inhabitants of the city. Almost all of them were pointing and watching the conflict above them in the sky.

The *Dawnhawk* hung nearby. Scryn swarmed over it, hellish red light illuminating the skyship. The irregular reports he'd heard were indeed gunshots. Fengel saw the defenders fighting off the flying vermin, and it seemed that they might be winning. Dead scryn hung from the gunwales and rigging, their black ichor staining the hull. Dead pirates lay about as well, a telltale hand or arm flopped out over the rails to signify their presence.

Fengel was hauled off the top tier to a terrace on the side. Natasha was pulled behind him. Their Draykin captors forced them to kneel before two of the strange, squat statues there. Then they were tied up with their backs to the stone and wrists tied tightly together around it. They were left there while the lizard-people returned inside the temple, presumably to finish re-dressing the other crew.

Fengel watched the city, the airship, the native lizard-men below. "This is your fault," he said to Natasha after a moment.

"Go suck on a loaded musket," came her reply.

There was a weariness to her voice. Fengel looked over at his wife. She looked tired.

The two of them gazed out upon the city and the struggle up above them.

CHAPTER TWENTY-FOUR

Mordecai roared. He lashed out with a two-handed blow, bringing his weight to bear. The blade of his cutlass hit the scryn in mid-dive, cleaving it in two. Momentum carried the corpse, and the pieces slammed into him bodily. Mordecai fought to keep his balance. The deck was slick with scryn ichor. The pieces of his last attacker fell down to add its own bile to the mess, still twitching.

He glanced up and around. Nothing else threatened him. The air was thinning as well. Against the odds, they were winning out. There were fewer of the attacking vermin around. There were also fewer of his own men and women still standing.

His arms felt like wood. The attack seemed to go on forever. Discipline amongst the crew dissolved the moment the first screaming sky-beast fell upon them. Then it was pure survival, blade and pistol at hand. Mordecai had tried to rally some of the crew together. Even now, though, he couldn't say if it had been successful. Fighting the scryn was like fighting an ocean—a hissing, screeching ocean that spit poison. Those crew he'd called together fell apart, and soon enough Mordecai was isolated, worried about his own survival.

Now the struggle thinned. "To me!" he called. "Everyone to me!" He took a swipe at a passing scryn, sent it tumbling to the deck with an outraged scream.

One by one the crew heard his call and came to him. Those still standing, at least. After a few more minutes of furious combat, the last of the scryn flit overboard to avoid them. Mordecai leaned on his sword, panting. A glance around told him that the crew were similarly exhausted. Some stared numbly at the devastation around them. Others just stood there.

Time to take control again. Mordecai raised his sword up high and shouted victoriously. Stunned out of their weariness, others took up the cry in ragged twos and threes. Mordecai let them feel their victory, then lowered his blade and examined the carnage on the deck.

The *Dawnhawk* was a mess. Dead scryn lay everywhere. Their stinking ichors stained the wood of the deck, the rails, even the ratlines and cables leading up to the gasbag. Reavers lay among them, groaning, gasping, or dead. A quick headcount revealed that they were at less than half their number, and none of those on their feet were unmarred or unwounded.

Mordecai called for order and picked a few likely faces out from the crowd. "Reaver Jane," he called. "Konrad." The two pirates looked up and made their way over. "Start getting people to clean up this mess. Get the Mechanist up here. Those propeller linkages look damaged, and we're not going anywhere without them in working order." Konrad grunted and turned away. Reaver Jane gave him an odd look.

"What about the wounded...Captain?" she asked.

He didn't like the tone in her voice. Jane had been staunchly loyal to Natasha. Would she give him problems now?

"See to them," he said. "Get them taken below and checked out." He turned away to give other orders.

The propeller systems turned out to be damaged indeed. Something had snapped a number of the linkage chains connecting the steam engines to the propellers at the rear of the ship. A stray pistol ball, cutlass strike, or enraged scryn, it didn't matter; they were stuck where they drifted for the moment. Other problems made themselves known. The gasbag frame had been torn, and one of the light-air gas cells was gushing its stinking contents down over the deck. It had to contend with the stench of dead scryn for most sickening odor on the ship, but Mordecai ordered it seen to immediately. An errant spark in the wrong place could be the doom of them all.

There was something else as well. Reaver Jane wasn't the only malcontent. As they recovered from the shock of the attack and their weariness, Mordecai saw more dark glances, heard more unhappy muttering. His hold on the crew wasn't as strong as he'd thought. They'd been unhappy with Natasha, yes. But they hadn't wanted to overthrow her, not really. He'd engineered the Crewman's Vote to take advantage of their emotions. Now though, they were having second thoughts.

Mordecai kept the crew moving, busy, focused on leaving. He was strict, though he used a lighter hand than he usually would. It wouldn't do have them resent him at the moment.

"Mordecai...I mean Captain!"

He looked up to see one of the Wiley brothers waving at him from the starboard rails. Mordecai didn't remember his name. But it didn't matter. Frowning, he sauntered over to the man.

"What?" he asked, putting a slight edge to his voice.

"Down there! It's Captain— I mean Mrs. Blackheart."

Mordecai gave him an ugly look, then peered over the side.

The Draykin still filled the plaza below. Most had moved back from below the *Dawnhawk*, avoiding the fleeing and falling scryn. Up on the temple just beneath them, a clutch of their warriors stood, spears in hand. They watched the airship above them. Now and again, though, one of them shot a glance toward a pair of humans tied to the statues on the terrace below.

Both of the captives were almost naked, wearing little more than scraps. Yet Mordecai knew them instantly. Natasha, he could pick out at a three hundred yards, in the night, probably even blindfolded. And there was only one man alive who would dress like a savage, yet still insist on his hat and that ridiculous monocle. Captain Fengel.

Tied up and held by lizard-pygmies, the two were quarrelling. Mordecai wasn't even remotely surprised. What did surprise him, though, was that Natasha was still alive.

Other crewmen were flocking to this side of the deck. Wiley's words had carried. They looked over and called out in surprise. Before long everyone up top was gabbing amongst themselves. Some of what Mordecai heard was quietly regretful. That wouldn't do. He clenched a fist atop the rail and turned, mouth open to order the crew back to their tasks. Then he stopped.

Isn't this just what I had railed against? He meant to leave. To take off, fly away and catch an aetherline, never looking back. Leaving Natasha behind him. She was an enemy now, and he was just...leaving her here. In some ridiculously contrived, dire situation from which she could never escape to cause him trouble again.

Oh. Oh no. That won't do at all.

One of the lizard-people stepped out of the temple mouth. It wore a shining golden headdress, obviously in some sort of commanding role. The creature pointed at Fengel and Natasha, and shouted something in its gibbering tongue to the guards. They leapt to obey, untying the captives and hauling them back inside.

Mordecai tapped his fingers on the rail, thinking.

The tromp of footsteps on the deck behind warned him. He turned to see Konrad, approaching him. The face of the aetherite was set and dour, his bushy blond beard outthrust. A long, ugly scryn-sting from the recent battle made him look even more ferocious. Others followed the aetherite and stood at his back, Reaver Jane and a small knot of several others. They looked defiant.

"Captain," said Konrad. "We should not leave Natasha behind so. We voted her down, yes. But not off the ship."

Mordecai smiled at him. "You know what, Konrad? I was thinking the same thing. See to the wounded, and prepare a number of ladders to go below. Reaver Jane, get that powder keg bomb Natasha wanted up here. Get it finished. I want those savages below us scattered." He faced them all, catching the gazes of those who hadn't approached him. "I may have erred, dropping the former captain below." He made a flippant gesture. "Something poorly done in the heat of the moment. But don't worry. We're going to go take care of Mrs. Blackheart. Maybe we can sort something out once we're back home."

The relief on their faces was palpable. Mordecai made a note of each and every one for later. For now he needed them all. For the trip back...well. Accidents happened, and so did executions. They scurried off to see to his orders. Mordecai watched them go, then turned back to gaze down at the temple.

I am not *going to make the same mistakes.*

CHAPTER TWENTY-FIVE

THE SHINING CRYSTALS SHE WORE GAVE OFF NO HEAT, but Lina's face was still flushed. "Do I have to do this?" she asked Rastalak.

"Chirr!" said Runt.

"You bear the accoutrements of the lost Voornenhai, the Great Ones. They are quite regal. I must revise my earlier statement. I believe this might work. You look to be one of their kind come again."

Lina shifted the pleated golden skirt at her hips. "The Great Ones could have done with a bit more modesty," she said darkly.

They stood in a long, vaulted hall. The walls were of the same smooth stone as the towering buildings that made up the majority of Yrinium. Niches were cut into the walls at either hand, each containing a strange artifact of alien construction. There were headdresses, bracelets, and other clothing. There were weapons like long spears, broad-bladed swords. And there were still stranger things whose purpose Lina could not identify; mechanical armatures shaped like men, covered in armor too fine and delicate to be worn by real people. Light came from a small, golden orb held in Rastalak's hands. He'd pulled it from one of the niches, then sang to the thing until it bloomed with golden illumination. He held it like a lantern as they walked through the old vault.

The Draykin had led her down beneath the ruin into the bowels of the earth. Through half-collapsed tunnels and bizarrely formed passageways, they had finally come to this secret place. Rastalak seemed to know it well. He regarded the objects within reverently, and performed a small ritual when removing objects that might serve to disguise her.

That was the plan, at least. The Draykin worshipped the old dwellers of the city as gods. Rastalak thought that if she dressed and acted as one, then maybe she could free her crewmates and steal the gemstone. All in all, it seemed a pretty weak plan, but they had to do *something*.

The lizard-creature gave her a golden headdress, bracelets, a wide, pleated skirt, and sandals. All were made from some deep-golden metal that was warm to the touch. The headdress was wide and studded with gemstones as well. She put them on obediently, the headdress flaring to light like Rastalak's little lamp as soon as she placed it on her hair. She felt funny, but the head covering was still only slightly warm to the touch, and the light did not obscure her vision. She went for more clothing, only to realize that she had nothing to cover her torso. Rastalak told her that the Voorn did not wear such things.

Now she stood in the middle of the hall, covering herself and glaring at the Draykin. Runt coiled in a nearby niche. Lina wasn't *that* upset; the reptile only seemed to care about her partial nudity out of artistic interest. But still, it was embarrassing.

"Yes," Rastalak said. "I think that this will—"

A deep boom sounded somewhere in the city above. The vault shook slightly with the vibration of it.

"What was that?" asked Lina.

Rastalak peered up at the roof of the vault. "I know not. Come."

It ran back to the opposite wall, where an opening led back onto the stair they'd descended. The Draykin replaced the lamp, taking her hand and pulling her along. Runt leapt up crying, soaring after to land on her shoulders. Lina grunted at the weight of her pet but did not have time to adjust; her companion pulled her relentlessly. They ascended, clambering up the smooth-cut, corkscrew stairs, their way lit by the halo of light around her head. The trip back up seemed far more quick than their descent had been. The strange architecture gave way to half-collapsed tunnels after what seemed only moments. Then they were once again in the ruin up above, shafts of sunlight falling through cracks in the ceiling.

Rastalak paused to listen. Over her panting Lina heard something as well. Gunshots, and enraged roars.

"Those are cries of battle and rage," said the Draykin. "My people struggle. Come."

He sprinted out the vine-covered entrance. Lina followed. She blinked back tears at the sudden brilliance of the city outside. Breathing was harder in the hot and humid air. The roars and screams were clearer here, echoing out from the Plaza of the Gods. Rastalak disappeared through the overgrowth. Lina cursed and ran after his lithe form.

Bushes and branches pushed at her, trying to yank the headdress from her. Lina held the heavy thing on with one hand, cursing and muttering. Runt chirped its encouragement. The overgrowth became a thick tangle. *I can't make it through this. Too thick here.* Then the bushes gave way.

She rammed into Rastalak, standing on the far edge of the lot. The little Draykin stared ahead. Lina followed his gaze and stopped as well.

To their left and right rose the towering spires of the Voorn. But directly ahead lay the Plaza of the Gods; they stood on its very edge. The space was huge, half a mile on a side. Little statues carved of stone dotted it, all similar to what Lina herself now wore. Past these squatted the Temple of the Voorn, the huge stair-step pyramid that dominated the center of Old Yrinium. The *Dawnhawk* hung above its peak, rope ladders dangling down. Beneath it was chaos. The mob of Draykin that had gathered to watch the skyship now howled and screamed and threw spears. They tried to ascend after a clutch of sky-pirates fighting a retreat up the stair to the yawning entrance to the Temple. Near the base lay the wracked and ruined bodies of the Draykin. Some crawled and cried out, their friends and loved ones tending to them.

Lina thought of the explosion they'd heard. *A cannon? A bomb?* One figure on the stair stood out. Clad in black, with a pistol in one hand and a blade in the other. *Mordecai.*

She turned to Rastalak. "We have to hurry! That's Mordecai. They're going to kill the captain!"

The Draykin lashed his tail back and forth. "It will not work! My kin are too angered, too agitated. What has happened here?"

Stuff it, then. Lina took a breath and pushed past Rastalak onto the flagstones of the Plaza. She forced herself not to run. To stay calm. Still, she felt terribly exposed. The Draykin mob ahead were enraged. And she didn't even have a shirt. She had Runt. But the scryn seemed...inadequate.

Regal. Regal and holy and like the Goddess come down to this Realm from the one Above. Lina pressed her palms together in prayer, forced her footsteps to a measured calm. She shook her arms and wrists slightly at every other step, so that the bracelets on her wrists jingled musically. As she passed the statues in the Plaza, they seemed to smile at her, more clear and elaborate in the brilliant halo of light emanating from her headdress.

Halfway across the Plaza, no one had taken notice of her. Three-quarters of the way, and the pirates were atop the landing before the temple entrance. They disappeared inside as the first of the Draykin below looked right at her.

Lina stood almost at the base of the stair. The air stank of gunpowder and blood. Before her lay the dead and dying. They screeched and hissed, clawed at their wounds to hold them shut. The lizard-people had tried to kill her twice now, but still, she felt for them. Those who tended their wounded kin looked up at Lina and cried out in alarm, then fell silent.

The shrieks from below reached the mob on the stair. Those at the back of the press glanced over their shoulders, only to stop. Like a wave, the Draykin paused in their pursuit of Mordecai to turn back and stare at Lina. Lina forced herself forward, held her breath as she walked out among the dying Draykin. The attention of the living and the stink of the bloodied dead made her queasy. Heart in her throat, she mounted the stair.

Oh Goddess. Oh Goddess. What am I doing here? Hundreds of eyes were locked upon her, tiny chips of coal in reptilian faces. She climbed the stair toward them, focusing on the slow measured pace of her steps, her breathing, the rhythmic chime of the bracelets on her wrists. Even Runt stilled, sensing the danger.

She approached the mob. Fifty feet ahead, then forty, then ten. Lina swallowed, wondering what she would do when she reached them. She couldn't go around them; a goddess wouldn't do that.

The first of the Draykin knelt at her approach, shuffling back to one side. They turned their heads away from her brilliance as she drew close. Lina wanted to cry out in relief. Others followed as she climbed until a path was cleared all the way to the top. Cries and shouts echoed out of the temple mouth just ahead. Human shouts. Lina almost leapt forward, but forced herself to be slow, be steady. To be a goddess.

She moved past the last of the Draykin mob and mounted the landing at the top of the stair. Lina was unable to hold herself back, and all but ran into the mouth of the Temple. The space within was deep and dark. And far from quiet.

Lina stood on a wide ledge suspended out over a vast and empty space. To her surprise, the temple was mostly hollow. Stone stairs descended to her left and right, to further ledges extending from the stone walls that circled the interior until they met. Fiery red light shone up from the depths of the temple, where molten lava boiled and seethed. In the center towered a tall spire wrought with carvings and bas reliefs depicting the same figures as the statues outside. At its peak a wide ledge supported an altar beneath a gleaming, shining jewel. Four wood and rope suspension bridges branched out from the outer ledges to varying points up the spire.

The temple was far from empty. Atop the spire stood a single Draykin with a massive golden headdress, the Lorekeeper Rastalak had mentioned, gibbering and hissing in outrage. Lina's crewmates stood at the base of the spire, wearing only loincloths and red paint on their skins. They fought with Natasha's Reavers, just coming over the closest rope bridge on Lina's left. Sarah Lome held their foes at bay with a pair of Draykin spears, one in each hand. The rest of the Reavers tried to cross the shaking and twisting bridge, while holding back in turn a clutch of Draykin guards. Mordecai stood between the two fronts, shouting orders and taking the occasional hack at a lizard-creature. Maxim and Henry Smalls held another rope bridge on the opposite side of the spire against a handful of Draykin guards and acolytes. The little steward jabbed about with a stolen spear, and the aetherite clutched a dripping handful of caustic white light. Above them, on the winding stair of the pillar, raced two figures.

"Give it up, Captain!" cried Henry Smalls up at them. "We need to leave!"

Captain Fengel, clad only in a loincloth, tricorn hat, and his monocle, fought with Natasha Blackheart to get up to the landing atop the spire. Natasha, similarly clad, fought back.

"Out of my way, you harlot!" he yelled. Fengel shoved his wife aside and scrambled hands and feet up the stair.

"Idiot!" growled Natasha. "It's mine!" She grabbed her husband by the ankle, half-tripping him long enough to scramble over and gain the lead.

"Strumpet!" Fengel cried.

"Fool!" came the reply.

"Enough!" cried Lina.

Her voice echoed throughout the chamber. Everyone looked her way, then stared. For a moment the tableaux held, everyone frozen in furious action. The Draykin shaman hissed something low, then stared in wonder and dropped to his knees. The other guards did so as well, stopping wherever they were, ledge or bridge or stair.

"Who the devil is that?" cried Mordecai.

"Miss Stone?" called Fengel. He and Natasha lay on the steps, hands wrapped around each other's throats.

Lina she flushed as she recalled her costume. "Yes," she said.

"What on earth are you wearing?"

"Please, sir," she said. "This won't keep them at bay for long. Forget the gem, we have to go!"

"Ha!" laughed Natasha. "That's one of your crew? And after all your talk of modesty."

Fengel turned his attention back. "Like you're one to talk!" He released his wife, knocked her arms aside, and scrambled past her up to the top of the spire. The moment was broken. The Draykin stood still, but Natasha's Reavers and Fengel's Men threw themselves at each other again with abandon.

Natasha jumped up and raced after her husband. The two of them reached the top of the stair almost at the same time, only to find the Lorekeeper waiting. The little Draykin held a short spear and was hissing fiercely at them. It was dangerous, but short.

Fengel blinked and circled right. Natasha circled left. The Lorekeeper tried to keep them both in its view, and backed up until it was almost against the altar supporting the shining gemstone of the Lantern. Lina's captain looked at Natasha. She met his gaze and gave a slow, almost imperceptible nod. As one they leapt forward at the Lorekeeper.

The Draykin hissed and faced Fengel with its spear. Natasha caught it across the side of the head with a strong right hook. The headdress went flying. The Lorekeeper yowled and fell back, dropping the spear and falling likewise to the stone at their feet.

The headdress arced through the air, brushing just against the Governor's Lantern. The gemstone rocked, then rolled off the altar to fall on the wide stone landing. It rolled for the edge.

"No!" cried Fengel. He bent over and rammed an elbow into Natasha's stomach. Her breath left her and she fell back, stepping onto the fallen spear of the Lorekeeper.

Natasha slipped and went down. She tumbled over the lip of the ledge, grabbing ahold at the last second with one hand.

"Ah!" she cried. Then, "you horse's ass!"

Fengel stood in indecision. The gem came to a stop, balanced precariously on the ledge a few feet away.

"Leave it be Captain!" cried Maxim. "The thing is *cursed*!"

"It's right there!" wailed Fengel. "If I don't get it, she will!"

"I don't want the stupid gem," snarled Natasha. "I want my ship! I just don't want *you* to have it!"

A gunshot echoed throughout the chamber. The stone next to Natasha exploded. She yelped and slipped further. Everyone looked down to where Mordecai stood alone on the bridge, the remaining Reavers wholly on the spire now. He glowered and lowered his pistol with a curse.

"Mordecai," yelled Natasha. "You whoreson bastard! Wasn't it enough to take my ship from me? If I'm going, I'm taking you with me. I don't know how, but I swear I'll do it!"

Mordecai glanced at the other Reavers, some of whom were staring back at him. "Just trying to save you from your husband," he said. He sheathed his sword, tossed his spent pistol over the bridge and drew another. "Now, hold still while I save you again."

The Draykin below were caught between staring at Lina and casting ugly glances at the pirates. *This can't hold for long.* "Captain!" she cried. "Leave it!"

Natasha yelped as she slipped a little. The gem rocked on the ledge, back and forth, over the abyss. Fengel looked from one to the other.

Then he made a choice.

Natasha slipped free. She shrieked. Then Fengel was there, grabbing her wrist with one hand. He grunted, grabbed her with his other hand, then dragged her over the ledge just as the Lantern went the other way.

The gemstone tumbled. It fell down in a long arc, passing Maxim, Henry Smalls, Sarah Lome and Reaver Jane. It fell down toward Mordecai, taking aim again with his pistol. At the last second he reached up and caught the thing with his free hand. It shone.

Mordecai Wright stared at the thing incredulously. Then he laughed. "Really? After all this? Well, why not." He shifted it to one side and took a shooter's stance, leveling the pistol in his other hand at Fengel and Natasha.

Then his bridge gave way.

The ropes supporting the suspension at either end snapped all at once. With a surprised curse Mordecai fell away, his gun going off and the ball shooting wide.

The Lorekeeper scrabbled forward over the edge. It screamed out in denial as the Governor's Lantern, and Mordecai Wright, fell into the abyss at the bottom of the temple. The little Draykin priest began to go into hysterics.

"Captain," cried Henry Smalls. "We have to *go*."

Fengel shook himself, saw the Draykin, saw Natasha, and gave a frown. He helped her up to her feet, and then ran. The pirates took that as a sign. Henry, Maxim, Sarah, and the others took the nearest bridge, running past the still-stunned Draykin onto the exterior ledges and up to where Lina stood. Natasha's Reaver's, bereft of leadership, joined in. Fengel and Natasha themselves brought up the rear.

Time to go. Lina turned and ran back outside.

The Draykin mob below had closed the path down the stair. They still stood on it, chattering and hissing to themselves, an argument or discussion it appeared. They pointed at the top of the temple, at Lina, as if trying to decide something. Lina didn't like that.

Even worse, the ship was gone.

Rope ladders dropped down in front of her. She glanced up to see the *Dawnhawk* directly overhead, having moved its course a little.

Lucian Thorne stuck his head over the side. "Hallo down there. Fancy a lift?"

"I thought you were dead!" cried Lina in delight. "How did you get off the *Queen*?"

The first mate made a small gesture with his hand. "The *Queen* drifted over one of those pointy pyramids. Net we were stuck in got caught on the tip and tore right open. Took a bit of a tumble, but me and the others are fine. Now, you'd best all get up here; the natives are looking restless."

Lina and the others caught the ladders and climbed. She made her way up to the top, where Lucian waited to pull her over the deck. He widened his eyes in surprise at her appearance, then moved her aside to help the others up.

"Apparently I missed the party," he told her. The missing twenty pirates stood about the deck, making ready to take flight, along with a few others from Natasha's crew. The Mechanists, old and young, ran back and forth along, tending the various mechanisms on the deck.

"We always miss the excitement," said Ryan Gae. His hair was mostly gone, and burn marks covered the side of his face.

"Looks like it was fairly wild," said Andrea Holt, an amused smirk twisting her lips.

Lina used Runt to cover herself, suddenly embarrassed.

The others made their way up three at a time. Lucian called for their navigator to get them aloft. Both Maxim and Konrad his counterpart ran back to the helm, shoving each other aside. Just as Natasha and Fengel came over the side, a great cry rose up from the Draykin mob below. Lina peeked over the gunwales.

The Lorekeeper was outside, pointing at the airship and screeching furiously. The assembled mob began to howl and stomp, enraged at being tricked. One of them ran out of the press and leapt at the nearest ladder. It almost didn't make it, but at the last second it snagged the ladder, and quickly began its ascent.

"Oh, fun," said Lucian darkly. He drew the cutlass at his side. "Navigator, get us up! I don't care which one of you!" Then he leaned to hack away the rope ladder.

Lina peered at the quickly climbing reptile. It looked much like the others, but there was something about it...

"Don't!" she said to the first mate. "I know that one!"

Lucian paused, blade held overhead. "What?"

Rastalak clambered over the gunwales and rolled to its feet. It held up its hands in submission. "Wait, this one would join you. I would speak to your leader."

Fengel and Natasha stepped forward at the same time. Then they glared at each other. "What do you want?" asked Fengel. "We can't take the Lantern away anymore."

Rastalak shook its head. "Te Salaas Voorn is no longer a problem. Ah! If only I had thought to do as you did. But no matter." It met Fengel's gaze with a frank one of its own. "I am still an outcast among my people. Take me with you."

Fengel frowned. Lucian peered over the sides of the ship and cursed. Then he began hacking away the rope ladders. "Get this ship up!" he yelled back at the helm.

Fengel glanced at Rastalak, then at Lina. Then he flushed and looked back to the little Draykin. "Very well," he said. "Miss Stone. Please keep Mr. Rastalak out of the way while we make our escape. Assuming that *someone* hasn't damaged the ship too badly." This last he cast at Natasha, who only glared at him in outrage.

Lina touched Rastalak on the shoulder and brought him up to the bow. Runt squirmed over her shoulders, upset and exhausted by all the activity. The pirates scrabbled up the ratlines to the lookouts above, or took their places at helm and along the gunwales. Slowly, slowly, the *Dawnhawk* turned and rose, the outraged inhabitants of Old Yrinium crying out below them.

Lina knelt on the bow, arranging Runt for decency as best she could. Rastalak put his hands on the rail and peeked over, stunned by the view. Lina smiled, recalling the first time she'd been up in the air. As they flew, a question that had been bothering her bubbled up from the back of her mind.

"Rastalak. How *do* you speak our tongue?" she asked. "I haven't heard any of the other Draykin do it."

The lizard-creature made a small hand gesture, annoyed at being disturbed. "I observed, and then learned it from Silas Thorn. Many other tribes of your people inhabit this land. Their tongues I have learned, too. The grunts of your kind are not overly complex."

"Chirr!" said Runt.

Lina opened her mouth to reply, then shut it. She shook her head, and watched the city in the valley as it shrank, shrank, and then disappeared behind them.

EPILOGUE

Fengel climbed up from the stairwell at the bow of the ship. He stood there a moment, feeling the wind as it played about the collar of his coat. Out beyond the rails of the *Dawnhawk,* the sun was setting.

The Yulan was behind them now. The passage from Yrinium to Breachtown had been uneventful. Both his Men and his wife's Reavers were too injured, tired, or sick of the whole continent to cause any trouble. Now they worked in mixed shifts, helping to take the airship home. They'd passed through Breachtown during the dead of night, exciting only a few bored watchmen. Then they were out beyond the bay and free over the Atalian Sea. Two days had passed since, and now it was evening on the third.

Fengel looked around and frowned. No one had noticed him yet. *Maybe I should go down and come back up?* He pondered the thought for a moment before shaking his head.

He strode down the deck toward the helm. Miss Stone was in her customary place, nursing her pet scryn with a bottle of hard liquor.

"Miss Stone," he said as he approached. "Everything is going well?"

The ex-prostitute looked up at him. Runt took the opportunity to grab up her hip flask. "Everything's fine, sir," she replied. "Nice weather. Calm."

"Yes. Calm."

They looked at each other for a moment. Then she blushed a furious red. He winced, then felt his own face start to heat. Half of the crew had seen her topless during the events in Old Yrinium. He still didn't understand exactly why she'd done what she had, or what had happened, really. That failed to make it less embarrassing.

"Well, then," he said as he turned away. "Carry on." He took a few paces away, then stopped. "Miss Stone?"

Lina grabbed the bottle away from her pet. "Yes?"

"What do you think?" he asked. "Have you had enough?"

Lina froze. Then she looked out beyond the rails to the evening sky and smiled. "I think," she said, "that I wouldn't trade this for anything else in the world. Captain."

He nodded and smiled at her, then moved on.

Fengel eyed the ship as he went. The *Dawnhawk* had taken a beating recently, but before long she'd be in perfect condition again. The Mechanists were busy working at all hours, it seemed.

Lucian came forward with a status report, both one he spoke aloud, and one he gave in a muttered whisper. Fengel acknowledged it, and made a sign with his hands as he walked past Gunny Lome, busy trading glares at Reaver Jane from across the deck. The huge piratess nodded slowly.

Henry Smalls came forward with the captain's evening tea. Fengel took the cup and sipped, the high, clear wind blowing away the rising steam of his drink. For a moment, everything was perfect.

"Captain," said Henry quietly, silver tray in hand. "Have you seen my big dagger? The one I loaned you awhile ago?"

Fengel shrugged, not really caring.

Henry sighed. Then lowered his voice. "Sir. Is it wise to relax so? I don't trust that she-shark or her people, not even a bit." He stole a glance around the deck. The Reavers and Fengel's Men tended to avoid each other. Even now, Fengel could pick out several cliques around the deck; the crews refusing to mix.

"It will be fine," he told the steward, placing the teacup back with Henry. "I'm going to have a chat with Mrs. Blackheart right now."

Henry stared at him. Then he nodded slowly. "I'll go get the physician's kit ready," he said, scurrying away.

Fengel paced down past the helm. Maxim and his counterpart Konrad were both on shift, as they had been since leaving Yrinium. The two aetherites argued incessantly, and refused to leave the other unsupervised at the helm for even a moment. So far they hadn't devolved into unleashing their spells upon each other, but they'd been up for three days. They were either going to kill each other, or drop into a coma. He shook his head and moved to the stern.

Natasha stood alone. She was properly dressed again, in long black trousers, a scandalously low-cut blouse, and a kerchief upon her head. She was looking out at the sky behind them and the ocean waters below, leaning on the railing.

He moved up next to her. "Mind if I join you?" he asked.

She turned and raised an eyebrow at him. The red paint that the Draykin Lorekeeper had painted them with had stained. No amount of washing had so far gotten it removed from either of their faces. For whatever reason, only the two of them had ended up so colored.

"Go ahead," she said.

Fengel watched the moon above the water, reflecting cool light across the horizon. "So," he said after a moment.

"So," she replied.

"There's not quite enough of either crew left to run the ship."

"Aye."

"I think, to make it back to Haventown, we're going to have to work together."

"Mhm-hmm."

They quieted again. An irritated shout came from up the deck. After a moment a lone scryn flew past the stern, a chrome hip flask in its maw. Fengel felt a moment of revulsion for the thing.

"Think there's something to that?" asked Natasha. She turned, leaned on the rail with one arm, showing him her bared throat and the low cut of her blouse. She blinked, long eyelashes fluttering.

He kept his posture ramrod straight. Then he sighed. "You're incorrigible."

"And you're stuck up."

He nodded. "Maybe. Maybe there is something to that."

"All right."

Fengel pondered a moment. "It would mean we'd have to truly work together. No more backstabbing. No more racing to get ahead. You'd have to stop caring that one of us is better than the other."

Natasha froze. Then she relaxed. "Same goes for you. A partnership. Equals."

There was mockery in her tone. Fengel frowned. He didn't trust it. He turned to face her fully, unconsciously falling into a quick-draw stance. He stuck out one hand.

Natasha rolled around to face him fully, yet still leaning against the rail. She put one hand to the small of her back. Ostensibly to support herself, more likely to put the dagger there close to her grip.

She took his hand. It was soft, between the calluses.

"Partners," he said.

They shook once. Fengel watched her eyes for the smallest hint of action, the smallest movement. They were golden, and very lovely. She watched him in turn, hunting for weakness, maybe admiring the curve of his jaw.

They did not let go.

 END BOOK ONE

ACKNOWLEDGEMENTS

It's taken five years to get here. That's a long time, and there's no way I could have done it on my own. I'd like to thank my parents for fostering my love of fiction. I'd like to thank my wife, Shawna, for standing beside me and always giving me the most honest of critiques. Both of my first readers, Cheri Cross and Erik Hansen, have put up with a lot of bad writing over the years. To Willy Traub, Rachel Helmkamp, Harrison Paul, Laurel Amberdine; your input has been invaluable on this project. Thanks must be given to my editor at Indigo, Susan Defreitas, for all her hard work. And to Ksenia Mamaeva, thank you for your wonderful art.

Last, but by no means least, my Kickstarter backers. Thank you for your support and assistance, for being excited and interested in the work of a complete stranger. I hope this novel has succeeded in repaying your faith.

ABOUT THE AUTHOR

Curious about me and my works?

Learn more at WWW.JONATHONBURGESS.COM.